A LAND OF OUR OWN

The first book in the series
The Kingdom of the Free

By Matthew R. Bishop

Books by Matthew R. Bishop:

<u>The Kingdom of the Free</u> series:

A Land of Our Own (Summer 2013)

In the Shadows of Laeolin (Summer 2014)

<u>Legends of Elyria</u> series:

A New World Wakes (Christmas 2021)

Of Gods and Men (Christmas 2023)

For the history of our world
Is yet to be written,
It is we who decide
Whether we will be smitten,

By the anger we hold
And which binds us to thee,
O sword and shield,
Sad destiny

Map Of the Skaelin Lands
On the Continent of Skaen
In the World of Fengorian

The Frozen NorthLands
(Unexplored)

The Skaelish Land

To The Skaelish Land

The Frozen Meadows

Gensbadin

Battle of Gatsesilli

Gatsesilli

Ambush Site

Tyeagen

Behi's Village

The Blue River Highlands

Castle Stangfeld

The Eastern Mountains

Bellford

Tenibala Meadow

Gendim gets Lost

Pod Jakul

Sea Bastion

Gonaka

Gaolniuk Landing Site

Gaoln   Kon   Laen

The Cold Ocean

ACKNOWLEDGMENTS

I am in debt to everyone who has helped me reach this point. Everyone who has ever even inquired into "how the books are doing" or even asked me what my stories were about, or expressed any interest in them at all, has given me a reason to stay with them and work with them year after year.

It was my parents, Robert and Shelley Bishop, and the way they brought me up that has allowed me to develop such a wide scope for characters and places— thanks to them, the homes they have given me and the travels they have sent me on, my own experiences with real-life unique individuals and unique places are by far more vast and inspiring than those I develop in my stories. By giving me a childhood full of imagination and a life full of adventure, you made this possible. You two have given me my own stories to tell. Thanks to you.

I owe a great thanks to Mr. Dan Foley and Ms. Anna Grossman. Dan, you have been my "chief editor" from the beginning, and at every point your enthusiasm regarding my writing has alone been an inspiration. Your insistence through my high school and undergraduate years that I could succeed as a writer has led me to this point. Your dedication to professional-grade editing has given me an invaluable reader's point of view into my own work. Anna, our casual exchanges on writing and editing have really helped me bring myself into the wider world of writers, and without a few of your suggestions many of the best scenes in this book would be absent. Both of you have provided helpful feedback and detailed insights for my stories from the very first time I printed off a script for outside review as a freshman in college to this— the time of that script's publication, all these years later. I want you both to know that your continued support has truly been invaluable both to myself as a writer and to these books as stories. Thanks to you.

I also want to thank Divya Nallapuram and Cheyenne Romick for going over a full version of all three books in this series once. For your hard work and insight, I thank you. I wish to mention also John Woods, Jo Campbell, Elizabeth Linares, Dr. Halliday of Ohio University, and Tyler Carnelison for at some point helping either with one book or a part of one script. I also want to give Elizabeth an extra round of thanks for putting up with all the times I called her (always way too late or way too early) asking her to read part of a script or help me make some decision.

It was a small group of kids in high school who first suggested I publish, and without their idea I would hardly have considered publishing at all. After your suggestion, I began editing and revising books that I originally created only for my own entertainment. Thanks to you.

The community of writers, artists, and thinkers that I found at Ohio University gave me hope that I could find people to help me discover what these stories might become and encouraged me always to keep writing. Thanks to you.

Lastly, thanks to my dog Gracie, whose death came just as I was reviewing the final proofs of this book. For all the many seasons and years you sat beside me helping me write and listening to my thoughts, going through script after script in the porch of our Ohio home, I thank you. You were my greatest companion and a true source of inspiration, and you always will be.

I cannot possibly list everyone, everything, and everywhere that has in some way inspired or encouraged me as a storyteller, a writer, and a person— what I have listed here is only the most brief recollection of these things that I could come up with. The places I go and the people I see lend inspiration to my writing every day of my life. So to every good person I have known in my own story, I thank you.

Cast of Kings and Countries

Centreal
King of Gaoln, land of the Gaolnians
Advisors: Luncas, Denelu, Nowhawna

Nowhawna
King of Gonaka, land of the Gash
Capital City: The Glorious City
Advisors: Kio, Joel, Menuld, Sela

Seagraul
King of Laen, land of the Lonins
Capital City: Laeolin
Advisors: Skerun, Menuld

Sealibahd
Emperor of Phenen, land of the Phenese
Capital City: Saumo

Sendroun
King of the Skaelin Lands, land of the Skaelin.
Capital City: Cavfurt Stronghold
Advisors: Skerun, Menuld

A Land of Our Own is dedicated to the people everywhere around the world, living and dead, who have known what it is like to live without being free.

PROLOGUE

There was a single green leaf on the tree next to him, and it vibrated as the wind blew through the otherwise barren boughs. All around him, the forest seemed dead. But his smile was full of life, and his eyes of memories which kept that smile warm. When he spoke, it was with a frankness, an openness in his voice which astounded his audience and bade them listen well. His face was old and wrinkled, but there seemed to be some youth in it, radiating out from his eyes, which still recalled the eons they had seen, with all the hardships and prosperities that went with them. At first, as they gathered around him, there was a silence which would stun anyone unfamiliar with the storyteller, as many called the tall man in the long, billowing brown robes. But to anyone who had heard him speak before, the silence was the anticipation of the audience, who wanted to hear only his voice tell them what their own ancestors could no longer recall.

"How to sing of a single life,
When life's all but a game?
And how to show but one man's strife,
Among the towering flames?

How can I sing of a bud in the sun?
A flower in the morn,
Or one cut down, burned and buried?
The fault of one man's scorn,

Sing to me forces of this world,
The tales you would tell,
When one day gone is all we know,
There's nothing left to fell,

When all is done and all is said,
Think now of what remains,
What is the end, the outcome of
This raging endless game?

What's left of joy,
Once stripped away,
By men and wars and hate?

What can endure,
Whatever's left,
Once Time has fought with Fate?

"There was a song that, at the end of the story which I am about to relate, the whole world heard and recited as one. It was composed, an age before, by a man who dared to dream that one day we all would live in peace. Do not say it is impossible! I have seen such a day myself, and on more than one occasion! The song is one of my favorites of this world— and if you had heard the voice of he who sang it to all the world assembled before him, you would believe all humankind to be on the very eve of paradise."

The being took in a deep, slow breath, and closed his eyes. The wind came again, and he smiled as it caressed his old and withered face. His robes fluttered in the wind, then fell to the earth as the wind ceased, and he opened his eyes. You could see in those eyes the sadness of his ages, all gathered together on some common cue. When he spoke again, it was with a deep and resonant sound, as if the earth had opened its vaults and cried out its memories to the world. Across the meadow of people not a single person stirred, but all listened intently as the being began hoarsely:

> "Sing me a story,
> Tell me a tale,
> A song and a sound
> Louder than war,
>
> Carry me off to
> A place without cares,
> No hunger or pain
> Can follow us there,
>
> 'Till I reach that place,
> I'll stand here content,
> To ask but these questions
> With humble intent:
>
> If Love is stronger,
> More lasting than Fear,
> Tell me, God, how's it
> That we've arrived here?
>
> If this world is full
> Of such love, peace and joy,
> What keeps us from knowing
> What I knew as a boy?
>
> That a world with such bounty,
> And with so much land,
> That a species which smiles
> More than it reprimands,
>
> Must surely live in peace with one another,

Must surely see that in truth they are all brothers,

And no I can't comfort you,
Childless mother,
No I can't tell you
Why your son had to die,

I can make for myself
Some obscure reason why,
But I look in your eyes,
Reasons are lies,

And when next you come,
O heavenly light,
I pray you see us
Without any strife,

You'll see us then,
As we're meant to be,
As men and women
In unity,

For the history of our world
Is yet to be written,
It is we who decide
Whether we will be smitten,

By the anger we hold,
And which binds us to thee,
O sword and shield,
Sad destiny.

"I do not like marking history by blood and wars. I do not
enjoy marking it by high politics and the hostilities they create.

If I were to explain to you the history of this world and our race, as I do now, I would tell it not by these things— I would avoid them as much as I can. For we are not so much defined by what haunts us, or by what we hate, so much as we are defined by what we love, what stirs us, what drives us, what makes us who we are and so shapes this world and our place within it. Our history can be told, can be seen, in the love that exists when a lost couple embrace, or when they waste the day away under the hot high Trest sun. It is seen as a child is born, as a bird sings in the morn, as the waves break on the sand, as I hold, in mine, your hand.

"But what I have to tell you here is one of the saddest stories I have ever told. Every age has its height of happiness and prosperity, each its low points, where immorality and chaos reign, where barbarous kings rule the world to its own demise. I find, sometimes, that we must endure the harshest of storms and the most black and desolate of cold Sen nights before in the morn we wake to the calm and the sobering light. The storm before this calm can be long and arduous and terrible, involving deeds and misfortunes which I could hardly relate without taking you back in person and showing you the suffering which our world endured. But the calm that comes after— it is the most beautiful thing one could imagine.

Part One:
From a Land of Nothing

- Chapter One -

The woman was weak. With all her strength, she held the newborn baby boy in her arms, and forced her voice to come out— for her breath to say something important before it stopped and never started again. She looked into his tiny eyes— but they were so large, compared with the rest of him!— and she broke into a wide smile. The soldiers behind her yelled for her to get up and leave the baby, or they would kill her. They prodded her with their spears and urged her forward, on into that prison land called Gaoln. For a moment she lifted herself away from the noises and the points of those spears, and she let herself become immersed in the innocence of those deep brown eyes. Then she heard her voice cry out faintly, and when at first she started to sing, it was in that broken and hoarse voice of a person who is in the middle of emptying their heart, that giant reservoir of hopes and fears— and in this place within her mind, the infant boy she held would remember this song for all the ages of his life, however long or short.

> "All of life,
> All of life,
> But a wave upon the sand,

And the stars in the sky,
When they no longer shine,
I will be with you here,
Tonight..."

She did not awake from that dreamlike place, where she was alone and at peace with her new child. That faint voice which had sang those words so beautifully had simply faded into some calm and warm wind, which bore tidings of someplace more peaceful, where she could rest. She disappeared into his eyes, she fell into them, and that was it.

The baby boy cried. Before any guards could act, an elderly man stooped down and picked up the infant, and claimed it as his own. And the guards marched him on, into that prison land called Gaoln.

- Chapter Two -

Kamira, the small girl with the dirty blonde hair who was only in her eighth year of life, looked at Gendorn, the slim, lanky young boy of about the same age— but who always said he was older and "better" than the young girl. He was drawing something in the dirt, and Bendoraun, the shorter boy with the dark hair and the voice almost as deep as a man's, started to laugh. Kamira tried to move beside Gendorn to see what it was, but Gendorn shifted his body this way and that, not permitting Kamira to have a glance.

"Kamira," Bendoraun said between laughs, "Gendorn drew a picture of you!"

Kamira rolled her eyes. "He draws a picture of me every day! And every day it's worse!"

"It's because he's in love with you," Bendoraun blurted out. Gendorn jumped up and tackled Bendoraun, and they went rolling down the side of the hill, away from the lonely, barren tree which stood rooted on its crest. When they stopped rolling the two of them were perfectly covered in dirt and dust, and were laughing while Kamira looked down at them. Gendorn fixed Bendoraun with a stare.

"If you tell her that again, I'll tell Rwannah that you love her!"

"Rwannah's sick," Bendoraun said, "that's what her mama said."

"The next food ships are coming in ten days," said Gendorn, "Rwannah will be fine, but she won't be if you keep telling Kamira that I like her!"

"As if she doesn't know! Get off me!"

Gendorn let Bendoraun go, and Bendoraun smiled cunningly. He turned and ran up the hill, shouting "Gendorn's in love! Gendorn's in love! With you, Kamira!" Kamira laughed, and Bendoraun's smile stretched across his whole face. "Kamira, don't let him hurt me!" Kamira fell on the ground laughing.

Gendorn rushed up the hill after Bendoraun. Bendoraun got to the top and started to descend, and Kamira stuck out her leg to trip him. He barreled down the hill, away from Kamira and Gendorn, and when Gendorn got to the top he stood there laughing with Kamira, as Bendoraun sat in the dirt below.

On an impulse, Kamira grabbed Gendorn's hand, turned him around, and kissed him. Gendorn looked at her, his eyes wide in fear, but before he could do anything Kamira squeezed his hand and spoke: "I like you too, Gendorn." Gendorn's wide eyes stood still, but his face broke into a smile, and he squirmed around a bit, unsure of what to do, but altogether happy with the situation.

When they looked back toward Bendoraun, they saw, from their vantage atop the hill, a cloud of figures in the far-off distance, growing thinner as they marched southward across the flat dirt plain. They were carrying their pickaxes and shovels and other tools they used in their labor, but Gendorn and Kamira knew that they were not where they should be, down in the mines. The two of them looked curiously at one another, and then they rushed down the hill to get Bendoraun. "Come on!" Kamira insisted, "Get up and follow us!"

"Where are you going!?" Bendoraun whined.

"We don't know!" answered Kamira.

"Of course not!" Bendoraun bemoaned, "Why would you?"

"Just come with us!" Gendorn told his friend.

"Don't think I didn't see that kiss!"

"*Bendoraun!*"

"Well I did! Kamira, I told you he was in love with you!"

"*She* kissed *me!*" Gendorn proclaimed.

"That's not true!" Kamira spat, "he told me that if I wouldn't kiss him, he'd toss me into the ocean!"

"*Kamira!*"

"I can't blame him," Bendoraun said, "You are really pretty." Kamira blushed.

"Go back to Rwannah's house!" Gendorn yelled.

"*Guys!*" Kamira said tiredly, "let's go see where these people are going! Come on!"

As the three children drew nearer to the crowd, they noticed more and more people. From every direction they marched, all of them toward the south. They found it rather difficult to keep walking after the first hour, but the sheer volume of people convinced them that this must be an important gathering. They continued past noon, and then into the afternoon, and when they could move no longer they were sunburnt and thirsty and very tired. But they could go no closer— the crowd was thick now, and it was not moving anymore.

There must have been a million of them, the children thought. Kamira, Bendoraun, and Gendorn could not see beyond the thighs of any adult around them, but from the noise and the smell and the fact that the man who was speaking— someone who commanded the silence of all that crowd— had to shout so loud to be heard, they knew that virtually everyone in Gaoln had come to hear this speech. Behind them, other adults were shouting even further back, to relay the words of the speaker to the rest of the crowds. All things considered, it was not very easy to hear what was being said.

"Today," the speaker began, "the last Skaelin guard inside our territory disembarked for his home country, and they do not dare to oppress us any longer!" The crowd erupted in cheers, and when they quieted down the man resumed. "You see that ocean in front of you? This morning, the waves of that ocean and the wind of our kind fortune carried our enemies away. Never again will we watch our families be torn apart. Never again will we be subjected to arbitrary arrest, arbitrary torture, rape, starvation, imprisonment, murder. We burned this guardhouse today, the one that I am standing on top of!" The crowd erupted again. "And never will we allow anyone enough power to rebuild it!"

"What's he saying!?" asked Kamira, "I can't hear!"

"The bad guys are gone," said Gendorn.

"And they're not coming back," said Bendoraun, "'Cause they're not allowed to."

"Says who?" wondered Kamira.

"Says *that* guy!" Gendorn said, as if it were the most obvious thing in the world.

"Everyone else listens to him," Bendoraun said with a shrug.

"Well if I could just *hear* him," Kamira continued. The figure had started to speak again, and Bendoraun tried to jump up to see, but he could not make it past anyone's chest.

"Be quiet, Kamira!" he said.

"Shh!" Gendorn said to Bendoraun.

"You shh!" Bendoraun retaliated.

"You're both being noisy!" Kamira complained. The crowd seemed to be angry about something— they had started to interrupt the speaker. The three children couldn't make out any of it, but soon the whole place had exploded in yells and shouts. Gendorn took an elbow in the face, and Kamira was pushed over backwards. She grabbed Bendoraun as she fell, taking him down with her. Someone in the crowd was kind enough to take the three of them by the hand and make sure they didn't get trampled.

"What's happening?" Gendorn asked the man.

"Gaoln has a king! He stands against the bad guys who run this country, the ones who give us food and water."

"Why do the bad guys feed us?" Gendorn asked. He had always wondered that, and never understood the response. The man smiled at him.

"Because they can't let the rest of the world know that they are the bad guys. Only we know. That's why we're the ones who have to do something about it."

Gendorn nodded. "What are we going to do?"

The man smiled again— this boy was quite amusing. "We're going to escape, child."

"Where to?"

"To a land called Skaen."

"Why do we have to go to Skaen?"

"Because things are going to get very bad around here. Things are going to get very bad, very soon. And we would do well to get out of this wretched place before we've all been killed."

"Who would kill us?"

"Those same men who give you your daily food."

"I don't understand."

The man's smile faded. "No. I don't think any of us really do." Gendorn, fully confused, shut his mouth, and let the man lead Kamira, Bendoraun, and himself out of the crowd.

In the days after that, there were a lot of things very confusing to the children all happening at once. The lithae, those huge flying reptilian birds, whose gorgeous wings and shimmering bodies carried the most important people in the world across countries that would take weeks on foot, were always in the sky. In the dust Gendorn would sit with Kamira and Bendoraun, and up at these creatures and these very important people they would look. What messages did they carry? Where were they going, in such a hurry? Why— *why* did none of them ever come down to swoop them off their feet, and carry them away to a free land? Could it be that people so powerful and so wise did not even care for them? They passed their days away asking these questions, and never finding their answers.

At night they would wander out to the hill and look at the endless black of the ocean, or watch the waves on the shore when the moonlight revealed them. Except, of course, that tonight it was only Gendorn and Kamira, while Bendoraun was off at Rwannah's house by the request of Rwannah's father. Despite all the cold which pervaded the dark of a night on the edge of Sen, and in defiance of the bitter winds which came down southward from the Cold Ocean in front of them, Gendorn and Kamira, when their hands and arms interlocked and their legs wove together, felt just warm enough to be alright. Some of the wind was blocked by the hill, anyway, as they sat on the side opposite the ocean, and by the lonely tree. It was, on such nights, the only way to remain warm, and Gendorn, Kamira, and Bendoraun were used to sleeping like this as soon as the winds started to bring tidings of the coming colder weather. It was how they had survived as children. Kamira, who had a mother— Curileyn— was able to get the comfort of a second blanket on some nights.

So they were content to sit and enjoy their togetherness without any words— but it was far from silent. The wind was harsh and quite loud when it broke against them, but the crash of the water against the rocky shore of Gaoln was even louder. For a long while the two children sat and tried to sleep, but at some sudden moment they both decided that this was a futile attempt and that they would definitely not be sleeping on this night, for some reason or another.

Gendorn began to draw a picture, and Kamira leaned her head over his shoulder. "What is it?" she asked intently.

"A picture."

"*Of what?*" she asked most curiously, and a little bit annoyed.

"The other side," Gendorn answered plainly.

"Gendorn, what does it look like on the other side of the ocean?"

"I just said that I am drawing it right now, Kamira!"

"*Okay!*"

"There."

Kamira looked down. In the dirt before them there were three small figures with lines for bodies, lines for arms, lines for legs, and with little dots for heads. They were holding hands. Around them on all sides were these thicker lines which extended upwards and branched out, and there were some scribbles— "they're leaves" Gendorn insisted— in the sky far above their heads. "It's a giant forest," Gendorn told her, "and you can't even see the top! And you can eat everything. Every tree has fruit, and there are animals everywhere!"

Kamira smiled. "You're cute."

"I'm serious!"

Her smile grew. "Okay."

"Well I will take you there someday, and then I will show you for real."

Kamira's eyes lit up and she said, slightly more seriously, "Okay."

- Chapter Three -

It was on the next market day, ten days after the Governor of Gaoln betrayed the powers of the world and proclaimed that Gaoln would be free from atop the ruins of that guardhouse, when the children truly began to understand what was happening in their big wide world. It was a cold afternoon, for the wind was relentless and neither their thin blankets nor their cracked mud walls could defend them against the gale. It was the first day of *Tun-Sen*, the coldest period of the cold season *Sen*, which in this part of the world could sometimes last two hundred days of the year. It was an unfortunately cold time in which to begin the rebellion of Gaoln.

One hundred thousand people were out around the borders of the colony, going to or returning from the collection spots where they were to receive their monthly rations from the prison guards. The hours before the storm had shown no signs of pending disaster— the sun was bright behind the clouds. But the storm rolled in swift as a sloop into home's harbor, and brought with it great and terrible things.

The children, nestled in their huts, were awaiting the return of Gendorn's caretaker, an elderly man who had taken to looking after the two young orphans when Kamira's mother was not able to. He was a generous man whom Bendoraun and Gendorn had known for as far back as either could remember, who seemed to have raised them from infancy. *Gulaus*, the orphan boys called him— a Gaolnian word for a kind soul who takes the responsibility of others' lives as his or her own, usually bestowed upon elders who cared for orphans. As there were many orphans in such a difficult place to live, so too were there many such caretakers. Kanel was his real name, but few people called him this any longer, and no one seemed to know where Kanel was from, or why such a kind soul was in Gaoln.

The sky turned dark. When such sudden storms came, the guards in the border markets routinely opened up the barracks for the prisoners to hide in and wait out the snow and wind and rain. So the prisoners gathered around the barracks while the clouds turned black, and waited for the guards to open the doors, as they most certainly would.

But the guards hid in their barracks, and did not open the doors. It would have been a quick and easy thing to do, to grant refugee to these almost naked people caught in a great winter hailstorm. And yet no door was opened, no guard stepped outside. The prisoners banged on the wooden doors and the iron knocks, shouted and screamed in hysteria for someone to open the doors, climbed the walls and tried to find ways inside from the rooftops. The cellars along the streets were locked down too. People beat the wooden hatches with their fists until their hands bled and their knuckles opened up. They tried to pry the iron locks until their fingernails tore off. But there was not a door that would budge in these markets. The soldiers were under strict orders from King Seagraul of Laen and King Sendroun of the Skaelin, who were both angered over the collapse of their last guardhouses inside the penal territory. Under no circumstances were the soldiers to open any hatch in any market anywhere on the borders of the colony.

People began to run home, horrified of what might happen. Most made it to the nearby *pels*, where they huddled close together under mud and thatch roofs, so close that you could hardly get enough air to breathe. But there were almost one hundred thousand prisoners collecting their rations that day, and the pels nearest the markets, though large, could not offer a roof for so great a number. Then it came— the freezing rain. It came from the sky as sudden as a clap of thunder, and with such a roar. It soaked them to their cores in only minutes, through their torn shrouds of cloth that the prison guards called clothes. The wind howled and turned the rain under their skin into ice. Giant drops of hail pounded on them from heaven and knocked them down to the floor of the earth. Huge crowds of people cried frantically and tore at the skin of their fellow prisoners, trying to find a way under the overcrowded roofs. But those under the roofs could only watch, as their huts could not grow any larger, their roofs could not expand.

In several places, there was such a fight to get into the huts that houses were torn down, leaving dozens more out in the rain. The anxious and strong pulled the weak out of homes and took them as their own. Vast groups of people dropped their rations and ran as fast as they could back to their huts when they saw the chaos unfolding in the pels nearest the markets. All through the country that day people under roofs watched as miserable mobs of slaves wailed in the cold, hopeless and without shelter, or tried to make room for themselves at others' expense. When the freezing rain truly did turn their insides to ice, their voices could no longer find a way out of their constricted throats. Their eyes couldn't bear to open against the cold wind and rain. Their hearts couldn't find the strength to keep beating. They fell to the ground and were soaked through. Over the course of the night, their bodies froze as surely as if they had been made entirely of water, and a thin layer of ice covered the piles of corpses the next morning and all through the following day. This was the Death Storm, and the Gaolnians who survived would always remember.

The next market day, thirty days later, Gulaus Kanel took Gendorn, Bendoraun and Kamira with him. Curileyn, Kamira's mother, came along, as did Bendoraun's friend Rwannah and Rwannah's parents. Altogether they walked through the caked mud toward the market. Gendorn and Bendoraun went off exploring together, running ahead of Kamira and Rwannah. At one point they came to an abrupt stop. Before them there was a corpse. They had seen corpses before, of course— such was a definitive part of growing up in the slave colony of Gaoln. But this corpse's face was particularly frozen. Its eyes were wide open, and Gendorn did not know that eyes could be so large as this. The mouth was open, as if it had been screaming and frozen in place. It seemed to be alive and shouting at Gendorn, shouting in rage and hysteria and madness. Gendorn stood there, unaware of Bendoraun standing next to him, and listened to the screaming for as long as he could.

The boys ran back to the company of their gulaus. He had taken them with him this day just for that reason, and so he smiled to himself when the boys came running back in terror. He gathered them together with Rwannah and Kamira, and looked across their startled faces. "They did this to us," he explained to the youngsters, "they gave us mud to build houses, rags for clothes, and dry fruit for food, and they told us to wait in the freezing rain for our bread. When we asked them what they could do to protect us from such a storm, they did not answer by giving us blankets or clothes or homes or food to build our strength and end our hunger. They did not open their doors to let us under their roofs. Do you know what they said, when the Death Storm set in? When people bashed on the walls, opened up their hands clawing at doors, trampled people to death trying to find shelter, and cried with their babies for some safe harbor? *Run faster, or go die.*"

Nearly ten thousand people died in the storm on that single fateful afternoon.

One week later, ships from Skaen and Laen showed up along the coast, and Lonin soldiers gathered inside of Gaoln on the three edges of the nation not surrounded by water. They waited for Governor Centreal, now calling himself the King of Gaoln, to make a move. Without armor or weapons for his slaves, and unable to receive emergency food supplies through the blockade, the ex-governor surrendered and left his people at the mercy of their masters. The soldiers rewarded the slaves with an extra month of rations, then went home. For seven years, the prisoners waited and did nothing, starving and freezing to death as they slaved in the mines in exchange for rations from their old masters, with little hope that things might change in any lasting or permanent way.

- Chapter Four: Seven Years Later -

In the seven years since that time when the man who now called himself King Centreal stood upon the ruins of the last guardhouse, Gendorn had grown from a boy into a young man in his sixteenth year. His face was still slim, his arms thin, his smile weak— he had the same signs of slow starvation that every one of them had. The house he was in, made entirely of mud, was hardly large enough for him to sit with Kamira and Bendoraun. His gaze set upon the faces of his two friends, and he realized how much they too had changed. Even malnourished, Kamira had grown to be almost Gendorn's height, and Bendoraun was even taller. Bendoraun's voice had grown deeper, and both boys had scruff growing on their chins. When Kamira smiled, she looked to Gendorn like the same excited child who he had known all his life. Kamira was the most slender. Bendoraun was the healthiest— for many years, he succeeded in pretending to be someone who in reality had already died, and so received double rations for part of his youth. Yet none among the three could hide their rib bones if they tried. Someday, Gendorn hoped, he could grow strong and large, to a healthy size, and Kamira would grow so that she didn't appear to be a stick curving inward. The opportunities for them to grow into healthy adults were quickly fading, however— along with all their other hopes.

He looked up to see Bendoraun's face— the same expression that he himself had, the same expression Kamira wore. "You think so too?" asked Gendorn.

"It seems obvious," Bendoraun said plainly.

"They plan for us all to die before the snows end this year," Kamira said.

"They aren't even giving us food and blankets for our work in the mines anymore," Gendorn said, "and I am sure we can't survive on the goodwill of foreign nations for much longer."

"But what's to keep this new plan from the same fate as the first rebellion?" wondered Kamira. "Who says the ships won't come back and keep us on shore? What's to keep those soldiers from coming back and blocking our exits? Who would give us the supplies we need to escape, after our first escape failed so miserably? It isn't possible."

"You don't really believe that," Gendorn stated plainly.

"How could I? If I did, it means I no longer have any hope for us. But sometimes I do think that. How could I not think that? We all do. I'm just tired of empty hopes."

"Does it even matter what we believe?" Bendoraun asked them all. "We have to leave, regardless. We'll die if we all stay here. That's our only certainty. All of our food is gone. Almost none of the young or elderly remain alive now, and healthy, working men are dying by the dozen each day. I have no doubt that they mean for every one of us to be dead by the end of this Sen."

Kamira ran her hands up and down her arms for warmth— her shirt had been cut around the arms so that her sleeves were open, and it was getting to that time of year again when the coldest winds came down from the north across the ocean. The first snowfall was not far away. She shuddered. "You mean to go with King Centreal, then? I heard these same promises seven years ago. I won't believe them."

Gendorn shrugged. "Anything sounds good enough to me. I don't see any choice in all this, really— we either follow King Centreal or nothing ever changes, and our slow extermination will continue. Whether or not the plan will work, whatever the plan is— all that doesn't really matter so much as the certain fact that we have to do something." He moved off the floor and sat next to Kamira, throwing an arm around her and drawing her closer to him. "You're always so cold. Are you sure you're okay?"

Kamira nodded. "I'm just very hungry, all the time."

"I know."

It wasn't that this Gaoln was a penal colony for thieves and pirates and murderers, as the nations which ran the colony claimed it to be— it was, by this time, a land overrun by the children and grandchildren of these people, who themselves had committed no crime. A great many people had been political enemies of King Seagraul of Laen, and had been thrown in Gaoln just two decades before. The children of these people and those people themselves, then, were both of fighting age. In the years that had passed since that day when King Centreal took command of the "nation" as some dared to call Gaoln, by renouncing his title of Governor of the Penal Colony of Gaoln and proclaiming himself King of Gaoln, Gendorn, Bendoraun, and Kamira had come to learn about Gaoln in more depth. Laen, the nation to the east, administered the colony officially, heavily supported by the Skaelin across the ocean to the north and partly supported by Las, south of Laen, and Phenen, an island nation that was too far away for them to even comprehend. Skaen, the continent that they were meant to invade, was divided between the Skaelish and the Skaelin a generation ago in the Civil War of Skaen. The Skaelin were the enemies of Gaoln, the ones who sent prisoners there and then starved them, whereas the Skaelish were uninvolved. The only country that was sympathetic enough toward Gaoln to take any action was Gonaka, to the west. They were the ones who sent in the secret supplies of food and blankets— and it was because of that sympathy that these three children, sitting inside that little mud house, were still alive on this day. The food, usually supplied by the Skaelin, had already stopped last year. They knew what was happening— their captors meant to slowly starve them out, and let them die over the coming snows of Sen.

One could not simply emigrate to this sympathetic Gonaka, for the Gash— those who lived in Gonaka— did not appreciate outsiders becoming citizens or indeed even working in their cities, and it would have been a terribly poor choice for the King of Gonaka to make. Furthermore it was outlawed under the terms of the Partitioning of Gaoln for any nation to accept a Gaolnian as migrant or refugee. Such action would provoke condemnation from certain nations, and would be grounds for being dismissed from the Council of Nations. And so Gaoln was effectively alone in its struggle for freedom, aside from what help Gonaka could provide in secret.

The border markets were what fed the prisoners of Gaoln. They lived on inadequate amounts of bad water and del, a sort of dry, red fruit, which was grown throughout the whole world of Fengorian and sold in abundance for next to nothing. In the past ten years the Skaelin had become more involved in overseeing the markets and had been sending more people to exile in Gaoln, while at the same time setting aside less and less food for the penal colony. This left the Gaolnians with less food per slave with every passing year.

There had been almost no rain this past Trest— the hot season. The buckets back in the pels— the units of four to seven mud-houses where these prisoners were forced to live— were empty. People's mouths were swollen. Some had taken to drinking the water from the ocean, and gotten sick. Others had gotten sick from the lack of food. Delirious men wandered until their corpses dried in the sun or were buried in the snow. Gangs of emaciated youths terrorized entire communities, and it was commonplace for Gendorn and Bendoraun to fight them off with the aid of their neighbors. Every boy and girl in Gaoln was raised as a fighter in this fashion. Innocence died young in such a place. The Sen before had been especially cold, and even for those who had survived hunger and thirst, many had died before the warmth returned the next year. Youngsters had gotten sick trapping and cooking birds, as there had been some kind of disease with them, and so many of the youngest children had already died out.

"I don't know what this 'king' of ours means, really," Bendoraun admitted, taking Gendorn away from this lengthy train of thought, "unless he thinks we'll do exactly what we did seven years ago. And I think you're right, Kamira— it will turn out the same. The Army of Laen will surround us and anchor ships along the coast, and they won't let anyone through— how can we escape when we don't have any ships? They just keep the ships out, keep their troops on the edges of the colony, and we're trapped forever."

"Well, if this plan fails," Gendorn remarked, "I think we should consider swimming across the Cold Ocean to Skaen."

"Great plan," said Kamira, "would love to swim across the Cold Ocean. Sounds fun." Gendorn pushed her playfully.

Kamira was still shivering. Gendorn shifted a bit so he could put both of his arms around her, and he warmed her up by running his hands up and down her arms— of course, now Gendorn himself was quite cold, as the wind was blowing into the hut through the cracks under the mud wall and it was hitting him first. "I just wish this whole season would come and go already," he said, "so we could be warm again."

Three days later Gendorn was sitting on that old hilltop near the ocean. He had come here alone to the dead tree, the last tree in Gaoln and a symbol of the life that once thrived in this land. The stories of the prisoners told them that this tree, now withered and fruitless, was once the most graceful and bountiful tree in all the world of Fengorian, and that its roots connected all the forests of Kon, from the Cold Ocean to the Southern Sea to the Endless Waters of the East and West. They said that it was a tree planted many thousands of years ago by the nurturing spirit of the Great Ancient of Creation. In the Age of the Great Wars, so much blood had been spilled in this land that nothing could grow here any longer, and the spirit of the Ancient dwindled and abandoned the land to desolation. So the territory began in the Age of Peace as a penal colony where nothing grew or lived by nature's laws. The only remaining life was what was left of this legendary tree. And so on days like these Gendorn would come here alone and think the deepest of thoughts, from the earliest of his days up until this very moment.

It was the same hill, he remembered, where Kamira had first kissed him seven years before, and where they dreamed of their freedom. He tore his gaze away from the water toward the figures of Bendoraun and Kamira, approaching from behind.

"Gendorn," Bendoraun began— he sat down next to Gendorn— "there were men who came into our pels just after you left— we came straight to find you. They said we're going to war."

"That's a joke."

"They're serious. They say we can defeat the Skaelin."

"What?"

"The king is going around and speaking with the people, and he came in just after the men left, and I spoke with him," Bendoraun said. Kamira sat down on the other side of Gendorn.

"It's true," she said.

Gendorn turned his head back toward the sea. "What did the king say, then?"

Bendoraun paused for just a moment, then recalled what the king had said to him. "He spoke, at first, to several of us, and he was very excited about it all. Everything he said seemed very important, and he made it sound rather obvious. He said that invading the Skaelin Lands is the only way to escape life in Gaoln, 'to break free of our bondage as prisoners without a crime. The Skaelin have determined that we are not worth their efforts to keep alive.' That's what he said— and then they're just going to use the same pels to house more prisoners, once we're all dead. Laen has agreed to it— that's why the food and blankets have stopped." Bendoraun let his friends think on this for a moment, and then he continued.

"The king told me that in one and a half moons we will sail away to Skaen. Then he started talking like he did seven years ago, but this time he was more aggressive, and he kept talking about this plan— 'this is not a rebellion', he said, 'it is a revolution. In Skaen we will find food and warm blankets inside real houses. There will be no diseases, and a steady water supply. We will be free, and with the opportunity to live a life that has been denied to us since birth, the kind of life which every man and woman ought to have a chance to enjoy.' I think he's gone mad. Even if we get ships, they won't make it out to sea. Enemy ships will come in from Laen or Las or even the Skaelin Lands."

"Have some hope," Gendorn said to his friend. Gendorn was trying to remain serious, for this was apparently a very serious conversation, but Bendoraun's impression of King Centreal was absolutely terrible. Bendoraun's voice would be very deep and his face would crunch up, his eyes would squint and his smile would become flat, as if he were angry. Gendorn had never seen King Centreal up close, but he could not imagine that any king would actually look or sound like Bendoraun's impression.

"I wonder what it is like to be free," Kamira mused, ignoring them, "and to have all the gifts that the king promises will be ours."

"'There will be a war,' he said," Bendoraun continued, "'only the fit men will go.' The women, young children, and old men would have to stay behind. The army will have to move quickly to surprise the Skaelin, and can not be compromised by people who cannot keep up." Bendoraun shifted a bit in the dirt. "Then I asked him why we had to fight the Skaelin, instead of the Lonins of Laen— Gaoln, as I understand it, cannot cease to exist so long as Laen supports it. And so he told me:

"'It's politics. There has to be a war, because we can't emigrate. We can't invade Laen. We would get slaughtered before we made it three days past their borders. The Skaelin are still on the retreat from the Civil War of Skaen, locked up in their castles. Their supplies are low and their routes cut off, and they're vulnerable. They have few men left of fighting age. They'll forfeit western positions easily so as to safeguard their more defensible cities in the Eastern Mountains. At the same time they are drawing closer to an outright alliance with Laen, and they are throwing more and more people into Gaoln. King Sendroun of the Skaelin now directly governs the border markets here. You've seen them— how undersupplied they are, how chaotic. The Skaelin haven't even supplied the markets in a year. If it were not for Gonaka's goodwill, we would all have starved to death already. They are the ones, even more than the Lonins of Laen, who are responsible for this starvation and disease, and they are the ones who every day deny us our freedom. And we can defeat them, Bendoraun. When we tried to claim our freedom seven years ago we faced an alliance of nations— this time we escape in secret, so that no one will know but those who are helping us. Our freedom is coming, and you can put your faith in that. We are losing a fight that we never wanted to be a part of— it is time to take the offensive.

"'There has been a tendency in the world lately to think of Gaolnians as some separate race, descended from pirates and murderers,' he told me, 'Gonaka does not believe this propaganda, and neither does Kale or Keay or Aniania, or the Skaelish. But Laen, Las, the Skaelin, and the Phenese— they do not think of us as humans. We have to show them that we are human, and that it is because of their wickedness and their negligence that we die. It is only their treatment of us which makes us less than human, but it makes us more deserving than they of all the good things life has to offer. We have to find those things, and we will never, ever find them if we stay here.'"

"Going to war?" Kamira wondered. "How can something like Gaoln go to war— Gaoln is not even a country, we have no army, we don't even have food— how could we feed ourselves? This is going to be a disaster! How will we even get to Skaen!?"

Gendorn threw his arm around her and drew her closer. "You won't be going, sadly."

"What? We'll be safer here alone? What if Skaen comes down here, and just kills us all?"

"If I could turn you into a man and bring you," Gendorn said, giving her a light kiss, "I would. But I can't very well override the king. Our success will rely on surprise and swiftness. And I'm quite sure that no living creature would have any reason to come to this desolate land."

- Chapter Five -

It was only a few weeks later when Gendorn and Kamira found themselves atop that old hill once again. This, they knew, would be their last night together in a very long time— and if Fate was not on their side, they would never have a night like this again. Gendorn sat there, one arm around her shoulder, the other laying flat upon the frosty ground. His head rested upon hers, which rested upon his shoulder. They both smiled faintly, wistfully, as if already gone, off into the orange sky over the sapphire sea. They sat in silence, watching the sun slowly fade into the ocean, the cool breeze blowing through the crippled tree, the cool ground just beginning to harden into its wintry surface.

Gendorn's hand pressed against something small and round and hard, and he turned his head and picked at the thing with his fingers while Kamira simply stared down to observe what might be happening. His fingers came out from the earth clutching what appeared to be a sort of seed— it was brown, and round, and hard, and smooth— the size of a child's clenched fist. Gendorn looked perplexedly up at the small and withered tree above their heads, the only tree left standing in all of Gaoln. "It doesn't make sense," he said to Kamira as they both broke into laughter. "But then I suppose there isn't a lot that does."

"Plant it," said Kamira.

"In Skaen?"

"Yes, when you get there, find somewhere clear where it can grow, someplace inside a forest that is empty and needs a tree."

"What if the other trees make fun of him because he's from Gaoln?"

Kamira hit him playfully, and Gendorn smiled. "They won't," she said, "they'll worship him for having made it out of Gaoln alive."

"Okay, I'll plant it somewhere, and I will name it Kamira."

"That's not a tree's name!"

"Why not?" Gendorn asked, pretending to be offended. Kamira hit him again. "Okay, what is a tree's name then?"

"Liberty."

"That's original."

"Stop! Okay, what would you name the tree?"

"Promise."

"What?"

"I'll name the tree Promise, and it will be our promise that I'll take you there someday, and it will be a promise of freedom to us, to everyone going to fight in Skaen and everyone else like you who is staying behind. Promise of a new country. Let's call it Promise. Unless you like Kamira better. But now that I've been thinking of it, Kamira does sound like an unattractive name."

She hit him again. "Okay, Promise it is," she agreed.

"You're such an agreeable person."

Kamira rolled her eyes. "You're trying to make me stop hitting you."

"I'm just trying to be sweet!"

Kamira pushed him, but Gendorn rolled over quickly and tackled her with one arm. In an instant they were rolling on the ground, tumbling over each other in the dust, laughing and playing like children again. When they stopped Gendorn was on top, and he leaned in and kissed her, and just like that Kamira let go and Gendorn fell down beside her.

When the cold wind blew in from the ocean in front of them, Gendorn tightened his arms, and Kamira cuddled up against him. She fell asleep like that at some point. He would not sleep quite as easily, for though he had told her many times he would return, he knew in his own mind that there were no certainties. Tomorrow they would embark for Skaen. It was at some late point when Gendorn began to cry— not out loud, but instead quietly and to himself. He didn't make any noise. The tears just fell, cold as the wind in the early Sen sky. He laid his head down just before the dawn and went to sleep.

The next morning was the first snowfall of the year, a heavy drizzle, most of which melted on impact. Curileyn, Kamira, and Kanel had all come to bid their farewells to Gendorn, Bendoraun, and the other soon-to-be-soldiers. Curileyn stood with her arm around Kamira while Kanel said goodbye to his two young boys. "Gendorn, Bendoraun," he said to them, "you, like all the children of Gaoln, have grown up far too fast." He paused, and smiled. "And you are the only hope in our world for some sense of justice and goodness." Kanel was old and frail, and it had taken some effort for him to walk here today. Gendorn and Bendoraun knew in their hearts that they would not see their caretaker again. They hugged him tight, and the old gulaus saw them again as infants in his arms. "My days are gone," he whispered to the boys, "and yours are yet ahead. Take care that it is freedom awaiting you, and not an untimely death." The children nodded. The man who had raised Gendorn from birth, and Bendoraun since the age of three, stepped away.

Kamira approached smiling— how could she smile, on such a dreadful day? Gendorn shook his head, dismissing the thought, and Kamira looked at him curiously. "I already want us to be in Skaen," he told her. "I want to get off this ship with you on the other side and just build a house far away from the shore, where we don't have to look back at this place."

Kamira smiled again, this time genuinely. She walked up and gave him a kiss. "Someday soon."

Bendoraun met them by the ships. The army was providing them with blankets and thick shoes, and, covered in these things, Gendorn could hardly recognize his friend. Together the three of them looked down at the ships preparing to embark. Kanel and Curileyn stood behind them, observing the youths who held the future of Gaoln. The little ones held hands in silence until the time came for them to go.

"When I come back, Kamira, we'll turn around and sail back to Skaen, and we won't ever have to worry about not having enough food, or about dying because we can't keep warm," Gendorn whispered to her. "And we won't be prisoners anymore."

"You shouldn't worry about him," Bendoraun interjected, "once the enemy army sees this beast they'll throw down their weapons and cry at our feet— we'll probably be back in a week or two. Maybe a month, at most."

"Thanks, Bendoraun," said Kamira, "but somehow I don't believe you."

"I never tell a lie," Bendoraun insisted. Kamira laughed.

"I'll miss you and pray for you, Gendorn."

Gendorn kissed her forehead and tightened his arms around her. "We'll be in Skaen soon enough."

The officers came out from the ships to gather the soldiers up. They walked together down to the water's edge, where countless other groups of people were delaying as long as they could to say their goodbyes. Everyone was in their rags— there wasn't a single person who had armor or a weapon. Gendorn and Bendoraun made an effort not to think too hard about what that meant. Kamira nudged Gendorn, and Gendorn extended an arm, grasped her hand, and locked eyes with her. Kamira opened her mouth, but shut it quickly. Then she tried again.

"Don't let them kill you, Gendorn. People die in war, you know."

Gendorn could hardly help but to smile. *Of course people die in war.* "We'll never be farther apart than a single night's dream," he said cutely. He was rewarded with her smile.

"I'll see you every night, then," she answered.

Curileyn and Kanel came forward to hold Kamira's hand. Together, they watched as the ships pulled up their gangplanks and pushed off. They watched as the oars dipped into the sea and began to churn the water. They watched as Bendoraun and Gendorn stared back at them, as their eyes grew too far away for Kamira, Curileyn and Kanel to look into, and then their faces, and then, in an instant, they were gone.

The sea was raging. The water splashed on deck, carrying small sheets of ice which had to be picked up and tossed back overboard. The winds were howling. The snow started to stick at some point, and became a problem. Buckets were emptied and used to bail snow and ice. Gendorn had never sailed before, and could not tell if this was regular or anything to worry about. For him, it was rather terrifying. He stared out to the storming sea, toward the unknown fate that lay in the unknown land he would soon call home, wondering if the ship would even stay afloat.

He wondered, briefly, how Bendoraun was doing on his own ship— it was a shame that they hadn't been placed on the same ship. He was probably rowing, Gendorn decided. Gendorn could not bring himself to row. It wasn't just his physical weakness, but the ocean which kept him on deck. He kept thinking that he would find something, some promised land in the middle of the sea— a place hidden in the waves that had been waiting for them. A place not yet inhabited, a land they could call their own. But there was nothing. And there was some flicker of recognition, once Gendorn realized this, that they were not only sailing across the Cold Ocean to escape and find their freedom— they were also going to war.

When the wind came again, he turned his gaze skyward. *Guide us, Wind*, he prayed, *and do not lead us astray*.

The sun was merging into the horizon. As the night grew colder his thoughts became dark, and the tears came back. As he rested that night he imagined the warmth of Kamira next to him, and it kept him smiling. Then the creaking of the ship would wake him, and he would feel cold very suddenly— and he was alone again.

This happened for the fourth time just before the dawn, and Gendorn did not try to return to sleep. He looked up at the deck's floorboards with weary eyes. As he sat up and walked out onto the deck, staring up into the starless night sky, his heart began to calm. It was still a ways away from sunrise, but the sky had begun to turn into that most unique shade of blue that comes just before the dawn. Clouds covered everything, and the fog dipped into the dark of the ocean. He took a deep breath of the night air, and let his thoughts fall away, until there was only himself and the ocean, and that fog which covered them all and kept them hidden from the rest of the world.

Just before sunrise a circle of sailors were sharing a loaf of bread and a small basket of del. He joined the circle, taking a chunk of bread for himself. The men were older than he was, and they talked for a while as he lost himself in thought, forgetting about his bread. A booming voice caught his attention.

"Hey! Boy!" Gendorn blinked, returning from his thoughts.

"Yes?" he asked.

"What's your name?"

"Gendorn." The man nodded to himself, and waited for the same question. None came.

"I'm Tejk," stated the man, giving Gendorn a friendly look. Gendorn smiled. "Nice to meet you."

"And you," said Gendorn.

After breakfast, the group split up. Most went to help row, but Gendorn walked back to his cabin. Tejk caught up near the stairs. "Weren't you the guy not rowing for the first day or two? Who was always staring off into the ocean?" he asked, smiling. Gendorn gave a light laugh.

"That'd be me."

"What was that all about? You think you're the only one who wishes there was an easier way? The only one who has people to miss? The only one who is afraid they might not live through this?"

"Nothing, really...no, it's not like that."

Tejk nodded. "Row. It helps you forget. And if you don't, you won't do very well in the coming weeks. You'll find that men here don't appreciate lazy boys. Do you believe in us or not?" Then he turned to leave.

"Tejk!" The man turned, surprised. "Look at me. Do you see my ribs? You could yank them right out, the skin hardly even clings to them." Gendorn lifted his shirt. "Before you go around yelling at people, try to be more thoughtful. I wouldn't last three hours on the oars before my heart gave out. So don't raise your voice to me again." Tejk smiled.

"There's the boy I wanted to see!" He tossed Gendorn a piece of dried meat. "Found it in storage. Get some beauty sleep and help us row when you want to be a man."

Gendorn, his face flush with anger, turned away to look back at the sea, and he heard Tejk's words in his mind: *Do you believe in us or not?* His own voice came in— *do you believe in yourself? In your freedom?* His gulaus spoke to him the loudest of all: *you are the only hope in our world for some sense of justice and goodness.*

He almost fell asleep right on deck when the first beams of the dawn peaked out between the waves, and struggled to make their way through the fog. He nodded, as if agreeing to something. "Keep on rising," he said beneath his breath. "And we will rise with you." He went below deck and rowed most of the day until that same sun set, and another night began. And as he rowed he imagined what he was rowing toward— tables full of food where friends sat all around him, a cottage with a great fireplace to keep warm all through the Sen, lofty trees outside where fruit grew even through the snow! He'd have it all soon, he knew, just as long as he kept on rowing. Every time he dipped his oar into the ocean, he would see those pictures in his mind, and those same emotions would run through him— and he *knew*, he knew beyond any doubt at all that these were the things he was rowing toward, that every dip in the ocean brought him closer to that common dream, to that happiness that one day they would share. He rowed that whole day, and then after a brief dinner he rowed through the night and into the morning. He would not stop until he fell asleep at the oars, he promised himself, because now he could feel what he was rowing toward— and it was getting very close.

- Chapter Six -

Cheers of excitement grew louder around him, breaking him from his thoughts. He opened his eyes to the barely noticeable sight of land. All around him people were laughing and smiling, and he joined them. That was Skaen, right in front of them, their new land to be. Skaen greeted them with tall green trees covered in snow protruding from the earth, rising from the hills and valleys, and shorelines reaching out to receive them and their dreams.

Tejk came up from below deck. He didn't laugh or cheer, but he smiled as he stared at that piece of land in front of them. Then he nodded. "What's that mean?" asked Gendorn. Tejk shrugged.

"We'll see. Let's go row."

When they hit land the cheers erupted again. People threw themselves off of the ships and sprawled themselves out on the land. People were pointing at the trees— most of those who lived in Gaoln had never seen a living tree— and were trying to climb them. Most of them had all disembarked, but Gendorn and a few others remained, staring off into the snow-glazed hills from atop the ships. In those forests Gendorn heard, for the first time in his life, the chirping of a family of birds. To Gendorn, it was every bit as beautiful and every bit as sure as the sound of his freedom coming. From the snowy trees huge flocks of white birds emerged to explore the sky, and it looked as if they were the very snow returning to the clouds. He felt it coming now— this was it. They would be free, and these beautiful birds would be the ones to sing their song of thanksgiving.

Tejk tugged his arm, causing Gendorn to almost fall over. "Come on, we have to divide up into our regiments," he said. Gendorn turned back around, following Tejk to the huge mass of Gaolnian soldiers. The regiments were quickly decided by pairing couples of ships. Gendorn's ship, luckily enough, was paired with Bendoraun's ship. They were to be the 53rd Regiment of Gaoln, led by Captain Luncas. Gendorn and Bendoraun exchanged confident nods.

The regiments went off for a brief introduction, and the captains took names. The men unloaded everything from the ships, splitting up all the supplies between the regiments. Some of the captains brought out boxes of rope and spearheads from the ships, and instructed the men to find sturdy sticks in the forest for spear shafts. A few had axe heads, and ordered similar instructions. Still fewer had small daggers. *Better than nothing*, thought Gendorn. *Hopefully enough*.

They were all camping close together, just off the beach and around the ships. Once everything was brought to Captain Luncas, he ordered the 53rd to set up camp. A few men who knew how to do this had been sent to instruct the regiments, and it took a long time to get everything right. Still, they had some time before sunset. Some of the men started scouring the forest for wood to make weapons out of, using the few precious knives some of the captains had brought to carve out shafts. Men were in charge of their own weapons, which was meant to act as an incentive to find the right wood for spears and such, but Gendorn just wandered off alone into the forest, driven by his instinct to explore and understand everything new around him.

He took a deep breath. He had never known this scent before, of the snow and the pines and the life all around him. For one used to smelling acrid water and dusty air his whole life, it was overwhelming. *Smells like freedom*, he thought with a smile. He hiked further up the hill, discovering a clearing on the top. Tall grasses grew here, frosted and covered in snow, glistening in the light that was just beginning to become orange. He let his breath show itself in the cold air, and let his thoughts grasp the concept that he was alive, that he was standing here in Skaen. He let his gaze turn to the sky, and let every burden in the world slip away as the gentle snow piled around him.

A disruptive kick broke his dream. "Almost sundown Gendorn, we need to get back. Keep sleeping in the snow like this and you'll die someday," said Bendoraun. He spoke softly, but it seemed like shouting to sleepy Gendorn.

"Of course I'll die someday, you damn fool," answered Gendorn.

"Not of this cold, not now at least. Come on, the sun's almost gone." Gendorn opened his eyes, propping himself up with his arms. He squinted into the distance, where he saw the last traces of orange light from the first sunset of Skaen fade over the hills, and the first light of night fill the first night sky, flowing through the forest and over the meadows and peaks and valleys of the land. And even now the snowbirds were flying through the air, like living snowflakes speaking to one another and heralding the beauty of this place. He couldn't bring himself to care about the camp, and fell back into the cold meadow grass. He had seen people all his life— but this was something new. The single tree by his head was the most majestic thing he had ever seen— something that rose higher than anything Gendorn could have imagined, something strong and ancient and patient. Bendoraun laughed.

"Alright, fine. We'll stay here tonight, but just tonight," he said. "And only because it's so amazingly beautiful. But it is cold, Gendorn!"

"We'll be fine!" Gendorn insisted, "We've got more blankets than we ever dreamed of, Bendoraun— I don't know where the army found such things, but we'll be warmer tonight than any night we've ever been."

"Alright," Bendoraun conceded. "How was the sailing? I can't believe how hard some of our crew rowed, seeing as all we ever get back in Gaoln is that withered old fruit. It is only the thought of their freedom that gives them strength— I saw their muscles fail them every day. They'd just fall over by the dozen, then get back up and row again— did that happen on your boat as well?" Bendoraun sat down next to Gendorn, but Gendorn was silent. In such a moment, he much preferred the silence. The stars were beginning to come out. Animals chirped and clicked, scattering through the pines. Gendorn stood, and began walking through the meadow. A nearby noise caught his attention, and he saw a little white rabbit. He smiled at him, and the rabbit, in turn, seemed to smile back. There was a light shroud of mist in the forest, which obscured his vision— but just beyond the rabbit, Bendoraun was walking through the mists. Bendoraun stopped when he got nearer, taking notice of the rabbit. Gendorn opened his mouth, wanting to say something, anything. But nothing came— he could not explain such wonder.

"It's like my dreams…" he finally said. He was no longer facing Bendoraun, but was staring up through the treetops and mists, into that crystal night sky. Bendoraun glanced up into the stars. It was his dream too, though he did not say it. Instead, he just stood there, his eyes closed and mind at peace, before he lay down in the mist. Lying there, the two friends felt so far removed from the prison of their past, and from the hardships of their future, that they could not bring themselves to do anything but sleep in the reverie that had taken them.

- Chapter Seven -

They walked in a peaceful silence, hill after hill. The only sounds were the songs of birds and the wind, dying down, picking up, dying down, over and over again. Eventually they reached the camps, and as soon as they entered the area of their regiment a man came barreling toward them with a rather angry look upon his face. He was a man only slightly taller than the average man, but he wore glistening red armor— orchalin, the metal used to craft weapons and armor— and he carried two real swords. Gendorn and Bendoraun had glimpsed this man before, when they had met the men of their regiment— he was among the most well-dressed in the entire army.

"Where the in the world were you two!?" shouted Captain Luncas, even as he walked closer toward them.

"This should be fun..." whispered Bendoraun sarcastically.

"What do you boys think you were doing!? You can't just leave the campground!" he yelled, stopping immediately in front of them. "Where were you!?"

"In the forest, exploring," answered Gendorn. Luncas glared at the boy as if he would kill him right there.

"You were exploring the forest?" he finally asked, in utter disbelief.

"Yes..." answered Gendorn.

"We have scouts whose duty it is to explore the forests. We also have enemies who remain unaware of our presence and who could follow you back to camp. We have soldiers whose duty it is to guard our perimeters. Do you know what your duties are, boys?" The two boys remained silent. "Maybe bringing kids was a bad idea..."

"We just like it out there, sir," said Bendoraun, "We've never seen such a thing. It's not like we were running away."

"That's why we came back!" Gendorn explained emphatically.

"Enough!" shouted Luncas. Some of the soldiers were watching, anticipating what would happen next. "Exploring the forest. What do you think would have happened, if you had explored your way right into a caravan or a scouting party or an enemy settlement? What would have happened if you explored your way just a bit too far, and couldn't get back? Aren't you aware of your duties and obligations? Of the risks you take when you walk outside our perimeter? While we were reviewing battle plans in our regiments, you two children were out prancing through the trees like a couple of damn bunnies." He closed his eyes, sighed, and shook his head. "I know I'll regret this later, but from now on, you two travel with me at all times. Come."

Gendorn and Bendoraun followed Luncas back to the regiment's campfire. "We'll talk more about this later. You can't just wander off like that. But right now we have to move. So let's go."

Gendorn picked up an old satchel by the fire, and Bendoraun did the same. "Go, we're ready," said Bendoraun. Luncas turned and stared at him. Bendoraun looked around nervously, failing to avoid his glare.

"Don't order me, child," Luncas said calmly.

"Yes!" answered Bendoraun, now looking straight down.

"53rd!" shouted Luncas, "Let's go!"

Bendoraun and Gendorn followed Captain Luncas, one on each side of him. A man named Alaisio, they soon learned, was following in between, directly behind Gendorn and Bendoraun. He was the tallest among them, and more slender, although he also seemed stronger than the rest and more nourished. Through the hike it became apparent that Luncas and Alaisio were very good friends, though they had just met on the way over to Skaen. They heard only bits of the conversation passing between this man and the captain— "lost all my brothers in the

war, and my parents in the Great Wars…" from Luncas, and
Alaisio's reply: "Still hoping that my son is alive in Laen…works
with the underground resistance there…No, absolutely no idea
where she is, though I suspect she was captured and thrown in
Gaoln…yes, one of the reasons…", to which Luncas answered:
"Always a mystery…never could understand the whole
thing…used to work against the resistance, before I became a
sympathizer…", and at that point Gendorn and Bendoraun
stopped listening.

Tejk was behind them, somewhere in the mass that made
up the 53rd Regiment of Gaoln. None of them had any armor or
real weapons, aside from Captain Luncas, who wore that
glistening red armor over all of his body and a thick orange cape
over his back. No one in Gaoln was allowed to have orchalin,
so they knew that their captain must have had some powerful
friends.

Gendorn and Bendoraun didn't speak much; few did. It
was too hard of a hike, with too many hills to talk. But despite
the extra weight of his armor, Luncas continued his
conversation with Alaisio. It wasn't until well after noon, just
before the sun began to dive into the hills, that Gendorn
noticed a slight limp in the captain's right leg. The more he
watched it, the more certain he became. Luncas was indeed
limping. He didn't say anything— he didn't want to insult him.
He'd tell Bendoraun later that night.

The night was quiet, aside from the rustle of the leaves in
the wind and the sounds of the creatures of the forest. It was a
tranquil night, no fights or shouts, not even full-fledged talking,
just murmurs and low whispers telling tales of times long gone
around quietly crackling fires. Gendorn stood outside the edge
of the camp, still within sight of the regiment's fire. Bendoraun
came up beside him, trudging quietly through the leaves.
"Captain was limping," he said.

"Yes, I saw. War wound perhaps?"

"Probably," agreed Bendoraun.

"Gaoln has never been in a war. I wonder where he got it from," said Gendorn curiously.

"No...then again, he's too rich for a Gaolnian anyway, that's obvious. I think he was hired by the king..." said Bendoraun.

"Maybe. We could ask him," suggested Gendorn.

"I think talking to him is a bad idea, in general," said Bendoraun.

"The king, I meant— I would not dare to say a word to the captain." Bendoraun nodded.

"Gendorn! Bendoraun! Back to camp now!" shouted Luncas from the campfire, gaining the attention of several nearby regiments. Gendorn sighed, to which Bendoraun laughed lightly.

"What are we, twenty paces from the campfire?" wondered Bendoraun mockingly. "He better keep a closer eye on us, or we'll give the position away, Fate forbid it!"

"Damn kids...quit running off!" snapped Luncas, as the two came nearer.

"Sorry, sir. Just exploring a bit," replied Bendoraun.

"Quit exploring then!" answered Luncas, rather meanly. "We have a lot of work to do, and you two had better shape up if you expect to travel with us. Next time you take your stupid selves into the forest, come back quicker, and bring with you sticks for sharpening or wood for burning. You missed the briefing of our first target. Got it?" said Luncas sternly.

"I'll give you the abbreviated version," Bendoraun said, turning to Gendorn, "don't die."

Luncas glared at Bendoraun, boring into him with his angry eyes. "Test me, and I will make sure you don't live through this first battle."

"Yes," agreed both Gendorn and Bendoraun.

"Good," said Luncas, "That means now! Firewood!" The two boys started and turned around, walking out into the forest.

- Chapter Eight -

It was three nights later when Gendorn and Bendoraun, after collecting firewood for an unusually long time, arrived at camp very late in the night, after most of the men had gone off to bed. They sat around the fire and tended it, talking about how life would be here in Skaen once the war was over. Gendorn and Bendoraun did not require much sleep, and on some nights would stay up until the dawn without really meaning to. "We'll each have our own bed, and in the middle will be the fireplace where we can sit around all day when it's too cold outside," Gendorn said, "I feel warm just talking about it!"

"You're warm because we're sitting in front of a fire."

"Partly."

A voice came out of the darkness, calm and steady, but threatening: "You wandered again."

"Yes..." replied Gendorn, turning toward the captain. The captain came into the circle of the fire, and sat down beside the two boys.

"You are very stupid. You're really, really bad at learning." Then the captain smiled. "You two remind me of myself sometimes. Do you have any idea how many times I almost died because of how damned stupid I used to be? I'm not going to waste my time chastising you today, Gendorn, Bendoraun, because if you don't understand what I said to you *last* night, then you won't live to see *this* night. Today you must not disregard my rules, you must follow my commands— your lives depend on it. It is important you understand that."

"Yes," replied Gendorn quickly.

"Don't give me that 'yes', Gendorn. Unless you do exactly as I say, exactly when I say it, exactly how I say to do it, exactly as I want, then you will die today." Gendorn nodded again.

"We understand," said Bendoraun.

"You don't understand," said Captain Luncas. "You think you understand. After today, if you survive it, then you'll understand. And then I won't need to treat you like children anymore, because you won't be children anymore." The captain took a look up at the sky, then nodded to himself. "It's time."

"Wake up!" he shouted. "Wake up!" Captain Luncas went over to the tents of the other captains and woke them, then the captains woke their regiments. Soon everyone was up, and King Centreal and Luncas got their battle gear on. As the troops lined up King Centreal moved himself to the front, and looked back at his regiments, beginning to speak.

"We are marching today to take control of Port Tekal. With this town we can receive shipments from across the ocean before the ice is too thick. Gonaka has agreed to send us some supplies if we can take the town. Make no mistake, the men who hold this town want you dead— they are your enemies, your guards, the ones who have imprisoned you and your parents and grandparents and siblings and children— these are the same people who fight to keep you in your prison, the same army which, fifty years ago, marched into Gaoln and declared that we and our descendants would never be free again. They hold this opinion now, fifty years later— that we, that you and me and everyone we care about— are not deserving of a real life, of our freedom. So what are you going to say to them!?"

The crowd roared. People threw up their sticks and clubs and other oddities which they would use as weapons. Hands were waving everywhere— the shouting would not stop. King Centreal's gaze was fixed down the middle of the crowd, and he raised his voice to be heard over everyone: "We will say to them that we will die before we live a life under you! We will die by your sword sooner than by the lack of food or blankets, we will die by your sword sooner than by the disease which you brought to our people! We will die before we will submit ourselves to live a life not worth living— and we will die before we allow people like you to tell us that we may not have the *privilege* to be free!" The crowd erupted again, and King Centreal turned around to lead the men toward Port Tekal.

Gendorn beamed— he felt more alive, more empowered than he ever had before. All around him he saw the men looking stern and focused and confident. They had all the strength of their dreams, the strength that in their weakness allowed them to row all the way here in the first place. And now they were on the march— the very march— to claim their freedom. Bendoraun, standing next to Gendorn, put his arm on his shoulder. "We're going to be free, Gendorn."

They hiked for the whole of the morning, before King Centreal shouted "Formation!" The captains arranged the regiments into a defensive, solid rectangular position, which grew more like a square as the trail died off and broadened into a plain field of snowy grass. Beyond the grass was the sea, and between the two lay Port Tekal, still hidden by the rounded hills. In formation, the army advanced. Soon the city was in sight, and their pace quickened steadily. The city alarms sounded, bells rang, and Centreal shouted as loud as he could, heard softly above the clamor: "Charge!"

King Centreal and Captain Luncas were up front, being the only ones with real weapons or armor. So when the city guards set loose a volley of arrows on the Gaolnian Army, they were the first to turn and shout for their soldiers to take cover. One of the arrows landed right in front of Gendorn, causing him to stop in step, before he was urged forward by the man behind him. Another arrow hit the man two in front, and Gendorn sidestepped to avoid charging over the dying man. At once he almost lost his senses, but Luncas's yells brought him back. Sighting opportunity, Gendorn bent down to pick up a dagger someone had dropped. Bendoraun did the same. "Now they don't stand a chance!" said Bendoraun, trying for a joke. Gendorn, whose eyes were fixed ahead and who had just seen someone's neck cut, could not manage to laugh, but the words echoed in his mind: *Now they don't stand a chance...*

Before he could realize it, Gendorn was tossed into the chaos of battle. A sword swung at him, swiping its tip less than an inch from his neck. He immediately shaped up, refusing to blink for fear of death. The man in front of him stared into him with blue eyes, devoid of emotion. He was a moderately tall man of medium build, with a scruffy face and a long scar on his left cheek. Suddenly Gendorn felt angry. The man did not look particularly hateful— just confused, as if he was not fully registering the situation. But this man had just tried to kill him! A survival instinct kicked in, and it came with an intense hatred of this enemy, like nothing Gendorn had known even in the harshest days of his youth. Again the sword swung, but this time Gendorn dodged it with a speed he did not know he had, ducking under and swiftly plunging forward, jabbing the tip of his dagger into his foe's unarmored chest, right between his lungs. He pulled out fast, and jabbed again, this time at his heart. The man wavered, his eyes half-shut, mouth half-open, heart bleeding into his punctured lungs, and then he fell. A sudden wave of relief washed over him, overwhelming a far darker feeling he could not yet identify. He paid it no mind.

Gendorn picked up his dead foe's sword, and quickly tore off his helmet— a beautiful, gleaming orchalin helmet, brand new, and a perfect fit. The sword was something less— an old rusty blade, nothing more. Bendoraun took notice of the sword, and nodded at Gendorn. "You ought to get up there with the king, Gendorn, with that sword there."

As soon as he finished speaking a mace swung toward Bendoraun's head. Bendoraun plunged forward in a frenzied hurry, piercing the dagger through the man's mouth. The man screamed and swiftly swung the mace back around, and it slammed into Bendoraun's head. Bendoraun fell to the ground just as a sword jabbed through the man's back. The sword twisted, and the man fell forward onto Bendoraun's body. The sword pulled out, and the man wielding it, Tejk, looked at Gendorn sadly. Gendorn had been getting his bearings, avoiding swings all around him. When he turned and saw this scene, he froze with his mouth hanging open. "I tried, Gendorn," said Tejk. Gendorn couldn't speak, or nod, or look at Tejk. His mind froze. *What happened?* And he only heard those words still echoing in his head: *Now they don't stand a chance...*

When he saw someone coming at him in the edge of his vision, Gendorn's reflexes returned. He turned around to parry the blade of an attacking swordsman. They met swords several times, before finally Gendorn was able to slice the man's arm. His foe winced, and quickly Gendorn sliced through diagonally across the man's unarmored chest. When the second man withdrew, Gendorn lost almost all sense of reality. He turned around to meet another foe, and lost his breath, seeing Tejk lying on the ground, where he had stood only moments before. His head was chopped off, and his decapitated body was surrounded by a pool of blood. There were these things that looked like worms inside of his head, and on his neck, but the blood covered everything. The very last thing Gendorn saw was a giant war club coming right between his eyes. His very last thought— some brief flicker of sense and memory and reaction beyond the immediate threat of death— was some vague and terrible sense that everything he'd dreamed would come true had suddenly vanished, and that everything he ever cared about would die.

- Chapter Nine -

He awoke in a meadow, cold and clouded, with a strong wind and a soothing rain. There were trees all around him, surrounding the clearing. He was lying on his back, eyes shut, but he could sense these surroundings. He was half-asleep, aware of the sounds of the forest and the meadow and the various creatures within. The roaring winds ruffled the trees and the meadow grasses. The rain was cold, soft, and soothing. Ice was scattered across the meadow. He laid there, letting the rain fall upon him, the creatures crawl, the winds blow, for a very long time. He was happy here, and a smile took his face. He saw everything around him without even opening his eyes— he simply knew it was there. He took a breath of that fresh wild air, and then opened his eyes.

But he saw no meadow. He heard no wind. There was no rain, no frost, no little creatures. Instead he found himself lying on the floor, surrounded by injured and seemingly dead soldiers, in an old, abandoned facility of some sort. The scent of blood was pervasive, thick and metallic. He tiredly lifted his head, very slightly, and screamed in pain. He let his head fall back down, but the pain in his head would not go away. The more conscious he became, the more intensely the pain grew. Recalling with ease what happened during the battle, he was thankful to be left alive. They must have won, otherwise he would not have awakened in this building, inside, surely, of Port Tekal. So hope still remained…it hurt to think, but it was hard not to. There were just too many thoughts to be thought! He wished himself back in the meadow, unaware of his growing headache. He realized then that the meadow he had been lying in may well have been Sendeilta, that mysterious place where souls and spirits fled upon the death of their earthly bodies— the happy place which existed between the first life in Fengorian and the lingering eternity in the Great Beyond.

The pain was tormenting him now, showing in every feature— he could not stop thinking about this horrid, agonizing pain! It had spread past his head, and he was having trouble breathing. His ribs and lungs felt crushed, his neck and shoulders were throbbing. His head was the worst— there the pain was so severe that he could hardly process his thoughts. Tears forced themselves out of his eyes, and he gasped for breath. Another gasp, and a few more tears, then he cried out. He tried to adjust himself, tried to get more comfortable, but his head would not move. It felt as if it was detached from his body, its weight exceeding the weight of the rest of his whole. He yelled out again, and gasped for another breath of air. Then, suddenly, the pain rapidly faded, and he closed his eyes, letting out two last tears, as he drifted back out of consciousness.

The screaming pain held no place in the tranquility of the forest, the sacred calm of the meadow. Pain did not exist there, nothing did. All senses relieved, nothing was heard, or felt, or seen, or tasted, or longed for or desired, or even sensed. There was no need for food or water, no desire for company, not even the realization of this lack of all earthly bonds. In this dream-like, heavenly place, Gendorn rested again for a long, long time…

His senses all returned suddenly, and he opened his eyes. The building was almost abandoned now, but he dare not move his eyes to see who else remained. He had no sense of time— it was dark out, but that meant nothing to him— time had lost place, and he didn't recognize the abandoned workshop he was in for a very long while. He recalled then the careless, boundless dream he had just awoken from, and longed to return. He thought this without any pain in his head, and debated whether or not to try and sit up. He rested for some time, still the pain he had felt the first time he had awoken did not return.

After a while he sat up, slowly and cautiously, and he realized he did have a bad headache— it hurt to move his eyes, to look around, and to blink. By the distant lights he could tell that the room was dimly lit by torches. This was his whole world, he knew nothing else, even what he saw did not register as reality— and he did not remember how he had fallen in battle. He started to sweat heavily, and was beginning to lose his bearings, when those realizations hit him. It was dark. What did that mean? He blinked again, and the pain in his head sharpened. A random word came to mind, *Gaoln*. What was that? He could hardly bear to think anymore, his head was hurting so much now. The sweat was drenching his clothes. *Dark! Night! What is night?* Immediately the thought was lost, an overwhelming sense of weariness taking its place. *The building!* A memory of consciousness flashed for a moment in his mind, then it too was lost in the void of heat, weariness, and pain.

The sweating suddenly stopped. It was dark out, it was night time. He had been hurt. In a battle, a war club had smashed into the center of his face, guarded by his nosepiece, the only reason he was alive now. His body began to cool. He recognized the building, but from where? He stood up, slowly, and the weariness returned in a much lesser sense. He looked around the room, relieved that it did not trigger the pain. His steps were weak and uncoordinated, like the steps of a blind man without a cane. The more he walked the better they got, and soon he was walking almost normally. He walked slowly, and was surprised to find Bendoraun lying down on the floor. A surge of hope came to him that he might still be alive, but it was quickly defeated by the cold fact that he was dead. But why then did they take him in? He knelt down beside his old friend, pressing two fingers strongly against his neck. He still had a pulse— he was alive. Hope came back, but then faded as he remembered the circumstances. Bendoraun was one of the very last people here, and probably had been unconscious since the battle, where he had taken a strike with a mace to his hardly-protected head. He was still fighting valiantly for his life, but that might not be enough. Time would tell, Gendorn knew, but he wished he could know sooner.

At some point it became the dawn. Gendorn had taken Bendoraun's pulse countless times, but never failed to find it. He looked up at the door as a man came in. The man, only slightly taller than Gendorn, spoke in an excited and eccentric voice. "Hello! How are you feeling? I wasn't sure anyone else was going to wake up, glad to see you did!" Gendorn was unable to explain what he'd been through, how he felt, so he said nothing. "I'll be right back!" said the man, turning to leave. He returned moments later with some fresh water and soup, which he offered to Gendorn.

Still unable to speak, Gendorn forced a smile, and gladly accepted the gifts. For a boy who had never eaten real food, the soup was unfamiliar, but it smelled like heaven, and the taste was something he had never imagined could exist. He held the first spoonful of it in his mouth for an eternity, cherishing the flavor and how filling it was. As filling as an entire day of rations back in Gaoln. He smiled, and a warm feeling came into his heart, a feeling that said he was the luckiest boy in the world. Alive, and with real food! He almost forgot his caretaker.

"You know him?" Zeal asked, nodding at Bendoraun. Gendorn tried to assert his voice, but only managed to let out a very faint "yes". He could not explain further, and didn't really feel like talking anyways— he was certain Bendoraun would never wake up. Tejk had died to save them, and somehow he felt that it had been a waste of his life— the life of an entire person, wasted to save another person, who died only moments later.

That was only in the conscious part of his being. The other part of him had died, or was still asleep. It could not register that Tejk had died. It could not even begin to imagine that Bendoraun had died. It could not dare to think that he, Gendorn, had killed two men. It could not think that this was a real war, and that this would be the way he lived until that war ended or until he died. "Come out when you're ready, the city needs some work. I'm sure we can find something for you to do," said the man.

Gendorn didn't hear that. Who were those two men? Where were they from? They were both many seasons his elder, probably in their thirties or forties, and their lives surely were richer than his own. Were they married— how old were their kids? What were their professions? What had they done with their lives? How many would cry, when their villages learned they would never return to them alive? Gendorn had killed them— he *killed* them. He ended their lives.

Those thoughts receded, and another came into his mind, of some other man's sacrifice— why did Tejk die for them, for

Gendorn and Bendoraun, for two men who were surely destined to die soon anyway, who knew nothing at all about war or peace or the world?

Shortly after the man left, Gendorn stood and exited the building. The man was right outside, leaning against the wall with his arms crossed. He had short black hair and slightly tanned skin, and he sighed, his eyes squinting in the sun, as Gendorn approached. "I've never seen anything like this…" Gendorn said.

"Neither have I," replied the man. The sun was bright, shining directly at them, and hurting Gendorn's head even more.

"What's your name?" asked Gendorn.

"Zeal," replied the man, "You?"

"I'm Gendorn. So where is everyone? And isn't it supposed to be snowing out?"

"Yes, very unusual weather considering the first snows fell in earnest more than thirty days ago. We can't figure it out, but the weather down here on this end of Skaen is warmer. Perhaps it is because we get more of the sunlight, as there are no mountains around this little peninsula. But, at any rate— the army already took the weapons and siege equipment, the armor too. They left three days ago."

"Oh…how long was I out?"

"Five days. The army put me in charge of watching over the injured three days ago, then they left. They didn't rest at all, they just looted the place and marched off."

"Bendoraun. How has he been doing?"

"The man you were sitting by? He's been out cold for a long time, I'm sorry to say. I don't know about him…" Gendorn nodded, having heard exactly what he had concluded himself.

"If he does wake up, he'll need water immediately," said Gendorn.

"I know," replied Zeal, "That's why I'm here." He smiled at Gendorn, and Gendorn nodded.

"If he does wake up, let me know?"

"Of course."

"So what should I do?"

Zeal sighed. "Are you okay to work?" he asked, sounding concerned.

"Maybe, as long as it's inside. The sun is really hurting my head."

"I heard you had a hard hit, lucky your helmet was there."

"My helmet, yes. Where is that thing?"

"We removed it right when we took you in. Check the smithy, maybe it was sent to be repaired. The nosepiece was damaged pretty bad, I doubt the army took it in that shape."

"I believe that," said Gendorn.

"You could work at the smithy. Headache, bad idea—nevermind. Hmm...I don't know, Gendorn. Most of what's left of the work to do is outside in the sun, or noisy indoors. Maybe you can see if the cooks need help preparing dinner for the city. I'll take you," said Zeal, already walking off down a street.

"Zeal, where are the native villagers?" asked Gendorn, surprised by his odd realization.

"Turns out the port was abandoned, only garrisoned by a small force, which we managed to defeat with quite a struggle. The walls weren't complete, so we overran the place once we broke through the guards who were defending the breaches. We defeated a guard force protecting a breach on the eastern side, so we rushed in and surrounded them, and took the city soon after. But there were no villagers here, and no ships at port either, so it's our stronghold now. Most of our army left to continue our march, so we'd be doomed if the Skaelin try to take it back. We're fortifying it though, repairing the walls and digging murder pits, and we trained some archers too. There were a lot of bows and arrows in the armory. So while the army divides into their divisions and combs through the Skaelin

Lands, we will receive shipments of supplies in through this port and send them north. And by the time that the allies of King Sendroun realize we've invaded his lands, the ice will be too thick for them to send aid. By that time, we'll have other ways of securing food— other cities here in Skaen, that is. It really is quite a nice plan. But, here we are! The chef's place— help out however you can. I'd better get back to the wounded," answered Zeal, turning to leave.

"Why was it abandoned? Does that mean the army has gone somewhere else, that they knew we were here?" Gendorn asked quickly, before Zeal could leave.

"Doubtful. One of the soldiers we found hiding in a warehouse told us they had been dismissed several years ago, in the Civil War of Skaen, but their homes had been destroyed in the carnage and their families killed. Some of the men went to farm new plots, and started their lives up again. But some of them decided they couldn't go back to wherever it was they'd came from, you know, so they were holding out here. The fort has been in disrepair since the invasion during the Civil War of Skaen, and reconstruction stopped after the truce was signed. So this may just be the safest headquarters in the country right now."

"They didn't want to go back?"

Zeal nodded. "It's hard to go back, when you have nothing to go back to, and after so much time in combat, a lot of people just lose their connections to a world outside the front lines. Returning to a burned village and a deceased family is, at any rate, an unhappy prospect." Gendorn stood silent for a moment, and Zeal watched for his reaction, examining the young boy who, so innocent and naive, had come to take part in what was surely a suicidal war.

"But they didn't even try to find their homes or families— they just gave up and decided to live in an old military fort, until the day they died?"

"They made their own village, Gendorn, because they didn't have a village left to return to."

Gendorn's critical look eased up, and he thought again of the men he had killed. He nodded at Zeal who, with a last careful look, turned again to leave.

"Need any help?" Asked Gendorn, as he walked into what appeared to be a large kitchen.

"You know how to make anything?" asked one of the chefs.

"No. You?" replied Gendorn.

"No. None of us do, what do they expect, it's not like any of us have cooked before, there's nothing in Gaoln to cook! And what in this world is a *gezru*? Every written recipe here needs a *gezru* of something!" said the man. "I'm a bit frustrated, sorry…"

Gendorn shrugged. "Give me orders."

- Chapter Ten -

"Gendorn! He woke up!" yelled Zeal, running into the kitchen. Gendorn looked up, wide-eyed and open-mouthed. "He woke up, only for a moment, I threw water down his throat, but he slipped away again before I could give very much to him. He was sweating horribly when he awoke…I should get back to them. I'm sorry my news isn't better, but at least it's something. Keep your hope, alright? But don't rely on it too much." And just like that, Zeal was gone.

Gendorn wandered out of the kitchen and into the harshness of the hot sun. Suddenly everything exploded. He was drenched in hot sweat, dizziness blurred his sight completely, and the throbbing pain in his head numbed the whole of his body. He lost his senses quickly, then he fell to the floor of the cobblestone street, unconscious under the blazing heat.

"This isn't the end of us," Spoke a familiar voice. Opening his eyes, Gendorn found Bendoraun standing right in front of him.

"Are you alive?...Am I dead?" asked Gendorn.

"I'm not sure. But I do not think we are meant to die— not yet. We have a long way to go. Many more battles lie ahead, and harder trials still— but we can't possibly be done so early, when we have so much to do," answered Bendoraun.

"What are you talking about?"

"I've been dreaming for a long time, and I've been waiting for you to join me."

"Bendoraun! You are dying! Wake up!"

"We are always dying, and always living."

"What ...?"

"It's true, isn't it?"

"Is this Sendeilta?" asked Gendorn.

"I don't know, I assumed Tejk would be in Sendeilta."

Gendorn's immediate sense of warning had faded quite quickly. He no longer felt the urge to get Bendoraun and himself out of this place, but instead felt rather content. "Maybe he's elsewhere, or maybe we're not in Sendeilta. Maybe we're just here to rest for a while " suggested Gendorn.

"Maybe, friend," said Bendoraun. "I'd like to think so."

Something shifted in the mist. "Do you believe in Sendeilta?" asked the voice of their gulaus, Kanel.

Gendorn shook his head in disbelief, while Bendoraun jumped frankly to the point: "So, *are* we dead?"

He emerged from the mists, his wrinkled face smiling heartily at the boys. "This is not Sendeilta. Your spirits have not yet left Fengorian— they do not wait to pass into the Great Beyond. It is simply a powerful dream, a dream that we are all dreaming. You have a lot to do back in the living world of Fengorian, Gendorn, and you as well, Bendoraun. But I am no seer. I know that hope can be a powerful thing, but it can also be a very terrible thing, and you must not keep too much of it," said Kanel, putting a hand on Gendorn's shoulder. "I came here for one purpose, and that is to remind you two boys that our world can be a very terrible place for those who hope. While this is true, it remains true also that without hope and the strength to follow our hopes, our dreams are never more than dreams. I see strength in you. I do. In you I see the stars shining after the storm in the night. So keep your hope, and if Fate is kind enough it will serve you well.

"You two are not meant to stay here, and I must return as well." He saw Gendorn's look of concern. The gulaus smiled. "I have a feeling we will all meet again." He turned to Gendorn, and inside himself Gendorn felt something stir— something which sent chills coursing through his body and rendered everything around him mute, except for this one powerful voice: "Be strong when the world around you falls to ruin. Be the best person that you can be. That is all we can ever do." His gaze shifted away from Gendorn. "Farewell for now, little soldiers."

"If you are dreaming, Gulaus," Gendorn said, "then you can't be dead."

"So you'll be coming with us," Bendoraun continued.

"I myself am not coming. But you will find that I am there all the same."

"That doesn't make sense," Bendoraun protested.

"No, not yet," Kanel said with a smile— then he shifted his gaze toward Gendorn once again, "but I think that someday it will be rather easy to understand."

Kanel disappeared into the very air itself.

Bendoraun felt nothing but thirst. Water splashed down his throat, but it dried up, and he felt no satisfaction. It happened again, and his eyes opened. "Are you okay?" asked Zeal. Bendoraun said nothing. "I'll get you more water," and Zeal ran out of the workshop. Bendoraun reached up to feel for blood, and cringed in pain when the tip of his finger touched the side of his head that had taken the hit. It was bandaged up, and the blood would probably be dry anyways. Zeal returned with more water, handing it over to Bendoraun, who tiredly lifted the small bucket and drank the water. Gendorn came in the room, standing in the doorway.

"Bendoraun..." Gendorn said softly, hardly able to believe his sight. Bendoraun could not look up to see him, it hurt to move his eyes. He could not talk either, hard as he tried, nothing ever came out. Zeal pushed past Gendorn, rushing to deliver the water.

"Gendorn, can you go in the sun yet?" he asked.

"I just passed out in the sun. I need a break," he answered, walking slowly over to Bendoraun. "It was very strange..." *Passed out in the sun...*suddenly Bendoraun remembered the dream that his thirst had made him forget. He tried agonizingly to speak, pushing his limits, trying to force his mouth open, to find a way to speak, but he could not. Every muscle he had, all the strength that was left went into speaking, still he could not speak. It tired him, and he felt a sudden overwhelming heat. His breathing got heavier, and he fell back down.

He drifted in and out of consciousness, never dreaming, simply skipping through time. His senses were still present, but very dull. Some time later the pain had waned, and he sat up and tried to speak. Gendorn kept urging him on: "Stay awake, Bendoraun," he told him. Bendoraun could not acknowledge this, through motion or speech— the words themselves hardly registered in his mind. Zeal left to get more water, returning moments later to splash it down his throat. This happened, in between bouts of sleeping, for one full day, before finally Bendoraun was conscious enough to stand. He waved his arms around, trying to maintain his balance. His legs gave way and he half-collapsed before steadying himself.

"Dream..." he managed to murmur in a low, raspy voice. Gendorn smiled, and looked at him curiously for a time before replying.

"Yes...the dream."

"What's going on here, stay with me Gendorn..." said Zeal. Gendorn laughed.

"It's nothing, Zeal. Don't worry. Certainly nothing to worry about..."

"Alright," said Zeal. Gendorn turned to Bendoraun.

"Can you speak?" he asked. Bendoraun did not answer—it hurt too much for him to think and move; he did not want to admit that he might actually be able to speak. Zeal continued fetching water for some time before Bendoraun spoke again, this time to Zeal.

"Thank you..."

"You're welcome. I'm Zeal, your medic. You're Bendoraun, I know."

"Maybe you should sit down," said Gendorn.

"Need strong legs," replied Bendoraun.

"Okay, but don't break your bones. You're lucky to be alive right now," said Gendorn.

Bendoraun's expression was plain, and he made little attempt to speak. "I'm feeling better...thank you for the water, Zeal."

"Of course. We are very relieved that you're alright. Gendorn was about to go mad," replied Zeal.

"This is Port Tekal, then?" asked Bendoraun.

"Yes, this is Port Tekal. It's almost time for dinner. You two rest here tonight, and I will bring you some food. I can show you the city tomorrow with some of the others if you are both feeling better then. But for now, stay here, and just relax. Walk around whenever you are well enough, but do not push yourselves too far." They both nodded. "Alright, then. I will see you both tomorrow evening."

The two boys spent the night recovering, standing and sitting and walking around and trying to regain all their muscles and to gather all of their thoughts. True to his word Zeal approached them the next evening and offered to show them to where they would dine. Bendoraun and Gendorn followed Zeal down a crooked old cobblestone alley, which led to a large boulevard full of old shops, guilds, and inns. They were all in disrepair, having been abandoned for decades. All of them were completely empty inside, and the boys could see this through the space where doors should have been. At the end of the boulevard they turned towards the docks, and went into an abandoned storage room full of people, most of whom looked as if they had a fair deal of injuries. Several were missing arms or legs, but there were none among the survivors whose head injuries were worse. One man had lost an eye and wore a patch, another man walked bent over backward because part of his stomach was torn. Noses were generally crooked, as a rule, and bloody clothes seemed to be the fashion. The three of them sat around an old crate and waited for dinner.

Part Two:
The Thin River Highlands

- Chapter One -

"How do you feel?" asked Gendorn.

"Bad. But I'll get better, right? I mean, how do you feel?"

Gendorn shrugged. "Better than you, I'm sure."

"So how are we going to meet up with the army?" asked Bendoraun.

"That depends on when you leave," said Zeal. "Centreal left me a map of their planned route; your path to intersect with them changes daily. If you do not feel ready, you will not be able to join them for a rather long time, in which case you could remain here, if we can find a post for you."

Gendorn and Bendoraun traded glances. "Don't you want to stay here a while? See what the town is like? It's the first real town I've been to," said Bendoraun.

"Maybe a bit. But we have to catch up," said Gendorn.

"Why? Do you really want to return to the army? Think about this! We can be so much more useful here— we don't know how to be soldiers, Gendorn. I think our friend the captain would tell us the same thing."

"We will all leave eventually," Zeal interjected, "It's simply not safe to remain here at Port Tekal. Someone's bound to come by here and discover us, and we're supposed to keep as low a profile as possible for as long a time as possible. We just need to keep this port until we receive the shipments from Gonaka. They will outfit us with everything we need to form our own unit. But the fact is we don't have the food for so many people to wait until that time. So, in the end, you must leave before the rest of us do. Only the core guard units will remain for the shipments, and they must be in the best health."

"When will the others all be leaving?" asked Gendorn.

"When the shoreline freezes over. We're repairing and producing what weapons we can, and trying to figure out as much as we're able to about our enemy by reading the maps they've left behind," replied Zeal. "We're leaving group by group, though. So far everyone is leaving without armor and with only bows and arrows, and they have various excuses in case they're caught. Only those who left a day or two after the army bore any instruments of war."

"I think we should go back to the army. I have a bad feeling about staying here too long. It feels like we're waiting in a trap," said Gendorn. Zeal nodded understandingly.

Bendoraun looked at him skeptically. "We'll die if we return to the army. You know this. We're worthless to them. We can do something useful here."

"I have to go, Bendoraun. I can't stay here. Much as I want to explore this place, it's too easy. It seems like something is lying in wait for us. Our enemy."

Zeal nodded. "You have strong instincts, Gendorn, and you're right. Look at this place. We're in a valley on a peninsula. Should the enemy discover us, there will be no escape. We would never see them coming. We don't have enough forces to amply scout the area north of here while maintaining a defense in the south in case of a naval attack. We can't get out if we're cut off even in our northern route, because we don't have any ships. We aren't trained, and we have virtually no experienced leadership."

Gendorn nodded. "It's a beautiful location, but it's a treacherous one. We would never escape. We can't hold this as a fortress."

"And yet," Zeal said with a sigh, "this place is peaceful, and it gives me a place and time to rest, and fills me with calm. I haven't felt so at peace since   well, before Gaoln. Back when I was a freeman   "

Bendoraun seemed about to say something, but Gendorn said quickly: "As do I, but I'm getting anxious. I don't trust this place. I can rest, and should, for a time. But then I must leave, and I can't delay too long. You don't have to come with me, Bendoraun. If you're not feeling well enough you probably shouldn't."

"I know, and I may not," answered his friend. "Do you really feel that badly about this place?"

"Yes," Gendorn answered, "and there is something else— I just, it seems like there is more ahead, but that we won't find it here in Port Tekal. I've had that feeling ever since we had that dream."

"I had a different feeling after the dream, and it makes me want to never leave Tekal."

"You dream together?" Zeal interrupted, "you are quite strange, you know. Don't worry, I'll give you some time. They don't need to leave on the exact date. But they can't wait too long for you."

"How long should we rest, Bendoraun? Assuming you are, in fact, coming?" said Gendorn.

"See how we sleep, how we feel in the morning. How long was I out, Zeal?" replied Bendoraun.

"Six days. One more than Gendorn. It's a miracle either of you survived."

"Did we miss any battles?" asked Bendoraun.

Zeal thought for a moment. "It depends on how the army's doing, but by Centreal's expectations, you missed nothing big. They plan to raid some villages and then, after stocking up on food, arms, and other supplies, they plan to cut through the Thin River Highlands and turn around along the Frozen Meadows. They plan to take down the supply villages, cutting off resources to the forts and thus defeating them without the risk of face-to-face combat. At least not a lot of it. That's the plan for the next one hundred days, and then they will begin taking fortresses. But if the army is discovered and word gets to King Sendroun in his Eastern Mountain stronghold at Cavfurt? Well, then I suppose this will turn into a race," he paused. "You probably won't be alone, just see who else wants to go when you're ready."

They all slept well that night, except for Zeal, who had to tend to a man who had just awoken from three days' unconsciousness in the middle of the night. Gendorn and Bendoraun woke up with the light of day and the noise of early workers, both feeling much better, but still rather wretched. They felt sure they would be going through this for a long time to come.

"Ready to catch the army?" asked Bendoraun, lying over in his bed after some time spent struggling to stay asleep.

"Not really, this headache's horrible. I can't hike in the sun with this," said Gendorn.

"I'm glad. I would not have gotten up. I would have lain here, and said goodbye from my bed."

"That sounds about right."

"You missed the no-sun route, in Fenidaln Meadows," said Zeal, coming in with some water. "Now you'll have to cut through the Thin River Highlands." He sat the water down for the three of them to share.

"How was that man who awoke in the night?" Gendorn inquired.

"He fell asleep at sunrise, just in time for me to start working with the rest of you..." replied Zeal.

"My sympathy," said Gendorn.

"Yes, he's been drifting in and out since the battle, he can't seem to stay awake. Hard to tell if he'll make it, but if anyone still has a chance, it's probably him."

"Our blessings on him," Gendorn said. "How are we going to meet the army, then?"

"You could travel in the sun, but it's still a bit risky in your condition. One group's preparing to leave; they're going to cut through Thin River, the area I told you about. It's a nice route, waterfalls and cold springs. It will be cold this time of year, but as it is in a rather high area it receives a lot of sun and so will have nicer weather during the day, even if the winds might be rather sharp. There's not a lot of tree cover in some places. Unless you leave with them tomorrow morning, you two will have to take a longer route with a later group, and probably will have to meet the army at the turn-around in the Frozen Meadows. As its name implies, that will be a much less enjoyable route taking you to the northern reaches of Skaen, where few things grow and the snow never melts, unless you choose to remain here in Tekal until we can assign you to one of the smaller army divisions around the area. They will be acting under King Centreal's commanders." Gendorn scratched the thin beginnings of his beard, unsure what to do.

"Let's do it, Gendorn," said Bendoraun. "I don't want to hike to someplace called the Frozen Meadows. And I'd prefer to stay with the king himself and his army, the largest division, and trust his officers to train us well. The rest of the 53rd is with him, and as much as I hate Luncas, I trust him to keep us alive."

"He didn't do a good job with that at Tekal, but I suppose it isn't a very easy job. It is our only real choice, unless we want to freeze to death. Who else is going?"

"Nolor, Sheal, Hendall, and Wyan," answered Zeal. "We have some packs of food prepared, and some blankets and such, but you can carry no arms. If anyone finds you, you're out of work, your village suffered an epidemic and you had to leave— make something up. Anything that fits the story of a lost group of boys and men in the woods wearing clothes that smell from a continent away and looking like they've been starving since the day they were born. Also, you two, specifically, will have to think of something to cover up the stories of your wounds and to explain your bad headaches, if anyone is so inquisitive. You should hammer that out before you leave."

"Yes," said Gendorn. "Let's go get breakfast."

At breakfast they caught up with their four companions, and confirmed the details of their trip. Hendall had a map of their route, marked with landmarks to confirm the right path. After breakfast the day was spent packing and doing various jobs around the city. The other four had already worked out most of the logistics. Packed and ready, they had dinner after working all day, and returned to the infirmary to sleep.

- Chapter Two -

"Get up!" said Nolor. "Get up get up-get up! Everyone who's coming along, get up!"

"I'm getting up!" replied Gendorn.

"I see you on the floor, Gendorn!"

"You're seeing things," said Gendorn, with a hint of a smile.

"I think my head is working better than yours right now!"

"Fine, I'm up."

"Me too..." said Bendoraun, opening his eyes slowly. "Give me some time."

"I'm awake," said Hendall, walking into the infirmary. "Sheal and Wyan still sleep."

"I'll take care of them," said Nolor. "Make sure you all have everything you need. We leave after breakfast. Meet us in the kitchen. We'll be there soon. Say goodbye to everyone now, but be fast," said Nolor, leaving the workshop. Nolor himself had to bid farewell to his brother, who had been gravely injured and could not come along. Sheal, Hendall, and Wyan all had at least one friend to say goodbye to. Bendoraun and Gendorn only said bye to Zeal. After the others said their goodbyes, they also thanked Zeal, and said their final farewell. They left with all their things for the kitchen.

After breakfast they retrieved their belongings and departed Port Tekal, heading northward toward the Thin River Highlands. Outside of the gate were some fortifications which they had built after taking the city. Beyond these walls and ditches the field, and the hills beyond them, were still littered with decomposing bodies. As was custom across all of Fengorian, the bodies were to decompose and become a part of nature through burial, cremation or other means. The most important part of the process was to ensure that the physical soul could continue to grow in the world of the living. The most honored bodies would be buried beneath great ancient trees so that they could spend eternity nurturing the world. In some instances bodies were eaten, and indeed such had happened with most of these bodies, as the Gaolnians had been emaciated to their cores. In this way, the soul lived on in other human beings. Likewise, if the soul were to grow with trees and plants and be eaten by animals, then it lived on in new physical forms while the original soul remained in Sendeilta. Even when the bodies were burned, the remains and ashes were buried beneath great ancient trees, or tossed into the ocean to become a part of the mysterious abyss. For some people, it was more customary to throw ashes up into the air, to become a part of the wind, which ties all parts of the land and sea together, thus allowing the spirit to travel across all the corners of the world. The emphasis, respectfully, always had to be on allowing the physical soul to endure in Fengorian while accepting that the spiritual soul must leave for Sendeilta, although the physical soul was believed to have had spiritual energies.

Most of the remaining bodies had already been buried by the army in large mass graves, but as the army had to attend to other matters there were still a good number of bodies left which the regiments posted at Tekal were assigned to dispose of. As there were so few able men left in Tekal, and as defense was their foremost priority, the bodies lay there for the time being. The guards north of Tekal prevented anyone from chancing upon them, and stayed far enough away to make sure the scent of death could not reach anyone. As there were not enough men for digging, the soldiers took to burning. The bodies would only be burned in small numbers, so as not to give off a lingering scent of burning flesh which might alert the Skaelin to their presence at Tekal.

At first, Gendorn and Bendoraun, and the rest of their party, could hardly move. They just looked out at the field of bodies. Without a word, Nolor cast his eyes downward and took the first step out from the gate. Gendorn followed behind. As he walked past the bodies, Gendorn ignored the hands and legs reaching for him from their graves, he closed his eyes to the lifeless eyes which would have stared back at him. It hurt him— and he saw Bendoraun's expression turn grim as well— to know that Tejk was somewhere in this mass of bodies. When they got to the top of the hill, Gendorn stopped and turned back to look upon the site of his first battle. He gazed across the field where he so nearly lost his life, where Bendoraun almost died, where Tejk still lay. Where Gendorn had killed two men.

He turned around to find Bendoraun just behind him. Gendorn looked at him with that sort of expression which Bendoraun had seen only a few times before, when the two of them would sit around and discuss why they had been born in Gaoln, or how they might get out, or how the rest of the world lived and why they never cared about the people in Gaoln. Nolor and the others were already walking down the other side of the hill, but still, when Gendorn turned and spoke to Bendoraun it was in a whisper. "Bendoraun, why did you not want to leave Tekal? And what did you dream about when you were still lying unconscious, after I had already woken up? Before we had that dream together, I mean."

Bendoraun's eyes were fixed on the bodies arrayed upon the field beneath him. He did not avert his gaze when at last he did answer. Instead he looked into the eyes of the bodies, as if somewhere they might hear him. "I saw terrible things,

Gendorn. I saw bodies torn to pieces, impaled on tree branches, their blood dripping onto the snow. I saw people on fire, and entire villages burnt to the ground. I saw something running in the forest— I didn't know what it was, but it gave me such a terrible feeling. I saw us— you and me, Gendorn!— buried in the snow, our bodies frozen and motionless, in the middle of nowhere, with no one around us...I saw a terrible blizzard, and a cave that dripped blood, and a hundred thousand Skaelin warriors coming to destroy us....and then I saw something that really startled me. It was Kamira, and she was so happy to see me, but all around her these images blurred together. I heard a million people screaming, and one man laughing. I saw great piles of bodies burning, and one flag flying. I heard one gentle voice doused out by the *swoosh* of ten thousand arrows. I saw you, and you were crying and bleeding from your face, and Kamira was crying, but she wasn't with you, she was somewhere else...somewhere strange. It's all strange. It was all real. All of it. It *felt* so real." There was another silence. "This is going to be a very difficult journey. Things are going to get very dark for us." The wind blew Gendorn's hair back, ruffling his old tattered rags. Without a word, the two of them hiked down the hill, Port Tekal fading out of sight behind them.

It was a sunny day, and they were warm, hiking over hill after hill— more because of their painful headaches, they supposed, than from any real heat that nature would be giving off. They took a brief lunch break near a half-frozen river, with gentle pools of water sitting atop the ice, then continued on until sundown.

They traveled all the next day along the southeastern edge of Fenidaln Meadows, which was south and west of the Thin River Highlands. Cold as it could be, the sun was hot to Gendorn and Bendoraun, who were still recovering. It would drown them in pain whenever they came to a clearing. It was hard for them to think under these conditions, so they rarely spoke with the others. Most of the trip was a blur to them. They set up camp a few hours after the sun started to sink over the hills, and quickly started a fire to cook their food and melt some snow. They went to sleep as soon as they finished eating, though Nolor and Hendall stayed up talking for a while as the crackling fire died off and the smoke faded into the wind.

Gendorn could not sleep. Despite all his weariness and pain, he could not manage to keep his eyes shut. Instead he thought of Tejk, of Bendoraun, of himself, of Kamira and Kanel. He thought of the pile of bodies on the field. He thought of the two of them among that mass who were the two men he had killed. He wondered how the army was doing, if those he knew were still alive, if the army was even still there. Perhaps they had lost already, maybe they were scouted and ambushed, maybe Gaoln's fate was doomed forever, and the Skaelin were marching to take over Port Tekal at this very moment. Maybe they would catch him, maybe all six of them would be killed, and he'd never see Kamira again— and they would never be free. They were so far away from their freedom, starving out here in the cold, lost somewhere in a hostile nation. How could he ever expect they might find it? How could he even pretend to believe?

Some small part of him just had to. He tightened his arms around his chest, smiled, and rolled around to his side under his blanket— as if Kamira were there next to him.

He was almost asleep when Bendoraun turned over and said: "Gendorn, have you been listening to Nolor and Hendall?"

Gendorn shook his head. "No, what have they been saying?"

Bendoraun let out his breath, then took it in. "That there's scouts around here. That means the Skaelin have found the army. Listen…"

Gendorn let his thoughts fall away, and tuned his hearing into the crackling embers of the fire, where two voices softly lifted up into the sky. "We'll split up, if we know they're on to us," Nolor was saying. "We'll have to keep them quiet. We can send one team to take care of the scout, and the other team can lead us out."

"I can take care of him myself," said Hendall, "but I'll give you the map, and you can lead the others."

"If there is one scout on our trail," said Nolor, "it means that there is one scout ahead of us as well. Isn't that right?"

"If they think we are a part of the army, that is right," agreed Hendall.

"But why would they? In any case, our best defense is to keep quiet."

"Silence is never a defense."

"What is, then— leaving a body in the forest for everyone to see?"

"We would bury it," said Hendall.

Nolor sighed. "What were you exiled for? Out of curiosity."

"Fighting against Laen. I was an officer for Gonaka fifteen years ago, during that skirmish they had in Kale. Why were you in Gaoln?"

"Because my parents decided to torture a soul. I was born there."

"What did they do?"

"Something to do with disliking the King of Laen. The King of Laen decided he didn't like them either, I suppose."

Hendall nodded. "Well, you'll sleep tonight, and I'll stand guard. Tomorrow night we'll switch. If he approaches us, we'll keep calm. If he becomes aggressive, I'm going to kill him, and then we'll have to split up, because the scouts will be coming from different directions and if we're all in one place they will ambush us. Until that point we will not attack, nor will we discuss anything about any army."

Nolor nodded. "Alright. I'm going to sleep."

Gendorn woke up cold the next morning. After a quick breakfast they began their hike across the cliffs and frozen river gorges of the Thin River Highlands. They stopped for lunch at a waterfall that led into an icy lake, surrounded by steep jutting rock walls. After a few moments they set out again, navigating through the maze of canyons using Hendall's map. They emerged from the maze to find a small band of what appeared to be Skaelin scouts eating lunch across another frozen lake. Nolor quickly hid the map and they casually hiked by, exchanging greetings. The scouts appeared totally unconcerned— Nolor took it as an indication that the Gaolnian Army had not been discovered yet, and that if they had word was slow to spread.

They set up camp once they reached a safe distance from the Skaelin scouts. Feeling better than he had since Tekal, Gendorn wandered off after dinner, climbing up a series of cliffs to watch the sun set through the trough of the canyon valley. He sat on the ledge of the highest cliff he could find, and breathed in and out as he witnessed the orange light fade to pink, and then finally turn into a violet. His eyes turned distant and thoughtful. "What a beautiful place…" he said to himself. "But what an unsettling world…"

The days passed uneventfully, Gendorn and Bendoraun steadily healing. They kept hiking until they reached the tallest cliff in the Thin River Highlands, which was where the army would meet them. Most of the divisions were off to the east and west raiding villages for supplies, and this was the path they would send most of the army through when advancing north. They set up camp there a few hours after noon one day, and waited for the army's arrival.

- Chapter Three -

The village guard, altogether only slightly larger than a single Gaolnian regiment, stood valiantly at the front wooden gate before a large part of the Gaolnian Army. The Gaolnian soldiers, who stood facing their opponents, wore pieces of armor and carried with them maces or axes or swords or clubs— only a few of them still had no armor or had improvised spears as weapons. They stood in a perfect formation, and were completely silent. Each man held his weapon like a man who knows how to fight— they had been practicing every night since landing in Skaen.

From afar the Gaolnians shot a volley of arrows toward the village guard, and some of them were hit. The guards charged, and were met with another volley of Gaolnian arrows. More fell. The guards were running now, as fast as they could, and another volley of arrows struck them. The village guards did not make it to the top of the hill.

They stripped the guards for armor and weapons. The notes of the dead— papers folded into soldiers' armor which detailed debts and last requests and such— were taken to the village, where they were claimed. The food stores and armories were emptied and distributed to the army, as well as a number of blankets and some pack animals— chuel, which resembled a cross between a donkey and a camel, and selk, a Skaenish variation of the elk which, although instinctively wilder and more aggressive and so often employed in war, could be used in caravans if domesticated. When they had taken everything they needed, the army surrounded and burned the village, and then departed.

This subdivision had been gone for ten days now, and had raided and razed five villages. They had another six villages left to go on their planned route, and fifteen days. Then they would regroup for a short time and reevaluate their situation. Leading this particular subdivision was King Centreal himself, with Captain Luncas and the 53rd by his side.

One sunny afternoon the king called Luncas to his side to confide in him. Before their eyes a village burned, and to see the smoke of burning homes and burning bodies through the clear sunlight was as surreal an experience as the king thought he would ever see. He turned abruptly to face the captain.

"I'm tired of burning villages, Luncas," said the king.

"I know, but we must do this. Think about how much these people will hate us. They'd ensure the Skaelin scouts find us, and if we're found, our campaign will be over before we can realize it. We cannot allow survivors, because survivors mean we will be discovered, and we cannot be discovered until we are strong enough to take down King Sendroun, or at least to coerce him into giving us land. And we cannot let the settlements be retaken, at any rate— we must keep the goods flowing into our hands while depriving our enemy of those goods," replied Luncas. "We need to make sure we remain hidden, and there is no hiding when people are running all around the countryside telling Sendroun precisely where his enemies are."

"We can salt the farms and it will have the same effect. Won't burning all these villages leave an easy trail for the scouts?"

"Our own scouts are spread too far to allow anyone close enough to see the fires. We have divisions all around us and we do not let anyone out of our sights alive. It is far more of a danger to have stragglers running off to the nearest forts telling tales of a foreign army that's less than half armed than it is to risk a little excess smoke in the air. Our mission is to cut supplies off from the military centers. That is what we are doing. It's them or us, that's how war is. Don't you think they would have killed us if they had the chance?" argued Luncas. "Look, I hate this as much as you do, my king— maybe not quite as much," he said, noticing the king's expression, "but I do despise it. I swear, we are doing only that which is necessary— once we have become strong enough to challenge Sendroun, to hold a part of his lands, to really secure them and keep them and manage them— then these tactics will no longer be necessary. Then we can be the farmers and crafters and traders and sailors that our people want to be. Until we have a land of our own, my king, we must be soldiers."

The two of them stood at the hilltop for a while longer, examining the fury of the flames, closing their ears to the screams that came from the village below. "Until that moment," Captain Luncas said, "we do only what we must to make sure that we succeed. If it helps your conscience, my king, think of it like this: had we allowed these villagers to escape and alert their king, we would all die— more lives would be lost, more families torn apart— and Gaoln would never be free. Should we continue this sort of attack upon but a few more villages, we will be fit to take control of some of the fortresses, and this killing, which to you seems cruel and needless, will no longer be necessary."

"These are not the people who threatened our nation," King Centreal said softly, almost to himself— "those people are being cradled and spoiled in the safety of their castles. These are chefs, these are smiths, these are artists and farmers and traders. They are not our enemy, Luncas."

"If we let them live they'll be our enemies," Luncas assured his king. "I know it seems wrong to you, my king, but this is war."

Centreal nodded. "I know little of war, but I never did like it. You know, when I was appointed Governor of Gaoln, I presumed I would be doing a good thing— guarding a prison of murderers and such. It took me less than a year to realize my folly— and now— "

"You find yourself leading a rebellion and directing a war that you aren't sure how to win," Luncas finished.

"Yes. I'll be counting on you a lot for that, Luncas. You've been a soldier since you were a boy, and you're the only one lower than Commander Denelu who knows how to win this war. I am forced to trust what you say. After spending the past seven years with you I am not quite sure if that is good or bad." Luncas smiled, but Centreal continued— "but I must trust you, all the same. Do not do anything that you do not have to do."

"I will not," the captain promised the king.

"As for now, well, I've seen too much of this burning villages business. We'll turn our path westward, and set our next target as a more real and defensible position, a fortress. I will not have my war being fought like this. We can achieve our goals and accomplish our objectives without all this murder, I am sure."

"I have just explained it to you——"

"And I was listening, captain. And yet I'm quite sure in my decision."

"King Centreal, if you send these men to take a castle it will be their death. We must remain on course. We cannot be discovered, furthermore—— we did not plan on taking a fortress for another month, my king!"

"What makes people so damned competitive anyways? People down in Aniania and Keay are practically throwing food away, and we have so little that we must go to war to avoid starvation! The food that is leftover when they are finished with their meals is tossed to the animals or into the forests for the wild ones, or even into the sea for the fish, while we stand here with our mouths open and no food before us." Luncas had no answer. "I don't mind killing people who point their swords at me, but half of these villager kids don't even know how to hold a sword. There will be no more discussion on the matter. We're changing course. We head for Latoga Fortress, we'll decide what to do then, once we make it our base," the king said firmly.

"We don't have nearly enough soldiers, or weapons, or armor. And we have almost no siege equipment, or anyone capable of making any. It would be a massacre," argued Luncas. "Maybe we should try something we have some chance of succeeding at, something like Port Tekal."

"Like what?"

"Well, first we need some engineers and materials, which we should be able to find at the next village. They produce for the entire area. It is an absolute necessity, my king. Then we could attack Fort Bellford, which is surrounded by farms and food sheds, a major producer of food. If we take control of the farms and the sheds and take all the food, we should significantly reduce the flow of food to the Skaelin strongholds, and give our own army a source of supplies."

"And that's less fortified than Latoga?"

"By far."

"Fine. We'll decide what to do from there," agreed Centreal. "Send messengers out to alert our other divisions of the change in course."

The sun had set hours ago, yet Gendorn remained atop the cliff. The snow reflected the sky. It was that sort of deep blue color which grows upon the whiteness under the moon as Sen goes on and the world cools. The trees seemed to glow with a violet radiance. In such a peaceful place, a memory suddenly came to him.

Kamira was next to him. Together they were watching the snow fall across the barren dirt plains of Gaoln. "What would you do," Kamira had asked him, "if you were sitting here by the water, on the other side of the ocean?" Gendorn turned his eyes to the ocean and considered the question.

"I would sit there, and I would ask you what you would do if you were on the other side of the ocean."

Kamira squeezed his hand. "I would answer, 'I would dream every day and every night of how we might live if we could escape.' I can't live like this, Gendorn. When the water's warm let's just jump in. Let's jump in and swim as far as we can, and if the winds are on our side maybe we can find something, or maybe we can just die."

He threw his arm around her and rubbed her back. "Don't say that, Kamira. This can't go on forever."

"Why not? If no one does anything."

Gendorn tightened his arms around her, and she felt them squeeze her. The snow was cold on their bodies, thin and old as their blankets were. The winds were getting bitter. This would be a very cold morning. He whispered in her ear, and they got up to return to their hut, where there was one more blanket.

Gendorn opened his eyes on the other side of the ocean. "I would sit here," he said softly beneath his breath, "and I would hold you, and we would just stare out across this place forever. And Bendoraun would come by and make some smart remark, and we would go back to his house in the valley on the bottom of these cliffs, where the wind isn't as cold as it is at the top. There'd be a fire inside. And we would be happy, and we would be free."

"Morning, Gendorn," said Bendoraun, as Gendorn approached the fire for breakfast.

"Morning," said Gendorn.

"We have some weird-looking plants and things for breakfast, so we decided to melt them and see how they taste all mixed up," said Nolor, mixing the food around in a pot over the fire. Gendorn laughed.

"Sounds good," he said.

Hendall was sitting down next to Bendoraun. "The army should pass through this point later today, maybe sometime around noon," he said, closing up the map he had been looking at.

"Let's hope so," said Sheal, "since we only have enough food for three more days."

Soon noon came and passed, and still the army had not arrived. Some of them grew nervous as the hours passed by, and then night was upon them. Figuring the army to be a day behind schedule, they had dinner, shared a few more stories, and went to bed.

The army awoke, anxious to obtain the promising power of fine siegecraft. By now most of them had one or two pieces of armor and a weapon, and they crafted arrows every night on the trail. Alaisio still had no armor or weapons, but had found a tall, fairly smooth, and very heavy stick he had been using in combat. It must have been a very strong wood, because it had already endured many strikes of a sword. They had a quick breakfast, then set out to capture the engineers.

They descended down the snowy hillside in perfect line formation, regiment by regiment, with King Centreal front and center, and stopped just outside the village. The Village Guard came out, prepared to defend and die. "Do not strike us," King Centreal told one of the guards, "we will leave your village unharmed, if you agree to cooperate with us."

"We do not have negotiative authorities. I'll get the governor," said one of the guards, turning to leave. The two forces stood still, awaiting the governor's arrival. Eventually the tall, well-dressed man arrived, and the negotiations began.

"Greetings, my friend," said the governor. "I am Hom of Venbal Village, I hear you wish to negotiate?"

"Yes, and these are my terms: I demand every siege engineer you have, all of the required tools to craft siege equipment, the greater part of your food stores, animals for our caravan and all the blankets you can spare. We also require everything in your armories, and clothing for our men. This is in exchange for the survival of this village and all of its residents," replied King Centreal. The chief sighed.

"I am betraying myself enough by forfeiting the siege equipment which doubtless will be used against our own countrymen. But will you also take our people from us?"

"It must be so— we need the engineers to operate the machinery and to help build more. We take only what we need."

The governor stood still for a while, looking at the king. "I will relay the message to them." The governor turned to leave, and returned moments later with six engineers and two apprentices, as well as several loads of siegecraft equipment and artillery parts. The villagers came up to meet the army, bearing loads of the things the army had requested. With a warning not to send out any scouts, backed by the threat that a small team of people would return to burn the village and kill everyone there, the Gaolnian Army secured the secrecy of the governor and the villagers. They left a small team of soldiers behind to make sure that word did not escape the village of what had occurred. With that the army turned and departed for Fort Bellford.

The days on the trail to Fort Bellford passed uneventfully. The engineers and apprentices taught several soldiers how to make basic siegecraft, such as catapults. After many days, most of which were spent simply gathering together the forces which would work together for this task, the army reached their final campground before the siege on Fort Bellford. Here they constructed the siege equipment. Food stocks were dwindling, so everyone went hunting before bed, but few found much of anything.

There were only a few people sitting around the campfire of the 53rd Regiment of Gaoln, which had taken heavy losses at Port Tekal. One of them, a captured siege engineer from the village, had been silent since noon. Captain Luncas had been observing him. It was around midnight when most of the company left for their tents. Alaisio, Luncas, and the man remained, and Luncas saw the chance he had been waiting for. "What have you been thinking about this whole time? I know it's a heavy question, but I've been wondering," Luncas asked him. The man looked up, surprised, and unsure how to address the question.

"You're not my captain. I don't need to answer you."

Luncas nodded. He *was* actually the man's captain, but he did not want to point that out. "Is that what you've been thinking of, then? The fact that I'm not your captain?" Luncas asked gently.

"No. I've been wondering why my family had to see me dragged away, what they felt like when I disappeared beyond the rise of Mull's Hill, and what my children will look like in ten years if I never see them again. I was wondering if my wife would ever find another man, if she ever could, after building a life together with me for these past fifteen years. Why, Captain Luncas? What have you been thinking about— how many bodies you've burned, how many families you've torn apart?"

To Alaisio, the captain seemed unusually quiet. But he began to realize this was just a side of Luncas that he very rarely showed to people outside his small and exclusive circle. To the public Luncas needed to appear authoritative and certain, to his superiors and his soldiers alike. He could never question what he was doing. He had to be firm, or the system would collapse— but alone, Luncas was as capable as any man of being unsure. It was never more than a passing thought to him. But it hit on that night.

"I have wondered about that before. It takes a toll," the captain answered at last.

"Then why do you do it?" asked the man.

"Why do you come with us? You do not believe in this war— why are you fighting it, and for your enemies?" The man turned angry, but he did not offer an answer. "I know why. You're afraid to die. You can't run away, because we'll kill you, and frankly you'd rather fight the war and live, than flee it and die."

"But what's the better choice?" came a voice from beyond the fire. The three of them turned to see King Centreal, walking up to the fire ring. "To kill, or be killed?" The king eyed the man sharply, his ears perking up in anticipation of an answer well-thought out.

"I'd rather die," the man insisted, "you can tell me to shoot at my own people, the ones who fought beside my father not twenty years ago, but I won't listen. You're not my captain, and you're not my king."

Centreal nodded. "You'll just have to keep us company then. And help us build machines."

"I won't build machines. I won't train new people."

"You'd rather die, and put your family through a lifetime of misery?" wondered Centreal.

"Than tear apart many families who I do not know? It is easy to make the wrong choice in such an impersonal decision, when I have never met the mothers of the boys I would kill. But I will not. They are my countrymen."

The king nodded. "Heroic. You know, I've talked to more than one dissenter today. And I've asked them all the same question, thinking they might be able to give me an answer, or at the very least to question themselves."

"I don't want to hear your questions."

The king shrugged as if this were of little importance. "I'll ask you anyway. Who were your parents? Where did they raise you? What did they hope you would do with your life?"

"Why do you pretend to care?"

Luncas shot the man a glare. "You should give more respect to a king."

Centreal shook his head. "He doesn't think I'm a king yet"

"You never will be," said the man.

"Answer my questions," Centreal continued.

"Or what?"

"You don't want me to have to answer that," said Luncas. Centreal put an arm around the captain.

"Don't threaten him, captain." Luncas nodded. "Man, answer my questions."

The man waited for a moment, then made his reply. "I was born in a village on the outside of the Eastern Mountains, in the foothills along the western ridges. My father was an engineer, and that is how I learned the trade. My mother grew spices and herbs and ran a small shop where she sold those to the rest of the village. It was just a very small village. My father was the only engineer, and he often worked for the village to the south also, so I learned to travel around a bit. I ended up where you found me just a few years ago, but the people I met there are wonderful people. Why does this matter?"

"Describe your home, the one you grew up in."

"Why does this matter?"

"Tell me."

The engineer sighed. "It was a small stone hut, with one wooden door which led into the single room. We had an upstairs but we never used it, it was just a very small attic under the rooftop. There was a fireplace in the middle at the end of one of the walls, and then there were some wooden chairs..."

"What would you do without that fireplace?"

"What?"

"What would you do if someone took away your fireplace? And then they took away your chairs, and then they took away your table, and then they took away your stones and your roof and gave you some mud. What if they took away your blankets and your bed, and then your water and your food, and then they gave you some mud? And what would you do when they killed your family and your friends and everyone you know? What if they took away your job, and they told you that you could never be anything again for the rest of your life? That you were only a waste of the resources that you didn't even have? What if they took away your purpose? And then, after doing all of that, they gave you a choice: You were going to be a slave, or you were going to die."

"I didn't take anything from you. But you have taken from me."

"I am asking you if, in our position, you would not feel obligated to object. And I am asking if, in the absence of any other possible way to demonstrate that objection and to regain everything which has been stolen from you and your children and their children, if you would invade another country."

"I would— "

"If you knew that if you did not invade and succeed, you would all die of starvation. What would you do? You see what I am doing, then— I am trying to give my people a choice, and I am trying to give my people a chance."

"I am not in control of what my government does."

"Then perhaps that is why you should join us."

"No! You are not killing King Sendroun, you are killing people like me. And that doesn't make sense to me."

"War doesn't tend to make a lot of sense," said Captain Luncas.

"Then why do you fight it?" asked the man.

"Think about the questions," said King Centreal. "I would be most interested in your answer. It's late, and I need to sleep. Good night, all of you."

Luncas nodded. He threw the rest of the water on the fire, and said goodnight to Alaisio. Luncas took the man by the arm. "Come on. Get to bed," he said. The man walked into his tent without another word.

Morning came in a moment, and still many thought this moment was too soon. The yet ill-equipped and inexperienced Gaolnian Army had serious doubts in its ability to successfully take what was sure to be a heavily garrisoned hold. In such hostile times, surely such an important location as Fort Bellford would be well-defended. But if Gaoln managed to take Bellford, they could obtain a steady flow of food and control over the bountiful and heavily inhabited hinterland. Everyone pushed their doubts aside as the morning drew on. There would be no time for it in battle. After a hasty breakfast, the regiments got in formation, hiding and protecting the siege equipment. Then they embarked on the siege of Fort Bellford.

- Chapter Four -

"I don't think they're coming," said Wyan. It had been four days since the day the army was supposed to meet them. "We can't stay here. We need to go somewhere where we can get food, we need to stay in a village," he continued. Nolor sighed.

"I know…"

"They must have taken another route, or maybe they changed course. I have no idea how we'll meet up with them," said Hendall.

"We risk the small chance of being discovered and killed if we seek refuge in a settlement," said Sheal.

"Why? We're just camping," said Bendoraun.

"Besides, we risk the greater risk of starvation in the wild," Gendorn said. "It's too deep into Sen now for anything around here to grow, and the animals don't seem to trust us."

"I can't imagine why…" said Bendoraun smartly.

"Well, what do we do then?" asked Wyan. No one answered. "Hendall, where's the nearest village?"

"Won't our injuries be suspect?" replied Hendall.

"I just assumed we could make something up," suggested Sheal.

"It was the squirrels," said Bendoraun. "First they came at me and Gendorn with their squirrel-maces and squirrel-axes…"

"Bendoraun," said Hendall, "please, this is serious. Some of our wounds are unmistakable to the veterans who fought in the Civil War of Skaen. We need a real excuse to get by them. There is another problem still: The map doesn't name settlements other than Port Tekal."

"We could go back there," suggested Nolor.

"That may be our only choice," agreed Hendall.

"I don't know…" said Wyan. "Isn't Tekal a bit far now?"

"It is," agreed Hendall. "It could be difficult to return. It's very long, and the weather has gotten worse. It may be the conservative choice, but it is also a risky one"

"We're dreaming anyway," said Nolor. "We can't make it to Tekal without any food. We've gone too far. And everything has died or gone away until Trest starts to come back around. That won't be for a hundred and fifty days or more— we've little idea of how long Sen lasts here in the central parts of Skaen. I imagine it lasts much longer than it does in Gaoln." For a long while there was a pensive silence.

"Let's explore the area and meet back here," said Gendorn.

"We could," said Wyan, "or we could search for food or villages on our way back to Port Tekal."

Hendall sighed. "There is a hill to the northwest of here. It shouldn't take us long to get there. I think we should go to the top. Maybe we can find something from the view up there. The trees all around here are dead. We could see any plumes of smoke at night coming from the fireplaces, and we could smell the fire burning. But," he paused to consider his own thought, "Port Tekal, of course, is to the south of us."

"If we do go back to Port Tekal," said Nolor, "we won't be reuniting with the army until they return to the south. We would be waiting in a trap, you know."

"It is a trap," agreed Sheal.

"If the main army starts losing ground, or is even discovered, the enemy could find out about Port Tekal and, well, 'expel' us," Nolor elaborated.

"The place is defenseless as it is. There aren't enough supplies going in for it to really hold out in the case of a siege," said Wyan. "And if they try to open new routes— "

"We're not planning a war here," said Hendall. "Tekal isn't safe, we've established that. But nothing is safe at this point. What is it, the hill or Port Tekal?"

Bendoraun, who had remained silent except for his jokes, examined the faces of his friends sitting around the fire ring. "Let's go to the hill," he said. Then he shrugged. "I mean, I don't know about the rest of you. But Gendorn, you sort of convinced me when we left that town. I would like to find the army. I don't want to go back to Port Tekal. I want to see the rest of Skaen, and I want to help us find the dream that we all set out here with, instead of just laying around in Tekal until the Skaelin do or do not come to kill us."

Gendorn nodded. "I agree with Bendoraun."

Nolor sighed. "I do too."

"Hendall," Wyan said, "what do you think?"

Hendall took in his breath and paused to think for a moment, then he looked up at Wyan and spoke. "I think we should go to the hill, and see what we can find."

"I want to return to Port Tekal," said Sheal.

"I think that is the wise choice," said Wyan. "We know it isn't safe there, we've all agreed. But it isn't the wisest thing to wander out alone in the woods, lost somewhere deep in these snows, without any food. At least we would be making our way south."

"I am not opposed to it," said Hendall. "But I do disagree. Yet if we are so adamant in these positions then we will have to split up."

"We cannot stay in the north, Hendall. You know that. And you could be useful in Port Tekal," said Wyan.

"Well," said Hendall, "I do not feel right about leaving the three of you here. But this map is useless to you."

"We'll be alright," said Nolor. "There must be villages somewhere around here."

"We have no idea if that is true or not," Wyan said. "You should come with us."

"We have to fight," Gendorn protested, "every man makes a difference, and hiding in Tekal waiting for the Skaelin to kill us won't help us at all."

"Don't make him keep saying this," said Bendoraun.

"Be quiet," said Hendall. Bendoraun looked at Hendall inquisitively. "Be quiet, everyone, and listen." There was hardly any noise, just the bitter wind in the trees. But Hendall's ears perked up, and he signaled for them to move. He gathered his things together and started walking northward, watching his steps, careful not to make a sound. The other five packed up and followed just as quietly.

"We're going to the hill," Hendall whispered to them, "there are some people behind us. And I don't trust them."

"What did they have?" asked Gendorn.

"Nothing. Which makes them inexcusably suspicious. They must have a camp nearby— or they set out for a very specific mission, and I don't like it," answered Hendall.

"They could have set out for a certain village, knowing the way by heart," suggested Gendorn.

Hendall shook his head. "No. The way they move— they aren't villagers. They spend their time out in the woods. They are looking for something."

"How can you tell this?" asked Sheal.

"I was in the Army of Gonaka before the Lonins captured me and shipped me to Gaoln. It was their idea of punishment for fighting against them."

"I've never heard of that," said Sheal.

"They only used that punishment for their most hated enemies, as it made the King of Gonaka very upset. I held off one of the cities against them, I was in charge of the wall defenses. They told everyone I was a pirate, and they branded me with the mark when they had me in chains. Then they shipped me off to Gaoln."

"That's why Port Tekal needs him," said Wyan.

"Be quiet," said Hendall. "They're following us, but not at a fast pace. We need to lose them. What are we going to do if we get to the hill and they are still behind us?"

"We need an excuse," said Bendoraun.

"We need a plan, Bendoraun," said Hendall. "But now is not the time— they are always trying to listen to us. We need more distance."

And so they continued at their brisk but quiet pace for some time, while the sun was still high in its mid-day ascent. When they came upon the hill Hendall signaled that the men were still behind them, so the six of them set out around the hill, careful not to make their way up toward the top— that was a race which these men behind them would surely win. At some point, a quarter of the way around the side of the hill, Hendall put up his hand, and the six of them stopped. His ears perked up, and he stood perfectly still. Then he shook his head. "They've gone," he whispered very quietly. "They're trying to get to us, but I do not know where they are coming from." Then he shook his head, as if dismissing his own comment. "No...they're heading for the top of the hill. They've split up.

They're going to find us, wherever we are, with one or more men at the bottom of the hill to go after us. The one at the top can shout out where we are. We have to get out of here. This was a stupid idea— I am a fool!"

Hendall paused. He started off in some other direction, and the five of them followed. Presently, he stopped again, and whispered: "They've gone somewhere. We have to mislead them. We can't lead them anywhere we don't want them to go." Gendorn nodded. He knew that Hendall was referring to the army. "They will have sent one or two scouts back to report to whoever it is that they are reporting to by now. Which means they will find us and trap us and interrogate us, if they haven't already figured everything out. And that means we have to split up." Bendoraun opened his mouth to ask why, but Hendall cut him off. "Because, not to be morbid, but at least one of us must make it out of here alive to tell the army that they have been discovered. If we make it to Port Tekal that is good enough, because from there we can send out a team of people to inform the larger divisions which lie to the north and west. It is also well enough if we can find a place to hide around these villages, and then set off to inform the army and unveil ourselves once we get near enough.

"So we'll divide into two teams, then. I will take Wyan and Sheal back to Port Tekal. Nolor, you take Gendorn and Bendoraun to see if you can find a village around here to lie low in and gather some information, if you can, but leave to inform the army as soon as safety allows. We need to find the army and tell them that news has probably already reached the king, and we should tell our men still in the south that the routes to the north may be blocked. If the Main Army catches our men by surprise, our people will never be free, and it is as simple as that. Are we ready?" The rest of them nodded, then Hendall nodded again. "Alright. Let's go. Die before you let them capture you."

Hendall turned his back to them, and, with Wyan and Sheal, took off into the forest. Nolor, Gendorn, and Bendoraun turned westward away from the hill, and began marching quickly away from where Hendall last heard the scouts.

- Chapter Five -

"Prepare the trebuchet!" yelled the master engineer. He and his men worked to prepare the trebuchet while some others prepared and manned the catapults and ballistae. The infantry marched up the hill across from Fort Bellford, and waited just outside the range of the enemy siege equipment. The archers ran up and exchanged arrows along the outer perimeter. Soldiers hauled up sacks of rocks they had gathered that morning or rolled up boulders the army had found on the way to the fort. The catapults and the trebuchet were loaded, and upon King Centreal's command, a heavy array of boulders and rocks pounded against the sturdy walls of Fort Bellford, just beyond the gates themselves. The aim was to sever the walls from the gates, thereby opening two channels of entry and discouraging the defenders from manning the gates, which would be vulnerable and exposed for a third offensive. The army used the ballistae to aid the Gaolnian archers, knocking down multitudes of heavily armored foes, but the Skaelin ballistae aimed at the trebuchet in an attempt to disable it. The siegecraft and archers kept going, but the double gates of Fort Bellford refused to yield. Part of the Gaolnian infantry advanced and laid down against the ground, right up against the outer walls, throwing up shields to catch falling arrows. Meanwhile the Gaolnian archers engaged the Skaelin archers who were posted on the top of the walls, directing fire away from the infantry. The catapults redirected to the inner walls and advanced up the hill. The move was a gambit, as it endangered the catapults and relied on the Gaolnian archers to protect them, but if the offensive was effective and they kept their siege equipment fully functional, they could take the castle by the next week's close, given decent conditions. It was no secret that the army did not have enough food to wait much longer than that.

Captain Luncas and the 53rd marched together with several teams of infantry toward the walls. Suddenly the captain stopped, and looked ahead. "Alaisio, look at that," said Captain Luncas, pointing to a man riding a selk appearing to have just exited the backside of the castle. Already the animal was running fast as it could.

"Someone running away to inform the king, no doubt," noted Alaisio, "we don't have a chance at stopping him, he's already too far gone."

"I know. I'm going to see if our runners can call a team of soldiers to intercept him. I'll send someone off. But see where he came from— the backside of the castle? Our shadows are hidden by these castle walls, so we can sneak back there without being seen. Stay against the wall," said Luncas. Without replying, Alaisio followed the captain around to the backside of the castle.

Overhead the two soldiers could hear the shouts and commands of their Skaelin enemies. Behind them, infantry rushed forward to meet the Skaelin soldiers who had come out of the castle and were trying to dismantle the Gaolnian artillery. Silent and dark as their own shadows, Alaisio and Luncas navigated their way to the rear of the castle.

Part of the castle seemed to protrude out from the wall, and Luncas smiled. "It's a camouflaged back door, and in his haste that man didn't even shut it! I knew this place wasn't this fortified when I left it. They're still working on rebuilding the walls! Fools..."

"When were you here?" asked Alaisio.

"Visiting a friend," answered Luncas. Alaisio nodded, suspicious, but not really caring. "Go tell the others, and don't get shot!"

"Yes, captain," replied Alaisio, skimming the wall back to the front. He passed the word along to King Centreal, and on the king's command, one of the regiments slithered around, row by row, and formed a two-by-two line just outside the door. Three more regiments did the same, and soon there was a thin line of people surrounding the wall. Under command of the master engineer and King Centreal, in a single swift motion the siegecraft switched fire to the top of the castle, taking down companies of archers and attacking the ballistae, while the infantry stormed into the castle through— literally— the back door.

They could not move. The dark corridors of the castle only allowed two or three men to fight at any one time. Captain Luncas insisted that he be first. With two veterans who had served in other wars, the captain led the way into the halls and cut paths through the Skaelin infantry who rushed down to stop the invasion. As they climbed a stairwell they were met by a row of archers, and had to fall back. It took half an hour of running back and forth, and almost out of the castle, before a team of heavy infantry with greatshields could be brought to the front of the single-file line. They pushed the archers back and entered a small courtyard inside the castle's center. In an instant, a hundred Gaolnians flushed inside and stood by the captain, including the king himself. "I have another thousand men on the way," the king said, "I will give them instructions when they arrive in this chamber. Lead the attack, Captain Luncas, for one day you'll be commander and our men will need to trust you. This castle will be ours by tonight."

Captain Luncas nodded. "It will be, my king— have no doubt."

Captain Luncas led the now five hundred men in the courtyard toward the top of the castle, and when Centreal's men arrived he sent them to the basement. There, one hundred trapped Skaelin soldiers threw down their arms and surrendered, and were taken as prisoners to become Gaolnian soldiers. The catapults and ballistae ceased fire. It turned out that Bellford was being defended by no more than a few hundred soldiers. Where were the others? The Gaolnians could not consider such questions for the moment, important as they may be. The Skaelin on top, having nowhere to pull back to in case of further loss, and hearing word of what had transpired below, were forced to surrender as well. Victory had come, thanks to good timing, good fortune, and a huge advantage in numbers. Fort Bellford now belonged to Gaoln.

The dining room was opulent. The wood seemed to sparkle with a luster of its own and the chandeliers above seemed to give off that beautiful sunlight that one sees as its last rays are fading into the night. King Centreal sat around the largest table, in the center of the great hall, going over their next moves with Commander Denelu, Captain Luncas, and several other important and more experienced captains, all of whom had convened here together and brought their companies to the fort in order to secure the area and establish it as a base.

"I never expected it would be that easy. I am very relieved," said King Centreal.

"It is our fortune that we saw the door and that man who got away," agreed Captain Luncas.

"It may not be such a good thing, that man," objected one of the other captains.

"Our runners failed to intercept him," King Centreal explained to Captain Luncas. "We couldn't find a trace. Wherever he was going, he intends on getting there very, very quickly. And he knows exactly what he is doing. King Sendroun will soon know where we are. We cannot leave too large of a company here, because we need to take as much ground as quickly as we can. The Skaelin Main Army will be upon us soon. They can be here in forty or fifty days time, and I would like to have more than Tekal and Bellford when they come for our blood. We still need a stronger supply chain and more secure routes for trade and movement, as well. We cannot survive this Sen unless we take care of those issues. They will come prepared for a siege, make no mistake— and under the current conditions, we cannot outlast them."

"The Skaelin are sure to increase fortifications in the strongholds around Bellford, now that they know our location," Luncas told the king, "We have to return to raiding villages and gathering supplies, and we must not let them know where we are headed. We cannot go north at this time, my king— should the Skaelin Main Army reinforce this area they could trap us in the Frozen Meadows, and that would be our death."

"He's right, my king, it's our only chance to bypass the counterattacks and fortifications that are bound to result," agreed another captain. Centreal sighed.

"I will be sending out some regiments to secure the hinterland and make sure that we have a steady surplus of everything we need," said Commander Denelu, "and a team of well-armed and experienced men will be stationed permanently here at Bellford, so you shouldn't worry about Bellford. We will keep it secure. But keeping too many people here is harmful to our offensive and also unnecessary. If we can hold Fort Bellford at all, we can hold it with a moderately sized group of experienced soldiers."

"That all sounds well enough," agreed King Centreal.

"Now," began another captain, "there is the matter of where the Skaelin Main Army will be directing its force. They might be expecting us along the Central Path, or they might assume the Central Path would be too risky for us. They may be expecting us in the hill forts of the Eastern Mountains instead, thinking we wish to besiege them where they are strongest."

"Well they can't fortify both, they're too beaten still from the civil war to spread themselves that far," argued another captain. "They're going to pick one, and so must we." Centreal sighed, and Luncas held his breath. No one broke the silence, the thought, the decision that may very well determine the survival of their nation and its people. Then the first captain spoke again.

"The Central Path is guarded by towers, and the trade route is secure, but the trade routes in the mountains aren't even known to us. They could easily get supplies back and forth without us knowing, and they know that. They'll use that."

"Unless they're expecting that..." proposed Captain Luncas.

"There is not a nation in all the history of this world that has taken the battle to the strongholds of the Eastern Mountains and returned the victor," Commander Denelu said. "There are few nations in the history of the world who could have won had they tried. We are certainly not among them."

"And at the same time, they value that position more than any other, and would never desert it should they suspect it threatened," Luncas pointed out. There was another silence, and then the king spoke:

"They would know what we're planning. No one would believe that we would try to take those strongholds. We take the only road that has hope for our success. After confusing our enemy and returning to village raids, we will attack the fortresses along the western border, which are the strongest and most productive castles in the Skaelin Lands outside of the Eastern Mountains. We make for the Central Path."

The morning snow fell gently onto the light green grass and across the fields which stretched into the plains and hills far beyond the castle. Alaisio stood at the top of the ramparts, looking out. Captain Luncas came up from behind him. "It's pretty, I know," said Luncas, "but it's so damned cold! Sometimes I wish I lived down in the islands— but then, I think I would miss the snow." Alaisio didn't answer. Luncas knew something was wrong— Alaisio may be slow to respond at times, but he never ignored a friend. "What's on your mind?"

Alaisio closed his eyes. "I used to live in the islands."

Luncas raised an eyebrow, and examined him curiously. "Well, that was an interesting story. Could you tell it again?"

Alaisio made a point not to laugh. "Lendah and I used to live there. We had a home on Goba, west of the mainland, deep in the forest. Just south of the Mountain. We had a son, Ciso. Lived there for years. Ciso's twenty-three right now. He wanted to join the war, but I asked him not to, and he listened. He's all I have left of the family— Lendah disappeared in the city one day, when we went to the market on the coast. We never heard from her, don't even know if she's alive." Alaisio paused. He let his breath out into the air, and watched it dissipate in the falling snow. "I think she was kidnapped. Pirates, probably. There are a small number of them still. And if she ever escaped the pirates, the authorities would have thrown her in Gaoln for piracy anyway. It never made sense to me, you know? I suppose that's why I am in this war— because I realized how many people out there were just like myself."

"Where is your son?"

"When Ciso went to the Academy of Laeolin, I was alone in the house. It was time to move, I decided. But then, I didn't really want to move anywhere. I joined the war because I believe that what is happening to Gaoln is a terrible thing, and because I think Lendah might be in Gaoln. Ciso, in Laen, learned to hate that government, to hate what Laen was doing to Gaoln. Many students there are against the regime— but many more are for it, because all the radical leadership against Seagraul has already been eliminated. But I am trailing off.

"It's just," Alaisio continued, "this snow. It reminded me of how far away I've gone. Away from the islands and the warm winds of the deep rainforest. And it made me wonder where they are— Ciso and Lendah, what they're doing. I just hope Ciso hasn't been captured— anyone who tries to foment dissent against Seagraul is liable to be thrown in Gaoln. And with our own invasion of Skaen, who knows what that means?"

Luncas nodded. "I hope Gonaka and its king will prevent that. King Nowhawna of Gonaka is afraid of openly displaying his allegiance. But I wish he would get over that damn fear and see just how much of his help we really need."

"You think we do?" wondered Alaisio.

"Alaisio, without Gonaka, Gaoln has no chance of succeeding. We could take this half of the Skaelin Lands, don't get me wrong, and we could hold it. Until Laen comes, which they will, unless King Nowhawna can stop them. Wars aren't fought between just two nations in this day and age. But how did you hear about our invasion down in the islands? I thought we did a rather good job of keeping it a secret."

"Few secrets escape me."

"That doesn't answer my question."

"I have friends in Gonaka who knew of my plight, and thought I would like to join the effort. I've a question for you, captain. What did you mean back there— I've been meaning to ask you this— when you said you've been here before? Frankly I don't know if I believe you, that you were here visiting a friend?"

"It was in the war. I fought for the Skaelin."

Alaisio accepted the fact as if it was of no importance. "Why are you fighting against them now then?"

"Because now they are wrong."

"You're not the kind of person I would envision as voicing a moral objection against your superiors. What made you change your mind?"

"It was moral. But it was," he sighed, "more complicated than that. I had personal reasons, you would say."

"Moral objection? Personal reasons? From Captain Luncas?"

Luncas nodded. "We must be selective about when we listen to and obey our morals. I do believe we are aiming for a greater good, and that to attain that greater good there must be many sacrifices, and many actions which will go against our own morals."

"You are a confusing man, captain. And I still do not believe you. You are the most amoral man I have ever met." The captain smiled. Alaisio was tempted to ask his captain if he thought the villagers he had killed would share that same view. But he knew when to remain quiet, and when to question his captain. "What are these personal reasons, then?"

"Someday I will tell you around a warm campfire, Alaisio— the whole story. But I am very cold, and this snow is thick."

"We should go inside." Luncas nodded. They went inside and down to the floor level, where people were sleeping practically stacked atop one another. With a blanket and a spot on the floor, they made it their home.

The Gaolnians spent two full days at Bellford, and it was an emotional scene to say the least. Men of middle age who had never been outside the prison colony wandered with open mouths and wide eyes down streets lined with food and clothes and merchants of every sort for any niche. Great buildings rose up inside the walled town, with oil lamps that danced through the night casting their light down alleys that never truly slept. Even under military occupation, the soldiers saw lovers sneaking out under the oil lights, and the sound of music came from more than one or two inns. There were a great many men in the companies assembled here who had never before heard the sweet sound of music. There were slave hymns that they would sing in Gaoln, of course, but there had never been an instrument in that sad land for as long as anyone there could remember. The sound that caught Luncas's attention was a soft, dirge-like song, appropriate for a town recently conquered. It was a sound hauntingly similar to the slave songs of Gaoln.

The streets were mostly empty, as there were few townspeople intent on meeting the soldiers. The great boulevards and person-wide alleys alike were full only of

Gaolnians, but even they spoke in hushed tones, as the atmosphere around the castle was sure to be tense. So when the music started up from one particular inn, playing one particularly intriguing song, the Captain of the 53rd stopped dead in his tracks three streets away. The sound was of a soft flute, and there were no words yet— it was just the slow sound of rolling highs and lows and lingering somber notes. The captain felt a chill rush down his spine, and something inside of him came alive. He knew this song, as well as any military man should, and far better than most. It was the harrowing sound left over from the Age of the Great Wars, and such was the age that it recalled.

Luncas stood outside the door to the inn. He looked up to read the sign— *The Bellford Stable*. An odd name for an inn anywhere else in the world, but it was not uncommon here in Skaen, the captain knew. He could hear the music from here, and it would not be proper for a Gaolnian captain to listen to this song in a Skaelin inn. When someone opened the door to enter, he saw the crowd inside. There must have been sixty people stuffed in the common room, huddled around the hearth or around wooden tables with burning lamps illuminating their faces. Not one among them was speaking, or paid any mind to the captain by the doorway. Their faces and attentions were fixed on the flutist by the fireplace on the far wall. Another man stood next to the flutist, and his voice picked up gentle and somber as the flute:

"Sing me story, tell me a tale,
A song and a sound louder than war,

Remind me of a time long ago,
When as children we asked why we all have to go,

Why do men fight, and why do men kill,
Why do they hate, why do they kill?

Where am I going, and what will I find
If I pick up a sword and claim it as mine?

Those questions we asked when the world was still young
Their answers are buried six feet in the ground,"

The chill crept back under Luncas's skin. He felt two or
three tears crawl out of his eyes, as he saw images flash in his
mind— images he had shared with no one, and had no intent of
doing so. He lost himself in these pictures of the past, until at
some point the singer gained his attention back when he started
up again with one single stanza, simple and soft:

"What one man remembers he never can tell,
His eyes know all the stories that his lips will never sell,"

The chill rushed through him as never before, and the
singer's voice rose in crescendo:

"In the ruin in the smoke
Our answers cry out,
They beg us the questions
We'll no longer ask,

For what soul is still brave enough to ask such a thing—
Why the darkness in our hearts is allowed to escape?

Why the fire's let loose and we watch the world burn,
Oh what is this fire, and why must it burn?

Well they started a war just to watch people die,
They burned it all down just to watch the fire's light,

And the king's damned glory's not worth such a sight,
To see a mother crying night after night,"

His voice slipped a little as he sang this next verse, in a far gentler tune, almost as if singing to himself:

"The man in me died in a field where men lie,
In the land now called the Sleeping Meadows,
The only thing left is the child inside
Whose questions come up late into the night,"

The singer did not pause for even a second, but dropped his voice instantly even further now, to the slow and somber note in which he had begun the song:

"He reminds me of a time long ago,
When as children we asked why we all have to go,

He can't understand it in his little boy mind,
Why do men fight, why do men die?

He keeps asking and asking, night after night,
He won't let me sleep as I relive the fight,

He reminds me of a time when the world was still young,
And where graves now lay a great forest did rise,

Great cities stood once where there's now nothing but ash,
A family lived and dreamed in a field turned to trash,

He tugs on his mother's sleep robe one night,
And he asks her why he's asked to grow up and fight,"

The flute dragged on, grew softer, and then finally stopped. The singer went on alone:

"The man in me died in a field where men lie,
In the quiet, serene Sleeping Meadows,

The only thing left is the child inside,
Whose questions wake me all through the night."

The inn was struck into complete silence. The flutist packed his instrument in a case, and the singer rose next to him. Together they turned away and headed for the stairs. Luncas watched them, along with the entire crowd. There weren't any laughs or harsh voices, no drinks clanging or hands slapping cards on a table. There was just the silence. Luncas turned his back to the inn and made his way back to the keep.

It was getting colder every night, and the snow, by the third day after leaving Bellford, was now almost up to the knees of some of the shorter soldiers. It had not relented for the entire march, and moving was slow. The animals went up front, for they were used to the snow, and lived in these parts— they could create trails for the men. The infantry sparred every night, practicing and honing their skills whenever possible, through all of the snow and wind. Around noon of the fourth day they arrived at the small village they had aimed for. The army surrounded the settlement, demanded all their food, weapons, armor, blankets, and animals, and rounded up the siege engineers. They took all the inhabitants captive, arming them and telling them that they now were soldiers of Gaoln. A large number of the villagers resisted, and held out in the center of town. But when King Centreal sent in the regiments to clean them out, only a few of those resisting escaped alive. Those who did were captured and, in turn, without being given any weapon or armor, were told that they were now soldiers of Gaoln. King Centreal left to brief the new recruits on why they should fight for Gaoln's independence, while, against his orders, some careless soldiers set fire to the village and watched it burn.

- Chapter Six -

Nolor, Gendorn, and Bendoraun stood still. It was hard to see through this heavy snowfall, which had seized upon them in an instant and eliminated their line of sight. The three of them all had that feeling that someone was watching them and following them, waiting for them to move. Did these people not want to hurt them? Were they just going to wait to see where the three of them went?

They continued hiking through the mid-day, when the snow began to dissipate and the sun, for a moment, came out into the afternoon sky. They could see clearly through the barren trees. They could see the two men behind them who were keeping their distance— yes, waiting to see where the three Gaolnians would lead them.

It was in the evening when the two men began to run forward. The three soldiers tried to run away, but they were not fast enough. When the men gained on them, Nolor became separated from Gendorn and Bendoraun— they could not all run along the same narrow path through the trees. The two men behind them both followed Nolor, while letting Gendorn and Bendoraun retreat further south. Without any hesitation the two boys kept running, and when they looked back Nolor was gone.

"He's beside us," Bendoraun assured Gendorn, "keep running. Those guys are behind us. They've just hidden themselves." The two of them kept running for a while. Gendorn tried to keep track of where they were running, but the clouds came back quickly and covered the sun. The sky grew darker and at some point Gendorn realized he had forgotten where they were in relation to the sun. The woods all looked the same— there were no big hills around here, just rolling plains. The two of them came to a frozen river and stopped. Turning all around, they saw no one.

"We lost him," said Gendorn.

"Nolor? Yes. He's gone. He went up that way somewhere," Bendoraun said, pointing to his right. "I saw the men following him." Bendoraun paused to regain his breath. "They must have thought that Nolor was the leader, and that he would take them to the army."

"He's got a better chance of doing that than we do," said Gendorn grimly.

Bendoraun shrugged. "Yeah."

"Let's keep walking. We've got nowhere else to go."

Bendoraun nodded. "I don't know how much longer I can keep this up."

"How is your head feeling?"

"Terrible."

Gendorn nodded. "Mine too." He let out a breath and watched it fade into the cool mist between the trees. "Let's keep walking. We have to."

"I'm shaking."

"We don't have another choice."

"I know."

"Keep going," said Wyan. Sheal wanted to reply "where?", to ask where his friend was claiming he could make it to— certainly not Tekal— but he found himself unable to speak. Sheal stopped, bent down, and allowed the freezing air to come into his lungs. "Don't stop, you can't stop, we need to keep going." Sheal looked down in shame. Again he wondered why, what hope did he have, where in this world did his friend think he was going, when did he think he would find salvation? But Sheal knew how Wyan would respond, and how Hendall would look at him, as if it were the most ridiculous thing to give up— as if they were actually close to Port Tekal.

Sheal collapsed into the powder. He closed his eyes, and began to lose all senses tying him to the troubles of the world. Suddenly he was in the same place, but could no longer feel the pain, the thirst, the hunger, the cold. None of it existed here, nothing mattered. In that one moment the voices around him sounded blurred and faint, and the falling snow seemed to melt into the air. Then something pulled him up, and he saw Wyan and Hendall standing there with their arms around him.

"Get up, Sheal!" said Hendall. "We need to keep going."

"Maybe we need to rest," said Wyan.

"We cannot," Hendall said, "we need to get out of the snow. The sun is still strong in the southern part of Skaen, and the snow will be less dense— we will have a greater chance of finding food. But we need to move."

Sheal regained his strength at some point in the day, tapping into his hidden reserves of energy, and they spent that night in their tent after the sun had set. Hendall showed them, with drawings in the snow, how to make a snow hut in case they needed to. "We used to build these during Sen when the campaigns against the Kingdom of Laen would last all year-round. The Army of Gonaka and the other Gash soldiers camped outside the walls. We were the front line," Hendall said. He paused to shake his head, "this army and its expedition are quite different from anything I've ever seen with the Kingdom of Gonaka."

The next morning they awoke with the sun. Instead of navigating their way back through the cliffs, Hendall, Wyan, and Sheal decided to go around them. They kept to the east of the way they had come up, brushing along the edge of the foothills west of the Eastern Mountains. The snow was falling lighter now, and the sun was out. Still, the cold was relentless.

The sun disappeared early that day, and the rest of their time they spent shivering in the cold. Their pace was slow. They were all very weak from the lack of food and from the cold conditions, and they were all tired and thirsty and not very hopeful altogether. The next night they found themselves not much closer to Port Tekal.

The next morning they hiked to the top of a nearby hill, where they could see out across the land to the south. The tiny rays of the dawn's light poked through the mists in the trough between two distant hills, and quickly spread to cover the troughs of several more hills. The sun itself would not be visible for a while. Hendall's tone had become softer in the past day and night. When he spoke to Wyan and Sheal, it sounded gentle and resigned, like nothing his two friends had ever heard from him before. It had been nearly two weeks since they had had anything more than scraps for food, or anything more than sips of water, and Hendall no longer encouraged them to remain hopeful. Their mouths could hardly melt the snow anymore, and it made little difference, at any rate. They were not even half-way to Port Tekal, but they could hardly lift their legs to keep themselves moving. The friends watched the rising sun for as long as it rose, but at some point the clouds returned and darkened, bringing tidings of a snowstorm, and that is when the last of their hopes failed them. Sheal and Wyan died slowly that morning in a dream where Gaoln did not exist and mankind had achieved its peace.

Hendall collected their notes inside of his coat. He remained there for a short while, then rose and continued on his way in a silence that he carried for the rest of his days.

He was alone. Where were the boys? Where were the people following him? He saw them go after him— why did they stop? Were they watching him?

It was a game, Nolor decided. These people who were after him, they didn't want to catch him. They wanted to terrorize him, to make him know that he was being chased— but why? What could they gain?

They must think that he knew something. If they kept chasing him, those men must think, then this man— who to those other men must surely be a scout of the Gaolnian Army— would eventually become too paranoid to function. He would start screaming for the men to come get him, just so the chase would end. Then he would be forced to tell the men everything he knew. Nolor shrugged. Of course, he knew nothing. That's why he was lost in the first place.

"Gendorn!" He shouted. "Bendoraun!" No response. "Gendooorrrrrrnn!" Just the wind. "Bendorrrauuuunn!" the wind howled. He took in a breath and let it out slowly, collecting himself for a moment. "Right," he whispered, "I just have to keep going..."

Nolor found it hard to keep himself motivated. Where was he going? What would he find there? What excuse could he possibly have for traveling alone in these conditions? It took enough effort for him to make sure that he kept walking in a straight line, and not in circles. At some points he would stop and think for a while, and consider handing himself over to those mysterious men behind him— then, at least, he might live. But he never gave in to those thoughts— he kept walking, through that day and on into the next, without stopping in the night for sleep. He could still keep track of where he was going by paying close attention to the knots in the trees and the way their trunks and branches bent. He had an unusually sharp memory. What happened to the boys, Gendorn and Bendoraun, he wondered? Their fate would be as bad as his own, surely. They were even worse off, he was afraid.

For a day and a night he wandered like this, and began another day in the same way. On noon of that day, he crested another rise, and saw before him something which seized the breath from within him. Not twenty paces away lay two tents, with their flaps open— inside were sleeping bags, food, waterskins, a firemaking kit— everything Nolor could have needed. There was even a long spear in one of the tents, the sort which is not exceptionally long and can be either thrown or wielded— it was for hunting. Nolor did not take a single step in that direction— he knew beyond any doubt that this was a trap. The two scouts would be surrounding the place.

One sudden realization made him change his mind: It didn't matter. Were he to refuse these things, he would be dead by nightfall. He clambered down the hillside, and the first thing he took was the water, although he used it sparingly— it hadn't frozen, which meant it must have been placed inside the waterskin earlier this morning, and that the men had meant to drink it all, as once frozen inside the waterskin one would have had to burn the waterskin to get the ice to thaw. Or was this some sort of special waterskin? It resembled nothing he had seen among the Gaolnians at Tekal. Perhaps they had ways of dealing with such things in such a cold place.

He ate for a short time, then packed up one of the tents and one of the bags, along with the fire kit, all the food and water, and the hunting spear. In an instant, he resembled a man who belonged in the wilderness. As such, he set off once more.

He was alone for the entire day, and the next night, and the next day. He came across one village, and then another, always skirting around them in the hills beyond. Another day passed, and then another, and he lost track of the days and the nights. His tent was thick, designed for Sen in Skaen— and his sleeping bag was warmer than anything he had known in his life. The spear had proved useful, for while there were few animals wandering about in these snows, there were one or two of them— their thick coats and fat protected them from the harsh cold. But the spear was more useful as a knife, for Nolor found that he could eat the tough tubers and roots he found buried in the snow if he stewed them at night. He did not worry about fires— he needed them at any rate, and the scouts knew where he was, Nolor was certain.

For two weeks he lived in the wilderness, maintaining his direction— he knew, if he hiked long enough, he would find himself outside of the Skaelin Lands and in the Skaelish Lands, and the Skaelish were less hostile toward Gaoln and did not utilize the penal colony. The Skaelish were enemies of the Skaelin, and if he could make it across the border, he would wait until the war was over. If he just kept going west, he would find himself in safety.

But toward the end of those two weeks his rucksack felt suddenly empty. He was without food, even though he had been hunting and gathering this entire way. He had been dangerously hungry for two days, and he was parched, as he had been unable to start a fire the night before and had run out of water, finding the snow a very poor substitute. When he crested yet another rise and noticed the smoke of village chimneys, he half supposed he was hallucinating. In the great valleys and hills before him stretched a settlement of endless magnitude. All around him smoke rose— villages and farms and small towns stretched out from the edge of his vision on either side to far beyond in the distance, and in that distance some looming structure rose from the earth. He caught his breath— it was distant, and hidden in the mist, but he was sure— this was a castle.

He walked closer as the day drew on, through towns busy with people, fields busy with farmhands, shops busy with craftsmen, and markets fresh with the smell of every food imaginable. For some long time he wandered through towns, but for most of the time his gaze was fixed on this castle, and the structure became larger as he walked on. Presently, he was under the very shadow of it— a titan fortress situated atop a hill, with immeasurable walls and a moat and farms and villages as far as the eye could see. It must have been the very heart of the Skaelin civilization. The castle rose up taller than anything he had seen. He slapped himself, then blinked hard. But the fortress still stood. Two guards intercepted him as he approached the outer gates.

"Why are you here, and who are you?" asked one of the guards. Nolor could hardly think enough to respond.

"I'm lost...I need water. Badly," he finally said.

"Genzut, go get him some water," said one of the guards. The other guard, Genzut, left.

"I need a lot..." said Nolor.

"Answer my questions boy, then you can get all you need," snapped the guard. This woke Nolor from his trance-like state, his mind now clear and lively, his dire condition demanding his attention. He was no longer half-alive, no longer half-seeing things or half-walking, but fully awake and alive. The man shouted again— "Who are you?"— Nolor could not bear it. His balance wavered, and he threw out his arms to catch himself— but when he hit the ground it was with a lot of force, and then his mind went blank.

"Get him water! He's waking!" yelled the deep, heavily-accented voice of a man. Who were they talking about? What was this voice, where was this place? Nolor's mouth was jerked open and water was poured down his throat. He gagged a little, but immediately felt much better. "This next batch is cold, sat outside yesterday," said the voice. Another rush of water splashed down his throat, but this time it was shockingly cold, the closest to ice he'd ever felt water be. The guard, that's who the voice was from! But was this Genzut or the other guard? They must have taken him inside. He wondered how long he'd been out for. But Nolor had no excuse for why he was here, where he came from, or why his body was covered in almost-faded slash marks. Now he realized the great danger he was in. He couldn't speak, not until he devised a story.

It was not long before Nolor opened his eyes. "Hey, you okay?" asked a man. It was Genzut, the man who had taken care of him. "Don't speak unless you think you can. You're being held here, in the east guest tower of Fort Gatsesilli, until you recover and finish the questions. Then you'll be free to go. I'm Genzut, by the way, the one who carried you here after you passed out. We have three guards who have been getting you water, and that's my blanket you're in." Another man returned with water and handed it to Nolor.

"You're awake, how are you feeling?" asked the man, speaking in a similar accent, which Nolor figured to be usual for this part of Skaen. Nolor drank the bucket in a single stream.

"He can't speak yet," said Genzut.

"Oh," said the man. The water kept coming for a long while, until finally Nolor devised his story.

"...Hi..." Nolor said, looking up at Genzut. Genzut smiled.

"He-ey! Good to see you didn't die on us! How're you feeling?"

"Good, and alive, thanks to you."

"It's no problem! Shang and Kule helped too, the other two of the three I told you about. Or do you not recall?"

"No, I recall. The first thing I remember was a voice yelling 'Get him water! He's waking!'"

"Well then, I guess I was right."

"Yes," agreed Nolor with a laugh.

"You probably haven't eaten in a while, have you?" asked Genzut. One of the others came back with more water.

"No."

"Hey, you're alive!" said the man, handing Nolor the water.

"Yeah, thanks a lot. Really. What's your name?" replied Nolor.

"I'm Kule. This is Genzut, and Shang will be here soon," answered Kule.

"I'm Nolor."

"Nice to meet you," said Kule.

"And it was very nice meeting both of you," said Nolor. "How long was I out?"

"Oh, a little over half the daylight hours now? It's night now," replied Genzut. Shang walked in with some water, then set it down when he saw the other buckets around Nolor.

"Morning, sunshine," said Shang, speaking in the same accent.

"Hi Shang, I'm Nolor. Thanks for the water, all of you, I'd be dead without your help."

"You're welcome," came the unanimous reply.

"Oh, food!" said Genzut.

"No food, either? Damn, that's one barely lucky boy," said Shang. "I'll get him some stew or something."

"So, how did you end up here?" asked Genzut.

"I was exiled from my village, sent away without food, water, or anything else. They claimed I was a thief, trying to save the precious skin of their stealing little son. I'd never steal in my life!"

"What village?" asked Kule.

"We call it Strongarm Village, it's on the Strongarm River just south of here. But not many people live there, and I doubt you could find it on a map."

"By Bellford, right?" asked Genzut.

"It's not too far from Bellford," said Nolor, trying to remain vague, "you've heard of it?"

"Sounds familiar— I've never been though. Who sent you away?"

"The guy who owns all of our land, we called him Mr. Lunos."

"It was his son?"

"Yes, I saw him, so he went home and told his father it was me who stole the plow."

"Did they not find it though? The plow?"

"Oh no, they found it. Lunos's son, Luile, threw it behind my house before he went home."

"And what happens if you go back?" inquired Kule.

"I'd rather not find out. I don't have much connection there anyways— my father was killed in the war and I never knew my mother. I figured I could find a job somewhere in Bellford, but I got lost on my way, and ended up— "

"Fort Gatsesilli," supplied Genzut.

"Thank you. Who steals a plow? It's not as if they would not have noticed my gaining a plow at the same time that Lunos lost one of his own— it's not a big place!"

"So where are you going?" asked Kule.

"If it's okay with you all I'd like to stay here, I really have nowhere else to go."

"I don't see why not," said Genzut. "As long as your story checks out, you could just get a job around the castle. There's a lot of mining jobs open, orchalin and stone deposits surround this place. We have a huge stone and orchalin export market. That's what makes us self-sufficient, as long as there's food to buy with the profits."

"Yes, we do some farming ourselves also, the land in these parts is great for dench and lan. Wheat also, we have a mill and top quality bakers," added Kule.

"I'll see what I can find in the morning," said Nolor.

"Good luck," said Genzut.

"Thanks, and thanks again for saving my life," said Nolor.

"Just part of the job," said Genzut.

"Except when we're interrogating prisoners," said Kule. "Or beating them."

"Or killing them," added Genzut.

"There's that too."

"Anyway," said Genzut, "you're welcome." Shang returned a little later with a bowl of stew, some bread, and more water, then the three men left for their chambers, leaving Nolor to eat and sleep in the comfort of Fort Gatsesilli.

- Chapter Seven -

The smell of smoke was in the air. Gendorn and Bendoraun, their senses alert, looked for any burning fires, but they found nothing until they came to the top of a hill. From there the two of them could see a great distance westward, where the ground dipped and leveled off into a plateau. There was no fire— just a smoldering pile of ruins— a village recently burned. They watched the buildings smoke. Bendoraun— whose painful headaches and outbreaks of sweat almost kept him from hiking— spoke suddenly: "We did this. This was our army."

"It may have been, but there are others who could have done this," Gendorn said. "Let's go down to them. They are our only hope."

The sun had almost set now, and only a few people wandered the streets in the village. Everywhere Gendorn and Bendoraun looked, they saw despair. Many of the buildings still smoldered. Great warehouses and granaries lay flat, buried in the snow. Houses lay bare and deserted, stripped down to their stonework with their roofs torn asunder and collapsed into the rooms. They passed a woman who stood outside a burned building, her bare feet in the snow, her gaze fixed on the fiery ruins, unmoving. They passed a young boy who sat by another house, his gaze every bit as intent as the woman's had been. In the center of the village there was a clearing, and the black and grey ash could still be seen through the sheet of snow. Where a dozen market stalls and a hundred people should have been, there was one man amid the wreckage, surveying what had been his village. It suddenly seemed wrong to Gendorn, for him to ask this man for help. It wasn't right. But he exchanged a look with Bendoraun, and they both knew that they had to find help, even if it was to be found in the burning wake of their own army. The two soldiers approached, and Gendorn appealed to him.

"Sir," began Gendorn, "we have been starving and freezing out in the woods for five days now. Please save us. We have nothing left."

The man looked at them, unsure how to respond, and a little suspicious. "Why?" he asked.

"We're dying..." answered Gendorn. His voice was weary, which helped convince the stranger.

The stranger sighed. These two boys, injured as they certainly were, wore the dirty slave rags that he had seen on some of the Gaolnian soldiers. But these were children without weapons or armor, and, more strikingly, without food or water. No sane man would abandon his only source of these,

and of warmth and shelter, in the middle of a frozen
wilderness. It made no sense that these could be Gaolnians.
Had they been injured, and left for dead by the army? If he
made the assumption and refused them harbor, it would mean
their death, regardless of whether or not they were Gaolnians.
He had seen a few desperate Skaelin men wearing similar rags
in his lifetime, and there was a chance that the two boys were
two such creatures. He would find out, the stranger decided.
"Alright…But our village was raided just the morning of two
days ago. The Gaolnian Army took all the food in the sheds,
and robbed the shops of blankets and coins. They stole some of
our people too— engineers, and let loose several fires in the
marketplace. They also took the selk and any other animals they
found. I can offer you very little, but I'll see what my neighbors
can spare." Bendoraun looked down, overcome with gratitude
and relief, unable to fully express it. They both thanked him,
and the stranger led them to his home, while Gendorn raised
questions about the army that had invaded the village in order
to avert suspicion.

"Sit down, I'll get you some blankets," said the man.

"Water…" said Bendoraun.

"You're right, that's more important. Hold on, I'll go to
the well." He took a bucket and left to fill it, asking his wife to
help out by making a warm stew, which she did. The man ran
back and fourth, delivering bucket after bucket of water, half of
which the woman used for her meal. She was oddly quiet
during her cooking, and the two boys did not know what to
make of this. The stew did not take long, and was delivered
with two blankets. The woman made a fire for them while the
man kept getting them water and filled up for the morning.
After they were hydrated and fed, they sat around the fire with
their two caretakers.

"I'm Synla, by the way," said the woman.

"And I'm Behk," said the man.

"I'm Gendorn."

"Bendoraun. Pleased to meet you. Thank you very much for taking us in," said Bendoraun.

"Yes, truly. Thank you very much," agreed Gendorn.

"I don't know what kind of human I would be, not to take two dying kids into my home. So what happened to you, and what's wrong with your head?" asked Behk.

"I was camping out in the forests, and I found Bendoraun lying on the ground, bleeding horribly. I bandaged him up, but he was unable to move. The blankets and our clothes I used for bandages. We're left with nothing but these rags we found, the rest of what we wore is a bloody mess somewhere in the woods." Behk's eyebrows jumped up and his eyes widened ever slightly, and Gendorn could tell that the man had heard something important in what the boy just told him. "By the time Bendoraun could walk, we were starved and out of food, so we hiked to the nearest village, here," answered Gendorn.

"I can't remember before this morning," added Bendoraun.

"Well we're glad to help out however we can," said Behk.

"We had some people who were with us, with me," continued Gendorn, "but they went to look for help— we don't know this area very well, and they're probably lost. Is there any way to send out a search for them? I hate to ask for anything more, but I'm very scared for them."

"We cannot afford a search party. The Gaolnian Army— do you believe that Gaoln has got an army?— destroyed our village. Our fields are ruined and our buildings are torn down. We'll have to move soon, to find new fields or move into the cities. We'd be worse off out there than your friends probably are."

Gendorn nodded mournfully. He knew Behk was telling the truth— the village could not afford a search party. And that, ironically, was the work of his own army. "Thank you very much," said Gendorn.

"Yes, thank you," said Bendoraun.

"You two need some sleep," said Synla. The two left, and Gendorn and Bendoraun sat by the fire. It was so nice and warm that Gendorn did not even want to fall asleep. Half a day earlier, Gendorn remembered, he had believed himself to be a dead man, lost in the wild without hope. And now he was in a home (a real home, just like they had always dreamed about!) with a warm fire, a hearty meal, and a limitless supply of water. How great his life would be, he thought, if only this house were his, and Kamira and Bendoraun and he could stay here forever. He would sleep tonight in a warm place, dreaming that when he woke, they would be together. It was more incredible than he had ever imagined— he had never been so warm in his life, and it was the gift of a man whose village was destroyed by his own army! The irony of this sank in deep, but it could not disturb Gendorn's cozy smile. He was going to live, and that meant he could still be free. He turned to say something, but Bendoraun was out cold, and would not be waking for a long while— Bendoraun was not the sort of person to wake easily from slumber. And so with such warm thoughts as these, Gendorn shut his eyes as well, and quickly fell asleep by the dying fire.

There had been an uprising that night, before the army had raided the village. More than a hundred of the Skaelin prisoners put down their weapons and refused to march on the town. Commander Denelu, who was informed of the situation, appeared before them to speak. He explained that the children of Gaoln needed a land of their own, for they had been born as slaves always dreaming to be free. The Skaelin men did not listen. They stomped on their weapons and spit on them, and answered that they would not kill the men who had fought and died beside them in the civil war, for Gaoln or against it. Neither of them seemed to understand the other well enough to resolve the issue. So the commander summoned Captain Luncas, his personal friend and confidant. Luncas, afraid that the rebels would defect if left alive, advised Denelu on what to do. On the orders of Commander Denelu, the soldiers executed every last one of the dissenters. The raid on the village that followed was almost mechanical. It was an atrocious and ruthless raid, conducted with so little regard for human life that the army forgot about the revolt entirely. The army left the village after their business was done, hiking until dusk before setting up camp. After dinner, King Centreal called a few of the captains, including Luncas, into his tent. Commander Denelu sat by the king's side.

King Centreal, by tradition, would be the first person to speak at such a meeting. But for a long while, the king did not make any movement. His advisors and officers sat around him in an awkward silence. When he had collected himself, King Centreal spoke.

"I don't want any more burning. Not only does it leave a clear trail for our enemies, not only is it cruel and needless, it is also harmful to us. This will be our country someday, these will be our villages," said the king. "These will be our people moreover, and I need— absolutely need— everyone who is now present to realize that. We are not annihilating this country, we cannot afford to nor would we benefit by doing so." Luncas huffed in frustration. "And I want no more execution of prisoners. Taking of prisoners should be limited. Recruiting of soldiers should be limited. The ruthlessness which we demonstrated today cannot remain the norm. What you two were responsible for, Denelu and Luncas, cannot happen again. This is not who we are, and this is not what we left Gaoln to accomplish. I'll not have us losing our own humanity in the pursuit of our freedom."

"I understand," said Commander Denelu.

"We cannot afford dissent among those who we hope will one day be our fellow countrymen," the king stated. "Our efforts, in many senses, have been so far counterproductive. We have weapons and armor and blankets and supply routes and engineers. Those were necessary for our end objectives.

But the means we used to get to this point we no longer need to employ, and we cannot afford to."

"What should we do then? We can't allow scouts to escape," said Luncas.

"We extort the supplies we need, and threaten to burn every village that sends out a scout. If we're scouted, we'll claim that we'll burn every settlement we find," replied the king. "It doesn't mean we will."

"We can try it," agreed one of the captains.

"I won't protest," said Commander Denelu. "After tonight, something needs to change."

Captain Luncas nodded, exchanging a look with Denelu. "Yes. I will agree."

"Good then. That is our policy henceforth," confirmed the king. "Luncas, Denelu, a word with you in private." The other captains left, and the three of them sat closely together. The king spoke:

"As long as I am king, I will never bear witness to these things again." He paused. "I have said it already: This is not who we are, not what we left Gaoln to accomplish. You men are experienced in the ways of war, whereas I am not. I, however, am experienced in running a state, and it is crucial that you realize this thing: This will become our state, but only if these people can serve us without revolting. We are not burning villages any longer. We are not going to systematically execute our prisoners!" Another pause. "You two can win this war, I have faith in you. But winning the country is another thing—winning the people is an entirely different effort. What you did today was one giant leap toward tearing this land apart, and making peace between the Skaelin and the Gaolnians impossible. I will not stand for it." The two men looked at their king in silence. "That is all. You are dismissed. Leave me."

Part Three: Gatsesilli

- Chapter One -

The room was rather small, but there were windows on all sides, and the advisors of King Sendroun, King of the Skaelin Lands, could see all around them. The conference room was on the second-to-topmost floor of the building where the king lived, and had a view of the mountains and valleys all along the ridge. On a clear day, one could see all the way to the ocean in the east, and all the way to the foothills in the west. King Sendroun sat at the end of the table, looking out at his men, and they waited patiently for him to speak. "I have called you here today for a very urgent briefing," the king began, "I have just been informed by a scout that the Army of Gaoln has taken Fort Bellford." There were a few heavy breaths, but no one replied at first. Then one man broke the silence.

"Gaoln has an army!?"

Sendroun nodded. "Yes. It appears so."

"But how? Who armed them? Who shipped them?" demanded the man.

"I have my suspicions. But I must speak to others before I act upon them. Right now, they alone are our enemy, and they alone must be dealt with!" exclaimed the king. "We also have not been receiving supplies from several western villages. It seems that their trade routes have been cut off. I do believe that this is the work of this same army. If we lose much more, we won't be able to feed our people, or our armies."

"How long has it been since the army took Bellford?" asked an advisor.

"The scout told me eight days, he rode as fast as the selk could take him," replied King Sendroun.

"They could be anywhere..."

"Anywhere within five, maybe six days of Bellford, for a marching army at full speed," the king said, "which is a great many places. It will take a rider at least another eight days to return back there. By then it will be ten days in any direction that they could have gone. It would take us ten days alone to gather our forces here. We should not underestimate their size either— it could be that they are in many different places at once, and in great strength. For all the routes they have cut off already, I estimate that there are at least three different divisions of considerable size and strength."

"We could set up a perimeter, cutting off the northern lands. Wherever they attack, we can close in on them," suggested one of the advisors.

"No, they could slip by," replied the king.

"Do you think the Skaelish will join them?" asked another advisor.

"I hope not..." answered the king. "They're raiding the armories no doubt, preparing to take the battle to us. We can't let that happen."

"Hah, I say let them, that puny rabble is no match for us!" said one of the advisors. "Regardless of their size. They don't know what a war is!"

"Not now, but they will be a match for us very soon at the rate they're going. They still outnumber us vastly, if the scout's report says anything— Gaoln would not have dared to attack us unless their rebellion was virtually unanimous. And with every raid and plunder they gain weapons, armor, and experience. No doubt they're capturing the village engineers as well, and making weapons of their own. We must go after them while we can still win," said the king.

"Where do you think they're going?" asked the advisor.

"We can rule out everything except the Eastern Mountains or the Central Path," said the king. "They would be wise to continue their attacks on the villages, but if they know we have sighted them, they'll know that in any open field of battle we would ruin them. They're going to try and hole up in some castles, or besiege us before we even know what's happened."

"They'd be mad to strike in either location..." said an advisor.

"Don't underestimate them, they gain strength with every moment," said the king. "And with it, we lose strength. We have to put them on the defensive and the retreat."

"So where do we go?" asked another advisor.

"It seems likely they'll try to take the holds and villages along the Central Path before bringing the battle to us. They need to take our commercial centers and the rest of our supply lines, because they know they cannot take the high forts that we occupy here. They're going to try and starve us out— that means we have to leave from here and defend those routes and centers. Bleed them out, and keep them in the open through the next Sen. The scout says he doesn't think he was spotted," answered the king.

"So the Central Path, then?" asked another advisor.

"Yes, the Central Path," replied the king. "To the strongholds of Fort Gatsesilli, Fort Gensballa, and Fort Tycagra. Send out all scouting parties to patrol the areas around the strongholds, I'll join the forces at Gatsesilli."

Over the next month the Skaelin Army assembled under King Sendroun outside of Cavfurt Stronghold. The assembled forces were a massive team known as the Skaelin Main Army. The Main Army would split into three groups after their arrival at Gatsesilli. Each group would fortify one of the three specified strongholds, and from there they would secure the northern and central parts of the country and confine the Gaolnians to the south shore of the Skaelin Lands. They would hold their position until the ice thawed, when they could attack the Gaolnians by both land and sea. Given these directions, the Skaelin Main Army departed for Fort Gatsesilli.

Gendorn didn't wake until noon had already passed. Behk had left to help clear some rubble, and Synla was absent also. Bendoraun slept soundly. For some while Gendorn laid in his bed, not wanting to leave, and feeling far too tired to do so. At last he arose, driven by some feeling he could not quite identify.

As soon as he opened the door, he froze. Across the street and right in front of him five men were working to clear away a pile of rubble. The stone face of the building still stood, but everything around it was ash, and the stone itself was darker, as if the fire had stained it. The men picked up a stone and moved it to a large crate which sat upon a giant two-person wheelbarrow, then they returned and repeated the process, over and over again. Without thinking, Gendorn walked toward them.

The men looked at the boy, but they must have heard about him from Behk and Synla, for they asked no questions. Gendorn paired himself up with one of the other men, and the six of them formed three pairs, each of which would lift one large stone and throw it into the crate, then return and do the same again. The work was hard, and it lasted for a very long time. But Gendorn could drown out the ache in his back if he just kept his focus on moving the rocks, one by one. At some point Gendorn realized that the sky was darkening, and then the men bid their farewells, and returned to their families— if they still had them— for dinner. Several of those whose families had been lost remained on the site and kept working, paying no attention to anything but the task they had assigned themselves. Gendorn stayed behind for a moment, alone with the cleaned area, now free of rubble. There was one man, who

Gendorn had not noticed before, and he was standing almost in the shadows, looking at the rubble. The man caught Gendorn looking at him, and seemed to be evaluating the boy— then he spoke. "Do you know how old this house is, boy?" Gendorn shook his head that he did not. "My great-grandfather built this, it's one of the oldest things in this village. My grandfather raised me here." Gendorn kept silent. "I've never lived outside of this village, but we'll be leaving very soon. We don't have enough food to survive the Sen. We'll be fleeing to other villages. Where are you from?" The man was looking at Gendorn's rags.

"Around," Gendorn answered.

"I see. Well, you're a kind soul for helping us in a time like this, and I hope we can do the same for you. Good luck to you, boy."

"And to you," Gendorn answered very quietly. He turned to leave the man alone with his ruined home. As he walked back to Behk and Synla's house, he felt something wrong inside of him— he did not feel much like a kind soul.

Bendoraun was awake, but still lying in bed, and he did not greet Gendorn— he was still too tired. But when Behk and Synla came in the door he sat upright and welcomed them home. The four of them had a small dinner and fresh cold water. They sat around the fire after dinner again.

"When do you plan to return? The village must be worried by now. What village was it again?" asked Behk.

"Oh, not any particular village," answered Gendorn, "I just camp around from place to place, get a job for a few weeks to stock up on some more food, and then camp again," answered Gendorn.

"Sounds fun," said Behk. "How did you get into that?"

"Well, my family didn't seem to want me around, and my father had been a traveling merchant— I had met a lot of people from other villages down in the south. So I just started traveling and selling things off, and when I would run out of things to sell I would be a hired hand."

"And where are you from?" Behk asked, looking at Bendoraun.

"I'm from…" Bendoraun began. But he could not finish, he didn't know what to say.

"He forgets random things like this, spends hours trying to figure them out. Whatever hit him must have hit him good," said Gendorn.

"I'll remember it…" said Bendoraun.

"No, you won't," said Gendorn.

"I know…" agreed Bendoraun.

"Well, do you have any family?" asked Behk.

"A mother, my father was killed in the War of Skaen. But she won't worry, I've been gone like this before," answered Bendoraun.

"I see. Well, Gendorn. You know the settlements around here?" asked Behk.

"Actually, I don't think I've been to this village before…do you have a map?"

"I do. I'll go get it."

"Behk was in the war also," said Synla, as Behk left. "He fought at Liono Den, was one of the infantry."

"We are all in his debt," said Bendoraun.

"Yes, I'm lucky he survived. Where was your father stationed?" continued Synla.

"He was garrisoned with the 21st," answered Bendoraun, hoping that would mean something. Synla nodded in sympathy.

"He remembers his father's regiment," Gendorn mused, "but he can't even remember the name of the village!" Synla smiled and gave a light laugh, and Behk returned with the map and handed it to Gendorn.

"There's the map. When do you two plan to leave?" he said.

"We need to find some work so we can get some blankets and food for wherever we go," said Gendorn.

"Don't worry about that. We'll give you nice warm blankets and adequate food, I just need to talk to the neighbors. Where do you two plan to go?" Behk asked.

"You should wash that wound, Bendoraun. I'll get you some water and new bandages," Synla said— clearly not following their conversation— and she left to get her things.

"Thank you very much," said Bendoraun. Gendorn pointed at the map.

"Here, Fort Gatsesilli. Do you happen to have a spare tent also?" he asked.

"Gatsesilli is too far, the village can't spare that much food. It could be ten days in this snow, if you account for getting yourself lost a few times, which you will. And I do have an old tent you two could have, I suppose," said Behk.

"Thank you," said Gendorn. "I really wish there was a way to repay you."

"It's nothing."

"So where do you think we should go?"

"If you're looking for a fortress, Fort Bellford and Fort Gatsesilli are both on the map, but only Bellford is close enough for us to supply. You could reach Bellford in only five days, it is the closest thing to a village castle we have, although it serves villages much further away than our own. But if the army took this village, it seems likely they have also taken control of that castle. In the worst case, you'll be walking into an active war zone, and we really should assume that will be the case, for safety's sake. If you want to go to Fort Gatsesilli I'd suggest getting a job in a village north of here to supply the rest of the trip. We could only spare enough for three days, I'd estimate, and that will leave you hungry on the trail for two days if you go to Bellford. If you want to reestablish yourselves, Gatsesilli is the place to go. You'll just need to stay in another village for a few days. I'll see what I can get from the neighbors. But there is one thing I've been meaning to ask you," said Behk.

"Yes?" wondered Gendorn.

"Synla and I see it as our duty to take in two people who so desperately need our help. And we will help you, because without our help you would die. But we need to know something, for our own sakes. And we need the truth. Are you deserters of the Army of Gaoln?"

"We are truly not," Gendorn answered without hesitation. He felt guilty for having been a part of the army— but they were not deserters. It was the army, Gendorn thought, that had deserted them. The thought hit him in an instant, and he considered telling Behk the truth. How could his own men do such a thing to this village, how could they treat people like this, just because that is how some other person, locked up in some castle, had treated the Gaolnians in the first place? He felt as cheated as any man by his having spent an entire life as a prisoner without a crime— but Behk and Synla didn't deserve lies, and that thought came to him suddenly as a simple fact. And yet when Gendorn thought of Kamira, Gulaus Kanel, Curileyn, and all the tens of thousands of others— when he reminded himself that the Army of Gaoln was his only chance at getting them here to Skaen, and out of Gaoln forever— he knew he could not tell the truth to this kind man. Behk nodded, leaving to gather the food and speak with his friends.

Bendoraun and Synla returned some time later, Bendoraun's head now clean and freshly bandaged. After a while Behk also returned, with more than enough food in his hands.

"The neighbors were more generous than I thought they'd be," he said. "Looks like you two are going to Gatsesilli after all. I'll get you both up tomorrow morning when I leave for the day's work."

- Chapter Two -

The boys awoke the next morning to see Behk towering over them, with gifts that they would remember for all the rest of their days.

Bendoraun and Gendorn had been wearing the same dirt rags for all their lives. New rags were sent for them every two years, as they were for all prisoners. Each laboring prisoner had a set of short rags for the hot days and another set of long rags. Prisoners too old, young, or weak to work had only the longer pair. They were all of a thick, coarse material, the color of mud drying into dirt under the sun. It was a color meant for the slaves of Gaoln. On board the ships, the fighters were given undergarments to be worn beneath the rags. These hugged them and kept them significantly warmer, which was necessary on the exposed high seas. Upon departing Tekal, the army had only given them modest coats, cut in places and not altogether effective in keeping out the cold. Even with those coats and undergarments, the rags of Gaoln never came off.

And now this kind Skaelin man stood before them, offering them fine collared tunics of red and blue, trousers of polished mahogany, warm fur hats that covered their heads and ears both, a stable tent all of their own, and two small backpacks with a map inside, tucked in between containers of food and water.

For the first time in their lives, the two boys took off the rags of their slavery, not with the intent of washing them outside in the rain, or hanging them to dry in the sun, but with the intent to fold them up neatly, tuck them away in their new backpacks, and say a sweet and long-awaited goodbye. They showered in a showerhouse near the village center, and donned their new clothes. When they walked out of the showerhouse, they stood looking at one another, and broke into smiles.

Bendoraun entered the house in the blue tunic, and Gendorn emerged moments later dressed in a royal deep red. They were stiff, and smelled very nice (especially now that Gendorn and Bendoraun smelled fresh themselves), and with the glistening red-brown trousers the two ex-slaves stood like princes. It was the clean fresh feeling of a new beginning.

Synla and Behk waved them out and bid them farewell as Gendorn and Bendoraun set off down the dirt road, in between the scattered ruins. When they took the first corner they saw beside them a row of houses which had been burnt— two of them had collapsed in on themselves and a few people were clearing the ashes. Up that road there were a few empty spaces where the rubble had already been cleared. Beyond that there was a group of men building a perimeter around the edge of the valley with shovels and axes— they must be making a ditch, thought Gendorn. Was that a perimeter, or was it to divert the water flow? He shook his head. A look to his left revealed another row of burnt homes, and beyond that a section of the village which had been completely cleared. Nothing was left on the eastern edge of town.

At the top of the hill, Gendorn stopped for just a moment. He turned around, taking a last look at the village that saved his life, and the life of Bendoraun. "Was this really us?" Gendorn asked.

"No," said Bendoraun, "and it's not going to be."

"This can't be right. It just can't."

"It wasn't us," Bendoraun said again. Then he lowered his head. "I don't know how we could fix it. I feel terrible, having been a part of all this the whole time— even though we weren't with them. Do you wonder how different it would have made us, if we had been a part of this?"

"I'm glad we weren't. I hope I'm never a part of such destruction."

"What will we do, then? Rejoin the ranks, and not fight? I'm beginning to wonder whether we should rejoin the ranks at all. I don't want to go to Bellford, Gendorn, because if our army is there, I don't know how I can look at them with respect. They won't be the men I thought I was sailing with a month ago. We need to win, but like this? And I still think of those dreams I had back in Port Tekal. We're only going toward the worst of them, I know it. I want to go back to Tekal, now that I've seen what this war really is. But when I think of Tekal...I don't even know if they will still be there, really."

"Everyone in Behk's village will have to leave soon. There's no food left. They can't farm," Gendorn paused. "It's ironic how similar his situation is to our own, in some ways. Kamira wouldn't tolerate this, I know that. She's too good. She'd walk up to King Centreal and Captain Luncas, sit them down, and tell them straight to their faces that they've gone mad, and that this isn't how the rebellion was meant to happen, this isn't how our freedom should be found. She'd lecture them for an hour, and by the end of it she'd have all the Gaolnians ready to pronounce her dictator."

"She does have that assertive quality," Bendoraun agreed.

"Assertive?" Gendorn laughed. "Aggressive, and nothing less."

"Come on" said Bendoraun. "We have to get walking. We'll figure out what to do when we are safe in Gatsesilli."

The night was peaceful. Gendorn and Bendoraun knew where they were going. They had a tent and warm blankets and food over the fire. They had a map. They had left that morning from a home— a real home!— and they would arrive at a castle, tall and strong and surrounded by fields, in just a few days more. Gendorn missed Kamira more tonight than he had in a very long time. But his thoughts were distracted. When he closed his eyes, sometimes he would see her face. Other times he would see some imaginary picture of the Gaolnian Army marching into that small village and burning the houses down. He would see Synla and Behk out in the streets, sobbing and weeping. He would see them inside their house, cowering in some corner.

Other times, he might see the same images, but he would feel no remorse. *Burn the villages down* would echo in some corner of his mind. *Should have killed them all at Tekal and not thought about it for a moment.* When these thoughts came, it was because another, far darker, more dangerous layer of images burned in his heart and mind.

These were the worst when he heard the snow turn into rain for a brief hour on one particularly warm afternoon. It started off slow, and then rose to a force. Lightning crashed. In that split of a second when the light revealed the expanse of the forest, he saw terrible, terrible shapes. The emaciated bodies of children lying in the dust, the freezing rain covering them. Crowds of people shouting and sobbing, begging for a roof. Two wide open eyes staring at him, the life draining out of them. A troop of children running around their gulaus, the elder showing them the remains of the Death Storm's victims, explaining to them why their world was this way. Somewhere in this explanation the images faded, and he remembered asking another question to another man, not too long before the storm. *No one knows.*

When the rain stopped, all was clear. But sometimes in the morning he would turn his head around, prepared to see one thousand starved and frozen corpses sprawled out before him. He never did see such a thing— he had not since that day in Gaoln. But he lived every second in fear that he would, if only he turned his head once more.

For most of the journey, the hatred he had grown up with, for all the men and women who had allowed him and others like him to suffer their whole lives beyond any imaginable suffering, battled against the simple fact that Behk and Synla were good people. He spent most of the days after that in an overwhelming silence. Bendoraun, he noticed, walked in a similar silence, his head cast downward, his eyes reflecting a thought he could not ever find the words to fit.

"Do you ever wonder, Gendorn," asked Bendoraun, one week into their journey, "what it would be like to grow up in a village like that? I mean, we talked about this all the time back in Gaoln, I know— what we would do if we had a land of our own— but we had never seen an actual village. Now that we have, I can put myself in that home. I can see myself as a neighbor, as a worker, as a child of the village..."

"Yes," said Gendorn abruptly. Bendoraun looked at him.

"What?"

Gendorn shook his head. "No, nothing."

"Don't say that to me, I'm your best friend."

Gendorn almost smiled, but couldn't. "I know. I'm just thinking about the village...Maybe this isn't the whole army. It only takes a few regiments to take a village, I would think. Maybe it was just some angry and stupid and careless captain who gave an order without the consent of anyone above him or anyone around him. We saw one village. That doesn't mean the whole countryside is in flames."

Bendoraun nodded. "You're right, see? We shouldn't jump to conclusions. Especially when our options are so limited in any case."

"Right."

"We should still go to Gatsesilli, though. If the army is still fighting at Bellford, it would be dangerous for us to be there. We need to be able to rejoin them outside of a battle, not during a battle."

"I agree. It might take some time waiting, but it will be worth it."

And yet as they passed through the woods north of the village they saw no activity. No Skaelin scouts, no Gaolnian scouts, no refugees, no soldiers, not even a passing caravan full of food or merchandise headed for one of the castles or nearby towns. The entire forest seemed abandoned. Rather than comforted, the two boys were worried and disoriented: What could possibly cause the forest right outside of Bellford to be so entirely devoid of people? In any case, it did not make them wish to stay. They headed north to Gatsesilli as quickly as they could.

After a week they found the trail becoming more winding, and the hills, which they had climbed the entire way, began to slope downward. Upon the crest of one rise they could suddenly see endless farms and villages arrayed before them, and a castle looming upon a distant meadow plateau. For almost an entire day they hiked through small towns and settlements, bustling with cottage-shops and expansive farmlands and stone quarries and large, multi-story housing such as the boys had never seen before. These things, common as they were for Gatsesillians, stunned the young soldiers into silent awe. To see a large and complex society functioning as such was something they had only imagined up to this time. Workers hauling stone was the only familiar sight. Carpenters, farmers, bakers, craftsmen, traders with roadside shops— these were all brand new, and very exciting. They felt a deep desire to explore more, but to retain their disguise they acted unsurprised and continued onward.

And then, suddenly, that great fortress in the meadow stood tall before them. The grey castle stood as something strong and invincible, its great turrets reaching for heaven, and the boys stopped dead in their tracks. What a wonder to behold!

On all sides of the fortress were more expanses of farms and mines or very small groups of workshops, reaching outward until they touched the very edge of the forest, and even then cottages had been built deep into the woods. The spires of Gatsesilli towered above the trees by at least triple their height. There was a small wooden fence along the edge of the forest, and from a gate in that fence two guards approached the two boys. The guards eyed both suspiciously. "Who are you two, and what business do you have here?" asked one of the guards.

"I am Bendoraun, this is Gendorn. We come here seeking a new residence, our village was robbed of its food and its fields burned by a large band of thieves," answered Bendoraun.

"We have only one meal's worth left, please let us reside here," added Gendorn.

"A village was robbed? What village? This is news indeed," inquired the guard.

"The village of Okanu, to the southwest of here. There will probably be more refugees in the near future. We didn't send a scout, they threatened to kill every citizen if we did," answered Gendorn.

"How long ago did this happen?"

"I don't know, somewhere around twenty days ago, maybe a few more. I have no idea where they are now," replied Gendorn.

"I'll send a scout to verify your report, thank you for this news. Welcome to Gatsesilli," said the guard.

"Thank you," said Gendorn, bowing his head. Bendoraun bowed too, and they crossed through the gates into the mighty city of Gatsesilli.

"Look at that, Bendoraun," whispered Gendorn, bobbing his head to a man in the distance carrying some sacks down the hillside.

"Is that...Nolor?" asked Bendoraun.

"Let's go see. We grew up with him," replied Gendorn.

"Of course," said Bendoraun, "where are we from?"

"Okanu, if they inquire."

"Nolor?" asked Gendorn, as the two approached him.

Nolor turned his head, and dropped the sacks of flour on the ground. "Gendorn! And Bendoraun! How did you two get here!?"

"We'll tell you when you're done with your work, it's a long story," answered Bendoraun.

"Yes, well, my story is a bit unsettling as well. I get the feeling we are not entirely through with those men who were following us. I'll meet you two in the dining hall. Ask a guard for directions, you two can stay with me in the tower. Dinner's at sunset. I have to get back to work. I'm a baker's assistant now. I can make bread, Gendorn! We have to talk at dinner! Fate has blessed us that we're all alive."

"It has. We'll talk to you then," said Gendorn.

"Goodbye," said Bendoraun. Their spirits were renewed—they were not the only ones who survived their endeavor! Nolor returned with the sacks to what must have been his boss's bakery, and Gendorn and Bendoraun went up to the castle for instructions, wide smiles on their gleaming faces.

"Excuse me, sir," said Gendorn, walking up to a guard posted just outside the gates. "Could you show me where the dining hall is?"

"I could tell you. It's the middle room of this floor, and the middle room of the second floor. Do you have a place to stay?" answered the guard.

"Yes, we're staying with a friend for a while," replied Gendorn.

"I see. Dinner's at sunset."

"Thank you."

Sunset came soon, and Gendorn and Bendoraun were among the first to enter the hall. It was an enormous and elaborate hall, polished wood on all sides and wooden floors, and balconies along the second floor which acted also as roofs for the outer part of the first floor. The middle was open and had only the third floor high above as a roof, and an opulent chandelier hung from the center, casting its light down onto both floors and every corner of the dining hall. Grand stone fireplaces stood at each end of the great dining hall, and their fires roared to warm the room. Once more, the two boys were stunned into silence and awe. What a place!

Gendorn and Bendoraun had little money, only what they managed to scavenge from the Port Tekal treasury. They bought some Skaenish fruits they'd never had before, and split a loaf of bread. Fresh cold water came free with every meal. Nolor entered amongst a large crowd, and stood in line for a while. He came out with another variety of fruits and a small biscuit, spotted them, and sat down at the table.

"So, how have you two been?" asked Nolor.

"We've been...well, alright I guess," answered Gendorn.

"We have a lot to catch up on," said Bendoraun. Nolor nodded.

"Did those men follow you?" Nolor asked.

"No. We had no one following us," Gendorn said.

Nolor smiled. "How sure are you of that?"

Gendorn and Bendoraun exchanged glances, then Gendorn shrugged. "Well, did they follow you?"

"Yes, in fact. But then they waited to see where I would go. I believe they are somewhere inside this castle. I never caught a look at them."

"Was this the first place you found?" Bendoraun wondered.

"Yes," said Nolor, "where did you two settle down?"

"A little village to the south of here," Gendorn answered, "We...well, we can discuss it later."

"We were very lucky," added Bendoraun. "We found a village and two nice villagers who gave us all we needed."

"They gave us a tent and a map also, and these backpacks too," added Gendorn.

Nolor smiled wide. "Fortune is with you, no doubt. I almost died myself, passed out at the city gates in the middle of interrogation. Woke up in the guest tower, which is where I'm staying."

"That must have been a new one for the guards," said Bendoraun.

"I believe it might have been. We should move up to the room," Nolor said, as a group of men came to sit down at the table across from them. The two boys nodded, finished their meals in silence, and returned to Nolor's room in the east guest tower, where they were free to talk.

The room was hardly large enough for the three of them to sleep in side by side, and was furnished only with a small cot along one wall and a tiny wooden chest tucked away in the corner. Standing there, Gendorn felt a claustrophobia he'd not felt since leaving Gaoln. It was somewhat of a shock, after having left such a grand dining hall and having seen the riches all around the castle. He shrugged it off. "What's this job?" he asked Nolor.

"Baker's assistant. I deliver sacks of flour from the mill stores and clean things, and I operate these machines that help make bread faster. They have some really amazing machines here. You can grind huge piles of grain into flour with these levers and pulleys and other contraptions. You have to see how it works! It's a fairly nice pay, if you two want to help some other baker."

"We'll search the place for jobs tomorrow. Is it alright if we stay here until one of us gets another place?" asked Gendorn.

"Or until we get kicked out," said Nolor. "I wasn't given a timeframe."

"Good. Now— what are we going to do?" asked Gendorn, "I mean, what are we really going to do? We can't stay here. What about Kamira? What about the rest of the Gaolnians and their freedom?"

"Don't worry, friend," answered Bendoraun, "the army is sure to come here, and even if they don't, we will overhear something about their location. If the army comes here, we'll just hide and hope they win. If they do win, we'll ask for Luncas and rejoin the ranks." He paused a moment, then went on. "Do you really want to rejoin the army? Look where we are. Look around us. We can leave this, and join the army, and make no difference at all, because we don't know how to be soldiers. Or we can live the life we have wanted to live this entire time. And we will find a way to smuggle Kamira in here with us. Do you really think the three of us can make a difference in the war, Gendorn? We can't do anything more for them, we are only three inexperienced soldiers. We've found the finish line. We don't have to go back to the start. And I know you're worried about Kamira, but we already broke out of Gaoln once. We'll find a way to get her out— we will, Gendorn. The army can win without us, and then we will find Kamira." Before Gendorn spoke up, Bendoraun started again: "Gendorn, we can not make the difference— "

"We have to, Bendoraun! And maybe we can prevent some of those things you saw in your dreams. And we can stop the army from killing people like Behk and Synla. We can stop the burning."

"You know we can't. Is that what this is about?"

"We can't get Kamira without the army, either! We have absolutely no way of reaching her unless we find the army. The army wants to get everyone out of Gaoln. No other group of people on earth would be willing to sail into that prison. Without the army, everyone we left behind in that terrible place will die. We have no choice!"

"Enough talk about that," whispered Nolor, "remember where we are."

"We'll figure it all out," said Bendoraun.

"We have to go back to the army. I can't let our dream die. We cannot stop until we are free— all of us."

"We will hear of where the army plans to put those who remained behind, where they will sail. And we will meet Kamira there."

"It's impossible, either as a prisoner of Gaoln or a citizen of the Skaelin," Gendorn protested. "Bendoraun, I despise what happened to Behk and Synla. I know we can do something about it. We are wrong to think it was a mistake. Listen to your feelings, Bendoraun. You know it was not a mistake. We have to stop this. And I will not leave everyone we've known in chains and sit idly by while the army wins our freedom for us. I will not live here, passing my days in happiness and freedom, while Kamira sits on the shores of a prison colony wondering which will come first: Freedom or death. And I will not live inside some warm castle with food at my feet when the rest of our countrymen are starving in the frozen wilderness with little more than roots for dinner. We will fight and die beside them."

"We won't make a difference in that anyway, Gendorn, to be realistic. She will be here or not, we will win or lose— we cannot make the difference."

"Don't you believe in a place for us? For all of us? Won't you fight for it?"

"Hey, watch what you say!" whispered Nolor. "Come on, let's give it a rest for now. Are you trying to be overheard?"

- Chapter Three -

It was a calm day in Laen. In the capitol city, Laeolin, the merchants and traders were hawking their goods on the wide white stone boulevards, calling out to poor travelers and rich businessmen alike. Singers and musicians lined the corners with their bowls open for coins. In the alleys, the homeless were burning wood in metal baskets to keep themselves warm. The morning had come, and the smell of fresh bread from the bakeries had already reached every nose in the city. It was an altogether busy day, and so it was as well for the king of this great place. He had an important meeting today.

Skerun, the Skaelin Director of Ambassadors, waited before King Seagraul for his reply. "Gaoln has gathered its prisoners, King Seagraul," the ambassador had said to the king. "They landed in the Skaelin Lands before the first snow. They have been attacking our villages and raiding our armories, and have gained enough strength to keep us trapped in the Eastern Mountains, if we fail to defeat them now."

"Gaoln has escaped?" the king had answered curiously. And Skerun could not quite tell why the king was not more disturbed by this information than he appeared to be. King

Seagraul was quiet for a very long time. Through his window at the top of the palace he could see the people moving about the city. "Would you like some cakes? I've just sent a man down there to get me some cakes. Raspberry. Quite nice." Skerun eyed the king, who understood that the ambassador would require a more directive response. "That is news indeed," the king said. "Gonaka will have to pay. I suspect their hand in this. We will have a victory of it in any case, I am sure, and I am quite confident that the Gaolnians will think twice of another rebellion. I've already got a sense of our options, but what do you suggest we do?"

"My sources tell me they plan to seize the holds along the Central Path. I fear the Gaolnians are too many, and we are too few. I have come for your help," answered Skerun. The king smiled knowingly.

"You want Laen to join the war, in alliance with the Skaelin, to defeat Gaoln?"

"I do. I do not see why you should hesitate— you were the foremost proprietor of Gaoln, you have quite an interest in subduing this rebellion!"

"We just got out of war with Gonaka. Many of our best leaders perished in the battles. Our land and sea troops are at the weakest they've been in a hundred years. And the Gaolnians cannot win this war, either way— to not intervene is to let them die, and I am quite fine with that."

"But you are still strong enough to march with us and defeat the Gaolnians. Gaoln is your problem, King Seagraul. You cannot keep them imprisoned and then, when they break out and invade your ally, sit by and watch. What will the world think of you?"

"Possibly, but our relations with Gonaka haven't improved very much at all. What if the Gash take advantage of this, what if they attack us when we send our men to Skaen? And what if Gonaka allies itself with the Skaelish, against the Skaelin? What if they both ally with Gaoln?"

"I realize that is a devastating possibility…"

"A grave possibility, my friend. Our nation does not have the strength to take that risk. I am very sorry," said King Seagraul.

"Don't you wonder how it was that pitiful Gaoln mustered the strength to attack the Skaelin? Who do you think supplied their food, who gave them their ships to sail across the sea, who taught them the geography of Skaen, who put this hope in their minds?" said Skerun. The king awaited an answer, knowing Skerun would deliver one. "The Gash. Gonaka did this, and King Nowhawna. The Skaelin spies in Gonaka have been working to uncover the truth behind this war." Skerun took a breath, then resumed speaking.

"What if you weren't alone? Maybe I could gather some of our allies to help our cause? Though I fear time is very crucial in this war, so I would request a litha." Seagraul looked at his old friend in admiration of his fervor.

"Fine, fly to President Leyus of Las, and you can fly on our litha. See if they will answer your call. If they do…so will I," agreed the king.

"Thank you, my dear friend. I promise you this is a wise decision. These Gaolnians will not stop until that whole country is burned down," said Skerun.

"How do you know this is the doing of the Gash?" asked Seagraul.

"Well, that is a more interesting tale…"

Skerun rested that night in the palace and woke shortly before sunrise. He woke Seagraul and the king wished him well, but decided against leaving his bed. Skerun stood in the courtyard observing the beauty of the great black and purple flying reptile in the pre-dawn light. As there were few lithae in the world, they were reserved for such important missions as these, and heralded grave news more often than not. He was not happy about the times being so grave as to require its use.

Skerun arrived at the courtyard of the Palace of Las around sunset, when he was greeted by two guards and escorted to the President of Las.

"Greetings, President Leyus," said Skerun, entering the President's Chambers.

"Skerun, how have you been?" said Leyus. The guards were sent away, leaving Skerun and Leyus alone to talk.

"Worried," replied Skerun.

"What bothers you?" wondered the president. And so Skerun explained the situation once again.

"I talked to King Seagraul, and he says if you will help us then so will he," explained Skerun. "Please, my president. The Gaolnians will ravage the entire countryside and starve out every city. We have to help the Skaelin."

"I've always secretly held my sympathies for Gaoln, you know that," said President Leyus. "Even if I am forced to abide by the nation's will, and support the penal colony."

"Throwing them back in that penal colony would not be necessary— there are other solutions. And I do not intend on letting Gaoln happen again. But sitting back and watching people die is not one of the solutions."

"I'll have to talk to the representatives. Give us a while," answered the president.

"I fear I do not have a while..."

"Do not worry, I just have to pass it by them, but I give you my support. It is yours. As long as we are agreed that the Gaolnians will not be made to return to Gaoln. If we have to throw them across all the nations of Fengorian, so be it, if we need to take some land from Laen or the Skaelin, so be it, but I will not force them back to Gaoln. Not only is it immoral, but it is impractical. You know they would die before returning to the colony, after they've come so far and fought for so long."

"I know. I am sure we will all be able to agree on some accords, once we bring King Central and King Sendroun together at the table for negotiations."

The next morning the Council of Las met with the president, and after a morning and partial afternoon of debate, the decision to send troops was made. When the ice began to melt and the harsh cold of Sen began to lift, one hundred thousand Las soldiers would gather at Port Cindyll, where they would wait for the ice to finish melting. As soon as passage to Skaen was safe, the troops would be sent to the king, where they would be given further instructions. Meanwhile, the connection of Gonaka in the war would be further investigated, and envoys would be sent to confront them with the matter.

This was relayed to Skerun, who flew back to Laen and relayed it to King Seagraul. After a short discussion among King Seagraul, his advisors, and Skerun, it was agreed that eighty thousand Lonin troops would be sent to gather at Port Syndona, where they would patiently wait for the ice to thaw, and then set sail for Skaen.

"I want you to be the envoy to King Nowhawna of Gonaka, Skerun," explained King Seagraul between bites of his bread. Skerun looked up at him with surprise.

"I thank you. I was hoping for that opportunity. I will present the case well, I assure you as best I can. I know Gonaka is behind this." The king nodded. "I'll leave tomorrow, then?"

"Tomorrow morning," confirmed the king.

That night, there was another man already en route to Gonaka. He arrived before the dawn at the Courtyard of Gonaka, and sent an immediate request for the king. The request was granted, and the king, hardly dressed at all, arrived promptly, knowing the coming of this man meant important things had to be discussed very quickly. King Nowhawna of Gonaka was a tall man with a long red beard, and he looked quite odd standing there in his thin night-robes, with his usual, scornful look upon his face. In contrast, the somewhat shorter old man who stood before him— whose beard was almost as long, but entirely white— wore a hesitant smile. The king grunted. "What is it, Menuld?"

"It's Laen," Menuld said, with a touch of humor in his voice. "It is always something with Laen, is it not? Why do you always ask that question, when the answer does not change?" His humor was lost on the sleepy king, and Menuld adjusted his tone of voice. "I received word some time ago that Skerun tipped them off on what happened, and that Skerun is trying to bring Las and Laen together to defend the Skaelin Lands. Gaoln is dying, is what it is, my king. The rebellion teeters on the edge of failure."

"Well, this was bound to happen at some point."

"You will have to make a settlement."

"Yes," agreed the king, "well, we will all be making a settlement here, that is the hope."

"Las and Laen will not want to settle."

"I am aware of that. Are you suggesting something, Menuld, or do you intend on only telling me things I already know?"

Menuld sighed. "You don't understand. We have to make a settlement, at any cost— any cost!"

"I do not believe that Las and Laen are foolish enough to attack Gonaka, or to actually invade Skaen. If they did, it would leave their own lands more vulnerable and wide open for attack. I am not overly concerned. What is more important is that this issue is finally resolved, and for that to happen we need to have a real solution, not a fast and simple one."

"I will try to convince King Seagraul of your wisdom, my king," said Menuld, "but I fear that it will be of no avail. Wisdom, as you know, is lost upon King Seagraul more often than not. I urge you— we must make a settlement, no matter what. An envoy will be here from Laen soon enough. And if, when he departs, Gaoln is still an issue unresolved, then Laen and Gonaka will be at war."

The king shrugged. "We will see about that."

Sure enough, when the orange rays of light began streaking through the cold crisp sky of the morning, Skerun arose to start the day. He set out as the circle of the sun was poking out above the junction of the land and sky away to the east. He mounted the litha and flew off into the morning, soaring over northern Kon as he made his way to Gonaka.

He flew westward for four days from before each sunrise to after each sunset, and arrived in the capital city of Gonaka—called quite simply the Glorious City— under the stars of the fourth night. When Skerun landed in the Courtyard of Gonaka he was received warmly by two guards, each of whom had seen Skerun before, and brought into the palace. After only a short time King Nowhawna of Gonaka emerged, and the two left for a private audience chamber, a small, simple room with a table, lamp, and a marked-up map of the Glorious City nailed haphazardly to the wall. Skerun sat down and wasted no time. "My friend King Nowhawna," the envoy said bravely, "I know that you supplied the Gaolnian Army."

King Nowhawna, not surprised in the least by the frankness of Skerun's comment, replied simply: "What proof do you have of that?"

"I learned from a friend that the army was given food, clothes, blankets, and maps of Skaen. All of these came from Gonaka," said Skerun.

"Who is your friend, and how can he make such claims?"

"He is a wise and patient man, and he happens to be correct. I do not mean to point the finger, King Nowhawna, but I cannot deny what I learn to be true, and I must act upon it," said Skerun. "You and I both know Gonaka's motives. There could be few other options."

"I am sorry, but your evidence is not firm. I am not sure of what to say, Skerun," said King Nowhawna.

"Admit it. Just because your ships bore no marks of nationality does not mean they did not belong to a nation."

"Skerun, I should remind you that it was we who first introduced the idea of requiring every ship on the sea to bear a mark of nationality. Gonaka is not intent on making war, I assure you. You know our stance on the issue of Gaoln— I thought you were on our side."

"I was, although my king has never been and never will be, and so I cannot be as lenient with you as you would like. But I am not for war! That to me is not a viable answer to the question of Gaoln. Why you thought terror and crime could be solved by murder and invasion is beyond me. We were making progress convincing Laen— "

"Laen would not yield to reason! Aniania and Phenen and Laen and Las all were stubborn and steadfastly foolish!" said King Nowhawna.

"I understand your thoughts, although you too were just as steadfast, and now, my friend, I fear it is you who acts foolishly. Come to some accord with my king and with King Seagraul, and this will end."

"Gaoln would have been enslaved! The Skaelin were siding with Laen more dogmatically than ever, as if they had some personal vendetta against Gaoln! But we do not want this huge war!" declared the king.

"You do, my friend. Do not try to deceive me," replied Skerun.

"I seek the freedom of Gaoln, as you once did," the king replied calmly.

"I seek it too, I seek freedom for all who are born in captivity. Yet I would not seek to accomplish this by invading the Skaelin Lands! You must understand that King Seagraul takes as much offense from this as King Sendroun. You play too risky of a game."

"Gaoln would never have ended. It had to rise up itself."

"I do know, and I argued many times for the freedom of Gaoln. But you must understand that war cannot be the answer. I have seen this war myself. It is not a prison escape, it is a pestilence that plagues the world, one that claims the lives of hundreds of thousands of people if it goes unchecked, for even now, I tell you, I swear to you— even now, plans are underway which will drag this war on and cause it to claim many more lives. It must be contained. Please listen to me," pleaded Skerun. There was a silence, with only the background noises of the furious winds picking up outside and the clattering of feet outside the hall.

"We should establish a government," King Nowhawna began, "between the Skaelin and the Gaolnians, and include them both. And we must move all the Gaolnians into Skaen. And we must make sure they are protected."

"The Skaelin, Las and Laen all remain unwilling to make that sacrifice. The Skaelin must be the only legitimate government, and King Sendroun alone must rule over Gaoln. The Gaolnians will be confined to settlements— "

"Absolutely not," said King Nowhawna, "if this is the proposition you have come to give me, then leave right now, and do not come back!"

Something like a shadow moved in the corner of the room, and Skerun and Nowhawna both shifted their focus to see what this disturbance might be. The shadow stepped into the light, and suddenly Menuld stood before the two men, looking at them as if they were two children bickering. "Would it be alright," he asked politely, "if I were to try and mediate this little difference of opinion?"

Skerun's eyes narrowed sharply. "Menuld, why are you here?"

"I came earlier this morning, to speak with the king. If you will allow me to speak, I would love to enter this discussion. I do believe this war must end, and I really mean that. The Gaolnians have destroyed too much in their quest to remain undiscovered and unchallenged. And when the Skaelin meet them in battle— well, I cannot fathom such terrible things."

"It has already begun. Can it be stopped?" asked Nowhawna.

"You can stop it. You can not get involved, there may still be a chance," said Menuld.

"And leave the Gaolnians to die?" asked the king.

"The Gaolnians will not die. They are strong enough now that they can create a nation of their own, inside of Skaen, and keep it from Sendroun's army. The alternative, of course, is to put the balance of the world at peril," Menuld said casually. "A contract must exist between those who are now fighting to be free and those who lived in the Skaelin Lands before, a contract which both Laen and Gonaka will have to abide by."

"This war will end with Gaoln's unconditional surrender," Skerun reaffirmed.

"You see?" King Nowhawna exclaimed, "I cannot sit back and allow those whose freedom my country fought for, for so long, to be destroyed. I cannot let their cause fall into the crags of the earth, never to be found. What would happen, my dear Menuld, to the people of Gaoln, the ones left behind? What will happen to the forces when they surrender?"

"Please trust me, as your king did before you, and his king before him. I would not deceive you," Menuld reassured the king, "our intervention in this war must be avoided, whatever Laen's ambitions may be. The path of war is terrible and ruinous."

"You see, King Nowhawna," said Skerun, "even Menuld the Wise, Menuld the Patient, Menuld the Peaceloving cannot agree with your ambitions. Let it end."

"Under my terms, this war will end," the king answered.

"Under my terms," Skerun argued, "this war will end."

"The fight is hopeless!" The king exclaimed once more, turning from Menuld to Skerun. "This war was fought for a purpose, Skerun, and until that purpose is met the war will not end!" The king turned back to Menuld. "You have not answered my questions. I have advisors too, Menuld. And they dislike the idea of leaving the Gaolnians to die in the deep snows of the Skaenish Sen."

"What have your advisors said, then?" asked Menuld.

"The world without this war is a terrible thing. Las, Laen and the Skaelin are set up for an alliance, whether you acknowledge that or not. Gaoln is set to become the prison for all those who oppose the alliance. And make no mistake— Gaoln as a penal colony would not end, not so long as the tyranny of Seagraul and Sendroun remains. For the world to become balanced, for the good of these people, far more than your few hundred thousand, we must take the course of action which we have planned for."

"I'll have no talk of penal colonies or of turning back the tide of rebellion— Gaoln should never have existed, and it will never exist again, unless it exists as a nation of free people," Menuld said, "But you have the power to stop this war! You have the goodness within your heart and mind and soul, if only you would reach it, if only you would tap it! You can stop this war."

Menuld turned to Skerun. "And you!" he exclaimed, "you should be ashamed. You know that Gaoln's dream of freedom will not die so long as Nowhawna is King of Gonaka and Centreal King of Gaoln, so long as the Council sits in Kale and there remain those who fight for what is good. Your unrealistic demands are nothing if not a statement proclaiming that war is your own preferred course of action. If King Nowhawna is to make concessions, they must be reasonable— that means you must be reasonable!" Skerun did not reply— his eyes locked with the gaze of King Nowhawna.

King Nowhawna was silent again. *You can stop this war* echoed in his head. He moved his fingers aimlessly around the desk, and heaved a heavy sigh. Was it his place to put an end now to what had been set in motion so long ago? Was it his duty now to destroy the fruits of the toil of his fellowmen and his ancestors? Would he plunge the world into chaos, or would he seal its fate— for good, or for ill? Where would the roads presented now take him, where would they take the entirety of Fengorian?

"I know what to do," said Menuld.

"You may think me rash, and you may be right. But I do not think you know. You know much, I do not doubt that. But you do not know it all, and you cannot see all the roads, you cannot notice where they go," said King Nowhawna.

Menuld replied softly, selecting his words with care. "I know this, my king, that this war will be the death of you, of many tens of thousands of your countrymen, of many hundreds of thousands of this world. More innocent blood will be spilled in the world of Fengorian than was spilled in Gaoln during the last of the Great Wars. But this, only, if you choose the path of war. This decision is yours. Do not falter, for in it lies the fate of the world, and I do not say that lightly. You and Skerun must both listen to me, and right now you are the only sane actor here. You must begin to make peace by accepting peace."

"Very well. I will agree to a peace, Skerun, but I am setting down my terms right now, right here: Every Gaolnian will live in Skaen, every government will be shared between the Gaolnians and the Skaelin, every settlement will be accessible to both Gaolnian and Skaelin. Veterans who choose to live in isolation may do so and be rewarded if necessary. But no lands will be restricted. They will be one people."

"King Nowhawna," Skerun answered, "I will state my terms clearly, given to me by King Sendroun, King Seagraul and President Leyus: Gaolnians will be barred from government offices, Gaolnians will live in separate settlements as non-citizens administered by Skaelin officers stationed in guard houses, Gaolnians will not be allowed to leave these settlements at any time unless by the order of the King of the Skaelin Lands, Gaolnians will not be eligible for military offices, Gaolnians will have no say in who reigns as king, Gaolnians will be required to obey Skaelin commands in all cases whatsoever— "

"Skerun!" Menuld burst out, "do you want this war to end, or are you trying to tempt King Nowhawna into killing you right here? The end of this war will be a product of mutual negotiation, and to be frank, most of your terms you must drop. King Nowhawna has elaborated that the purpose for which this war was fought in the first place cannot be forgotten."

Menuld shook his head a bit, then looked straight at Skerun. "Please, just realize what lies in front of you. Realize you have a chance for peace. It is enough that King Nowhawna is willing to consider peace."

"Absolutely not. The terms I received from King Seagraul cannot be negotiated under any circumstances."

Menuld turned to the king. "Will you reconsider?"

"This world does not know peace, not yet. I cannot take your way, Menuld, nor am I able to adhere to your advice, wise as it may seem to you, and wise as it may be, in its own right. I will not let the Gaolnians escape a prison in one land only to find a prison in another land."

Menuld turned to Skerun. "Non-negotiable," Skerun said abruptly. "Gaoln must be subordinate to Skaen."

"Skaen and Gaoln can only exist together," said Nowhawna.

"Then our discussions are over," said Skerun.

"Are our hopes of finding some agreement to be cut down so quickly? I pray to Time and Fate that this is truly for the best, as you are both so convinced that it is," Menuld proclaimed, "And I hope you, Skerun, and that idiot king of yours learn some common sense!" Skerun, offended, rose and left without another word. The king watched him leave, then turned in anger and stormed out from the opposite exit. Menuld stood there, sighed, and whispered to himself: "So this is how peace fails…"

- Chapter Four -

Two months of raiding towns and villages came and passed, until the army decided it was safe to reveal their most prominent locations once again. They continued gathering resources by their new extortion policy, where they left villages unharmed but left with virtually everything the villagers had as their own. The Gaolnian archers trained at the border of the camp every night, and infantry sparred whenever possible, even on breaks during the marching if they had the energy. Engineers practiced their mathematics and assembling of crafts every evening while the rest of the army set up camp and established perimeters. The army grew stronger and stronger, and began behaving as a truly cohesive unit. And so they passed their days, until finally they were ready to reunite the subdivisions and lay siege to the strongholds along the Central Path. The largest division, led by King Centreal, set its sights on the fortress of Gensballa.

Centreal's force was massive, and indeed he did not intend on letting Gensballa put up a fight. With the castle besieged, the routes between the Eastern Mountains and the Central Path would all be under the control of Gaoln. And so Centreal and his army surrounded Gensballa with all the force of the Second Division, and camped outside the walls waiting for their victory while inside those walls the Gensballanians struggled to find enough food to outlast the Gaolnians.

The days spent besieging Gensballa were put to good use. Warriors of all sorts practiced their arts from sunrise to sunset. There was fine weather on all but a single day, so the sparring and the shooting and the building was relentless. As much as the Gaolnians knew the Gensballanians would be fortifying their castle, they felt that they themselves were the ones gaining in strength with the passing days.

There was a noise one morning— it woke Alaisio up. He was alert and on his feet in an instant, and along with every other man posted outside Gensballa he stared up at the hill toward the chiming of bells ringing out through the dawn. Upon the treeless hill that Alaisio and his fellow soldiers glimpsed in the distance were at least a thousand warriors mounted on selk— the Knights of the Northern Plains.

The Knights of the Northern Plains were the most elite cavalrymen in Fengorian. Because it was so hard to train selk for war, not many good cavalry divisions existed. But selk were very vicious animals, and feared by every soldier. Once the cavalry was out, the gate closed again. But while the Gaolnians were running to get their defenses together, the Gensballanians showered them with arrows and boulders and bolts. In the chaotic scene, through the thick morning mist, it was impossible to organize a real defense. Yet a team of infantry, backed by archers and a few catapults, went out to meet the knights. Captain Luncas led that team, leaving Alaisio in charge of the regiment.

Alaisio's mouth dropped. He stopped moving and stared straight ahead. He heard the captains in front shouting to hold the lines, but Alaisio appeared uneasy. "We should be falling back, not holding these lines," one of his soldiers said to him.

Alaisio knew the man was right, but he didn't have time to consider a better plan, and he knew Luncas would implement one as soon as the opportunity presented itself. So he followed the orders of the other captains. "Hold the line! Go support Luncas!"

To Alaisio, it looked as if the cavalry simply ran over the front lines of the infantry. It was not a contest. Their animals, native to the snows of Skaen and the northern reaches of Kon, could dash through the snow where a man could hardly trudge. Their advance was slowed only gradually. The cavalry broke off and began to enclose the front lines of the advance, and Luncas— who managed to survive, but found himself surrounded by enemies on all sides— ordered the fall back after fighting for only moments. It was not long before the advance infantry was in a full rout. The knights pursued them until they came under enemy fire, then they redirected their attacks. Swooping around the back of the main army, the knights mowed over the rear archer units and trampled the trebuchets and engineers.

King Centreal called back the infantry. Many of the knights had fallen, but the Gaolnians had taken a terrible and devastating blow both to numbers and morale. The advance infantry were now descending from the hilltops down onto the Knights of the Northern Plains, while the small defensive lines Centreal managed to organize held firm as the cavalry ran through them. The front line of cavalry was defeated, but new waves tore through the formation, even as the advance infantry finally reached the knights. Just as it appeared that the Knights of the Northern Plains had nowhere to go and nothing to do but stand and fight, a number of Gensballanian archer regiments— who must have been hiding somewhere in the fog— fired on the outer lines of Gaolnian infantry. Alaisio could not get his bearings— his men were being attacked from left and right by the archers, while in front of him a thousand mounted warriors rushed to meet them. Never in his life had he been so scared.

And then, *again* as if from nowhere, more than two thousand Gaolnian warriors came out of the mists, cutting down the Gensballanian archers and holding a line against the Knights of the Northern Plains. Captain Luncas came running down one of the hills, and stopped when he saw Alaisio staring at him, dumbfounded. "Alaisio! Where is your regiment!?" Alaisio looked at him in silence, his mouth hanging open, then he blurted out:

"Captain Luncas, where were you, and how did you do that— how did you hide two thousand warriors!?"

"You pick up on these things. We tracked the archers from the rear and picked off their scouts with our own marksmen. I see you need some more time before you're given command of a regiment."

"Yes...I think I do..."

"Well enough. Come with me, and let's end this."

By the time the mists cleared, the Knights of the Northern Plains were defeated. Most of them had escaped back around to the city, some fleeing altogether or galloping off to alert other settlements. The Gensballanians hadn't even lost half of the knights they sent out, but they had destroyed most of the trebuchets, a third of the catapults, and had cut down and killed hundreds of infantry and hundreds more Gaolnian archers.

The Gaolnians wasted no time. They fortified their perimeter vigorously, with tall stakes at the edges of their land and murder pits around the engineer camps. They reformed regiments so that every able captain led a full team fit to their skills and experience. They waited. Gensballa might come again, and with them their famous knights, but they would find a defensive line as hard as the walls of their own fortress. What the Gaolnians lacked in strength, experience, and training, they more than compensated for in their great numbers and the power of their will.

It was four mornings later when the gates of Gensballa opened. Captain Luncas took a team of people in, with Alaisio by his side. When he entered the city he was suddenly struck by some realization— this city was empty, almost as empty as Tekal had been. And for a city ten times the size of Tekal that meant something was terribly wrong. It wasn't that the doors were shut and locked, or the windows barred, or the children hiding from the soldiers— it was, instead, the fact that those people who should be hiding from the army simply were not there at all. There was a silence pervading the entire city, from wall to wall, and hardly anything moved save a small team of defending Gensballanian soldiers who had opened the gates on the command of their superior.

Luncas led Alaisio and the rest of the 53rd up to the top of the open castle, where he surveyed everything around him. This day was sunny and clear, and he could see for miles around, as the trees that populated the plains of Gensballa, this far north, were short and thin. Far away to the south he pointed, and Alaisio nodded. There must have been ten thousand people in the caravan there, half of them soldiers. They were riding south. "They're a day ahead of us," Alaisio said.

"Four days, my friend, unless we plan on leaving all our armor and supplies behind us," Luncas answered. "The Knights of the Northern Plains were a diversion so that everyone in the city could escape. And can you tell me where they are going?"

"To cut us off."

"Very good, Alaisio. You learn quickly. They will reinforce the forts south of here and try to cut us off from our supplies. That will leave us trapped here in the northern reaches of the continent, a land which certainly cannot support so many men as we have brought with us. They mean for us to starve before these snows melt. And that is still a long time from now. This far north, we could be under the snow for another hundred and twenty days. If we return south, the snows will melt in half that time. It is the difference between success and complete failure. Wherever we go next, we will find a much greater level of resistance than we found at Bellford or here at Gensballa."

"What will we do, then?" Alaisio wondered.

"Take counsel with the king."

After dinner the next night the fireplaces throughout the citadel of Gensballa were lit. The smoke rising from the titan fortress joined with those rising from the small abandoned houses where many of the soldiers had taken up residence for the night. King Centreal sat in a rocking chair by one such fire within the deepest halls of the citadel, surrounded by captains and commanders, and, of course, by Alaisio, now counted as a friend by both the captain and the king.

"So where are they heading now?" asked King Centreal.

"If they're retreating to the nearest garrison southwards along the Central Path, they'll end up in Gatsesilli," answered Captain Luncas. "Unless they march to take back Bellford."

"Gatsesilli is a good prize, my king," another captain chimed in.

"It is," Luncas agreed, "with Gatsesilli, we, in fact, will be the ones confining Sendroun and his armies to the south. It is also the largest city between the Eastern Mountain Strongholds and the western part of Skaen."

"Onward to Gatsesilli, then," King Centreal said. "We will leave a good team of people here to ensure that Gensballa is not retaken. The force will be strong enough to assert total control of the territory and to make sure that by the end of the month this fortress and all of its villages are ours. If the Skaelin try to retake it, our surrounding divisions will collapse in around Gensballa and we will destroy them. Keep the villages in tact and keep the people alive and happy, we need their labor, their obedience, and their harvests. The rest of us," he concluded, "will march southward, to Fort Gatsesilli."

In the morning light the king prepared to leave. Before the army began the day's march, however, a rider— tired, beaten, easily the most miserable man the king had seen since the battle— emerged from within the mists. The man rode up to where the king waited, and then fell off. "King Centreal," the man began, "The Third Division is gone. Commander Suri, he's dead."

The king was silent for an awkwardly long time, the confusion showing on his face. His expression changed in an instant— he shouted back in a fury: "Gone? What do you mean 'gone', man? The Third Division is sixty-five thousand people! They can't be 'gone'!"

"The Skaelin Main Army, my king— they've made the trek from Cavfurt stronghold. They assailed us for fifteen days, twenty days— on every front. They ambushed us in the forest, *everywhere*, on every front, all at the same time. The offensive must have stretched from Benaballa to Gensballa. It spanned the entire country! We tried to get to you— "

"Tried to— " The king stopped talking— he began walking around in lines and circles, throwing his hands up and making terrible expressions with his face— "'Gone'! Gone!"

"My king— "

"Where is this army of theirs now!?"

"My king, they've regrouped in their center. They are retaking Bellford."

"They took Bellford!?"

"I am afraid they will. They are launching daily attacks from Benaballa Castle, south of Bellford, and control a great swath of land north of the castle where they prevent supplies from reaching the castle. We still hold Bellford, but by the time I return, I might find it in Skaelin hands. Denelu is making them pay dearly. The Main Army must be devastated. They have nothing left to fight with."

"You know as well as I do that's a lie! The Main Army would never jeopardize themselves so badly, to attack us on open ground if they are weak. It means they've still got most of their strength left. Spirits, how many of them can there be!? *Sixty-five thousand people!*"

"We may be able to contain them. But the Third Division is gone. Two thirds are dead."

"They aren't attacking us here at Gensballa?"

"No, my king. They want to draw you down to Gatsesilli. They want you to come there. It must be some sort of trap, my king— "

"Well, good for him! We just happen to be on our way to Gatsesilli at this very moment. We'll send out teams of men to cut off the fortress ahead of us, and arrive in force at his gates— then we'll see about his taking the Third Division!" The king looked around, hurt and confused and angry, then turned back to the messenger. "How in this world does one just march up and eliminate a force of sixty-five thousand people!?"

"These are hardened fighters, my king. Veterans of the Civil War, most of them. The survivors of the division will be joining us soon. They number almost twenty thousand, but they are shaken and defeated in spirit."

"They'll have their revenge."

- Chapter Five -

"So how are the mines?" asked Nolor, sitting down with a plate full of what had become their regular diet— a full serving of fruits, meats, vegetables and bread.

"Am I supposed to be enjoying it?" replied Gendorn. For all his complaining, the diet and the work had done well for him over the months at Gatsesilli. Well-fed and well-worked, Gendorn had evolved from a starving boy to a man building some muscle. He was surely the strongest of the Gaolnians by now, though of regular size by Skaelin standards.

"You found the good one, Nolor," said Bendoraun. "I wish I could have your job."

"I know, I love it. I love this place. I wish I could stay here…" answered Nolor. "It's just so fascinating, to see how it all works."

"More fascinating than hauling up stones all day, I'd imagine," Gendorn said glumly. Again his friends smiled, amused at Gendorn's discomfort.

The three Gaolnians had been in Gatsesilli for more days than they could count, but they weathered through four blizzards, and knew that they had passed more than fifty (but definitely not more than one hundred, they agreed) days since their arrival. They passed the days as freemen— they worked with smiles on their faces from before the dawn until after the sunset, for every night when they came home to the inside of the castle, there was warm bread and water and always some fruit or another, and large fires burning in the mantles of the great halls and common rooms. Their first taste of freedom was a sweet one.

For Gendorn, it was only ever bittersweet, and never more than a false and temporary state of being. Bendoraun noticed that at night his friend would sometimes wake up and take walks around the castle, although Gendorn never explained this.

The three of them ate every morning and every evening together. Their shared identity kept them very close when they found themselves surrounded by Skaelin soldiers.

They became accustomed to looking out the window of the high tower where they slept, of searching the sky for stars when the clouds tried to cover them, or observing as the slow passage of dawn commenced from the depth of night. And when the snowstorms came, the three of them would go down into the Great Hall with their blankets and sit around telling stories and sharing hot drinks, as if they were children who only wanted to feel warm when everything was so cold outside. Gendorn, Bendoraun, and Nolor did not speak much with the others at Gatsesilli on these nights, as their stories would not stand up to the increased scrutiny of the guards, who were now on the lookout for the Gaolnian Army.

The elation they felt at being free was abruptly cut down when they were reminded of something on one particular evening. They were sitting around the dinner table, as usual, when trumpets and horns broke off their conversation, as they blew from somewhere in the castle halls. The gates were opened, and a detachment of the Skaelin Main Army marched into the dining hall of Fort Gatsesilli, four by four lines of heavily armored soldiers. At the front of the foremost line came a tall and burly man wielding a spear twice his height and a shield that reached to his neck. The three men sitting around the table could not understand the gasps and expressions of amazement all around them, until they heard someone exclaim "King Sendroun!"

"Fellow people of Skaen," The king began, without waiting for anyone to gather their bearings, "You have probably heard

word of something moving about the countryside, burning
villages and terrorizing our people. It has sounded, to most of
you, like what you heard before the civil war. But this is quite
another thing altogether." The crowd was attentive, every man
in the hall listening with their eyes fixed on this suddenly-
appeared king. "The Gaolnians have risen up and rebelled, and
have sailed from their colony to our shores. The Army of Gaoln
has been attacking us since the beginning of Sen. I have taken
the Main Army to fortify Fort Tycagra, Fort Gensballa, and
this, Fort Gatsesilli."

"Sorry, sir...A scout arrived here earlier this afternoon,"
said one of the officers in the room, standing and bowing to
address his king, as was custom. "We sent someone to reach
you, but he must have been intercepted. The Gaolnian Army
has cut off Gensballa. We cannot march past them, as they have
perimeters secured all around the fortress. They plan on cutting
them from their supplies and then marching on the fortress
after it's been besieged for weeks. Centreal's division marches
to Gensballa even now."

"You, you're sure?" asked the king.

"We sent a scout to verify the report, but that's what we
heard," confirmed the man.

"Well then, we have even less time than I thought. And
even less strength. I have brought a thousand warriors with
me— the fastest men among them, and the rest are still ten
days behind me. I will send runners to inform them. We will
send a message to King Centreal, one which will draw him to
our very gates. Forget about Gensballa, and forget about
Tycagra also, the whole of the Gaolnian Army will be here
upon our door. We have a while before they can reach us.
Which Gaolnian division is nearest to Gatsesilli?"

"The Third Division, my king."

"Destroy them. Send out the Main Army and make sure
that the Third Division does not exist in three weeks' time. The
Main Army will return here in six or seven weeks. I will be
sending men to reinforce Gensballa, but we will let it fall, and

let them believe they have a chance of taking Gatsesilli as well. Once their force moves south, the detachment we leave east of Gensballa will sweep in and reclaim the fortress. When they arrive at these gates, the Main Army will be back here waiting for them," said King Sendroun. "They will be trapped in between our two fortresses, without supply lines and without shelter, and we will bury their bodies in the snow."

"Could you brief me now, my king?" wondered the officer. "I am afraid I will not be in the castle tonight."

"You will be in the castle tonight— no one is leaving these walls. We cannot risk anyone coming into contact with the Gaolnians. But the plan is simple," said the king, and he signaled for the officer to join his own men. Gendorn, Bendoraun, and Nolor, at the table next to King Sendroun and the officer, perked up their ears and pretended to make their own conversation, to appear uninterested in the designs of Sendroun. A good while after the king left, the three of them returned to Nolor's room.

"How are we going to warn them?" asked Gendorn, as soon as the door shut.

"An escape may be our only way," replied Nolor.

"If it is, will we take it?" asked Bendoraun.

"...I will," said Gendorn. He paused a bit, but Bendoraun noticed he was about to speak and waited for him to finish. "It's not just Kamira, Bendoraun. And it isn't just the struggle to be free— it isn't just about a better life or even survival. I also need to know that what the army did to Behk and Synla's village had some reason behind it— that there was some cause for such an action. Otherwise...how can I call myself a soldier of Gaoln?"

Bendoraun lapsed into a brief silence, before he conceded: "I need to know too, but it's hard to believe we will find an answer. Can there be a reason?"

Gendorn nodded. "There has to be. And I know you will come. If the Skaelin plan succeeds, you know what happens. Are you with us, Nolor?" Nolor sighed.

"Yes…I am with you. But how will we know when they're here, or where they're camping?"

"I don't know. Try to listen to whatever the soldiers say," said Gendorn. "The scouts are flooding this place. We can only hope we overhear where they are, and when they get there. If we don't, there's nothing we can do."

Bendoraun nodded in affirmation. "Just have patience."

"In the meantime," Nolor suggested, "we will be as curious as it is safe to be."

It was the morning of some six or seven weeks later, as the three of them were walking through the hallways, when they next heard word. The king was speaking to what appeared to be another officer. "Our scouts returned yesterday. Gensballa's report of being conquered has been confirmed. We have also confirmed that the Army of Gaoln should be camping a good march north of here tomorrow night, at the rate they're going. We'll be attacked in two or three days if they're headed for Gatsesilli, which we think they are," said the officer.

"I see. Then our plan shall be set in motion. Tomorrow night we will confirm their location, and follow through with the preparations," replied King Sendroun. "The bulk of the Main Army has just now returned and has had only two nights' rest. Let's hope that's enough for them."

"Good. I'll inform the others."

"Hear that?" murmured Gendorn, as soon as the two men passed out of hearing range.

"Yes," replied Bendoraun, in the same soft whisper.

"Quiet," whispered Nolor. "And yes, I heard."

"Good then. Tomorrow night," said Gendorn.

"Tomorrow night," agreed Bendoraun. Nolor heaved a sigh.

"Tomorrow night," he agreed.

The next night came quickly. They had dinner while nervously awaiting the scout's confirmation of the Gaolnian encampment. They had to eat slowly, but eventually the scout returned. The king walked into the dining hall and announced the army's plan to ambush the Gaolnian Army later that night. Most of the men dining in the castle were officers of some sort or another, waiting for that report, so they listened carefully to every word. King Sendroun said the gates would be locked and the bridges be drawn until they returned. One regiment of native Gatsesillian guards was left to ensure that no one attempted to leave Gatsesilli until the Skaelin Main Army returned. The king then took his leave of Gatsesilli, promising his return. Gendorn, Bendoraun, and Nolor quickly finished eating and returned to Nolor's room.

"We should each take different routes, that way it's more likely at least one of us will get through," suggested Bendoraun.

"Maybe we should go together, so when we do get caught, there's a better chance we'll get through anyways and overpower the scout who catches us," said Nolor.

"How will we even get through? The guards are blocking all the stairways, we can't get up to climb over the walls," said Gendorn.

"We need an excuse, in case we get caught," suggested Nolor. "Any ideas?"

"No," Gendorn said, dropping his head.

"None," said Bendoraun.

"I know," Nolor beamed, "My boss decided to eat at the bakery for dinner, wanted to be alone. We're going to warn him about the gates closing. Okay, to make it believable: We can't let him wait for the bells to chime and tell him that the gates are closing, because he left earlier this afternoon to visit a friend south of here who he hasn't seen in a while— something simple. He was planning to come back in the evening and be here at night, but there is a chance he will be locked out and he doesn't have any friends outside the castle because all his work caters toward the castle's residents, and those are where all his friends live. He can't sleep in the bakery, because he has a fear of sleeping outside castle walls. That's why he moved to Gatsesilli and sleeps here every night, inside the North Tower. He does sleep there, so that will check out, I know. I can make up a traumatic experience to make it seem plausible. It's not hard."

"You're an excellent liar," Gendorn said, "except that for a man who spends half his day working outside the castle walls, you would expect him to know at least a few people who live in the farmhouses and shops out there."

"Thank you," Nolor said, and he looked genuinely pleased by his ability to lie. "We'll have to go with it anyway. Maybe he's just an angry person who doesn't want to socialize with people outside the castle. Make him sound arrogant. Let's hope the guards don't know the bakers too well."

"Good then. We'll ask to go out the front gates. If we're lucky, they'll let us right out," said Nolor.

"What if they escort us?" asked Bendoraun.

"Hope that they don't," said Nolor.

A while later, deep into the night, the sounds of men marching on the stone floors of the castle and gathering in the halls echoed up the stairwells and into Nolor's room. He listened intently until the sounds faded away, then turned to look at his two friends. "Time to go," said Nolor.

"Let's go then," agreed Gendorn. Bendoraun was silent. They left the room and hurried down the stairs to the front gate, where they were stopped by a guard.

"The gate's closed. Go to bed," the guard told them.

"I have to get out there, I won't be long. I'm a baker's assistant. My boss needed to talk to his friend, wanted to be alone. He will just be getting back now, and he sleeps in the castle— I have to get him, to tell him the gates are closing," Nolor frantically explained.

"He'll realize that eventually, being locked out and all," said the guard with a laugh.

"He's going to be scared, seeing the whole place deserted and all the gates locked up. He'll lose his mind," said Nolor, his speech furious and worried, "you can't keep him out, it isn't safe, and we didn't even know that these gates would be locking— the Gaolnians, if they get here— "

"He should have heard the alarms, shouldn't he?"

"He should have, but he might not have listened to them— his friend's father just died, and the village is quite a ways south— "

"Fine!" The guard said resignedly, "but you're not allowed out, so I'll go. You stay here until I get back. Which bakery is it?"

"The one between the granary and the armory, by the stone mines to the south. He might be wandering off near there though," answered Nolor.

"Alright, wait here," said the guard. He lowered the bridge and opened the gate. "I'll be sending another guard to come watch the gates for me while I look for this man, so don't get any ideas." With a quick look of skepticism, he left to look for the baker. Nolor, Gendorn, and Bendoraun waited a short while after he left. Gendorn peeked outside and Bendoraun looked around inside. No one was around. Nolor looked at Bendoraun questioningly.

"Be quick," whispered Bendoraun.

They sprinted silently down the hill, up the rise across from it, and then across the frozen plateau which was home to the villages north of Gatsesilli. Their dark clothes camouflaged them in the night. Soon they entered the stealthy protection of the hills and forests surrounding the flatland, lessening their pace to a comfortably swift jog. They kept a safe distance from the Main Army, but kept them in sight. They were still unsure what to do when time came to warn the Gaolnian Army. How would they possibly sneak through to warn the soldiers? Surely they would be caught and killed...

"I'll go up front," whispered Nolor, "follow them from the side. I'll get as far as I can, and signal you when I see the camp. We'll run around back and warn them of the ambush."

"Don't get caught," said Bendoraun.

"Thanks," said Nolor. He ran off to the far right of the army, shielded by trees and darkness. He could see much further than the army, being high atop a long range of hills. From there he waited until Gendorn and Bendoraun were close enough, then signaled them to follow.

They had been running along the ridge for some time in the darkness when Nolor pointed out two shadowy figures in the woods below— on the opposite side of the ridge from the army. He turned around and whispered: "Those are the scouts who were following me in the forest. They followed us here, I knew it. And now they are going to stop us from warning the army."

"Bendoraun and I will take care of them," said Gendorn.

"Don't be stupid, Gendorn," said Nolor. "The two of them would kill you and Bendoraun before you can reach them. They're probably traveling with bows and arrows or some other device. If they get the shot, they'll kill us where we are."

"What do you suggest then?" Gendorn replied. For a moment they continued running in silence, then Nolor spoke again.

"We absolutely cannot let the army see us, and they are going to play safe— they might kill us, or they might not, but they definitely need to alert their army that we are here and trying to alert our own army of their army's ambush. What we need to do— and this is all we can do— is run as fast as we can, and not let them persuade us to go down the other side of the ridge, where their army could see us."

So for some time they continued running along the ridge, until they realized that the two Skaelin scouts were splitting up ahead of them. One of them was heading to the other side of the ridge, where the army would see him— he was going to alert the Skaelin! The other one continued running forward. Nolor responded in an instant, talking as soon as he started to turn to his left and run toward the opposite side of the ridge. "I can't let them get to the army," Nolor said, "I'm going after that scout— keep an eye on the other one. Whatever you do, you must get to the Gaolnian Army."

"Move quick," whispered Gendorn. They ran as fast as they could toward the camp under the cover of night. The other scout had disappeared, and Bendoraun and Gendorn could not be bothered to find him. They ran until a handful of Gaolnian sentries intercepted them, knocking the wind from their chests and throwing them on the ground. Gendorn and Bendoraun looked up, and said quietly "The Skaelin are coming!"

They set out with the sentries toward the camp. The two young soldiers went in waking and warning everyone they could. One of the first people to rise was a startled Captain Luncas emerging from his tent. He had been awake, resting inside, and had come out when he heard Gendorn.

"You're alive!?" he whispered. "Where in the world were you!? Wandering in the forest for a hundred days!? What is wrong with you!?"

Gendorn turned around. "The Skaelin are coming, the whole army! Wake everyone up and get them out of here!" explained Gendorn. "Don't be loud! They can't see us yet, we don't want them to hear us!" Luncas ran through the camp, shaking tents and whispering for people to wake up and grab their arms and what armor they could. As more people awoke, the camp became a chaos of frenzied runners trying to wake whoever was left, while most of the men were already hiking up the side of the hills, trying to get away from the camp. Soon the last soldiers were grabbing their weapons and armor and evacuating the camp opposite the direction of the Skaelin Main Army. They remained silent, and hiked to the top of the highest surrounding cliffs and hills. They continued into the valley just below it, to avoid being sighted by the Skaelin Main Army when they advanced, and waited for their scouts to signal that the Skaelin were in sight.

The scout was fast, and he darted through the trees towering all around him, his figure just as dark. It was difficult to see through the shadows beneath the thick canopy, but towards the end of the ridge there was a clearing. The scout ran into the clearing and waved his hands around and shouted while he ran toward the army, but he was still too far away for the army to hear him, and the moon was not shining all the way through the clouds. Nolor picked up his pace, almost falling down the side of the hill as he chased after his former pursuer.

It was not long before the scout was at the bottom of the hill, under the now clear sky, in full view of the army without a single tree in his way. Out of the army, marching through the meadows in the valley, came a man sprinting towards the scout. Nolor, who was forced to stop and stay hidden along the edge of the forest, watched in terror as the army picked up pace and split into divisions. The scout turned around to look for Nolor— but Nolor was already gone.

Gendorn and Bendoraun waited in silence beside Alaisio and Captain Luncas. Some of the braver men had stayed a while longer to haul up food and other materials without which the soldiers would die, and which, left unguarded in the camp, would make for a better target than the Gaolnian soldiers themselves. The official command had been to remain on guard at the top of the hill or the side of the even-higher cliffs, but King Centreal knew that without the efforts of those men down in the camp, the soldiers would die of starvation sooner than they would of any sword.

It was from atop the cliff above their own heads that Bendoraun and Gendorn heard a soldier shouting that the Skaelin were coming. The word spread down into the valley, and the men gathering food either ran up the sides to join their captains or took positions below the hilltop. The Skaelin were in a hurry, Luncas knew at a glance. Through the torchlight and the moonlight he could see them, and they could see him too. The Skaelin Main Army surrounded the camp and set up a large battery of artillery. The Gaolnians took the time to equip their weapons and strap their armor, and set up a makeshift artillery battery of their own. A short while later, a combination of archer and artillery fire was released on the Gaolnian camp. After a few more volleys the ground troops were sent in to kill off the rest of what they thought were the Gaolnians. Once the infantry were at the lowest point of the surrounding hills, the site of their camp, the Gaolnian Army emerged from hiding. The artillery bombarded the Skaelin infantry at the base of the camp, while the Gaolnian archers fired walls of arrows down on the Skaelin archers. The Skaelin artillery down in the camp was unable to fire up the steep slope of the hill, and so served no purpose in attacking from their less defensible position. The Skaelin, now, were put on the defense— the Gaolnians had escaped their own camp and trapped the Skaelin inside of it.

That was only for the part of the Skaelin Main Army that the Gaolnians were aware of. The scout, who had returned to the forest in search of Nolor, ended up getting lost between the trees, in the shadows of the thick canopy. Nolor, skimming the edge of the forest, followed a larger division of Skaelin regiments marching quickly around the edge of the valley. They carried no torches and they stayed close enough to the forest that a Gaolnian, looking from afar, would not be able to distinguish them from the darkness surrounding the meadow's edge. But Nolor saw them, and in silence he followed.

Along the edge of the Gaolnian camp the Skaelin Main Army stood. On the opposite side, along the hills and cliffs towering above, the Gaolnian Army waited in patience. Nolor knew what was going to happen, without even watching. The Skaelin attacked the camp, destroying the tents and blankets and supplies and stealing whatever they wanted— they poured arrows and boulders down over everything and pretended that this was a full attack. The Gaolnians bought into it, and retaliated. As the Skaelin advanced up the side of the hill, the Gaolnians met them half-way. At that time the men that Nolor was watching started to come up around the side— they were going to attack the Gaolnians on the cliffs from behind, cut them off and surround them. The Gaolnian Army would be finished.

Nolor waited until the men he was following marched further around the edge of the forest and circled back behind the cliffs, then ran off behind them and scrambled up the hills. He reached his own lines gasping for breaths. "It's a trap!" He warned the men, "They are behind us and coming in from all sides! They mean to keep us here until we've all been killed, or to trap us and starve us out on this cliff!" Nolor's regiment, toward the top of the hill, sent a runner to King Centreal. With a command and a wave, King Centreal directed one division to monitor the rear-left, and another the rear-right, while the other two divisions would fight at the front where the Skaelin were right now advancing.

King Centreal stood tall upon the summit of the highest cliff. The moon was close to him and it shined upon him, so that all the Skaelin could see him, and King Centreal, from such a vantage point and in the open moonlight, saw all the enemies surrounding him. The Gaolnian artillery moved some teams to the rear where they held back the Skaelin, and many of the archers switched over to help them. Gendorn, Bendoraun, and Alaisio, under Luncas, moved to the rear, while Nolor and his regiment stayed fighting at the top of the hill. For a long while the Gaolnians maintained a perimeter around the cliffs, and the Skaelin were not able to advance. But the Gaolnians saw them as great masses of shadow moving behind the cover of the trees below the cliffs, masking themselves from the moonlight so as to cover their numbers. How many there were, no one atop the cliffs could say. Gendorn was quite afraid to ask.

Bendoraun and Gendorn were not in the fray. They, alongside Alaisio, were toward the top of the cliffs, not far from King Centreal, and they waited there for their call to battle, when they would replace a regiment which was fighting down below. They could see the expanse of forest and hills below them covered in Skaelin soldiers. They stretched as far as they could see. The Gaolnian catapults were launching rocks and boulders across the entire vista, and giant stones littered the ridges. The archers were ripping through the lines and waves of Skaelin soldiers as they tried to advance up the hills. All of this Gendorn watched, and he heard them shout and yell under the open sky— then they would die. He would blink, and at times he would see Tejk laying on the ground somewhere, a pool of blood all around him. Then a field of bodies that reminded him of Port Tekal. Other times he would see the meadow empty, a river running through it, and he walking by its shore alongside Bendoraun and Kamira.

He was called to action. With Alaisio and Bendoraun, he started down the hill. Toward the front of the line Captain Luncas joined the three of them and led them to the battle. They fought next to each other— they fought the same enemies and looked into their eyes, all the same— and they watched them die together. They killed together. They heard the shouts and saw the rage in their enemies' eyes; they saw the same swords swing at their faces, the same curses hurled at them. They watched their fellow soldiers die next to them, shouting "Gaoln will be free!" They came away bleeding and tired, but above all with a shock that disabled them from thinking about what had just happened.

King Sendroun was dumbstruck. His infantry, weighed down by their armor, was losing ground and falling back down the side of the hills on every front. When the Gaolnians pushed them back far enough, however, they came within range of the Skaelin catapults and ballistae. When they were hit, the Gaolnians withdrew back out of range, and the Skaelin renewed their assault. Yet now King Sendroun was unsure of what to do— they could not win the battle up the hill, and the Gaolnian archers were doing more damage than the Skaelin archers—

they could not simply let them battle it out. They could only win if they themselves found higher ground and lured the Gaolnians into an offensive. For a short while Sendroun continued the attack and tried to lure the Gaolnians out of their hilltop and clifftop positions, but the Gaolnians would not be fooled. Wave after wave, the Gaolnians held firm. Before the sun rose King Sendroun ordered a retreat back to the other side of the ridge. To Gendorn and Bendoraun it looked as if the enemy soldiers were weaving themselves out of the forests and out from the bases of the hills back toward Gatsesilli. On their way out they set fire to the Gaolnian camp in as many places as they could, targeting the food supplies more than anything. King Centreal, who from atop his own cliff ordered the Gaolnians to pursue, saw King Sendroun himself and many of his officers escape with a large part of the army as they disappeared back into the clearing which led to Gatsesilli.

Captain Luncas joined King Centreal at the top of the cliff, in time to watch Sendroun's figure fade into the night. As their figures disappeared the light rose from that same direction, hailing the new day. "We've won," said King Centreal, "but we've lost almost everything. We will need to hold down Gatsesilli and get shipments in from the other forts and towns we've occupied. We cannot continue the advance until the supplies come in." Captain Luncas nodded. "We are out of food."

"We will work it out."

"Gendorn, Bendoraun," said Nolor, coming up from further down the hill.

"I'm so glad you made it!" said Gendorn. "Nolor, you've saved the army."

"We all did, Gendorn," Nolor answered. "I talked to King Centreal, told him what we heard about the three garrisons. He's sending divisions out to Gatsesilli and Tycagra. I'm not sure which of those we'll be heading for ourselves."

"Hopefully they won't be able to hold them long, with the Main Army defeated," Gendorn said to Nolor.

From above, Luncas had heard the exchange. "They aren't defeated," he assured Gendorn. "Not yet. And without any food, we're a long way from a sweeping victory, as much as I hate to admit it."

The light of the morning shining down on the valley revealed the destruction wrought by the Skaelin. The Gaolnian camp was burnt to ash. Hardly any tents were intact, and there were only scattered remains of clothes and blankets and food. The Skaelin had lost a significant part of their army, but the strength of the Gaolnian Army had been pulled out from beneath them, and the Skaelin attack had rendered the Gaolnians immobile. The men were depressed as they left the camp— there was not much to salvage. Seldom was a word heard. King Centreal made the decision to continue on toward Gatsesilli and to besiege the Skaelin there— they would be able to secure supply routes from the north and west while they waited for Sendroun to retreat. "I am leaving Commander Denelu in charge of the siege of Tycagra and another captain in charge of securing the supply lines," King Centreal explained to Captain Luncas, "and you will come with me and the rest of the army to Gatsesilli. We will besiege the Main Army in both its locations at once and keep them from their resources. We will go a few nights short on food, and short on blankets," he told the captain, "but we will make it, and we will not let King Sendroun out alive until he surrenders and hands over control of this land."

- Chapter Six -

It was not more than a week after that large battle between the Gaolnians and the Skaelin when Nowhawna summoned Menuld into his chambers and presented him with a mission. "You will go," the king told Menuld, "to make sure that King Seagraul does not invade Skaen. Play in to his game— he is scared of Gonaka invading Laen, you must justify that fear, and convince him that aiding the Skaelin will expose him. Keep him down, Menuld," the king told him, "the end of this war lies in your mission. Use the destruction at Gatsesilli to your advantage— make it seem like the Skaelin are on the verge of defeating Gaoln, and that Sendroun does not need Seagraul's help in either case. You did well trying to make these negotiations work, but our efforts at winning over Skerun and Seagraul will be plagued with difficulty."

Menuld nodded. "I will make it clear to Seagraul that the situation does not require his intervention, my friend and king."

Four days later, Menuld landed his litha in the Courtyard of Laeolin and walked into the King's Chambers. "Sen is not a short enough season, I fear," he said to King Seagraul.

"What do you mean?" asked King Seagraul.

"Come, walk with me," said Menuld. They left the palace, choosing a path through the snowy forests outside. "The Army of Gaoln has been active. Three spies snuck out of Fort Gatsesilli. They warned the Gaolnians of a planned Skaelin ambush. The Gaolnians barely got out in time, but they did. The Skaelin Main Army did not kill them all, but they were able to torch most of their food and shelter and supplies. The Gaolnian Army will die in the cold. They cannot be relieved. The war has already been lost for Gaoln. And the truth of it is that the ice will not thaw for some time, so you cannot cross the Cold Ocean regardless. By the time your ships can sail, King Seagraul, the Gaolnian Army will already be lost."

"You know this?" asked King Seagraul.

"All of it," confirmed Menuld. Seagraul sighed.

"Then, what do we do?"

"Nothing, King Seagraul. The war is over."

"I cannot believe that the problem of Gaoln is gone so easily. I would be the happiest man alive, and this war might be over. But, Menuld, I don't believe you are telling the truth."

"The survivors will be sent to a collection of villages that will be built especially for Gaolnians, and those in Gaoln will be transported over to the villages— "

"So there will be survivors!"

"Only if the Gaolnians agree to surrender."

"The reports that I heard were different."

"Of the battle? Yes, the Skaelin Main Army was defeated, but in either case, the end is very near, and your intervention will make no difference and, in either case, will arrive too late. The ice is too thick— you cannot sail. The Skaelin may be low on numbers, but that is a much better situation than being stuck outside in the snow without food, blankets, or proper shelter."

"What did King Nowhawna say?" the king asked.

Menuld sighed, closing his eyes and shaking his head. "He said...they will not tolerate the captivity of the Gaolnians..."

"We knew that, Menuld. What he did say about Skerun's accusations?" Menuld knew that Seagraul was testing him— Skerun had informed the king of the outcome immediately after the talks.

"He denied them. He did deny them, but he seemed, nonetheless, to be in support of the Gaolnians."

"He's behind it. You know it, Menuld."

"I know," said Menuld. "But we can't fight fire with fire and expect the fire to go away. We have to forgive Gonaka's transgressions and address the issue at hand in the most diplomatic and peaceable manner possible." For a while the only sounds were the wind and the crunching of the earth beneath their feet. It was a clear day, the sun shining down through the trees upon the snow. Finally Seagraul spoke.

"I worry about Gonaka," he said, pausing in his tracks as he thought to himself.

"I understand. I think Gonaka worries about you, too. I suggest you stay on guard, but do not provoke King Nowhawna's hostility," advised Menuld. The king nodded.

"What do we do about the Gaolnians?"

"We have to make sure that they do, ultimately, coexist, because there is no other real alternative. They could inhabit two different states, or one state led by both the Gaolnians and the Skaelin. But whatever we decide on, we should include King Nowhawna in the process, and we have to include King Centreal and King Sendroun both as well. You can't send troops, you know how vulnerable you would be here in your own country once your army leaves these shores. Peace is the only practical option."

"For their own security, and for the security of the Skaelin," King Seagraul answered, "we should demand that the lands be returned to the Skaelin, and the Gaolnians return to Gaoln. If they refuse, we kill everyone left in Gaoln."

Menuld stopped in his tracks. He let his mouth hang open and his eyes search for some hint that the king might be joking. After what must have been a full minute, the elderly man looked at the king as if he were a misbehaving child. "Are you completely out of your mind?" Menuld shouted, and waited intently for an answer. Another minute passed. The king shrugged, embarrassed, but by no means apologetic. "No, I will not condone that at all. We should bargain with them. We can offer to deliver those who remained behind to New Gaoln, so they can all be together— in exchange, we will work together to set up a government run by the Skaelin, with certain precautions taken of course, to ensure the ongoing freedom of the Gaolnians, and to ensure they are in no way unjustly persecuted for what they have done. Those who have behaved atrociously will, of course, be punished, but we cannot reprimand the entire population and expect obedience," Menuld advised. "You are advising holding the lives of one hundred and fifty thousand people for ransom!"

"I will not tolerate this rebellion," Seagraul said, "I will not work with the murderers of my ally— would you work with the killers of your friends and family?"

"I would, if it meant a real and lasting peace. You must learn to forgive. The only way to end this kind of violence is to forgive and move beyond the atrocities committed," said Menuld.

"The Gaolnians must learn to forgive! In their hate and rage they kill endlessly!" proclaimed the king.

"That is war, and that is why we must ensure there is peace to follow."

"But how is that best done? By trusting a nation of thieves and pirates, or by demanding obedience to ourselves?" said the king.

"They will never obey Laen again. It's out of the question. And they'll only listen to the Skaelin if they have equal rights as the citizens living there now. Please, you must understand. You cannot act aggressively when Gonaka is so close to war. Certainly you see where this can lead!" insisted Menuld.

Another pause. "Menuld, much as I trust your advice, I do not trust those who you trust. I must seek my own way. I am trying to prevent war, but sometimes the best way to prevent a war is to bluff," answered the king.

"Someone will call your bluff. This is too big now to bluff. It has gone too far. Accept what has come, do not concern yourself with the past, for that is done— concern yourself only with the present and future."

"I think forceful persuasion is the best way. I truly believe that if they are as virtuous somewhere in their hearts as you make them out to be, they will relinquish what has been obtained by the slaughter of thousands, and return to their loved ones in Gaoln," said the king.

"Would you return to Gaoln? Really? Work with them— don't you see? The chance to end it all is upon us. The chance to end the debate about Gaoln, the chance to end the rivalry between Laen and Gonaka, the chance to stop the war in its tracks, if only you would will it, this all could become reality!"

The king sighed. "The rivalry between Gonaka and Laen is long and deep, and it cannot be ended by compromising on Gaoln. And that is another issue altogether, one which I am not willing to compromise on, as I have stated before, beyond certain boundaries. I have a plan though, and perhaps, if the plan goes just right, this all can be settled," replied the king.

"Abducting the Gaolnians as hostages will not resolve the issues at hand!"

"We need our ally, Menuld!"

"The Skaelin are weak! They, as allies, are helpless!"

"The Gash are trying to weaken our side, don't you see?"

"You are blinded by your hostility and your suspicion! Please, open your eyes to the truth! And even if you are right, you are playing right into Nowhawna's plan— once you send forces to Skaen, Gonaka will conquer your own kingdom!"

"I see the truth. The truth is that while our allies have been losing strength, Kale and Gonaka have mustered theirs. Now the Gash have set the Gaolnians loose upon our ally, the Skaelin, and while they have gained a powerful ally who may even befriend the Skaelish, we have lost what was once our most powerful friend! All in an attempt, long in the making, to finally gain a last upper hand in the clash between Gonaka and Laen!" claimed the king.

"No! Please, forget the past— this is not some conspiracy to topple your nation! The Great Wars ended long ago. Don't bring them back, Seagraul. This is about Gaoln and the Skaelin, and in order for this issue to be resolved peacefully, both sides must be consulted, both sides must agree. It will become a conflict between you and Gonaka only if you invade Skaen to aid the Skaelin. We can foster the birth of a friendship between Laen and Gonaka, if only we are willing and able to come to a mutual agreement between the Gaolnians and the Skaelin! Don't you agree?" said Menuld.

King Seagraul made a disgusted, contorted face. "Gonaka. They will never be our friends."

"You have too much bitterness. Let it go. The future can be bright, if only you allow it to shine," said Menuld reassuringly. At this King Seagraul paused, giving deep thought to Menuld's arguments and advice.

Then the king sighed. "Menuld, Gonaka gains on us an edge sharper than we can bear, a flame that grows hotter and closer to us as they grow in strength. I will not allow my friends around me to be slaughtered by my enemies, and so I cannot heed your advice."

"But the war is already over, if only you would let it end!"

"I will not. I will not accept defeat, on behalf of my country, on behalf of my allies, on behalf of the Skaelin. I will challenge Gaoln, I will challenge Gonaka, and I will challenge any other who dares to conspire against the order of the world along with them. I will invade Gaoln and take all the prisoners as hostages, demanding from the escaped outlaws the return of the Skaelin lands. If they refuse, the hostages will be executed, and we will prepare to invade Skaen," said the king. "We worked too hard for Gaoln, Menuld— we've come too far."

Menuld took some moments to gather the gravity of the situation, to observe his surroundings, to select his next words. Finally he asked: "Can't you find some middle ground? Can't you work with anyone other than your established friends?"

"Already they have gone beyond the terms of my compromise."

Menuld shook his head. "O weary world..."

"O weary world, indeed. But I will not be the victim nor the laughingstock of my foes."

"Rather you would be the laughingstock of wisdom and the pity of good will," answered Menuld. "You mention the taking of one hundred and fifty thousand hostages as if it is a matter for only some quick debate between friends. Seagraul, you are playing around with fires that you will not be able to control. You once said the same thing to an evil man, I recall, and you were the flame to burn him down. Will you burn yourself? Can even you not stop this?"

"I am still the fire of the revolution. I am only fulfilling our nation's destiny. I am only serving our people."

"A wildfire cannot tell between right and wrong. It can only burn."

"Enough. You have offered your advice, and I thank you for it. But I know what I must do," proclaimed the king.

"I will have no part of it," said Menuld.

"So be it," answered Seagraul.

- Chapter Seven -

That night King Centreal sat around a large campfire with his captains and commanders. Luncas sat by his side, and by Luncas's request, Alaisio, Gendorn, Bendoraun, and Nolor were also present. King Centreal turned to Nolor for his first question: "Did they mention anything about any other places?"

"Yes, a few," Nolor answered. "After Fort Tycagra fell, if it came to that, the Skaelin planned to retreat further south down a series of fortifications along the Central Path, before making a final stand at Seun Bastion. Sendroun sent messengers throughout the Skaelin Lands to gather what's left of their military. They plan to assemble a force almost as large as the Main Army, and meet them at Seun Bastion for the final stand," answered Nolor.

"Where's Seun Bastion?" asked one of the newer captains.

"The south end of one of the peninsulas along the southern shore, essentially in the shadow of the Eastern Mountains," Luncas explained.

"I don't understand," Gendorn said, "if we know they are gathering at Seun Bastion, if we know they plan to flee there should they be defeated at Gatsesilli and Tycagra, why don't we just kill the garrison there, hold the fort, and then kill them when they arrive? Deny them the fortress."

"It's too risky," answered Alaisio.

"They might not show up all at once," explained King Centreal. "If that's the case they'd scatter after the loss of the first party, and we cannot let them drag this war on, we have to finish it before the snows melt in case of aid from Laen. It is our good fortune that they are ignorant of our knowledge of their plans."

"Why are they gathering there?" wondered Bendoraun, "The ancient citadel strongholds of the Eastern Mountains have never been breached and are completely self-sufficient. Wouldn't they be better off there?"

"Seun Bastion is very well-fortified, almost as well as some of the hill forts to the east," Luncas answered him, "And no single city is prosperous enough to support an entire army. Seun Bastion is the closest it gets. They can receive shipments as soon as the ice thaws, so we have to break them before then. And of course the main reason is that the peninsula it fortifies and the fortifications themselves are designed so that the range of artillery and arrow fire forms a sort of pouch shape, and in the center you can be hit from three sides of fortifications. The arrow fire will be intense, and there will be a terrible cost in casualties for the Gaolnian Army. Additionally, as the waters off of Seun Bastion do thaw sooner than the waters off the coast by the eastern strongholds, they could be relieved by an ally if we do not break them soon enough. Seun Bastion, in fact, is a rather good choice. They know that even if we take Seun Bastion, the strongholds of the Eastern Mountains will remain theirs, and that in any case if they withdrew now the war would be over. They know we cannot take the fight to the mountains. They are trying to prevent the loss of their greatest southern port town. So even in the worst scenario they still have a nation of their own in the east. We will have to reach a peace agreement with them at that point, rather than bring the attack to the Eastern Mountains. And I do think they will be ready for peace— there is a lot of pressure on King Sendroun to end this war."

"In the meantime," Centreal continued, "we cannot allow another siege to occur, in case they are counting on being relieved by an ally. That was, I will admit, the shortest siege I have ever been a part of, short of having someone from the inside unlock the doors and let us in. If we find ourselves in that situation again, we could be waiting for weeks, or months— and the Lonins would surely relieve the Skaelin, I suspect. No ally would dare intervene if Sendroun falls at Seun Bastion. We have to finish this quickly, or we will not finish it at all." He took a breath, then looked up around at the faces staring at him. "Let's get some rest."

The captains and commander left toward their tents. Bendoraun and Gendorn left with Alaisio and Captain Luncas, but Nolor remained behind. He had been silent since speaking his part at the beginning of the conversation, and had since lost his gaze somewhere in the fire— he was entranced with the dancing flames, with the feel of the heat on his face. King Centreal looked at him for a brief moment, about to leave— then turned and spoke.

"What happened to you six out in the wilderness?" he asked. "Gendorn and Bendoraun told me about themselves, but after the six of you split up, how'd you end up at Gatsesilli?"

Nolor was slow in his response. "The others— Hendall, Wyan, and Sheal were their names— we don't know what ever happened to them. Sheal was a good friend of mine when I was younger. I sort of grew up with him. Hendall was great with directions, I can't imagine he would have gotten lost. He was a very reliable man. But those scouts followed us to Gatsesilli— that's how they wound up informing their army just as we were informing you. I passed out during the interrogation at Gatsesilli, so a guard named Genzut carried me in and nursed me to health. He was a good man, Genzut..."

"I would have liked to have known them," said Centreal.

"I'm glad that I did," said Nolor.

"I hope all the best for your friends, soldier," said Centreal, getting up to leave. As he walked away, Nolor was left alone by the fire, and he resumed his staring into the dancing orange and yellow.

He took a breath of the cold air, and threw his hands closer to the fire. "I hope you've found a place to rest and live in peace, I really do. But if you have not— rest in peace all the same," Nolor whispered into the air and the smoke, "I'm just glad you got out of Gaoln before you died."

Part Four:
Dust to Dust

- Chapter One -

The cold wind woke her up. It was dark outside the mud hut, and nothing stirred. Inside the other huts, people cuddled together under blankets to stay alive. She turned her head and opened her eyes, and outside her door she saw an old man lying sideways in the dirt. His stomach had caved in, and in the moonlight she could see even the undersides of his ribs. His mouth was open and his shallow, craven cheeks dipped like valleys in between his rotten teeth. His eyes were wide, and they were almost larger than his head, as shrunken as it was. His beard was long and thin. Tomorrow, Kamira knew, she and the others should begin the journey to the Cold Ocean, where they would throw his body into the water and pray for it to land in Skaen. As the tradition went, there would be another elder to oversee the ceremony, and he would bless the body with his prayer. "Though in this life you were but a slave," the elder would say to him, "may the next life set you free."

But this ceremony would not happen. It had stopped almost completely seven years ago, when people started dying by the dozen every day. There were those who still trekked to the ocean for the ceremony, if they could make it. But it was, Kamira knew, now mostly a thing of the past. Burial had stopped also. There were none left strong enough to bury their elders. More often they were eaten, for this was the measure that survival required. It was the new tradition for the elder present at the meal to begin by giving a new sort of prayer.

"Now your body comes to us, and we will carry it as we go. And when one day we are free, free also you will be."

She whispered these words beneath her breath. Tomorrow, she would be among those eating this body. At first, the idea had disgusted her. She, like most of the others, in fact, refused her first meal. But then, so many of those who had refused died shortly after of starvation, or lingered on barely alive. There were none now who could survive in Gaoln without taking part in such meals. They were always civil and respectful, and those who knew the deceased always talked of them and how they lived, and gave consent for the meal, knowing that they were doing only that which was required for Gaoln to be free. Kamira closed her eyes and fell back asleep.

Curileyn, Kamira's mother, shook her gently. Kamira woke again to see the people gathering outside around the body. Mother and child walked together to join them. The eldest male said the prayer. The deceased had been a pirate without relatives, but his friends spoke of him well. "We will carry you with us to freedom," they said. "And when we breathe the air of a new life, may you breathe as one among us. May we always live and die, in bondage and in freedom, as one people."

And so they did. Every face that died she remembered, and she made a point to memorize their names, their stories, their memories. She knew pirates and murderers and thieves from every corner of the world. She knew heroes and martyrs who were exiled for their protests against villainous kings. She knew elders from the Great Wars and old widowed women. She knew children who had no stories of their own to tell. And she carried all of them with her.

There were always the wild rumors. The insane would run around and say that some army or another was coming to kill them all. Sometimes a man would appear and say that everyone was free, that the Gaolnian Army ruled all the continent of

Skaen. People learned to disregard all rumors. But sometimes the lithae would fly overhead and the Gaolnians would wonder if anything was actually happening. They flew back and forth between Laen and Gonaka, and the rumormongers proclaimed that Gonaka was forcing Laen to surrender control of the colony, or that Laen was threatening war. But nothing ever happened, and so she and her mother passed the days with the rest of the Gaolnians, awaiting either freedom or death.

Far off to the east, where Gaoln ended and Laen began, Juron stood at the edge of life and death. Behind him things grew and lived, plants sprouted, flowers blossomed, people lived by smiles and laughs as the seasons passed by and time went on. But in front of him, the only life was that of those imprisoned captives condemned to exile, hunger, and disease. There were no trees, just caked mud and earth. He looked up right then, and for only a moment contemplated that one sky connected them both, and one earth underneath. His eyes were still, looking on at the legacy of the Great Wars and the Pirate Wars, and perhaps it was that truly, for a moment, he felt some tinge of uneasiness, of regret, of sadness. Deep inside, he doubted if the king's plan would work, and he questioned his motives. But he was afraid to speak out against Seagraul, to appear weak in front of his soldiers and uncertain to his king. The obligation he felt to fulfill his duty, however wicked, was stronger than his hesitation, and this sense of duty he obeyed.

"Fellowmen of Laen!" shouted Juron. The lines of soldiers grew attentive as Juron turned to face them. "In front of you lies the desolate land of Gaoln, where the wicked and condemned live in exile. For Laen we capture all who dwell here, and return them to Laeolin, where they will be held hostage until the issues with New Gaoln are resolved. Do not kill anyone unless you are attacked— and I am not just talking about a slap in the face. That is a direct order from the king. But capture everyone. Take your ranks now; group yourselves with your fellow soldiers and your captains. Each regiment will go separately into Gaoln, taking a predetermined route. Be swift, time is very crucial in this operation. We will meet along this border in one month, and wait another month for everyone to be returned. Go— our mission begins. Do not fail me, do not fail Laen."

One of the soldiers nudged his captain, and whispered "It's true, then? The legends about the Great Wars?"

The captain turned, but before he could respond, Juron was in front of them both. "First, you do not speak when I am speaking," the commander said, "and second, yes, it is true. So much blood was spilled here during the Great Wars that nothing now may grow. The earth, they say, still holds the blood of a million men and women, and refuses to allow its beautiful trees to grace this desolate place. That is why it was an ideal place for the prison colony in the first place. You should brace yourself to see terrible things, soldier, and to see savages behaving like animals in ways you cannot imagine. These are not people like you and I— people cannot grow here, the same way as trees cannot grow here."

"May I add something, Commander Juron?" asked the captain. The commander nodded, and the captain turned to his soldier. "They say that once, this was home to the most verdant forest in Fengorian, with trees of a deeper brown and leaves of a richer green than even the most legendary forests of Aniania or Keay or Goba. This land had rolling hills and cliffs with waterfalls, and upon every hilltop one could look out and see either the ocean to the north or the endless green to the south, east, and west. The People of the Forest, this breathtaking expanse their most ancient and beloved home, lived every day in celebration. And the tree which stood in the heart of this place, which stood guard over the land and sea both, which protected and gave life to the People, was the tallest, the strongest, and most ancient tree of all the ages— in the tales of our ancestors, the tree has been there since creation itself."

"And it is gone?"

"There is one tree in Gaoln," the captain told him, "and they say that it is an old and withered thing upon a small hill by the sea. That is the ancient tree which, despite the curse of the land and the blood of a million, still refuses to die and yield to the will of Time and Fate."

"That is enough," said Juron, "This land is cursed because so many loyal Lonin soldiers died here defending what is good against the evil of Gonaka, and it is only the dregs of the earth that inhabit it now. There is no need to speculate on old tales about how beautiful it once might have been, or who lived here in ages long gone. Our mission is to retrieve those who have been deemed unfit for life in the civilized world, and we will be treating them as such." The captain nodded, and without another word filed in behind his commander.

- Chapter Two -

Luncas and the 53rd did not have far to move. The great looming towers and thick citadel of Gatsesilli stood only a day's march from the battle. But they could not be seen through the blurry haze of the snowstorm. "I heard it in the night," Alaisio said. Luncas looked around, but he could not find the source of the voice. "It's going to be a bad one," he said.

"How would you know? You've never even seen the snow before, you islander!"

"It seems bad to me!"

From behind him, Luncas heard a voice, and as it came out to him he turned to face the king— but although he heard the king's voice, all he saw was a black shadow several feet in front of him. "Is that you, Luncas?"

"Yes, my king."

"We can't make an offensive in this weather. I'm going to keep the guards up and around the artillery, and the catapults will keep battering away at the walls. It won't get done today. We have to camp out around here and make sure that no one breaches our line to get more supplies into the fort."

Captain Luncas looked across the snowscape— he knew the king was right. "Our supplies should be coming here in less than a week."

King Centreal nodded. "I know. We'll be fine. We'll lose some good men, but there is nothing to be done for it. We just have to wait it out. And you can bet that they aren't going to attack us here, not when they've got firewood inside that warm little castle. They are going to try and break the siege to get more supplies into the fort so that they can hold it longer. I am going to go around back with the better part of the army, and make sure that doesn't happen. I need you to command the rest of the regiments that will be guarding this side of the fort and looking out for signs of our own supply trains coming in."

Captain Luncas nodded. "Will do, my king. Will I be overseeing the engineers?"

"Yes. Send a runner if you need me, but we will be in contact. There are networks of caves stretching all the way from here to Tycagra, so we should have some roofs even before the new tents get here."

"My king?" Centreal turned to look at Luncas. "How many tents are we expecting?"

"You're not expecting one for yourself, are you?"

"I am hoping to have one for my men."

"Perhaps. Perhaps not. We will have to rotate tents, captain, and learn how to make shelters. For now, find some caves."

Captain Luncas sat with his regiment inside a shallow cave, which provided just enough roof to keep them dry in this blizzard. The wind had gotten even stronger, and the trees were bending over. He had ordered all the regiments to stand down where they were, and to find the closest shelter. "No use letting them die of the cold before we even get to the soldiers," Luncas said. Runners kept the siege alive, making sure that the lines didn't break and that the Skaelin were not anywhere in sight.

Inside the cave it was just Luncas, Gendorn, Bendoraun, and Alaisio. The rest of the regiment had to join another regiment under a larger shelter. Captain Luncas made a little fire, and the four of them huddled around it. "Captain," Gendorn asked, "won't the Skaelin be able to last longer than we can? They have a castle, and more food. So what are we doing here?"

Luncas grinned. "As long as we make sure that they don't get any more supplies than they already have, we will be fine. Our men are coming."

The blizzard continued through the night. Gendorn and Bendoraun lay awake for the first hours of the darkness, unable to sleep. The wind was howling and blowing inside their cave. But Captain Luncas made sure they had enough blankets to survive the night, and Gendorn kept the fire going after the captain fell asleep. When he looked out into the night, outside his cave, Gendorn imagined shapes in the wind. In the bending trees he saw figures of humans, stretched tall and thin, screeching under the sky. When the trees would stand upright and look at him, they took on the shapes of Behk and Synla and Tejk and Kamira, or even Bendoraun. Then they would move and become twisted, and Gendorn would hear them moaning and shouting, and chills would run across his skin. *Help me*, he would hear them say— *I am dying in the cold.* He would shy away, and cover himself with his blankets, and wish that the day would come. He turned to his friend— but Bendoraun was asleep. He turned the other way— Alaisio was too, and the captain was snoring. So Gendorn threw the blanket over his eyes and waited for the dawn.

The wind was still blowing when he heard the captain's voice behind him and Alaisio next to him. He threw the blanket back over his head and waited for a while, but he couldn't shut his eyes again. When Bendoraun shoved him— almost outside the cave and into the snow— Gendorn jolted up and threw off the blanket. "Okay, I'm up," he said. Bendoraun nodded.

"Our plan for today, boys," said Captain Luncas, "is to stay inside this cave."

"Do we have enough scouts out there?" wondered Alaisio.

"Oh, you'll get your turn to play the scout and run around in the snow, don't worry," the captain answered. "And yes, we have enough on all sides and we are in constant contact with King Centreal. I myself should be getting word very frequently throughout the day, and we are not far from two different lookout points if we need to check on anything. Our line is secure."

At mid-day a runner arrived. "King Centreal's auxiliary regiments to the south have intercepted a caravan heading for Tycagra," he told Captain Luncas. "They captured the caravan and are bringing it here for our own supplies. Commander Denelu's men have established a siege around Tycagra, and they are waiting like us."

"Thank you," Captain Luncas told the messenger. The man left, and the silence returned.

They spent that night again in the cave. Again, Gendorn found himself unable to sleep. And again the figures haunted him. This time they took the shapes of the two men he had killed at Port Tekal— they would be moving and alive at one moment, and then still the next, and the falling snow became the blood falling from the trees that were their bodies. Gendorn sat upright with his eyes fixed on these figures, his face bare of any expression. Alaisio's voice broke his trance. "You are seeing things."

Gendorn turned to look at Alaisio, and nodded. "Yes."

"I see things a lot." Gendorn did not answer. "It's a problem that many of us experience."

"Who do you see?"

"My dreams can be very dark. Sometimes I see myself lying still, from the air, as if I were a bird looking down upon the dead body of Alaisio. Sometimes it is my child, but he is young when I see him, only a boy. And I realize that my whole life has just been a dream, that he never lived beyond four years. Other times it is Lendah, the love of my life. And then there are those whose lives I have taken, and they can be the worst of all.

"The dreams will follow you, and you will find it impossible to appease them, impossible to end them. You must learn to sleep, or you'll never rest again until you die." Gendorn turned to look at Alaisio, and found in his eyes a note of sincerity that he had never witnessed before. He said nothing, but nodded that he understood. Then Alaisio continued: "So get some sleep. You'll need it."

- Chapter Three -

Another week of siege brought the supply trains in from Bellford, and the blizzard had passed by that time. The Skaelin had surrendered after failing to intercept the Gaolnian caravans, which were heavily guarded. Gendorn and Bendoraun slept well and warm inside the castle with most of the other soldiers that night, and when they woke the army was preparing to leave. Just before they left Gendorn and Bendoraun ran to the top of the castle and looked out, and everywhere they looked on that clear bright morning they could see the snow-covered hills and the white forests stretching on forever. When they returned to the castle floor they found most of the soldiers ready to go. The army hiked until the sky above was the deep sapphire of night, then quickly set up camp. Gendorn and Bendoraun had fire duty for the regiment that night.

The air was still but for the sound of various forest creatures mixing with the quiet conversations of the soldiers and the scent of campfires just beginning to fill the night. It was a cold night— but Trest wasn't too far away. Soon it would get warmer. Usually the ice would have already begun to thaw along the shores of southern Skaen, but this year it was still frozen thick.

Bendoraun started off into the forest. Gendorn followed behind, stopping to pick up fallen sticks and twigs and such, as Bendoraun searched for a good tinder tree. "I can't find any tinder, we'll have to use twigs. Is anything dry?"

"No, it's all frozen and snowy. Check that tree, see if anything's there," replied Gendorn, nodding at a fallen tree not too far away. Bendoraun hiked over, trudging through the snow and lifting up some heavy sticks.

"We'll need an axe for this Gendorn," he said, returning with the sticks.

"An axe? How large is this fire?"

"I want to see if clouds can catch on fire," answered Bendoraun. Gendorn nodded at his friend, as if he had gone mad.

"I'll bet you that the trees above us will catch fire before the clouds do," Gendorn said smartly.

"I'll take that bet."

Gendorn laughed. "Nevermind. You win." They returned the wood to the stockpile by the regiment's fire pit, dug out by the other soldiers. They left to gather more wood, returned, and continued, chopping fallen trees, gathering fallen branches and twigs, until finally, when everyone else's fires were lit and lively, they returned for the final time. Luncas looked at them both stupidly as they laid down the last load.

"Okay, but I'm going to sleep," the captain said, "regardless of how roaring that fire is and still will be when the sun rises."

"It will be," said Bendoraun.

When they finished setting up the fire, Alaisio took out a pair of stones and some serrated metal device. After working for a while, a few sparks finally caught, and the fire sparked and grew. It grew and grew, and continued to grow, so much that some of the soldiers were deprived of sleep that night due to the heat or the uneasiness over the undying flames. But for most of the night that wasn't a problem, because the entire regiment came out to sit around the fire. They were not the only ones— they were joined by many other people from many other regiments, and as the night progressed the crowd grew with the fire. There were laughs and shouts throughout the night, and dancing on the outskirts of the crowds which gathered around the flames. King Centreal was there, partly to ensure things didn't get too rowdy, and so were Nolor and some other members of his regiment.

Around the circle of people closest to the fire, Gendorn stood next to Bendoraun, Nolor, Luncas, and Alaisio. For the first time in a long time the five friends stood together and smiled, and were genuinely happy. The cold season was nearing its end, and the weather would be warm. Food would be easier to come by. They would not have to make so many raids— the war itself was getting closer to its end. The time when Gendorn, Bendoraun and Kamira would live together in these hills was not far away.

The king approached them at one point, and his smile burned warm as the fire. "You've given us hope in our dreams," the king said to Nolor and the two boys. "And the day will come when people all around the world tell the story of how the prison colony of Gaoln became the Kingdom of the Free. And they'll remember your three names and what you did for us on that night, in those hills north of Gatsesilli. I just hope you know that. When you look around tonight and see us dancing, Gendorn, Bendoraun, Nolor— we are dancing because you have given us the reason to believe and the chance to succeed. May you always take that with you as you travel through life. This celebration is yours. Our freedom is yours."

The king left, and throughout the night other crowds came to congratulate them. They called them heroes of Gaoln. *Gulaus Gendorn*, *Gulaus Bendoraun*, *Gulaus Nolor*, the crowd cheered around the fire. Captains and commanders would raise toasts to their names, always addressing them as *Gulaus*, and soldiers prayed for their health. People sang and danced for them. People gave them weapons and armor and food and blankets. They vowed to name their children Gendorn, Bendoraun, and Nolor. And throughout the night the three heroes of Gaoln stood silent with Luncas, Alaisio, and on occasion King Centreal. Luncas wore a smile that none of his men had ever seen before. Alaisio was stoic— there was only the small rise at the corner of his lips to reveal his deep satisfaction and pride in his friends.

Somewhere deep in the night, Gulaus Gendorn stared into the burning embers at the base of the fire. Around him the celebration was alive, but it was only the three heroes with Luncas and Alaisio sitting front-row around the great fire. Bendoraun looked over at his friend. "What is it?"

"A lot of things burn."

"Are you thinking of the village again?" wondered Bendoraun. Gendorn did not answer. "Do you ever want to go back?"

"Yes. Or to Gatsesilli, or even to Port Tekal. Someplace we can rest and be away from all this," his voice turned to a whisper, "We're heroes, right? And I am proud, and so happy for our people. I don't know if I have ever been so happy since we first sailed away, and all our dreams were fresh. But those villagers are our heroes, Bendoraun, and without them we would have died. Therefore, without those villagers, our army would have been ambushed, and we would never be free. There is something dark and ironic about this."

"Fate works in mysterious ways," Bendoraun said.

"Is this how freedom works?" Gendorn wondered. "Is this what it feels like? Are these dark times the memories that we must bear as the cost of our freedom?"

"Did I just hear that?" said Captain Luncas bluntly. "Gendorn, you should be very proud of what you have done. What we do costs lives, but it saves more lives than it costs. Let that knowledge comfort you when you doubt yourself. And know that you are a hero."

"Captain, why did the army burn that village?"

Luncas looked at Gendorn as if he were some immature child. "People kill, Gendorn, and people die. War is a mechanism that we use— all of us. It may be brutal for you, but it is simple and true." Alaisio, who had kept quiet, held the gaze of the fire. As Gendorn looked across to Captain Luncas, on the other side of Alaisio, he saw on Alaisio's face the shadows of dancing flames. His eyes, for a moment, seemed to be brought back to life— they glowed with some kind of radiance. He turned around, and was about to leave when the captain stopped him. "Do you disagree?"

Alaisio nodded. "I think that it is less important which mechanisms exist in our world, which ones people and their countries use— I think the more important things are the mechanisms we should try to use, we dream of using. People kill, and people die— people live their whole lives as prisoners, Captain Luncas. People are born as slaves when they should be born free. It is the way the world is, not the way the world should be. I thought that was what we were fighting for, captain. The way the world should be."

"That is what we fight for. It is not as clean of a fight as we might wish."

"I know," Alaisio said softly. To Gendorn, Alaisio never seemed so defeated before. He walked back through the crowds, and Gendorn turned back toward the fire.

"I have to get the soldiers who don't even know what a soldier is," said Captain Luncas to himself. "Questioning war! One does not question the sun, do they? One does not question the way the world turns or how the winds blow or when the tides come upon the shore. And yet here he is, saying that war cannot be the answer to our problems, when our problems have no answer but war!" He shook his head. "Of course, I get stuck with them."

"Captain— "

"It is because they have the resources to keep us alive, Gendorn. If we had not taken the village we would have died, because these villages are our food and our health, our blankets and clothes, our lives. Would you walk up to them and say, quite politely, 'excuse me, sir, but I am invading your country to kill your king because he has been slowly starving my people to death. My friends and I have no food or blankets, as we are poor and come from Gaoln. Would you mind giving us all of your food and clothes, so that we may besiege your country's larger cities until your king surrenders and we cut off his head and put up a new government in his place?' I do not think that would go over very well!" Gendorn turned away, and was silent. The captain was not done. "I am tired of people talking about this war as if it had been a choice of ours to make— Gaoln did not have choices, Gendorn, you were born and raised as a prisoner in that place, you should know more than any other! We had an opportunity to claim our freedom. It was the *only* opportunity presented to us. We took it. *You* took it! And you were right to do so!" Gendorn remained silent, and the captain turned away.

At some point in the night King Centreal started to dance with some of the captains, and a circle formed around him. Gendorn, Bendoraun, and Nolor brightened up as they watched the circles of laughing and dancing men take form around the king. Captain Luncas was somewhere behind them, back toward the fire— they had lost track of him. King Centreal continued dancing for a long while, until the captains started forming their own circles, and then Centreal disappeared into the crowds.

Gendorn and Bendoraun walked further away from the fire, and in the cold forest they found Alaisio slouching against a tree, staring into a frozen pond. "What is it, Alaisio?" Bendoraun asked gently.

Alaisio took an eternity to deliver his answer. In the silence preceding it they could still hear people laughing and dancing, and the fire was roaring high. "Do you two ever wonder why you lived? My son Ciso was convinced of this— that there was a reason for every person, a purpose to fulfill. There are a lot of places where you should have died along this road."

Bendoraun nodded, and, to Gendorn's surprise, replied "I wonder about that all the time. I believe it also— there has to be a purpose, and we were only waiting for ours. Why didn't we die in Gaoln, why didn't we die at Tekal, why didn't we die in the cold wilderness in the middle of Sen far to the north?"

Gendorn cast his eyes down to the earth. "I wonder that sometimes, really. But I don't know. I don't know anything about how to run a country, or the world, or how to conduct a war without killing needlessly. What help could we be? It doesn't make sense that we were meant to live. I think of Kanel sometimes, you know. I hear his voice. When I took those walks alone in Gatsesilli— we must have been there for 120 nights, at the very least— sometimes I'd pretend I was speaking with Kanel. *You are the only hope in our world.* That's what he told us just before we left. His last words. Then, in the dream, he said we were supposed to do things."

"What's this?" wondered Alaisio.

Gendorn shrugged. "A dream we had. We were almost dead, and we had this vision of Kanel— the man who raised us— it was as if he wouldn't let us die. "

"Maybe we will know those things someday," said Bendoraun, "why we lived, I mean. You are something special, Gendorn. There aren't a lot of people in this world who would have left that fortress, or that village where Behk and Synla live, to return to a place like this."

"I would have stayed— "

"But you didn't. And you wouldn't let me stay, or Nolor."

Gendorn turned away. A roar of laughter erupted from the crowds, and the dancing started up again. Closer to himself, he could hear the animals of the night all around him, chirping and scurrying around in their snow-burrows. This was the time of year when the animals were just coming out again. The wind was still and dead, the night above him was clear and full of stars, except for one single cloud that loomed above him and the giant plume of smoke from the fire. The smell that lingered in the air, the scent of campfire in the bitter Sen, had become familiar to him now. It almost felt like a welcoming home. "Do you still believe in finding a land of our own?"

"I don't know," Bendoraun admitted. "Too many of us have lost sight of the dream which gave wind to our sails and bore us to this land. I believe we are meant to be free now. But maybe the safe and happy place we dreamed of cannot exist for us. You remember the visions you had when you were rowing to Skaen? Can they still come true?"

"Well," Alaisio said softly, "it looks like I started quite the debate. There aren't a lot of people in this army who take issue with killing the Skaelin— they imprison us, they starve us, they exterminate us, they enslave us. Yet most of the people we fight are ignorant of the plight of the Gaolnians, a product of Sendroun's efforts at controlling what his people hear. That is one thing Ciso fights against inside Laen. I do worry about him. At any rate, I think you've already found the answer to why you lived. You two saved our army. And that means you saved everyone back on the other side of the ocean. One day soon, all the Gaolnians will be free, and they will have you two to thank. If you ever doubt yourselves, just remember that."

"We were so sure of ourselves," Gendorn said, even quieter than Alaisio, "when we set sail from Gaoln. Why do I feel guilty after saving our people?"

Alaisio nodded. "You will experience that a lot, Gendorn. It's part of growing up— learning to question yourself and reform your ideas of good and bad. There are too many people who, at some point in their lives, make the decision not to listen to themselves anymore, not to question and rethink their words and actions. Do not become one of those people."

When Gendorn looked into Alaisio's eyes, he saw that same glimmer that he had seen the night Alaisio had told Gendorn about his night terrors. "I won't," Gendorn said.

- Chapter Four -

King Seagraul scratched his chin while he thought for a moment, then he looked at Skerun. "I am concerned about this situation," he admitted, "and I think it is time we pay more attention to the end of this conflict. Fly to Phenen, and see if they will offer additional forces. They voted against Gaoln on every account and are terrified of pirates. They have a lot of incentive to fight for us now. And now that Las has pledged assistance, Phenen should be easily convinced. They'll keep some of the land, if they want. When the ice thaws we need to be able to send out a fleet that the world has never seen before. With all our ships and soldiers on the way, and enough left in Laen to defend against any ambitions of Gonaka and Kale, the Gaolnians will have no choice. After we tell them how their families are being held hostage in Laeolin, they will embrace surrender as if it were their only chance for salvation, and this whole thing will be over. Gaoln will be back to how it was, and we can stop this worrying. And then we can discuss what to actually do with the prisoners." Skerun nodded. He rose to leave.

It was not long after King Seagraul had sent Skerun to Phenen when the king returned to the Palace of Laen and met with several of his advisors. A while into the discussions a guard entered the room, and whispered something into the king's ear. Seagraul arose from his seat with a stern, almost worried expression, and immediately left the room for his chambers.

Sitting there, in King Seagraul's own chambers, in one of King Seagraul's own chairs, next to King Seagraul's own bedside, was the man he hated more than any other man in the world— Joel, the Director of Ambassadors for Gonaka. For a moment King Seagraul stared at the man, as if he might murder him— and then he noticed another figure on the opposite side of the room, slouching against the wall, his arms crossed, long beard flowing over his chest, staring at King Seagraul— Menuld.

"Listen, Seagraul," Joel began, with an unconcealed disdain in his voice, "pull back your forces or you'll have other, more powerful foes to confront than Gaoln." Their eyes locked, and King Seagraul sighed.

"Must it be this way? Can't you just stay out of this war? We only want to help our friends, the rightful owners of the Skaelin Lands," he said. Joel scoffed.

"You don't want to help anyone, you liar of a king! You want the lands for your own, you want a claim there so you can someday grow more powerful than us and so Laen once again would have an edge on Gonaka! We won't let that happen, don't take us for fools!"

"Ah, but you are fools, Joel. We all are. And especially you, you have more enemies than you know," said the king, with a touch of humor.

"Las, Laen, Phenen maybe, and the Skaelin, if they continue to resist, that is. Against what? Kale, Gonaka, Gaoln, and maybe the Skaelish," replied Joel.

"Perhaps you do know," said the king. "But perhaps you overestimate the loyalty and the fervor of your allies."

"Perhaps," Menuld intervened, "you overestimate the fervor of yours."

King Seagraul looked unconcerned. "And what, precisely, do you mean by that, Menuld?"

"Phenen will not be joining you, King of Laen. I have been speaking with Emperor Sealibahd III. He is rather disgusted by your decision to hold the Gaolnians hostage and threaten their mass slaughter. He seems decidedly against such an action, and is now, come to think of it, leaning more toward joining the war on the side of Gonaka and Kale. It was a waste of your time to send Skerun on that mission. He will be coming back disappointed."

King Seagraul made no reply, and did not allow any expression to take hold of his face.

"Call back the forces, King Seagraul," Joel said plainly.

"How, Joel? They've already set sail."

"Our intelligence says otherwise," Joel answered. "So do the 120,000 people waiting to set sail and the thousands of ships still in your harbors. You're getting worse and worse at lying, you know."

"Perhaps our army is bigger than you realize."

"Do you ever stop telling lies? Use the litha to call them back, even if they've already set sail— that is no excuse!"

"Why? That you may gather your strength for another attack? We're doomed if we stay here, Joel. Don't pretend you don't think to gain an ally against us for future conflicts by releasing the Gaolnians into Skaen."

"We want no war, not if you back down! This is not about us, it is about Gaoln! And no, correction, you are doomed if you leave! Do you really think Gonaka and Kale will sit idly by and watch you slaughter more than a hundred thousand hostages? When your army crosses the Cold Ocean to Skaen, our forces will be waiting at your door. And the moment you leave, we will come in."

"King Seagraul," Menuld interjected once again, "if I may try to be the voice of reason— "

"As is ever your aim," the king said sardonically.

"— as is always my aim— might I suggest that you do not kill the prisoners, thereby saving all their lives, and in doing so you forbid Gonaka and Kale to have a legitimate reason to invade you— in doing so, you will also keep them in check by maintaining a stronger presence on the ground." He paused, then concluded: "Really, it is the only logical choice. By confining the war to Skaen— that means all of us keeping out of it— we are, truly, confining the war— "

"There is no confining!" Seagraul shouted. "No confining this war— this war is a pretext for another war, the final offensive against Laen, I see it now— I know you supplied the ships, Joel, and I know you aim at establishing your own colony in Skaen— "

"We seek a free state," Joel said.

"You seek power," the king answered plainly.

"King Seagraul, I do not have the time to bicker with madmen like you. You will pull back your forces and continue negotiations, and you will stop threatening to kill those hostages, or you have the armies of Kale and Gonaka to answer to."

"And your allies," Menuld added, "they are not as supportive as you would like to think."

"So be it."

"Is that your final decision?" asked Joel.

"It is."

"You're too rash, Seagraul. Far too rash."

"Perhaps we all are."

"No," said Joel, "just you. Goodbye."

"Goodbye, Joel. Goodbye, Menuld."

- Chapter Five -

Crying voices stung the bitter wind as it blew through the dust of Gaoln. Angry and protesting elders were beaten to a pulp. Women were stripped, whipped, and raped in the mud while they screamed and tried to escape. Kids ran like mice in between the soldiers. The captain of the regiment tried to calm the Gaolnians and coerce them into obliging. At some point the Gaolnians allowed the Lonins to tie their hands, and when the pel was fully captured, the soldiers moved on with their captives, westward along the coast, continuing their duty. Such was the scene throughout all the land. Pel by pel, regiment by regiment, the youths, women, cripples, and elders of Gaoln were captured by the soldiers of Laen.

Screams to the east worried Kamira, and she looked out into the snowy wind, blowing dust in her face. "What is it?" asked Curileyn.

"I don't know," answered Kamira.

"Should we leave?"

"Should we?"

Her mother paused. "We should. Come, we need to go. I was worried this might happen."

"What might happen?" wondered Kamira.

"We've been invaded. Come," said her mother, taking Kamira by the hand as she led her back into the pel to warn the others.

Together, Kamira and her neighbors trekked westward, away from their homes. Out across the dust plain they walked, the snow blowing against their backs. Yet even as the mud huts behind them grew dimmer in the distance, in front of them shapes took form and grew. Curileyn bowed her head in resignation. "I was afraid this would happen," she said.

"They've surrounded us," said an elderly man.

"Yes," agreed the mother.

"We should go south," suggested another older man.

"They'll be south of us too, but for now it seems the best solution," agreed Curileyn.

"We can't confront them. If we must, we should all split up and try to escape through the lines. We are not weighed down by possessions, and can easily outrun them, if we are determined enough," said the man.

"Yes. Well then, south we go."

And so they hiked south, praying that their enemies to the east and west could not see them through the storm. For that day, that night, and the next day, they hiked through the cover of the elements and the darkness of the night. The second day revealed they had escaped the vision of their enemies to the west, and their enemies to the east had not yet reached them, even if the screams from the east continued. They knew their enemy had surrounded them. It was the most logical tactic for whatever their foes were contriving. A mass slaughter, perhaps. Laen had finally grown tired of the debates, thought Kamira's mother. And so at last they had decided to take a final measure for themselves, to end the debate by killing the Gaolnians. She wondered then, how was the Gaolnian Army doing? Were they, too, being as harshly suppressed as this?

For Kamira, that was the only train of thought. Was Gendorn in this same situation? Had the forces of Laen joined the Skaelin to end their rebellion and kill them all? Was Bendoraun alive? Were any of them alive? Perhaps every one of them was dead. She'd never see Gendorn again. Their promised Someday would never come. In the darkness she cried, hushed by her friends and family, but unable to halt her tears. And now they were coming for her! By night and day grief consumed her, as it did to all the others, and indeed, she was only one of all too many who wept and wailed in the dust of Gaoln.

It was a sunny day, but the air was sharp and bitter, and the snow as cold as ever. Gendorn walked by Bendoraun, talking quietly with him, as Alaisio and Luncas spoke together in front. The 53rd marched on the outside edge of their larger division, so that through the trees they could see only three or four other regiments. But through the gaps in the trunks one man came riding a selk, quickly and with purpose. Luncas turned to look at the man as he stopped in front of the captain.

"Captain Luncas, a message from King Centreal!"

"Well, what?"

"I delivered this message to King Centreal moments ago, and he ordered me to relay the message to you: Scouts report that they have sighted King Sendroun himself near Benaballa Castle! The sighting occurred just last night. Denelu's company still holds Bellford, but in relieving the siege there, we here are left as the only company able to engage Sendroun."

"What are the king's orders?"

"We make for Benaballa Castle!"

Ten days later the horn of the king sounded, and the Army of Gaoln awoke. They surrounded and besieged Benaballa Castle, pounding it with catapults and trebuchets, until the walls broke and the gates opened and the Gaolnians poured inside. The walls should have held out for the better part of a week, and had not withstood even a day's barrage, a fact which aroused the suspicion of one particularly inquisitive Captain of the 53rd regiment of the King's Division.

Luncas led the team of men who stormed the castle, killing or taking as prisoner the few guards present. When the affair was over, the captain stood alone in the entryway, the hallway which ran down the middle of the castle, and listened. Alaisio walked up next to him, and asked: "What is it?"

"The same noise that we heard at Gensballa, my young soldier."

"What is that?" wondered Alaisio.

"Silence."

King Centreal threw another log on the fire and sat back in his chair, picking at his dinner plate. "Do you think they may have changed course? Where could the king be, how far could he have gone?"

"I'm not sure. All we can do is hope they're at Seun Bastion," answered Captain Luncas. "There are three forts within four day's ride. It is a rather bad place to have a king on the loose."

"Are you sure that is what we should hope for? Seun Bastion is a tough take, and the garrison will be very strong."

"Are you suggesting a different path?"

"Maybe," answered the king.

"I don't know," said Luncas with a sigh. He knelt down to blow on the infant flames, steadily spreading the fire. "Where would we go?"

"Is there another course they could take?"

"Lonavag Fortress. A walled castle in the forests just off the road that leads from the Central Path to Seun Bastion. They could continue to Seun Bastion from there and only lose a few days' time. If we're wrong, however, we're only giving them more time."

"I don't like this, Luncas. It was too easy. It's all too easy. Something is very, very wrong here. Gatsesilli was not so far back. If the Skaelin were going to surrender this fort so easily, they'd have just left before we got here. Our men have been scouring the lands south and west and east and north, and nowhere can we find a trace of Sendorun and his army. How can a king and his army hide? And why would they, when they have such defensible positions as Gatsesilli? Couldn't they have stockpiled enough food, as they knew we approached? Are they that short on food? Are they as poor off as we are? There is something dark about all of this that we haven't seen yet."

Luncas gave a dark laugh. "All we know is that the army is gathering at Seun Bastion. That's our ultimate target." The king ran a hand through his hair.

"It's too early to take the bastion."

"Is it? It only gets stronger with time. Perhaps that is where they are sending all of their food, to hold the bastion until relief comes from across the sea. The Lonin forces could land north of us, and the Skaelin could press from the south. We would be trapped in the peninsula. If we take it now we'll get most of the army down, and the Skaelin will be left scattered and largely confused. We've accumulated a lot of power, and more than half of the Skaelin will probably be there by the time we are. If we wait too late, we put ourselves up against a full garrison with possible reinforcements by the sea, if the waters melt early. We should advance immediately. And we should leave twenty thousand to the north to attack any reinforcements from the rear."

"What about the king? We need to take him down. He'll never surrender to us. He must be at the bastion when we invade it."

"If we surround half of the leftover Skaelin forces at Seun Bastion, King Sendroun will not be in a good position. He'll recognize that," the captain insisted.

"True, but if he concludes that Fate has begun to favor us he will retreat to the Eastern Mountains, where he can continue to lead and inspire resistance for years and years after we secure the other territories. We do not want to scare him, he is powerful when cornered. Rather, we want to kill him and his possible successors. Let's take tomorrow to think on it. We're staying here the next night anyway," suggested King Centreal.

"Agreed."

- Chapter Six -

"Good morning, Luncas," said the king, coming out to address the captains in the field where they had assembled.

"'Morning," replied Luncas.

"Alright," began the king. He pointed to a group of captains across the room. "Take your regiments across the ford to the east village. And you," he continued, signaling to another group, "take your regiments northwest to the village opposite. Luncas, you and I, along with regiments so far unassigned, will take the town to the southwest. Everyone take what you can, we'll need it all, and report back here by nightfall if possible. Those not included in this briefing are to remain on watch in the castle. If combat is delayed for any reason, and you do not expect to be back until sometime tomorrow, we will have auxiliary regiments posted here at Benaballa, so just send a runner up as soon as you're sure on which course of action you plan on taking." The captains went to their regiments and the army split up, then each company began their march.

It took a good while, but eventually the edge of the town was within sight. "Set up the engines," said the king. "Do not fire unless I give the word. This town is going to take one look at our forces and surrender, I'll wager." Most of the villagers did not even wait to see if they would fire the catapults or not, however— they simply picked up their things and fled. The army, now far beyond the point of hoping they would not be discovered, did not bother to prevent their escape. The village was almost entirely empty when the first volley of arrows shot out from the forest behind the Gaolnians, between the trees, and hit the rear of the Gaolnian line.

From where the arrows had come, a deep and resonant voice yelled behind them: "Charge!" Suddenly, an endless mass of Skaelin soldiers emerged from the forest all around the Gaolnians, and sprinted towards them.

"Hold them off!" yelled King Centreal.

"My king, is Benaballa safe?" questioned Alaisio.

"I don't know," answered the king, parrying a sword. "Archers fire into the forest! Keep your eyes open for any clear shots!" he commanded. "We'll have to try to meet the army there tonight, but we should camp somewhere else," he continued, still parrying blows from the apparently very skilled swordsman. He ceased speaking for a while as he fought with the man, but some other Gaolnians came to the king's aid, so he turned back to Alaisio. "Our plans may have been completely ruined, to be frank. I'll bet the other regiments are being ambushed as we speak. Just stick together and follow orders, and we'll be alright."

"Alright," said Alaisio. He had his doubts, though— there were only a small number of Gaolnians here, after all, and there seemed to be an endless stream of Skaelin soldiers— they kept coming out of the forest from every direction.

Before they could register what had happened, the Skaelin lines charged them from all sides. The 53rd, toward the front of the lines, moved ahead of King Centreal and beside another regiment to protect him, and they received an attack from the most skilled of their Skaelin opponents.

Bendoraun dodged a blade and let his fellow Gaolnian take on his attacker, while Bendoraun himself ran to help Gendorn— Gendorn was hardly defending himself as two Skaelin axemen were cutting him off from his line. Bendoraun attacked one of the men from the side, but another group of Skaelin swordsmen came bearing down on Bendoraun, and now they were both surrounded. Alaisio and Luncas were trying to get to them, while Luncas kept shouting "Pull back, back to the line! Get back here!"

Alaisio caught up with Gendorn and helped him get free, and they pulled back beside Bendoraun, who was still surrounded by three men. The 53rd ran up beside them, and helped keep the Skaelin at bay. "Retreat now, steady, hold the line, bring the line back— back to the king, just behind us— there we go..." Captain Luncas was saying. They got back to the line, but found that wherever they went— even right next to King Centreal— they were surrounded and outnumbered by the Skaelin.

Another wave of arrows came out from the forest and landed, from the sky, in the middle of the Gaolnian circle. "Return fire!" King Centreal shouted, and the Gaolnians nocked their arrows and set them loose. A great many of them got caught in the trees, and most of those that didn't landed without any real impact. King Centreal looked around for an exit, but the Skaelin were closing fast on all sides around them. "Pull back and push the line to the south!" he commanded, noticing that the line seemed weakest to the south— "Get out of here, but keep your lines!"

King Centreal heard the voice of King Sendroun burst out of the forest: "Don't let them escape! Kill King Centreal! Do not let them go!" The Gaolnians kept pushing the line south, losing many men— and the arrows kept coming at them. From every direction the Skaelin continued to press the attack, pushing them back.

After some time the Skaelin line to the south opened up, and a thin line of Gaolnians began making their escape— but from every side they were swarmed by the Skaelin, who kept shooting them from behind the trees or picking them off from the sides. With time that stream of Gaolnians widened, and more of them made their escape.

Bendoraun and Alaisio ran along the edge of the escaping line of Gaolnians, parrying blows and blocking arrows with their shields. To their left, Gendorn and Luncas ran alongside them. At one point the Skaelin line moved up, cutting Alaisio and Bendoraun off from Luncas and Gendorn. Gendorn and the captain turned to help set them free, but the line of Gaolnians tried to move them forward, and right next to him Luncas heard the command of King Centreal: "Get out of here! Regroup in the hills and hold our position somewhere where we can defend ourselves— get out of this forest, out of this valley!" The captain ignored the king for now, and pressed his attack against the line of Skaelin that had come up to kill the rest of his regiment, with Gendorn beside him. He would not leave without his men. But the Skaelin, ahead of them, moved up again, and now the 53rd found itself cut into two pieces, with both of those pieces surrounded.

They fought to try and bring themselves back together, but the Skaelin kept pouring in and drawing them further and further apart. When Captain Luncas took a moment to find their location, he noticed that Alaisio and Bendoraun were no longer in sight— they had been caught far behind, immersed in the Skaelin lines. The captain turned around to face Gendorn. He spoke quickly, and without any doubt— and only the slightest hint of sadness could be heard in his voice. "We have to leave. Get out of here— follow the king."

In a scattered mass the Gaolnians ran through the forests, up and down hill after hill. The Skaelin followed, just as scattered, swiping away and picking off the leftovers of the Gaolnian party. After quite a while, the command came from

King Sendroun to let them go. The Skaelin had them in full rout.

"Luncas!" yelled King Centreal, reaching the crest of the next hill.

"King!" replied Luncas, darting up to meet him.

"Take your regiment and alert the other two parties. I've sent runners ahead but I fear they won't make it alive. Tell them to hurry and make way to Fenidaln Meadows, make sure at least some of them know the way to lead the others. If there are none, lead them yourself, but hurry, I need you in the meadows to discuss the plans. Seun Bastion is off for now. Don't get caught," said the king.

"I will, as soon as I find my regiment..." said Luncas.

"No time, they could be regrouping for another attack even now. You must hurry! We'll keep a watch for them— you're not the only one in this situation, don't worry, but we have to keep functioning!" replied the king. For a moment, Luncas was silent.

"Very well, I'll meet the rest of you in Fenidaln Meadows. Don't get killed." Luncas turned to lead the remainder of his regiment back to Benaballa, where he could relay the orders.

Trudging quickly through the hills, he wondered where the rest of his regiment was. Was this all that was left? Had there been such a severe toll? Roughly half of the 53rd that had set out that morning remained to march alongside him. The snow was falling faster and harder, turning into rain as it came down to the earth. Trest was beginning. The sea to the south would have mostly thawed by now. If the rebellion did not succeed by the time the waters thawed, it would most certainly fail altogether.

While he led his men toward Benaballa, he lost himself in his thoughts. The scout that had come to him on that day— he had not seen the man before. It was not entirely odd, as men were changing regiments or divisions every now and then. Had this been a trap? And, the more looming question— was it still a trap?

"Bendoraun's not here," said Gendorn with tired breath, struggling to keep pace with the captain.

"Neither is half of our regiment, including Alaisio," replied Luncas.

"Nothing we can do?" asked Gendorn.

"Nothing, we have to hurry— the nation of Gaoln is more important than our friends."

"Right..." said Gendorn, slowing his pace. He paused, looking up at the cold sky. *Bendoraun*, he thought to himself— *where are you?* And it seemed that the only answer given was the wind which suddenly blew against him, urging him onward, away from the battle and away from his friend.

- Chapter Seven -

The figures ahead appeared as dark shadows clouding out the dawn. The party stopped in their tracks, debating their next move. The shadows, meanwhile, drew closer, and from the east the screams grew nearer. Kamira's mother bowed her head, looking down at the dusty earth. "This is it. We have to run. We have to split up. That way, maybe some of us can escape. Maybe one of us can tell the world what's happening here," Curileyn said.

"The world? Don't you know yet?" another woman answered, "The world does not care for us. To the world, we are sons and daughters of thieves, pirates and murderers. The world would not be disturbed."

"They care. But they cannot act, or at least, for a long time they have been unable. Now, things are different," Curileyn insisted.

The second woman scoffed. "Clearly. Now they care for us. That is why they have come to rape us and kill our children, and to enslave us until we die!"

The wind picked up for a moment, blowing fiercely against them, sprawling dust and light snowflakes in their faces. Kamira closed her eyes, thinking of Gendorn. What else could she possibly think about? While he was out there, fighting for their freedom, she was here, and about to be captured and killed— and Gendorn, Gendorn wouldn't even know. She held her mother's hand, and yet she wanted to let go of it, only to imagine she was with Gendorn instead. She loved her mother very dearly, but she could not help but think such thoughts. Her mother, meanwhile, seemed to trail off in her own thoughts, but every now and then her grip on her daughter's hand would tighten, and she would look down and smile at Kamira. Kamira smiled back, and her heart was content, if only partly, and her burden, if only a portion of it, was eased.

"Shall we go?" inquired an elderly man, whose long white beard was flowing with the breeze. Several of the people nodded. Kamira's mother looked down at her, and she looked up at her mother in return. Her grip tightened, and Kamira smiled. And as she ran through the dust and through the wind with her mother, as fast as she possibly could, she was filled, for a moment, with some sense of hope.

Her mother ran quickly, and Kamira trailed behind. She shouted for her mother not to go slowly simply for her— she shouted that she should run, because she might just stand a chance at outrunning all her pursuers. "I can't leave you!" shouted Curileyn.

"You can outrun them!"

"I won't leave you!" She stopped dead in her tracks, and Kamira caught up. She took her hand, and they kept running, Curileyn always in the front, urging Kamira to run faster. Secretly, Kamira was glad her mother stayed. The figures took shape to the south and to the west, and screams grew even louder to the east. The men ahead of them were the most menacing figures Kamira had seen since her childhood, when she remembered the uprising against the prison guards. These men were crude— they were dirty and covered in dirty armor and dirty weapons, but the shine of the red metal was the color of bright and newly drawn blood. When Kamira saw it glimmering through the cloudy haze, her whole body erupted in a shiver. Together, they ran toward this mob of soldiers. As they ran, some of them were tripped, some were knocked unconscious, some were slashed and beaten, then taken away to be tied up. There were yells coming from every direction. Kamira dropped her mother's hand.

"Go, mom. Go."

Curileyn reached for Kamira's hand, but she avoided it. "Give me your hand!"

"Run!" Kamira said. She dashed off in a separate direction, praying her mother would not follow. Curileyn, fighting back her tears, avoided a trip and the slash of a sword. Kamira did not make it half-way through— she was hit on the head with a small orchalin buckler, and punched in the stomach as several men swarmed over her. They tossed her body around like it was a piece of meat as they tied her up. She burst out wailing, her breathing heavy and despaired, but she almost smiled as she saw through a gap in the soldiers her mother running beyond the rear of the lines.

"Get the woman!" shouted one of the men. Several of the soldiers dropped their gear and took off running, and to Kamira's despair, they seemed to be gaining on her mother. She was not lucky enough to see the end, however, as she was thrown on her stomach, kicked in the mouth, and her hands bound together behind her back.

- Chapter Eight -

Bendoraun shook his head, and Alaisio nodded that he had seen. Together, they walked out from behind the brush and into the field. There were only a few scattered Gaolnians still there— the Skaelin had dispersed, disappeared into the trees out of which they had emerged only moments before. The entire meadow and its surrounding hillside forest was strewn with bodies— the bodies crushed the plants that grew and the shrubs which were poking out of the snow, and lay strewn across low-lying branches, the blood still slowly oozing out. The snow was red, and the rain, for all its power, could not wash away the color that had spilled into the earth.

Bendoraun let out a breath, and he watched it linger in the cold air for a moment. "Are they dead?" he asked his friend.

Alaisio shook his head. "I saw them get away, I saw them run beyond that hilltop— " he nodded toward the hill to Bendoraun's right— "but if they died after that, I would not know." He turned his head and, in a much louder voice, yelled across the meadow: "What regiments do you belong to, and where have they gone?"

One of the men stood up and replied: "We have lost all our regiment."

Another stood up behind him, and proclaimed: "I am the Captain of the Fourteenth Regiment. I have located only three of my men, and they wait for me at the hilltop there. We lost contact with the rest." The other soldiers, so they told Alaisio, were lost and could not find their captains or comrades.

"Should we gather notes?" One of the soldiers asked.

"No," replied the Captain of the 14th. "We do not have the time, and this place is dangerous— the Skaelin did not march all this way to attack us once and then leave on their merry way."

"King Centreal cannot tell if Benaballa is safe," Alaisio said to the captain. "Should we send a team?"

The captain shook his head gravely. "Benaballa is not safe, and the king will know this. He'll send a message around to meet elsewhere, and push onward— we will forget Benaballa if we still plan on reaching Seun Bastion. But I cannot tell where we would meet."

"Alaisio," Bendoraun said softly, "we should leave this place, I do not feel safe here."

"I know," said Alaisio. "We really need to find our captain…"

A man appeared just then at the crest of the hill where the Gaolnians had fled, and he peered down at the scene. "Gather whatever notes you may, but we cannot linger here," said the man, "all the Gaolnians are regrouping at Fenidaln Meadows. I will take you all to one of the captains who knows the way, and we will travel there together, then reform our regiments."

"Well," Alaisio said to Bendoraun, "traveling with fifteen people in a hostile land isn't the best way that could have ended— but then, I suppose it isn't the worst."

"Yes," said Bendoraun, fixing his eyes on one of those bodies of his fellow Gaolnians who had been thrown up into a tree and impaled on its branches, "it is not the worst..."

"Luncas!" shouted a man from afar, jolting up to meet him. "Soldier?"

"A runner."

"Good then, the king will want you to relay a message: All forces are regrouping from the ambush at Fenidaln Meadows. Any word from the others?" said Luncas.

"None. How many were lost? Is the king alive?"

"Centreal is alive, but we don't know how many we lost. Hopefully most of them are just lost, rather than dead."

"Okay, we'll be on our way."

"Be on guard."

The runner left in a hurry, and Gendorn turned to Luncas. "Are we ever going to find them?"

Luncas, from atop the hill, could still see bodies hanging in the trees and blood running like streams through the ditches in the valley. "Don't get your hopes too high, Gendorn. Stay strong."

"I swear it is," Alaisio said under his breath, as he stared at the two men several hilltops away. Their figures, dark as the trees under the newly cloudy sky, were hardly visible— yet Alaisio felt certain. "It is— who else would be standing there casually conversing with one other man just after being ambushed?" Alaisio asked. "It's got to be Luncas."

"Well, I'm sure the Skaelin would feel comfortable conversing casually— they just routed us, after all!"

"No," Alaisio said firmly. "It's Luncas. We're meeting him."

Bendoraun rolled his eyes. "If you are sure," said the Captain of the 14th— Captain Dunral was his name— "then we will follow you. But if you are wrong, you are sending us all to death."

Alaisio shook his head. "I am not wrong."

It was as Captain Luncas was turning around, and about to leave, when he heard his name being shouted out from afar. "Captain Luncas" a stream of voices cried. "Captain!"

Luncas turned back around. "Alaisio?" And in the trees, at least four hilltops away, he could see a band of maybe fifteen men moving quickly toward him. They disappeared when they descended into one of the valleys below, and then popped up again, and then disappeared again— and all the while Captain Luncas waited with Gendorn, who stood next to him wide-eyed and hopeful.

At last, the men arrived at Luncas's side, panting and utterly out of breath. "Well, good time to get tired," Captain Luncas said scornfully, "now when the Skaelin come, they won't have to bother chasing us again."

Alaisio managed a grim smile. "Wouldn't want to inconvenience them, you know."

"No!" agreed Luncas, "wouldn't think of it!"

Gendorn went up to Bendoraun and shook his head. "It is perfectly like you to get lost at every possible chance, isn't it?"

"Me?" said Bendoraun, "what happened last time was *not* my fault."

"Well, be glad we found— "

"*We* found you," Bendoraun corrected him.

"I am sure that you were of critical use..."

"Glad to be back too."

"I am more glad than you could imagine— I would not last a single battle without you."

Bendoraun smiled. "I know."

"I heard we are regrouping in Fenidaln Meadows?" Alaisio asked Luncas.

"We are, but our regiment has been assigned to inform the other groups. We're spending the night here, hopefully the others will report and we can leave in the morning," answered Luncas. "The perimeter is safe— we have auxiliary groups all over these hills, searching for soldiers who have lost their way. But the Skaelin are all around us, so I will not be sleeping tonight, and I ask that several other men keep watch with me. We will be in very dangerous territory these next few days— *very* dangerous. Commander Denelu will soon be leading the forces south— "

"Who's in charge up north then?" Bendoraun blurted out.

"King Centreal has appointed someone new to oversee operations in the north. Commander Denelu and all his regiments will be coming along with us to Seun Bastion, where they will help command the army. Where are these men going?" Luncas answered, waving a hand at the men standing behind Alaisio and Bendoraun.

"I am Captain Dunral of the Fourteenth Regiment of Gaoln," one of the men said, stepping up next to Alaisio. "I have lost all my men. I am unaware of the situation. Should we travel with you, Captain Luncas?"

"I know the way to Fenidaln Meadows," said one of the soldiers behind him.

"If you are sure of the way," said Captain Luncas, "then you should leave for Fenidaln, and get out of this area with haste."

Hearing that, Gendorn and Bendoraun exchanged a worrisome look. "I'll be leaving, then, and leading these men to the meadows," said the captain, "we will see you in Fenidaln, Captain Luncas."

"Good luck, Captain Dunral."

The men left with Dunral, and Alaisio turned to face Luncas again. "Of course we would be the ones to spend the night right next to where we were ambushed! Bendoraun and I thought we would be safer with you, Luncas! We should know better by now."

"I'm sure you'll learn someday," the captain replied.

It was well after nightfall when the last group arrived. Luncas relayed the information of what happened, and they made sure to keep all the Gaolnian regiments away from Benaballa, which had now been retaken by the Skaelin. They awoke with the rising of the sun, and had a fast, meager breakfast, before setting out into the rising dawn, southward down the Central Path, toward Fenidaln Meadows.

- Chapter Nine -

Skerun jumped off the litha and walked across the courtyard toward the palace doors. King Seagraul came out to meet him. "I saw you coming," he told his envoy. "Please tell me that Phenen has pledged support."

"The emperor vows he will only join our war if Las or Laen is directly attacked by Gonaka or Kale."

"Menuld and Joel surprised me as soon as you took off. They told me this would be the answer I would receive. They are the most frustrating devils in this world, I swear!"

"What will you do?"

"We cannot send forces and risk an invasion by Gonaka or Kale without Phenen's support. We have the hostages already, so the matter is unimportant."

"So..."

"So we will send a message to this so-called King of the Free, that traitor Centreal. If he does not relinquish his claim to the lands in Skaen and return to Gaoln, the hostages will be executed. Send the message immediately. Send a small team of soldiers to wait on standby. If Centreal is unwilling to surrender, they will do their job, and put a new king in place—

one who is more responsive to our demands. We'll force them to surrender, either way, and if somehow they manage to elude us, well then, they'll have to attack us, won't they? If it's an invasion the emperor requires, it is an invasion he will get. And we will draw him into the war on our side, in which case we will also win."

"You're luring them to invade your own country so as to gain another ally?"

"I do only what is necessary, and nothing more. Send the soldiers as soon as the ice has thawed, and keep them hidden. If Centreal's answer is to fight, then we'll replace him with someone more docile. And if he escapes us, he'll have a war waiting for him on this side of the ocean. That is all."

The king turned to leave, and Skerun stood there dumbstruck. In the months leading to this day he had begun to notice a change in Seagraul, but now it struck him suddenly that this was a madman. "Lure an enemy army to invade his own country because he is afraid of some escaped prisoners," Skerun mused to himself. "Where is this going...?"

Part Five:
The Battle at Seun Bastion and a Message from the Sky

- Chapter One -

Gendorn, Alaisio and Bendoraun had never seen Captain Luncas so tense before. He was constantly alert, which was somewhat like him to be— but he was so alert that when he heard the crunching of leaves in the forest or the light scampering of feet, his eyes would come right out of their sockets and his head would twitch faster than lightning, and he would survey his entire surroundings before he would be satisfied. It was not easy, traveling with so few men in such a dangerous place, and knowing, furthermore, that they were at the very tail end of the Gaolnian regiments making their way to Fenidaln Meadows.

Captain Luncas stayed up later these nights, and he would stand guard alone outside the ring of firelight, working to adapt his vision to the night. Sometimes Alaisio would join him, and there were a few nights when Gendorn and Bendoraun, together, relieved the captain of his duty. But he looked more tired every day.

It was on one particular afternoon, the first hot and sunny afternoon that they had experienced since their departure from Port Tekal, when Captain Luncas, as he had so many times before, ordered the caravan to an immediate halt. He held up his hand, and signaled for silence. Unlike any previous incident, however, the captain hopped down from his wagon onto the ground, and began surveying the scene with more caution in his eyes— and a hint of fear— than Gendorn, Alaisio or Bendoraun had ever observed before. In the silence that ensued he whispered to his men: "Take out your weapons."

"Let's walk along the edges here," Gendorn said to Bendoraun, "and see if we actually find anyone."

"Keep a keen eye," Alaisio said.

Gendorn and Bendoraun walked along the edge of the path, and Alaisio walked with another man along the opposite edge, while Luncas remained behind, scanning the scene. Bendoraun and Alaisio were signaling to each other— there were very small walls and structures of wood and mud and stone along the edges of the path, and they went deeper into the forest. Gendorn eyed the scene skeptically— he could not see or hear anyone around. And he knew they had delayed themselves too much already. They had to get to Fenidaln Meadows.

"Let's not overreact now," Gendorn whispered to Bendoraun. "Our soldiers have been passing through here for more than a week now, our people, correct?" He advanced steadily, unwavering in boldness. "They've been gone for days, look at this— these ashes are old. Our people scared them off, no doubt," he said. "They cannot hide here while ten thousand men march this path, and expect not to be detected. They've gone."

Gendorn went to turn around, when out of the corner of his eye he saw a flash— some swift movement, and then a horrible, terrible, miserable onset of pain, a pain which overtook his entire body and sent him writhing on the ground, screaming and crying. And in that instant he saw nothing, nothing at all, except red blurs when he opened his right eye— his left would not open. Bendoraun jumped over Gendorn's body and ran towards something, and from the other side of the path he heard Alaisio and Luncas come running. Sword against sword rang out in the air, and the sounds of arrows set loose—

the sounds of arrows hitting their targets, penetrating bodies—
and then the sounds stopped. Luncas, who was bleeding on the
side of his arm, was the first who bent down next to Gendorn,
followed shortly by Bendoraun and Alaisio.

Gendorn was twitching wildly and shouting, and he moved
his hands up toward his head. He felt around where it hurt, he
felt the shaft of the arrow sticking out of his head, he felt the
blood dripping down his body— and he had that instant feeling
where he knew was going to die. He screamed again, then lay
down, and, but for his struggling breath and his convulsions, lay
motionless on the floor of the earth. Bendoraun, hovering over
his body, saw that the arrow, lodged inside his head, had gone
through the side of his eye.

"Get him in the wagon!" commanded Captain Luncas.
They laid Gendorn down inside Luncas's wagon. "I've done this
before."

"You've removed an arrow from a man's head?" Bendoraun
wondered.

"There isn't a lot you don't do after forty years of war."

"Did the man live?"

Captain Luncas did not answer— instead, he said again,
"I've done this before. I want you men to be ready— get out all
of the bandages and the clean clothes we have, and get water,
and that vial I have in my bag over there, Alaisio— get that.
There is no way we can do this without Gendorn losing his eye.
There will be a lot of blood— you need to do exactly what I
say exactly when I say it." Alaisio and Bendoraun nodded, and
the captain nodded— as if to reaffirm himself of his own
words.

Removing the eye require Luncas to cut some worm-like
cords behind the ball, and rendered Gendorn unconscious after
he seemed all tired out of screaming in pain, and after he drank
one of several liquids the captain asked Alaisio to fetch. The
arrow came out after the eye. Gendorn's head was entirely
covered in clean white cloth, although the bleeding did not
stop, not even days after the attack. So the captain kept

attaching more and more bandages to the wound, kept trying to apply more and more pressure— but the bleeding did not stop. For the rest of the way to Fenidaln Meadows, Gendorn lay inside Luncas's tent, and sometimes Bendoraun swore Gendorn had already died. At times Luncas would make him lay on his stomach with the wound down, and at other times he was told to lay on his back. But the captain, who checked on him continually, assured Bendoraun that he was alive, and that he was taking good care of him. Alaisio and Bendoraun, neither of whom knew anything about such things, nodded and went along with whatever the captain said.

To Gendorn, the world was a blur. His remaining eye was shut, and he saw only with his mind. In these visions he saw through time as easily as he saw through space. There were three child slaves sitting on the shore of a prison colony, drawing dreams in the dirt. They kept each other warm at night— they kept each other alive. There were great lithae flying overhead, and on their backs rode kings and ambassadors and commanders from a world away. There was lightning in the sky. There was a storm in the ocean. The soldiers of Gaoln drowned in the cold water, and all their ships sank, and they were never free.

Some of the visions were memories, others were dreams or nightmares or a mixture of all three. Sometimes the memories became twisted and dark. The three of them were sitting on that shore again, and they were drawing the same dreams in the same dirt. But there were screams and shouts from all around them. And when the three children got up and looked around, they saw an entire army arrayed against them. They had catapults and archers and great warriors riding selk, and they were destroying, raping, killing, stealing. Gaoln was dying. The three children jumped into the Cold Ocean to escape the soldiers, and everything turned cold and dark. And he did not see or think anything else for a very long time.

And then the sun rose. There were snowbirds in the morning sky. There was the sight of land from the ships. There were thick castle walls and warm blankets inside. There was a village that offered them shelter. There were captains and soldiers who helped keep them alive. There was a great fire with a great many people, and they were all calling him a hero of Gaoln, *Gulaus Gendorn*. Something in the back of his mind was burning— people were screaming. People were dying, and their lifeless eyes stared at him. It went black again.

The next thing he saw was the sheet of cloth overhead that covered the wagon in which he lay.

They arrived in Fenidaln Meadows not ten days later to find only a few scattered regiments there. Most of the men were out of the camp, scouting the countryside, setting up outposts, or searching for food and materials. A tall and burly soldier approached Luncas, recognizing him as a captain. "We await the arrival of a few more regiments, but I'm not sure how many. Our forces are more scattered than we seem to know. We believe Sendroun's army continued to make several attacks in addition to the one against Centreal, and we currently have many of our regiments sweeping the countryside in search of his army," said the man.

"We were attacked. Gulaus Gendorn has been gravely injured, shot through the eye. Where can we find someone to help us?"

The man's concern was apparent on his face. "Come with me, we will have a tent set for the gulaus."

Gendorn was lowered onto a camp bed inside a tent, barely conscious at the moment, but able to hear that they were discussing him. He was too weak to care. One of the men took off the bandages and began applying some sort of viscous paste to the wound, trying to force it around the edges of the shell of hardened blood which had surrounded his eye socket without opening the wound. Bendoraun, who sat beside him, whispered: "Are you awake, Gendorn?"

Gendorn let out a weak cry: "Gaoln."

"We could not have you fight," said Bendoraun comfortingly. "But do you really want to go back there? To Gaoln?" Gendorn did not speak, he just looked up at his old friend. Bendoraun saw in Gendorn's one eye the sadness of a man who knows he is dying, and he knew at once that Gendorn just wanted to see Kamira once more before he passed. He didn't want to die here. Bendoraun took his hand. "You will sail home with a few others, don't worry. You'll be back soon."

Even in his greatly weakened mental state, Gendorn knew that his friend, gulaus though he now was, had no power to order such a thing. Still, he had to smile.

"I will go with you...if I can..." said Bendoraun. Gendorn didn't have enough strength to respond. Instead, he reached into the backpack that lay by the bed, and pulled out— his hand slow, as if this movement required the most tremendous effort— what appeared to be a very large seed. It was almost the size of Gendorn's fist. He held it out for Bendoraun, who took it and eyed the thing curiously. "Where did you get that?"

"Plant it here, before I die. Promise. That is the name."

"Promise is the name of the seed?"

"Seed and tree."

"What kind of seed is this? It's huge!"

Gendorn's mouth trembled into the shape of a smile. "From Gaoln." Bendoraun's eyes grew wide in disbelief.

"Okay, I'll plant it. Before we leave these meadows. I promise." Placing his other arm around the injured man's shoulder, Bendoraun bid him farewell and exited the pavilion.

Alaisio was outside, with an apothecary to whom he had been speaking. When he saw Bendoraun emerge from the tent, he hunched his tall figure lower to better meet Bendoraun's eyes. "It is infected...I'm afraid..." Alaisio spoke softly. "He might not make it home in time...Nothing we can do...They are using that paste that you saw, and a few other things, they are trying…Not very hopeful…"

Bendoraun stood for a moment. He returned to where Gendorn lay, but found that he had drifted back out of consciousness. Would he wake up again, ever? He sat there for some time, observing his friend, before he rose. When Bendoraun turned around to leave, he found the king in the exit, waiting for him.

"What is it?"

"There is something else, Bendoraun. In the battle, Nolor's regiment was overwhelmed."

"Where is he?"

The king shook his head. "They were overwhelmed, Bendoraun." His voice was laden with concern, and the king knew his message was understood.

"What does that mean?"

"It means the entire regiment is gone."

The space between the end of that simple statement and the time when Bendoraun spoke seemed to drag on for some immeasurable eternity, in which Bendoraun struggled to understand what the king had said. And then he felt quite suddenly alone. After the silence Bendoraun quietly asked: "Was there a note?"

The king again shook his head. "The Skaelin control the area and they kill anyone on sight. They are concealing their whereabouts, and, in so doing, cannot allow even the note seekers to pass into their area of control. It is a shame upon their honor that they do not allow us to retrieve the last wills of the dead, but then, Sendroun is a very dishonorable man."

"Thank you, my king."

"I am sorry to bear this news, gulaus. I hope your friend Gendorn fares better."

"Thank you, my king."

"Goodbye."

When Centreal turned, he found Captain Luncas standing in front of him, waiting to speak. "What is it, captain?"

"Is there any news?"

The king pushed away thoughts of the many regiments that had not escaped, and forced himself to consider the latest developments in the war. His voice still carried that solemn tone of a man who really needs to get some rest. "Our forces were split and battered. Most of our regiments are seeking Sendroun's army, and on many fronts we are now fighting regiment by regiment in the forests. I have sent Commander Denelu to lead a force of thirty regiments who are blocking the paths to Seun Bastion and raiding supply trains. Hopefully this will act as a counter and ensure Seun Bastion is at least in somewhat of a weakened state."

"They won't try and pull out? They have too many forces already at the bastion?"

"Correct."

"How long are we waiting here in the meadows?" asked Luncas.

"Not much longer. We have information that King Seagraul and President Leyus of Las may be sending aid to King Sendroun. Which means King Sendroun must be dead, and this war over, before their troops arrive."

"What do we do if we spot Sendroun's army?"

"I do hope and pray we see them before they reach the bastion. If we find the king before the bastion, we send a force against him that he cannot imagine in his wildest dreams. If Sendroun's force enters the bastion unchallenged, we will find ourselves in a difficult position. It is critical that Seun Bastion does not become a prolonged siege. We cannot give Las and Laen enough time for their reinforcements to reach the bastion. It would mean the war, and nothing less."

"Then we will give them no time, my king."

That night was quiet. The Trest animals were out and about, celebrating the coming of the warm season with their chirps and cricks and clicks and their scampering little feet through the underbrush. The stars were bright in the clear sky, but the wind was cold, coming down from the north, reminding Bendoraun that Sen was not yet gone away. He shivered when the wind came, even with his great coat, but the morning, he knew, would bring warmer weather. He was alone in the dead of this night, in those hours before the morning, in the very center of the great camp, just outside Gendorn's tent— it was customary for the gravely injured to be kept in the center of any encampment, so as to protect them in case of battle. As gulaus he was in the center's center. And here in the heart of the Army of Gaoln not another soul stirred.

He knelt down and felt the grass wet his coat and pants. He touched the earth with one hand, and it was colder than the wind. It bit him, but he dug into it with his fingers, and he kept digging and digging and digging long after he could no longer feel his fingers. He saw them under the starlight, and knew how to move them, and that was enough. And when the hole was wide enough and deep enough Bendoraun took the seed out from the backpack and set it down inside the hole.

For a time he stood there. "I don't know what Gendorn was talking about," he said quite suddenly, "but he wanted to name you Promise, so it's Promise I'll name you. And I suppose I should make a promise, then. If that's what he wants. I promise that our people will see you grow to be a tree, one stronger even than the withered old thing we left in Gaoln. They will come here happy and alive and free, and they will look on your flowering boughs and your lofty branches and smile. They will remember the deeds of Gulaus Gendorn, who saved the army from ruin and salvaged our freedom. Maybe they will also remember Nolor and I, and they'll say 'Gendorn promised them a land of their own, he promised them their freedom, and he made them believe.' And one day, whether in this world or the next, I will come here with Gendorn and Kamira, and we will sit here and watch you grow to be as big as the dreams we drew in the dirt and the promises we made to ourselves." And even thinking these things made him smile.

He buried the seed, then stood slowly, keeping his gaze fixed on the spot. "I made a promise to you, so make a promise to me that you'll stand here as a testament to where we've come from, what we've been through, and where we're going— to who we are and who we want to be. A testament to what this all means. And a thousand years from now may you be even healthier than the trees that surround this meadow now, and let those who look on you remember Gaoln and the fight to be free. Let them remember your name. Let them remember your ancient father, the dead tree in the prison land of Gaoln where you were but a seed. It is here, in the land of promises and dreams, where you will grow."

He turned and, without looking back, went inside his tent and fell asleep.

- Chapter Two -

Bendoraun set his things down gently inside the wagon, and turned to face his friends. "Captain Luncas, I have to say, I wasn't quite sure about you when we arrived in Skaen. And at the end of it all, I'm still not sure."

"I was less than sure about you, Bendoraun— I almost tied you up in a tree and told the king I'd somehow lost you. And I mean that. Good luck to you," Luncas answered with a smile.

"Alaisio, I do enjoy your nightly stories and jokes around the fire, especially the good ones that you tell on the nights when Luncas isn't around." Luncas raised a brow and cast a skeptic glance.

"It's been a pleasure to have such an appreciative audience! I wish you all the best," Alaisio told the gulaus.

Last, he turned to King Centreal, who had come to see them off. "My king, thank you for your permission to let me help see Gendorn back to Gaoln. And thank you for allowing us to do so."

"You are Gulaus Bendoraun now, young boy," said the king with a warm smile. "It would have been wrong to refuse the request."

"We will return to Skaen as soon as we can," the young gulaus assured his king, "and will help organize the escort for the women and elderly to join us here in Skaen, as you instructed. I wish all of you the best of luck at Seun Bastion."

They bid him their best once more. Luncas and Alaisio helped load some more food, and then the wagon took off westward, away from the Gaolnians and the Skaelin Army.

The days passed on the road with Bendoraun looking out of the wagon as he sat with his friend, or up at the sky as he led the animals down the paths. He watched the sunrise through the trees, and saw it set beyond the hills. He watched the snow packs melt day by day and he looked down at the little blades of grass that grew where the packs melted, a wonder that Gaoln did not have. He smiled as he passed by plant after plant, life after life, wondering which one may be the last he ever recalled when he was trapped in Gaoln again.

"You remember when we said we might go back someday? To that forest, the one we went to when we first landed here?" asked Bendoraun. There was no answer. "Maybe we will, someday." The thought resided in Gendorn's struggling mind, as he faded back out of consciousness: *Someday...*

"...I think I'm dying, Kamira..." Kamira looked at Gendorn curiously, and took his hand in her own.

"We can all be dying. Or we can be living. The only thing that determines that decision is how you look at it."

"I'm not living anymore. I'm dying. I am."

"Well, we may as well all be dying then. If that's what you think it is."

"I'm weak, and I don't want to fight anymore."

"Remember what you fight for, Gendorn, and let that give you strength." They rested in each other's arms for a very long time, listening to the strong wind in symphony with the crashing sounds of the shoreline of that dust pile Gaoln. An old song played in his head, one he recognized, but had no idea where he had heard it. It was the song that made him feel warm and safe, that he heard only in his deepest dreams. He closed his eye and listened to the soft and loving voice that sang this song and as it grew, everything else faded. Kamira turned to a gust of wind and blew away. The grass disappeared beneath his feet. The crashing waves made no sound, then the ocean was gone and all was as nothing. The music began to fade. The song grew softer, but as it was almost gone, a voice cut across it, a distant whisper blowing in the wind...

"Gendorn..." The voice got stronger, another gust of wind blowing across the dust. "Gendorn! Get up! It's time to board the ship."

- Chapter Three -

The ground beneath Kamira's feet was dull and grey. The grass, which grew sparsely upon it, was discolored and faint, and it compacted into the earth under the pressure of three hundred thousand bare feet marching. They must be in Laen now, she thought. Kamira stared down at the earth, observing it. It was dying, just like they were. The world they lived in was simply too harsh.

She had not seen her mother, and hoped she had gotten away. If she had made it all the way to Kale, maybe she could find some help. But it was more likely she had been caught near the border and killed— she did learn that Juron had stationed guards all along the borders with Gonaka and Kale. Still, it would mean so much for her to have survived— it would mean that one of them, out of all the Gaolnians now hostage under King Seagraul, had escaped alive— that they, as a whole, would never be entirely exterminated.

They were not given food until mid-night, when they stopped walking. They had a brief while to sleep, then they were woken up before the dawn and forced to march again. They received no more food until sunset of that next day. They had been hiking like this for five days, by Kamira's count. They had hiked almost every hour of every day at an absolutely inhuman pace, and a large number of the hostages had died along the trail. Every now and then Kamira would lose herself in her thoughts, and her gaze would lock on the earth under her feet. The thing which brought her back to reality, every time, was when the earth beneath became the body of some very old woman or man, and she would be forced to march around it. On the sixth day she lost track of time, and many days after that they arrived in the city of Laeolin.

The sky was dark. In front of her the feet stopped, and Kamira halted. At the very front of the line, on a rise so that the prisoners could see him, stood a man in polished orhcalin armor, the red metal lined with some kind of glimmering blue trim, and a great billowing cape of blue with the image of a white seabird flying. The man stood facing them, and though she could not see his eyes, Kamira felt his hateful glare. The man introduced himself as Juron, their commander and captor. "You see that tower to the east? That's right in front of you?" Juron proclaimed. There was a tall black tower, surrounded by many buildings almost as tall and much wider and square. "That's the Tower of Laeolin. We're all going there, and if you try to escape, you will be killed. Is that clear?" There was no answer. "Perfect. Let's go."

The streets were flooded with people who had gathered along the sides of every alley and boulevard to watch the hostages march in. Some of them were cheering, others were solemn and silent. There were some who threw things at them and yelled at them. "Pirates," they called them, "murderers, thieves! Warmongers and criminals!" Kamira lowered her head— she did not want to give anyone an excuse to target her. But still, someone threw a small block of wood at her, which hit her in the head. She raised a hand to rub the wound, and almost began to cry. It was not a very hard hit, but she could hardly bear to be the target of such hate. The fact that these people would accuse her of murder, then throw things at her and laugh at her pain— when *they*, these horrible people, were responsible for her suffering, when *they* had created Gaoln in the first place, when *they* had started the fight— It was simply too much to bear. Her heart rotated between a violent anger for these people and a desparate, defeated depression.

One of the women in front of her spoke to Kamira, keeping her head low. "I'm from Laeolin, you know. Most people aren't like this— there are a lot of reasons not to like Seagraul as king. Some of them are against Gaoln, but they can't voice their opinions, because the government would send them to Gaoln for it, or kill them outright. Don't be quick to judge people. They're not all bad."

Kamira almost said nothing, but she decided to protest. "They all seem pretty bad to me right now. If they don't like it, they should do something about it, instead of just letting this happen to us!"

The woman smiled faintly. "The world doesn't work that like, honey, as much as we all wish it did."

The block of buildings surrounding the Tower of Laeolin, which stood alone in the middle of a circular courtyard, was where the guards led the prisoners. Most of them were sent to these buildings, each of which was guarded by a force of seven or eight armed and fully armored guards. "There are more guards posted around the city," Juron told them all, before he split them up, "so don't think of escaping. Every tower and gate is being manned, and they've all been told to watch out for escaped Gaolnians. Your best chance of survival— and I say this truthfully— is to take your chance that Seagraul will get what he demands and release you. Your chances of surviving escape are very, very slim." He waved his hands. "Alright, let's split them up."

Kamira, along with twenty thousand or so other prisoners, was sent to the Tower of Laeolin itself. The outside looked like a giant spire of twisted metal and stone protruding from the earth, and it soared above the other buildings. It was completely black, an obsidian that refused to shine. From the top, Kamira assumed, one could keep an eye over the entire city, and see the surrounding hinterland and beyond. Laeolin sat in a valley between very distant hills, so such a tall tower would have been necessary, she realized. On the inside, the air was cool and damp. She shook her head— the place looked so grim, one would imagine that it had been built just for keeping them hostage, and not as a lookout and a place for important meetings— that it had always been intended to be a symbol of intimidation, rather than a symbol of the glory of Laen.

There was no one but them inside. Every floor had been cleared. Kamira was in the front of the middle of the line, and so she went most of the way up the tower, but not to the top. At first she had ample room, but as more and more people entered, it became clear this would not be so. Soon she was shoulder-to-shoulder and chest-to-chest or back-to-back with her neighbors. When they moved, they had to move as a group, they were so tightly packed. She heard the doors close, at last, and the dark rooms became even darker. She was near the center of the room, but there was a gap in the heads where she could glance at the window— a small, thick thing, carved into the very stone itself. Outside, the clouds, she could see, were just barely beneath them. There was a single bird which popped out from them, and flew just above the grey horizon of the clouds. It lifted her spirits, to see that one bird fly— and for an instant, she felt herself smile. *Fly, bird*, she thought—*fly far away from here. Tell the world what they're doing to us.* But even as she thought this, she saw the tiny black speck of the bird dip again beneath the clouds— and she did not see it return to the open sky.

The morning after Gendorn and Bendoraun departed Fenidaln Meadows, from the direction of the rising sun, a litha— purple and black in its wings, black in body with a purple streak down its spine— flew fast toward the camp. It landed in the center field, an open space surrounded by huge pavilions, and a rider jumped off. The man, who carried in one arm the flag of the Skaelin and in the other the flag of Laen, was tall and kept his head up as he looked around. "Bring me King Centreal," the man commanded.

King Centreal appeared presently. "What is this?" he demanded.

"King Centreal, my name is Cero, and I am the Lonin Ambassador to the Skaelin Lands. I come today to issue to you the command of King Seagraul to halt your forces and return to Gaoln."

King Centreal laughed openly. "Yes, of course, we will return very shortly."

"Good. If you do not, of course, all of your family and friends back in Gaoln will be executed."

Centreal's laughter died, and he stared at the man sternly. "You will not touch the prisoners of Gaoln, *guard*."

"It's late to be saying that, seeing as we have already seized every last one of them and are now holding them captive inside Laeolin." The king could not find the words to make a reply— he could not even find his thoughts, his reaction. "We will need an answer before I can leave this camp. You will surrender these lands and return to Gaoln, and we will rebuild the guardhouses destroyed in the First Rebellion. Or you will stay here and pretend like you stand a chance at winning these lands, a chance at defeating Las, Laen, and Skaen together. As a consequence of the latter choice, your friends and families will be killed. You will not see them alive."

"Does it make you happy to deliver this message?" The king wondered, with a sound of defeat in his voice.

"It gives me satisfaction to know that this war is over, King Centreal, and that you have lost. Go back to Gaoln."

"Gaoln is no place for a home, Cero. You've seen that land before. Do not ask that we return to it. It is not a *home*."

"I would pity your plight, King Centreal, if I were authorized to pity. But I am not. You have the week to talk it over. Our men are sailing to the bastion as we speak, and your women, children, and elderly await your decision at Laeolin."

"I will need two weeks to hear word back from the other divisions, at the least."

"You have one week."

King Centreal stood before the assembled captains of his company. In the front of them Captain Luncas stood at attention, his eyes fixed on the king. Centreal was a man given to serious expressions, one who seldom laughed or smiled, but who felt the weight of kingship at all times. On this particular night, he wore an expression so grave that the captain could not even begin to guess what had caused him to call this meeting.

"I received a message from the ambassador Cero of Laen today. He has informed me that all the Gaolnians in the old colony have been taken to Laeolin to be held as hostages. The demand is quite simple— we must refuse ownership of these lands, return to the prison colony, and allow the guardhouses to be rebuilt. Laen and the Skaelin will own us once again.

"I will send runners to all the regiments outside Fenidaln Meadows. Every soldier will have a vote and a voice on our decision to either surrender now and forfeit all for the possibility of reuniting ourselves with our families, or to press on to Seun Bastion at the risk of losing our families.

"I am personally of the opinion that King Seagraul would never dare to slaughter so many innocent hostages simply to spite us. From a political view of things, it is in his interest not to do so— should he kill the hostages, he loses the only real leverage he has against us, and forfeits the chance of future negotiations. I also believe that King Nowhawna of Gonaka would never allow for such a thing. It would, furthermore, mean war, at the least, between Laen and Gonaka. It is in his interest to keep the hostages alive as long as possible.

"I also remind you all that our freedom is close at hand. If we sacrifice everything we knew in Gaoln, even if we sacrifice our families, then it is for the benefit of everything yet to come, for the benefit of the hundreds of thousands more who would have been born into that prison and condemned to a life where they await their death. I am, furthermore, of the opinion that should we return to Gaoln, all of us will be killed regardless, as was the situation prior to our invasion, when the Skaelin were killing us off with starvation.

"And yet the choice must be ours to make— not mine, your king, not yours, my captains— but every soldier who is among us now. We will gather the votes for two weeks, and if Cero cannot wait, that is his issue. Laen will hardly be able to reinforce Seun Bastion in that time— the icebergs, may I remind you, endure even after the first rains of Trest have fallen. We will be forced to march double-time to Seun Bastion as often as we can, for the march is thirty days from here, and in that time it is conceivable that the bastion could be reinforced by forces sailing north from Laen.

"I will issue one last warning, that this may be a trick for the Lonin forces to gain more time to reinforce Seun Bastion. It is possible, though I do not believe this to be the case. I know that King Seagraul is capable of such wicked deeds as have been reported— I have no doubt that this message from Ambassador Cero is real.

"Go then, captains of Gaoln— have a very long talk around your campfires tonight, and then the next night, and the night after that. And may Time and Fate guide our direction."

The captains stood there, their faces set in stone, their eyes uncomprehending. None of them obeyed their king's dismissal. Captain Luncas, usually the practical, quick-to-reply and stalwart type, struggled to understand what had been said. His usually commanding voice could not be heard in the silence of the nearing night. And then, breaking the silence, King Centreal spoke again.

"None of you have ever delivered a message so heavy, so dreadful as this, and it will not be an easy thing to do." His voice came firm but with a gentleness in it— this was a king who found himself needed by these captains, and who assumed his role as their leader quickly and ably— "You will need to be the comfort for your men. They will console and speak with one another, but will look toward you for leadership. As you have led them in battle and kept them alive, so must you tell them, if Fate decrees, what choices they should make. Many of you are more aware of the world around you than your soldiers, most of whom know nothing. You know that King Seagraul cannot kill these prisoners without terrible repercussions, and you know that his better option, even considering his own interests exclusively, is to keep the hostages alive. Your men will need to hear you say these things, or they will succumb to depression, believing that their families have already been sentenced to death.

"I assure you, I will continue to work with Gonaka on releasing the hostages. But we cannot let this war end. Go, talk to your men, and be frank with them— ask them how they feel, and you will observe their choices changing over the days. We will cast the votes at the end of the first week, and count them on the second. Cero will have to deal with our tardiness. This is no decision that you and I can make alone."

At these words, the captains began to turn around. They walked back to their regiments without a sound, without a muttering of any kind. When they arrived, their men, some of whom were laughing or sitting down and enjoying their dinners, wondered at the silence of their leaders.

Alaisio knew something was wrong. Captain Luncas had never showed his insecurities openly, but now Alaisio saw in front of him a man who grappled with some issue that Alaisio could not begin to guess at. "Tell me what it is," Alaisio said, and the captain looked up at him. *Seagraul is going to kill them,* Luncas thought. *Centreal is blinded by his years in Seagraul's service. He still sees some good in him, some reason. I met that vile king four times in my life, and upon every occasion I saw the madness in his eyes. He will kill them all, Alaisio— that is what it is.* Aloud, the captain answered:

"It is something with the prisoners back in Gaoln, Alaisio. We will wait until all our men have returned. And then we will speak of it."

King Centreal met again with Cero on one cloudy morning when the sun did not shine. "What is your decision?" asked Cero.

"The decision of the people of Gaoln is that we will press on and take hold of Seun Bastion, because we remain a people without a country and without a home, and because our children remain condemned to life in Gaoln unless we succeed in our current undertaking. It is our purpose to succeed."

"You will let them die?"

"You are a monster, Cero," King Centreal said, with the utmost distaste, "an abomination. If you lay a hand on one of those innocent people, you will see every town in Laen burned to ash, and the flag of Gaoln over every tower. And don't you dare try to convince yourself that this is not your fault. We are not killing them. The blood of those innocent people will always stain your hands and your heart, should it spill."

"I do not think that is possible. You are certain in your decision?"

"My people have decided. Go and warn your king— if he lays a hand on our people, we will come for him. And we will not stop."

The crowd of people— at least eighty thousand soldiers from the Army of Gaoln, some of whom had hiked for ten days to see this— had gathered to watch their message being delivered. The brief silence which ensued took the whole of the camp. Not a wind blew in the air, not a breath came from the mouth of any man. The world, for a moment, was still— then in an instant it came back, and the flapping of the great black and purple wings broke the still air. Two days after that, the army set out for Seun Bastion.

- Chapter Four -

The sailors lifted Gendorn, barely conscious, onto the ship, and set him down in the cabin bed. They looked back for a brief moment before setting sail. The land was warmer now— Trest had finally come to the shores of Skaen, and the wind was not as bitter, the ocean not as icy— the land was becoming greener. Bendoraun gazed at it all, and remained up on deck, hanging on the side of the rail, as they set sail for Gaoln.

The waves were rough, and the wind was strong. Gendorn had been lying in bed since the moment they boarded. For the most part, Gendorn was quiet. He was now steadily conscious, but slept easily. He was strong enough to talk quietly, but due to the rocking of the ship and the hard winds, could not walk. Bendoraun walked up to him with a small plate of fish and set it down on Gendorn's bedside table.

"Bendoraun," said Gendorn without opening his eye, "am I going to die?"

"No."

"Mm…" Gendorn said. "Do you believe in Sendeilta? Are we worthy of such a thing as eternal rest?" he wondered.

Bendoraun's eyes grew grave. "I don't know. Kanel didn't tell us," he answered with a distant smile. "Gendorn, you can still count the number of people you've killed on the palm of your hands, and every one of them was a soldier in a battle who was at least as intent on killing you as you were on killing them. Your spirit will come to me from Sendeilta, I know it, Gendorn— and you will remain there until we come to join you, and then together we will go into the Great Beyond." The boards overhead creaked. "But I've already told you, you won't die!"

"Maybe," said Gendorn plainly, "I just…I don't know. I won't give up, Bendoraun. I need to see Kamira one more time. But the thing is, I see her every time I drift away, and I just want to stay there, away from here. But I know that's not real. Was Kanel real? That dream, I mean? Could we go back there?"

"I don't know, but I know he was right. You have a longer life ahead of you, Gendorn. Hold on to it." A brief silence passed. "Your wound is infected," Bendoraun said bluntly. "I was talking to Alaisio outside. He had been speaking with an apothecary. They said it would be difficult for you to survive the journey back to Gaoln."

"Well I wasn't going to die there!"

"I know, I know. I'm just saying. You have to keep fighting, Gendorn. We only get closer to Kamira, but your dreams will never take you there, only this ship."

"Don't worry, Bendoraun," said Gendorn softly, "we'll make it home. But if we don't…"

"If we don't, I will always remember you, and I'll tell Kamira you thought of her every day. I'll make sure King Centreal never forgets Gulaus Gendorn of the 53rd. And when we're in Skaen, living freely, we'll remember you as one of our greatest heroes." Gendorn smiled again, but he was quickly falling asleep. Softer, Bendoraun said: "You made me believe in a land of our own, Gendorn. You made us believe. And alive or dead, I will always believe in you. We will all believe in you. Keep on dreaming, and we will dream with you." Bendoraun placed a hand gently on his chest, then rose and left the room.

The third day of the voyage, Bendoraun came to Gendorn in the morning again. Bendoraun sat next to him, watching him as he lay there. Gendorn turned over, and said weakly: "We should return to Skaen when we get Kamira."

"You need to rest. We're not going anywhere for a while, not unless the circumstances in Gaoln have gotten even worse since we left."

"Maybe. But just for a while. We can sit outside by the tree…"

"You need to stay inside and rest, with your back level and your eye closed! We have enough of that medicine the apothecary gave us to last for months, it's practically all we took back with us. And Kamira will not want you to travel again."

"I'll need food to recover properly, and we haven't got food in Gaoln!"

Bendoraun laughed. "You're hopeless."

"I know."

"You seem to be getting better."

"I am."

"It's because you're closer to Kamira. You two make me sick sometimes, you know?"

Gendorn managed a smile. "I know. It's quite noticeable."

"Well, good. I'm going to go help out on deck, see what needs done. Goodbye, Gendorn."

"Goodbye."

- Chapter Five -

A bird, small and grey with a streak of blue across its chest, landed upon the outside windowsill of a house upon a hill, one which overlooked the city of Laeolin. Ciso, from the desk he was sitting at next to the window, leaned over and looked at the bird. The sky outside was grey, the same color as the bird, and the clouds were thick, moving quickly through the sky. A storm was coming. The bird twitched its head sideways, and Ciso looked at it again. It seemed to be beckoning to him, almost knocking on the glass, as if trying to catch his attention. Ciso rose and opened up the door, walked outside, and leaned up against the house as he surveyed his surroundings. He could see great streams of people moving about in the middle of the city, though it was hardly visible through the fog and from so far away. He turned to the bird, as if it might tell him something important— but the bird only rose and flew off toward the city.

Ciso made it back to Laeolin before the storm reached its full power. He was wet when he walked inside the Welcome Hall of the Academic Institute of Laeolin, or, as some called it, the Academy of Laen. The air inside was cold— the walls were high and the roof seemed miles above, its cross arches almost out of sight. It was dark, with only the dim light of the torches placed far away from one another, spreading their light upon the dark stones. The wind inside died as the doors shut behind him. He began walking toward the end of the hall, but from the corner someone came out to speak with him.

"Forin," said Ciso, unable to hold his surprise. "What are you doing here? It isn't safe," he whispered.

Forin grabbed Ciso by the hand and led him into one of the side halls, through a small wooden door and down a skinny corridor. "We need to talk."

"Let's go to my room, then."

"It isn't safe."

"Isn't safe? What could be there?"

"There are people watching your room. They cannot see me alive."

"What? They're watching— "

"Be quiet," Forin said. "And come with me."

Forin led Ciso into a small dormitory room, with a small single bed and thick, bare stone walls. There was a very small fireplace along one of the walls, unlit and empty. On the bed sat two people, one very old whose beard was long and white, and another, a woman, whose age was betrayed by the many wrinkles on her face. Forin seemed younger than the old woman, yet Ciso knew that Forin must be almost as old as the man who sat on the edge of the bed, the one with the long white beard.

"Ciso," said the bearded man, rising to greet him, "it is a pleasure to meet you— I have heard much about you."

Ciso looked at the man, unable to appear more flattered or bewildered. "Oh, well, I— I guess I haven't heard about you..."

"Oh, of course! My name is Menuld, dear boy."

Ciso's eyes went wide "Oh— I'm so sorry, I didn't mean— "

"Not at all, it's nothing. But we can't tarry. I came here for a very specific reason and I do not have a lot of time. You already know Rajah?" Menuld pointed to the elderly woman sitting on the bed. Ciso nodded. "Good, I'll get on with it.

"You may have received information that King Seagraul was planning to abduct all the Gaolnians and hold them hostage in the center of Laeolin. Those hostages arrived more than a week ago and have been under constant threat of execution. King Seagraul is not the man I once thought he was. I never was his biggest fan, and I never really worked for him, I know— my loyalties always rest with the goodness of the world, and not any one nation— but the things he has said and done of late make me realize that King Seagraul is a plainly terrible man. He does not value human life, only the status of this false idea of 'Laen'— an idea that in his mind does not include the welfare of the Lonin people, but instead only considers the welfare of himself and his close friends.

"I have no doubt that King Seagraul has the potential to murder every one of these victims. The world is oblivious to that potential. King Centreal and the Gaolnians refuse to yield to Seagraul's demands, as is just, but, foolishly, they believe that King Seagraul would not execute the Gaolnians held in Laeolin."

"It would not be logical for him to do so," Ciso suggested.

"Logic is out of the question," Menuld answered. "Seagraul is no longer a logical man, he is consumed by his paranoia."

"What are we going to do?" Ciso asked. Forin came to stand beside him, and Rajah rose from the bed, coming to Menuld's side. Menuld continued.

"Forin and I worked with Ambaru, Malia, Numini and Ailo many years ago, as you'll remember," Rajah told Ciso, "when we were plotting the first revolution and the freedom of Gaoln. We have struggled endlessly in the shadows, unknown and unheard of, to combat Laen's aggressive agenda and its inhuman policies. That battle has been fought in the field of politics and speeches and protests, and has been lost by the state's violent responses of imprisonment in Gaoln or simple public execution."

Forin stepped forward and placed a firm hand on Ciso. Menuld looked into his eyes, and held Ciso's gaze as Forin spoke. "It is time to take that battle to the streets. Our next mission will be a dangerous one, and it will be answered with swords and axes and arrows. We have to free the prisoners of Gaoln. They are no longer held in some distant and inaccessible prison— they are here, in our city, Ciso. And they are about to be systematically executed, every one of them."

"What you need to do," Menuld proclaimed, "is to alert your group of followers. We know what you have been doing. We watch people like you. You need to tell them that the time to act is now. You need to lead them into freedom."

"Do you not have anyone else who can act?" Ciso asked him.

"We will be in contact," Rajah answered him. "We still have agents, you know, who work in the shadows, as I said. We will come out from hiding the very moment you do. We will free them together, and we will keep them safe. We have established safe houses throughout the city, and if we cannot use those, we have arranged for a few ships to wait for us in the harbors. We will not be able to save everyone," she said quite gravely. "Most of them will die. Most of us will die. This attempt, as I said, will be met with force— King Seagraul will perceive us as enemies and traitors of the state. He will try to kill us all."

"But if we do not act," Forin stated, "then we are useless and inept. All our lives we have fought for the freedom of Gaoln and for a just state here in Laen, a state that does not murder its own citizens. The breaking point is upon us. We act now, or fail."

Ciso nodded. Without a doubt in his mind, he drew himself up, and looked boldly— gravely— into Menuld's eyes. "We act now, then. I will alert the others."

- Chapter Six -

The army hiked for twenty-eight days before they were just north of Seun Bastion. They had lost innumerable men, as the Skaelin had attacked them sporadically throughout the journey with teams of hit-and-run regiments, the Skaelin suffering few losses themselves. The men had trudged through snow the entire way, but here the snow was thin and they could walk upon it as if it were nothing. The trees were taller and greener— altogether healthier, it seemed. They were three days from Seun Bastion.

They hiked until the sun was down, and then set up camp. Luncas was looking very tired, and was limping more on his bad leg, but Alaisio kept it to himself. The men gathered tinder, chopped wood, and after an hour, were sitting around the camps, making food and exchanging information on Seun Bastion.

When the men awoke they quickly packed up. They marched down the path that whole day, and set up camp in the early night. The captain did not complain, he kept to himself. He didn't tire as usual. He was still limping, but no expression of pain could be seen on his face as he hiked over hill after hill. There were no stories that night, as the men knew they needed sleep, and wanted it badly.

The morning of two days after that, grey shapes appeared on the horizon. The peninsula around them was thinning, and the sea was getting nearer. At some distant point it became even thinner, and the grey blocks in the distance marked the last bit of land before the Cold Ocean. "That's the bastion," Denelu told his captains. As they drew nearer the three sides of the fortress became visible, and the middle ground between those sides, where their soldiers would be under fire from all three walls, gave them reason for doubts and second thoughts. "We'll be pushing them back as soon as we can hit the ones farthest north, so hopefully by the time we reach the south wall there will only be one side of defense left. Follow my commands, and this battle will go over nice and quick." His men nodded. Luncas and Alaisio, behind him, did not appear quite as certain as their superior.

King Centreal stood behind the front line of trebuchets, with Commander Denelu and Captain Luncas by his side. Regiments of archers stood ready behind him, and the infantry were back behind the archers. Before them the mighty bastion reared up into a stormy sky, its large turrets and thick walls looking down at the Gaolnians with amusement. Wooden palisades and barricades blocked their route to the walls. On either side of them they could make out the hills giving way to the ocean in the distance, and the deep sapphire waters closing in around Seun Bastion.

The catapults and ballistae started firing at the earthwork, from where the first line of Skaelin defense fired back. "Archers half split and advance!" ordered the king. The archers split into two sides and flanked the earthen defenses, shooting at the engineers as they ran up beside the ballistae and catapults. The Skaelin had stockpiled shields along this outer line of defenses, so while some of the defenders held up huge shields, others fired arrows.

"Commander Denelu," said the king, "The Skaelin will try to halt the advance of our archers while they bring that artillery back behind their walls. We can't let that happen, because if they get to those walls we'll be forced to move well inside their range in order to force a breach. We can't act rashly, because they already have siege equipment and archers posted on the wall, ready for us to make a move. When we advance, they will not only defend from the earthwork, but attack from the walls. I need you to take care of this."

"And siege is not an option, we are sure?"

"Unless our spies are mistaken," said Captain Luncas, "Laen is sailing even now. They tell us that Seagraul has been sending messengers trying to gain additional forces, and that he was planning to sail as soon as the ice thaws. We cannot risk his landing before Sendroun is dead. We are under a severe time constraint to take this position and kill the king, and if we fail, we could lose our chance at winning the war. Not to put us all under too much pressure, or anything."

"Thank you for that, Luncas," the king said sarcastically. "Here's what I need to happen, and you two will be in charge of getting it done…"

Captain Luncas, due to the death of Commander Suri of the Third Division and his subcommander, was serving as a commander in this battle, and Alaisio had taken his place as Captain of the 53rd. In the rear, the 53rd saw ahead of them thousands of Gaolnian soldiers, and they knew that behind them one hundred thousand more lay waiting to advance. Around eight thousand were forced recruits who were actually Skaelin themselves, and every precaution had been taken to ensure they did not revolt. By this time, they had been thoroughly schooled in Gaoln's history, and were sympathetic to the situation. But it was a difficult thing to ask them to fight against their own country, in any case, and most of the Skaelin were being used as non-soldiers to construct engines or serve as field medics. Even so, from his view in the rear, Alaisio was ready to act immediately if he saw any sign of Skaelin resistance.

King Centreal issued the command to charge, but it was not only for an advance team. At once, the entire advance command, all those soldiers in front of Alaisio, marched forward. From corner to corner of the meadow, the Gaolnians rushed forward to the castle. Captain Luncas led the western wing of the army, sweeping around the earthwork. Arrows poured down at him and his men from the east and from the south, as they drew closer to the castle itself. Alaisio, leading the 53rd, trailed at the end of Luncas's company. Luncas split his forces into two teams, one consisting of two-thirds of his manpower and the rear team, led by a man from another regiment, which consisted of the other third of the company and trailed off to take control of the siege equipment and attack the archers. That team met with two-thirds of Denelu's forces, which attacked from the east end. The other third of Denelu's forces, as well as the two-thirds of Luncas's forces, attacked the infantry, which were forced to address the rapid Gaolnian advance from the east and west. Rather than cut them off in the south and thereby prevent off their escape, they worked together to cut off their north end, thereby separating the Skaelin infantry from the war machines while allowing them to flee back into the bastion. At this same moment, a team of eight thousand Gaolnians came out of the forest from the north, and marched down to where the advance company had waited only moments before.

The battle lasted longer than Centreal would have liked. For too long the Gaolnians were under fire from the archers and machines on the castle walls, and they suffered many casualties. But Denelu, in charge of seizing the machines on the earthworks, was relentless. He ordered a charge on the fortifications, and through sheer mass of numbers forced the Skaelin to abandon the defense. Most of the archers he killed, but a few escaped to join the infantry, under pressure from

Luncas. Commander Denelu secured the location and brought up engineers from the rear. "Trebuchets, concentrate your fire on those towers, take the enemy fire down! Catapults, hit those walls! Ballistae, hit the Skaelin infantry as they flee back to the castle, then refocus your fire on the walls!" he ordered. "Look for any vulnerable positions! Every castle has a weak spot, find it!" he turned back to the rear row of siege equipment, and couldn't help but smile. The Skaelin advantage— positioning their defense so that they could attack the Gaolnians from two locations before pulling back to Seun Bastion— had turned out to be their weakness. Now, King Centreal commanded two artillery divisions, while the Skaelin were forced to have only one division and continue their attack from only one location.

"Cut them off! Keep them away from the machines!" Luncas shouted. The distance between their new artillery and the Skaelin infantry was growing, and Luncas couldn't help but hope this first phase of the assault would be a clear and encouraging Gaolnian victory, despite their losses. Luncas was in the front, pushing the enemies back toward the base of the castle walls, where the ballistae were concentrating their fire.

"King Sendroun!" said a Skaelin commander.

"I am aware of the situation."

"Will you not let them in!?"

"Letting them in would be to let in Luncas and his company. Is that really what you're advising?"

"But my king, we need those infantry!"

"We need the Gaolnian Army to not get inside this castle."

"They will get inside! They'll get inside very soon! They've taken control of the field artillery, and they're tearing apart our defenses on every side of these walls!"

"We can hold them, commander. Our hall here is too open to let them in, too wide. Our defenses will take a long time to fail, but even when they do, it is better to allow for a minor breach where we can concentrate our firepower."

"You're going to abandon our infantry and let Luncas have his way with them! Let them back in the castle! You are giving this battle to Gaoln, my king!"

"Commander, I'm just trying to win it."

"Commander Luncas!" yelled Alaisio. Luncas rushed back to the center to meet Alaisio. "Our sub-commander fell in the assault, he put me in charge of your rear team," Alaisio told him.

"We're all sticking together from here on out. We need to take cover from this fire, we can't do anything until there's a breach in the castle. Sendroun isn't sending out any more forces, he's going to make us work hard once we get inside the castle."

"How many of us have arrow shields?"

"Not enough," said Luncas, taking out his own. "We should fall back behind the earthwork and hide in those caves behind the outer fortifications. I need to speak with Denelu to make sure we have enough captains for the engineers. I'll meet you back behind there. Take the men back— they'll get slaughtered if they stay out here in this field. But keep their shields up!"

Alaisio nodded. "I'll meet you back there."

Commander Denelu was already behind the earthwork when Luncas arrived. "We beat them back. Sendroun didn't let the infantry in, and we got them all. A few of them put down their arms and ran— we didn't pursue them," Luncas told him. "Do you need another commander?"

"I can handle the artillery for now. If Sendroun sends anyone out, I'll need your command to beat them back, but unless that happens you and the infantry should stay out of sight. We will assault the towers with the trebuchet companies, and— "

"Commander, those caves don't go under the castle walls, do they?"

"Of course not— how stupid do you think King Sendroun is?"

"Of course," said Luncas, "send a runner if you need me. We'll take cover."

Blood dripped through the cave ceilings. Alaisio and Luncas were both on the very outside of the cave, while further down in this particularly large cave another hundred or so men stood ready. Their small niche was above the rest of the cave, which afforded them some privacy. The wind could not enter the small hole and make its way down, but they still caught the fresh scent of the open air. Alaisio rose. "I'll be right back," he said, and he took a peak outside, then slowly came back down. "Yes, still standing," he said, sitting back down on the muddy mould he made. "And a thunderstorm will be here by nightfall."

"Good. I don't think it rains or snows enough here in Skaen," said the captain. "Very dry."

"Did you just tell a joke?"

"I never joke."

"Was that another joke? Doesn't it rain much in Laen?"

"Almost as much as it does in Skaen," he said. "But don't say that so loudly."

"I'm sorry. You don't ever talk about Laen, captain."

Luncas raised his eyebrows, then nodded. "Well, I suppose I should, then. I grew up in Laen, of course, and there isn't really a lot to talk about..."

"There seems a lot not to talk about, actually."

"There is." Luncas paused, and Alaisio waited for him to continue. "I entered the military at a very young age, you'll recall me saying. Of course, Laen wasn't really engaged in a full-on war since the last of the Great Wars. I spent some time chasing pirates around, battling the Confederation. And what I saw disgusted me— I hated those pirates, their disengagement with the world, how unconnected they were to ties of emotions which bind the rest of us."

"You have emotions?"

"I am telling a story." Alaisio was quiet again. "So yes, I hated them, and I believed that they needed to be punished— I believed in Gaoln, in the way that Laen and the Skaelin and Phenen believed in Gaoln. When the Pirate Wars ended I stayed with the Army of Laen and went to Gaoln."

"Went to Gaoln?"

"Yes. I was a guard. I watched over the prisoners of Gaoln, with a team of other guards, in a guardhouse. It was my responsibility," he said, in the softest voice Alaisio had ever heard him employ, "to make sure that they did not escape."

"And how did you end up facilitating their escape?"

"Well, I was only a guard for a short time before the Civil War of Skaen broke out, and I was hired as a captain for the Skaelin. I've already explained why I made that decision— the Skaelin were the victims in that war, those whose argument I believed was more justified, and they were under the leadership of a different, much wiser king. They had more money as well, which may have eased my decision, and there was also this particular girl I was interested in. That was a mistake— but anyway. It was a different country altogether. At the end of the war..."

"You went back?"

Luncas nodded shamefully. "I did. I still hated those pirates, and I believed that was who we were keeping as prisoner— I was surrounded by people telling me nothing else. I was one of the last captains of the guards in Gaoln."

"Were you there for the fall? And what made you change your mind?" Alaisio wondered.

Luncas took a deep breath, and let it out slowly. The air stank of death, but the captain paid no attention. "There was a man named Centreal, who had been appointed Governor of Gaoln." At this, Alaisio smiled. "He was meant to keep the prisoners inside of Gaoln, of course, but he came to me one day, in my guardhouse, and he began talking— he pulled me

aside, and spoke to no one else. He told me it was something
he needed the captains to know."

"'I've heard of you, Luncas,' was the first thing he said to
me. 'I know of your hatred of the prisoners here, but you are
unaware of your own ignorance.' He told me all the statistics
about how many people were actually pirates, how many had
even been charged with any crime at all— tiny numbers, of
course, out of the many innocents barred inside Gaoln.
Centreal lived with these statistics every day, thrown on his
desk in little brown booklets season after season, and over the
years they grew on him. I told him that I didn't believe him,
that he was a traitor, he was making it up. I was going to report
him to headquarters in Laeolin. Then he told me that I couldn't
escape. 'The revolution is coming,' he said to me, and it
sounded so eerily familiar to what Seagraul had told me when
he was taking control of Laen, it felt so wrong— 'the guards
are going to be killed. You make your own choices, Luncas,
and I leave this one to you: Join us or die.'"

Again, there was a pause, and Alaisio looked at Luncas with
a new kind of skepticism— had his own captain only ever
joined this fight because he had been threatened with death
when he refused to do so? Is that where the loyalty of Luncas
came from? "I took a walk one day," Luncas said suddenly. "I
took off all my armor and put on those rags that the Gaolnians
were forced to wear as clothes, and I walked around and
pretended that I had just come in, that I was a new prisoner. I
walked for days, through pel after pel, and I visited the markets
and the guardhouses, and the guards threw curses and death
threats at me and told me I wasn't really human. They said they
didn't want to see me, that I disgusted them. One of them
cracked my knee when I asked for some food." Alaisio raised his
brows in surprise. So that was how the captain got his limp.
From his own guards. Luncas continued: "I was gone for a
week. I saw two bodies lying in the dust in that short time, both
of them tiny little creatures, starved to death— their stomachs
had caved in. I spoke with many of the prisoners. One of them

watched their children die of the cold. One man told me how the guards had raped his daughters until they bled to death from the inside. Another told me how hard it was to have to choose between feeding yourself and feeding your father, when one of you has to die. His father died. He refused to eat. Died over the night. On the last day, I just sat down in the dust and let my thoughts overwhelm me. And I knew that I would fight for a free Gaoln, under threat of death or not. I could not spend my life guarding a prison full of innocent people. How had I been this naive the entire time? How did it end up that I actually believed I was doing the right thing by guarding these prisoners? I wasn't listening to myself, and I decided to change that.

"I found Governor Centreal in his house in the center of Gaoln, and I asked a guard to get him for me. Centreal looked out his window— he had the only window, and the only proper house in all of Gaoln— and he could tell me just by my face. He drew me up into his room, and we spoke in confidence. He told me that Gonaka was sending the largest fleet of ships this world has seen since the Great Wars to carry all of the Gaolnians who could fight over to Skaen, and that Gonaka would be supplying all the initial food and clothes necessary, and that they would provide as many weapons as they could. We could not let anyone else know that Gonaka was doing this, of course, and they flew no flags when the ships came to our shores. I stayed with him while the last guardhouses fell, while the soldiers were driven out of Gaoln. But Laen answered quickly, and they blockaded the entire coast. Gonaka could not get to us in time. It was another seven years before they came, before we made our escape.

"Alaisio, I tell you this only because I count you as a friend and a soldier who may someday be good enough to hold the position of captain, should this war drag on. It is also because you are not from Gaoln, unlike the rest of these soldiers. This needs to be kept secret."

"I understand. You lived with Centreal that whole time?"

"Yes, by which time he was King of Gaoln, by the mutual decree of Gonaka and of himself."

The conversation lulled. What more could Alaisio ask, and what else could Luncas explain? Alaisio caught the captain's eyes. "Is this really the end, then?" Alaisio asked.

"As long as Laen does not arrive on these shores, this is the end." There was another long pause, and then without looking up, Luncas said: "Well, now I suppose you know why I never spoke of my younger years to anyone here. It's sort of a necessity to keep my past hidden, you know. I used to be the enemy of every soldier who now fights for me. And I am trusting that you will realize the gravity of this secret."

"I would never betray you, my captain. Although I realize now that I am just beginning to understand you."

Alaisio looked up. The blood was beginning to drip around him— he would need to move soon. The ceiling of this cave was incredibly thin, Alaisio observed, and must be very permeable. But there must have been something solid in the rock to keep it from caving in. Overhead, Alaisio and Luncas could hear the sling of boulders and the firing of ballistae. For hours they sat there, listening to those sounds. Sometimes they heard people dying— it could be as loud as a scream and visible as the blood dripping through the earth, or as soft as a distant thump on the ground, or a sword clattering down on a rock. Inside the cave, the air was still, and people's voices were low and solemn. At some point they heard a soft rain falling down on the earth. It saturated the soil, and more blood came through the roof of the cave.

They stayed more or less that way for the next week, as the Gaolnians attacked and were repulsed and attacked again. The storm came and went and came again. The sounds of people fighting and dying started, stopped, and started again. The soldiers in the cave slept until their terrors came, and then a few of them would start writhing and shouting and all the men in the tunnels would wake up, and then they would fall slowly back to sleep. The same patterns recurred day after day and night after night. And the only difference was the slow and steady increase in the number of bodies in the field above their heads.

At one point Alaisio rose from his seat, as he had many times before, and peered outside. The field was covered with arrows, shields, and people lying in pools of blood. Broken siege engines lay strewn across the earthwork. Behind him, King Centreal still stood, issuing orders from his base behind the rear line of artillery. He must be growing tired, Alaisio thought. He was tired just looking at the scene. Then he saw something which especially stole his attention. Commander Denelu was walking— no, just trying to stand— with an arrow in his chest.

Alaisio fell back into the cave. "Luncas! Come see this!"

"I've seen enough."

"Denelu has been shot!"

Luncas bolted up and sprang outside the cave. He turned around to see Denelu falling to the ground, hit by another arrow. "Can you load a trebuchet, Alaisio?"

"I think so."

"Come with me— we're in charge of this now, it looks like."

- Chapter Seven -

The walls of Seun Bastion stood still. Commander Luncas, now in charge of the assault, stared at them, in all their might and legend, contemplating how they would fall. The sky above was cloudy and dark, and out to the southeast, from where the clouds were coming, there was a storm. It would be here soon. And with that storm from the south, Luncas knew, another challenger was approaching. They could not be allowed to land, if the Gaolnians were to survive.

Luncas sent a runner back to King Centreal. The runner returned shortly, and nodded at Luncas. As one, King Centreal and Commander Luncas refocused their artillery. Luncas's entire battery began attacking the northwest tower of Seun Bastion, supported by Centreal's trebuchets. His catapults moved up, supported by the archers. After continuing this for some time, a crack appeared around a window slit in the middle of the northwest tower. The barrage continued, and another hole appeared above it. Luncas and Centreal threw all their strength at that window slit, expanding the cracks as best they could, using every catapult and trebuchet that they had. The gaps grew too wide. The slit opened up to a hole as one of the boulders finally pushed through the stone. The barrage continued for hours, and then the tower crumbled down to the earth, opening up a small entrance and providing a route to the top of the castle.

"Charge!" yelled King Centreal.

"Charge!" echoed Luncas. The Gaolnian Army broke into a sprint to Seun Bastion, and when they got close the artillery ceased fire. Centreal ran up to join the charge, trying to direct its flow.

"Up the rubble! To the castle! Anyone who has shields, bring them out and help lead the way!" the king commanded. Centreal was still too far behind to help run the advance. Luncas and Alaisio, however, were near the front.

"I can't find my men! They were lost in the charge!" yelled Alaisio. "I have to wait for them!"

"They'll be swept up by another regiment or by the king— they know what they're doing! You can't just stand there, you'll be shot— hurry on up!" yelled Luncas, as he began climbing the rubble to the top of the castle.

"Fifty-third!" shouted Alaisio. An arrow whizzed by Alaisio's head, narrowly missing his neck. Luncas grabbed him by the arm and pulled him up, then let go and resumed climbing.

"Get up here!" he yelled. Alaisio nodded, and began to climb close behind Luncas. "Don't let it bother you, you can't think about it right now. They've been through this before, Alaisio— they'll be okay." Alaisio was about to respond when he ran right into Luncas, who was falling backward and staggering down the ruins. Alaisio dropped his weapons and caught him, holding on to the rock of the tower with one hand and to Luncas with the other. Luncas's left shoulder had an arrow sticking out of it— it had wedged itself in between the shoulder plates. Luncas was holding the wound with his other arm and trying to move his left arm around. His face was contorted in pain.

"Luncas!"

"Put me down you fool, keep moving! We issued a charge!" he yelled. Knowing a command when he heard one, Alaisio dropped his friend and sprinted up the rubble.

The climb was frantic. On the one hand, the crumbled stones provided shelter for the advancing Gaolnians. On the other, those very stones were sometimes large and awkwardly placed, and at certain points only one or two people could make it up at once. The Skaelin met them with full force. Arrows came down in the hundreds, and loose rocks were thrown down the sides of the crumbling tower. A barricade had already been erected in a tunnel that led into the interior of the castle, which had been opened up by the crumbling tower, and Skaelin engineers lit a fire at the entrance, prohibiting both a Gaolnian climb above that distance and an invasion into the castle itself. Balls of flaming pitch rolled down the ruins and were thrown into the Gaolnian advance lines. Not a single Gaolnian soldier had made it more than halfway up, where the Skaelin barricade had been hastily set. There was almost defeat in King Centreal's voice when he ordered the Gaolnian withdraw.

But he'd not be routed again. With a stern face he looked at the great fortress walls, and his mind was the harder between the two of them. His men ran back to the lines as fast as they could, and when the last of them reached him, he raised his hand, held for five seconds, then threw it down in the direction of the castle. Following the movement of the king's hand, one dozen boulders loosed into the air and struck the top of the castle, hitting archers and destroying war machines, tearing out murder holes and crenellations, rolling along the top and crushing their Skaelin adversaries beneath them. Bodies fell from the top of the castle, and then the Skaelin stood still once more, ready to meet an attack.

King Centreal smiled. If they were waiting for one, he would not disappoint them. The second battery released its load on the crumbled tower. The flaming entryway, the blockades, the loose ends and the crevasses where soldiers had fallen, all were torn away as the massive rocks sundered wall and tower alike. There now appeared two holes in the castle, one being almost at floor-level and the other with a clear path upward. From the second entryway, they could load ladders and send men up to the tops. With another wave of his hand, the King of Gaoln sent in the advance. Close combat soldiers supported by archers into the castle, archers to the walls, ladders to the top, climbers to the ladders, engineers reload. He smiled, watched, and waited.

The Gaolnians flooded the castle, pouring into both openings and sending waves of men up the ladders to the top. As Alaisio neared the top he himself felt a sudden rush of pain course through his arm and chest and shoot up to his head— he was hit in his upper arm, near the shoulder. His immediate reaction was to take it out, but he recalled Luncas's explicit warning to never remove a barbed arrow without supervision. Clenching his teeth, he kept the arrow in, and tried to flex his own arm so he wouldn't lose mobility, although it cost him in blood. He looked around, and everywhere saw people stumbling back down the rubble or being killed and thrown off, and soldiers charging up trying to avoid the bodies. He narrowly avoided one body that had fallen from the top and nearly landed on him. Beyond, though, the Gaolnians were establishing a position on the top of the castle. And behind him King Centreal was coming up with the rest of the Gaolnian Army. Another arrow whizzed by his side.

He reached the top, and immediately targeted the archers, who he knew would try and shoot Centreal as he came up with the rear advance team. He picked up a shield someone had left and started plowing through the infantry to get to the archers with a group of likewise determined soldiers. Many of the archers withdrew behind the infantry, but then the Gaolnians only broke through the Skaelin lines with more and more fervor.

Behind him, the Gaolnians were being massacred. Almost no one who ran up the crumbled tower made it to the top— there were too many arrows, too many catapults and ballistae trying to bring them down, and masses of Gaolnians would at times roll down the sides of the crumbling tower, tripping the soldiers who were trying to make their way up. Behind them, there must have been fifty thousand Gaolnians running toward the walls of Seun Bastion.

In the distance, further along the castle top, Alaisio saw King Sendroun. This was a man taller than Centreal, and of a wider build. He had a dark look about him, the concentrated look of a man who knows his mission. King Centreal had just reached the top, anxious to inspire his soldiers, and steadily they were gaining ground and cutting off the archers. Alaisio had looked too far and his gaze had been diverted for too long. The enemy's blade hit his wounded arm, sending him to the ground— and suddenly Alaisio found himself unable to move his injured arm. The man turned his sword around, ready to thrust into Alaisio's heart. Alaisio mustered all the remaining strength of that arm and blocked the strike with his shield, which dropped as the sword hit it. Alaisio screamed, and his wounded arm fell beside him, limp and useless and bloody. He quickly rolled and rose to his feet, parried the next blow, and cut his enemy's arm. His enemy dropped his shield, but wasted no time in attacking. Alaisio again parried, then drew up close to his enemy and put his blade next to the man's neck, looking him in the eyes. The man's expression did not change. Alaisio pulled his sword back, cutting his enemy's neck.

Soldiers on both sides cleared away to form an open circle, in which stood two opposing kings. As the ancient custom ordained, the two kings fought alone, without any interruption from either side. All along the castle top, from the walls and ramparts and from the highest towers, soldiers stood watching the two kings battle.

Alaisio looked for the captain, but could not find him. He climbed down the tower ruins, finding that Luncas was still in the cave-in.

"Captain," said Alaisio. "Are you alright?" There were large pools of blood around the captain, and he didn't seem too lively.

"After all I've withstood…an arrow will kill me? Not even a man, whose face I can see. Just an arrow?" answered Luncas.

"The kings are fighting," said Alaisio.

"…What are those wounds you have?"

"An arrow got my arm, and a blade hit me there. I might lose it."

"Well, that's just destiny telling us to stay together, isn't it? If you wish to watch the kings battle, go on."

"Is your leg okay?" asked Alaisio.

"It's been getting worse. I could hardly walk today. I don't know what's happening. Was it hit in one of those battles, or is it all this hiking? It feels…wrong. But with one limp leg and one useless arm, and an injury that will make me bleed to death here, I don't think I can lead the invasion. The king is up there now. I trust he'll live, and you'll be there just in case, won't you? Go get up there!"

Alaisio patted his old friend on the shoulder, then rose out from the cave-in. He climbed back up the rubble, watching the two kings duel from afar.

Sendroun lifted his axe and struck. King Centreal blocked with his shield, but the axe cut through, slicing his arm. Centreal jabbed his spear into Sendroun, but his armor deflected it. Sendroun lifted the axe to strike again; this time Centreal's shield held firm. Centreal knew he could not win like this. His shield could not withstand the axe. Swiftly he slid beside Sendroun and turned around, jabbing the spear tip into his enemy's uncovered waist, deep into his gut, and smashing his shield in the enemy king's face. King Centreal pulled out, but the enemy king did not strike in return. Sendroun lowered his axe and stared down at the bloody spear tip, dazed from the shield. He lashed out with his axe, but with his shield King Centreal blocked the weak attack, threw it aside, tossed the spear aside in favor of his short sword, and slashed his foe's face. Quickly, he jabbed the sword at Sendroun's neck as Sendroun tried to parry with his axe. Sendroun reeled around, saving his neck, and parried another blow. King Sendroun swung his axe at Centreal, but Centreal caught the blade in his shield again and tossed it aside, leaving Sendroun's torso open. Again he stabbed the enemy king through the chest, and Sendroun breathed out in despair as King Centreal managed to wrest the axe from his hand. King Sendroun fell to the ground, and the King of the Free looked down upon him. "You die for the children you killed," Centreal whispered, "And it is as simple as that."

Combat resumed. King Centreal turned around, seeing that all along the top of the castle, the Gaolnians were pressing their attack and taking control. Inside, the Gaolnians were taking control of the two floors opened up by the war machines. Seun Bastion would be theirs in hours at the very most. No foreign ally would now land on these shores. The

king was dead. The rest of the Skaelin leadership was hiding up
in Cavfurt, and they did not have the power to control the
outside world, where Centreal and his freemen now reigned.

Alaisio reached the top and pushed his way through to the
king. "My king, Luncas has fallen!" he told him. Centreal
turned around.

"Take me."

"Come."

"Your arm…" began the king.

"One of the soldiers below already cut off some of the
pressure with a light tourniquet and bandaged it up on the
inside. It will hold until we get back to camp," replied Alaisio.
They walked cautiously down the wobbly stones, making their
way to the cave-in. "He is in here."

Centreal went in first. "Luncas!"

"My king…" replied Luncas. "I can't move my leg or my
arm. I can't fight."

"We've won, Commander Luncas. The Skaelin have been
defeated. You stayed until the end. Gaoln will be free. Our
country will stand here alongside the Skaelin to the east and the
Skaelish to the west. Gaoln is no more, and the Kingdom of the
Free is truly born." Luncas smiled. "We will send you home,
Luncas. Or you may reside here in Skaen, should you choose."

The smile faded. "I have no home," said the captain and
commander. "I will stay here in Skaen. Everyone will call it
'The Free Kingdom' you know."

"Perhaps. But the Kingdom of the Free it shall be. We are
all free men now."

The bastion fell at sunset. The gates of Seun Bastion opened
up and five Skaelin officers emerged, holding up the flag of the
Skaelin Lands and proclaiming their surrender.

- Chapter Eight -

Throughout the camp a sort of silence prevailed, disrupted by grim murmurs and the occasional soft sob, and yet a sense of joy and relief granted by the final outcome of victory still pervaded the entire encampment. They laid the injured on the ground in tents. Among them were Alaisio and Captain Luncas. Alaisio was put on a crude wooden table, where a doctor carefully tightened the tourniquet and cut off his arm. Quickly, he and some soldiers covered the fresh wound in a soft, clean fabric, taken from the medical ward of Fort Gensballa, which kept most of the blood from seeping out of his arm, something which felt to Alaisio as if it was slowing his circulation around the amputation. There wasn't much they could do for the captain. He wouldn't be able to fight. His shoulder was hurt badly, and the doctors were worried it would cost him his life if there had been too much damage to the artery. In any case, it was far too dangerous to cut off the arm right where the artery passed through beneath the shoulder. His legs had been strained somehow when climbing the rubble, so he was not allowed to leave the pavilion.

King Centreal ordered a detachment of forty regiments to accompany him to fetch notes. The men laid down their weapons and packed up their armor. They put on round, earthen hats, to signal they were messengers, then they left to pick up and deliver notes, store them or carry them out, and count the dead.

The rain was pouring hard on the ruins of the old castle. Bolts of lightning shocked the ground and tore through the sky with thunderous roars. Together with the king and his personal detachment, the forty regiments— in addition to Luncas and Alaisio, on their own request, and Luncas having been released from the pavilion by Centreal's own order— gathered the notes, which grew damper and less legible as time went on. Commander Luncas came across one in particular that seemed to catch his interest. It was sitting in the open, sprawled between two bodies. The note could have belonged to anybody, and now it would be useless— such was the hazard of not tucking it in tight. The note had no burial requests or addresses to family or loved ones, no pay-off money certificates or any of the normal aspects of a note. As he read it, a chill wind swept around him, and he shivered.

~ I did not imprison you ~

Luncas approached Alaisio, who was standing tall atop the field, unbothered by the pouring rain, staring ahead as if he were in a trance. He almost showed the note to him, but then he truly saw him, standing there with one arm, gazing across the field tainted by the sins and the hatred and brutality of men. Alaisio had come here looking for something, the commander realized, that, at the end of it all, he still hadn't found. Alaisio bowed his head. "Captain?"

"Alaisio?" answered Luncas, walking closer to his friend.

Alaisio sighed, and took in a breath. He shook his head, gesturing out at the field. "What…" He looked down at his stub and laughed, a sort of dark and hopeless laugh, the kind that comes only when a person realizes they are powerless to change what matters. Thunder roared in the dark storm clouds above, and a streak of lightning flashed over the sea in front of their eyes. "What…"

The captain came up to his friend, and put his good arm on Alaisio's good shoulder. "It's okay," he said, "It's over now."

Alaisio seemed unsatisfied. He looked across the thousands and thousands of bodies strewn across the field, the pools of blood, the hunched-over figures collecting the notes. His face tensed just slightly. He made no reply, he only looked up at the sky as the rain pounded against his face, his body, and the earth all around him, as flashes of lightning thrashed about the dark clouds above, as the noises of the raging sea overtook him. *Over now…*

"They're free then," Alaisio whispered, "The Gaolnians are free."

"We do have that unique aspect of not being Gaolnian, and having been born free, don't we?" Luncas said curiously. "Yes, there is no Gaoln any longer. There is only the Kingdom of the Free. We did what we had to do, and those who died with us or against us needed to die— never again will Gaoln be a way for nations to terrorize their citizens, or an excuse for nations to fight wars. And the people themselves, most importantly of all— they are free. So ends the terrible tragedy of Gaoln, too long overdue. So is born the Kingdom of the Free."

The storm grew in intensity as the regiments continued collecting the notes. They would be sorted later, when the soldiers could escape the cold rain. Alaisio was grim now, reading each note as if it had been left by a loved one who had been murdered that day. His gaze would often fall across the field and upon the castle drenched in blood and rain, overflowing with broken weapons and armor and bodies. Luncas stayed by his side. The rain passed to the west eventually, where in the distance, over the sea, the thunder roared and the lightning dashed. After a few notes, Luncas sat kneeling on the grassy surface of the wet earth, and on an impulse he stood and read again the first note he had found.

As the soldiers collected the last of the notes and placed them inside the large bags they had brought for them, the storm seemed to pass further west, heading out of sight and hearing. It was still raining in the distance, out to the sea, when they gathered together and left the ruined peninsula for their camp. A dim moonlight through the dark clouds cast the bloody field and the tall, stony structures of Seun Bastion in an eerie, ambient kind of light. The roaring of the thunder grew more distant as the men hiked through flowers and bodies. Alaisio turned, looking with one eye over his shoulder at the site of Seun Bastion, as he crested the first large hill. He paused for a long moment. Then, with a heavy sigh and a closing of his eyes, he turned back around, and walked down the hill.

There was a celebration at the camp. People were eating as if they had all the food they'd ever want, and dancing around in circles as if the world had been saved and all was good. People would break into songs, songs they had known for generations or which they had just made up themselves— they were all songs abut being free, about finding justice, about a good life. *O Children* was the favorite of these, a song of freedom passed down as a lullaby to all the children of Gaoln. And to the tired and free soldiers in that meadow the harrowing stanzas filled their hearts. It was a song of being without a home, and now they had one. It was a song of being enslaved, and now they were free. It was a song of being nothing, and now they could be something. Above all this, it was a song of what tied these people together, people who had come from all around the world and had been shunned by every nation: Their common dream. And for the whole night through they did nothing but dream and rejoice.

There were those among the crowd who remained somber— those whose thoughts revolved entirely around the hostages in Laeolin, or the possibility of the Lonin soldiers coming to retake Seun Bastion, an unlikely event, or whose closest friends had just lost their lives. But the general consensus was that they had won— that the life which lay ahead of them was one of freedom and goodness, a life where they would find their peace. The dancing lasted until the dawn.

- Chapter Nine -

For a while, all Gendorn heard was the creaking of the ship, and he did not know how long he had heard this, how long he sat in bed. But at some point Bendoraun's voice broke the stillness of it all once again. "Can you get up, Gendorn?

We're almost to shore." Gendorn moaned, struggling to wake up. His eye twitched a bit, then shut again.

"Help me up," he whispered, extending a hand. Bendoraun took his hand, yanking him up roughly. "Ah…" Gendorn whispered, struggling to maintain balance. Bendoraun put his arm around Gendorn's shoulder, helping him out of the cabin. "It probably doesn't help that my entire lower body is asleep, I can't even feel my legs or feet."

"Hah," said Bendoraun, "You're just trying to play dead-weight." Gendorn grinned. He lifted his head, staring at the approaching shore, and as he saw it his smile grew.

"Gaoln…"

"Yes," agreed Bendoraun sarcastically, as if he had been longing for ages to return to this pile of dust. "Good old Gaoln…"

They walked down the plank, stepping again onto the dirt plain of Gaoln. The sky was the same shade of grey it had been on the morning of their departure. The land was just as dry and desolate. The wind was less chill— the cold season was ending, and soon the sun would shine warmly down upon them. Gendorn stood there, leaning on Bendoraun for support, with his one eye open and wearing an expression caught somewhere between elation and grief. Bendoraun pretended to be thinking about what to do for just a minute, and then his eyes grew wide, as if he had the most novel idea come to mind. "Let's go see Kamira," he said excitedly. Gendorn stared ahead weakly at the old hill with that single, barren tree. He could see it far off in the distance— the hill he and Kamira spent their last night on, the shore where they bid farewell.

"Yes," he said. "Let's go see Kamira. And then let's get back to Skaen. We'll find another nice little village, or a castle like Gatsesilli," said Gendorn, "And then we can really get some rest."

Appendix A:

Timeline of Events for
A Land of Our Own

Year 87 in the Age of the Great Wars: Menuld is born in a town outside the Glorious City, Gonaka.

Year 107 in the Age of the Great Wars and Year 1 in the Age of Peace: The Great Wars end. The Council of Nations is reestablished. The Council of Nations passes the Partitioning of Gaoln, establishing Gaoln as a penal colony to provide a solution to all the problems of the world, intended to allow the civilized nations to exist in peace without "the corrupting spirit of corrupted men". Nations are given unlimited possibilities in exiling citizens to Gaoln, but the original convicts include only war criminals from the Great Wars. Gonaka and Laen sign a "Perpetual Peace Agreement" which requires the other nations of Fengorian to intervene with force if either Laen or Gonaka become involved in any more wars of aggression.

Years 1-20 in the Age of Peace: Peace reigns in the world and there are no wars. The Council of Nations is stronger than ever, and its word is as law.

Years 20-42 in the Age of Peace: Resulting indirectly from ruined livelihoods and a series of bad harvests and small-scale invasions, violence returns to the world. The broken peace provides a setting where figures of ambition may challenge established dynasties. The Wars of Succession, the Pirate Wars, and the Civil War of Skaen shake Fengorian in a bloody chaos. States become more vicious toward outsiders and the number of people exiled into Gaoln soars during this time period. Originally most prisoners are pirates or ex-pirate captives, but increasingly Gaoln becomes a place for political prisoners, as allowed for by the terms of the Partitioning of Gaoln. By the year 42 more than half of those imprisoned in Gaoln are either born there or are there for political reasons.

Year 42 in the Age of Peace: Gendorn is born and brought into the penal colony of Gaoln from Laen, his actual birthplace, as the child of an important protestor. Growing up, Gendorn remains ignorant of this fact and of the life his ancestors lived.

Year 49 in the Age of Peace: The First Rebellion succeeds in destroying all the guardhouses and in forcing the guards to withdraw from Gaoln, but when Laen, Las, and the Skaelin blockade the penal colony and station forces around the border, Gonaka withdraws any offer of help and the rebellion ultimately fails. Governor Centreal proclaims himself King of Gaoln and vows that the second attempt at escape will succeed.

Year 57 in the Age of Peace: The Second Rebellion begins. Gaoln invades Skaen with the help of Gonaka, the nation which provides the ships and supplies necessary to make the journey and begin the assault. At the very beginning of Sen in the year 57 in the Age of Peace, the Gaolnian Army lands on the shores of Skaen.

Appendix B:

The Partitioning of Gaoln

It was dark that day, and the wind was chill. The end of Sen, the cold season, was near at the time, and Trest, the hot season, was beginning to ease its way into that northern corner of Laen, where by the Cold Ocean the weather hardly ever got very warm. But it was cozy inside that tall and mighty stone building, where around the table covered in candles the representatives of all the nations of Fengorian came together. When the rain began there was a stillness in the room, a silence where every member of that group examined the ideas they had in their mind without any exchange of words. The candles danced lower as their wicks melted down toward the table. One of the men— a man by the name of Menuld, who at the time was hardly twenty years old— rose from his seat.

"We have seen the death of two hundred thousand men." He said nothing more for some long while, as he waited for this to sink in. "That war, the last of the Great Wars, ended precisely ninety-four days ago. We have before us a proposition put to the Council of Nations, which emerged from that destruction. That proposition condemns to slavery all people bearing any mark of any pirate or gang. That slavery will be supervised in the land which the proposition names 'Gaoln'. This is the land which bore witness to the end of the Great Wars, and which saw them at the beginning more than a hundred years ago.

"They say that so much blood has been spilled on this land that nothing can grow there any longer. No water runs through the dust, and no trees grow in the valleys or the hills— the hills themselves are eroding with the wind, as the landscape itself turns to dirt. Everything is dying, and what now remains will soon be dust. Thirty days after the end of the last of the Great Wars there were less than a thousand people who had been exiled into living in Gaoln, and most of them have died since that time.

"You are proposing that we throw all the pirates of the world into this 'Gaoln'. You say that this will deter pirates; this will make them reconsider their lots. I would ask how you define a pirate, and how anyone could say, based on a mark on someone's skin, who is and is not a pirate, when every captive of every pirate is given the same mark as the pirate himself. The proposition throws everyone convicted of murder into Gaoln, if they are not to be killed by the state. But the last clause is what bothers me most, and I will read it right from the proposition, which I hold in front of me now."

Menuld looked down at the table. He took in a breath, and continued speaking. "I quote: 'Anyone deemed worthy of exile by any state supporting the proposition, granted either that the person is a citizen of that state or that he or she has committed the alleged crime within that state and has no state to claim citizenship over it or if they do that state is unwilling or unable to pursue persecution, may be thrown in Gaoln for any reason. These reasons include posing a threat to the state by inciting anti-state sentiment or actions, defying state law to a significant extent, encouraging others to defy state law to a significant extent, and lying to the state. The reasons why a person is subject to exile in Gaoln include but are not limited to those valid reasons.' And I quote again— this is from the very last passage of the proposition: 'Exile in Gaoln will be an hereditary punishment. The descendants of those who have committed crimes will not be allowed any appeal, but may be granted freedom only at the discretion of the responsible state or by the Council of Nations. All prisoners will be given no opportunity to make a livelihood for themselves, to trade with other nations, or to form political networks. Gaoln will be supervised at all times by the nations signing on to this proposition. Those who are prisoners in Gaoln will never, by any nation in

Fengorian, be allowed the opportunity to escape from Gaoln, and the Council of Nations and every independent state reserves the right to take action if any state allows the Gaolnians to escape or to seek refuge in their land. All basic necessities will be provided for as described in passages four through nine, and no other method of delivering goods or services to Gaoln or the Gaolnians will be tolerated unless agreed-upon beforehand by the signatories of this proposition.'"

Menuld looked around the room, but no one appeared ready to speak. "Well," Menuld continued, "it seems to me that this Gaoln idea is going to imprison a large number of innocent or wrongly convicted people and by its design will continue to do so in the future. It will condemn them to imprisonment without the right to have a livelihood, without the right to work unless that work comes in the form of state slavery, and without the chance to ever escape. Furthermore, this proposition condemns all of the descendants of the condemned to the same life under the same circumstances. It states that any attempt at rebellion, which to me seems the only viable option in life for anyone born into Gaoln or any wrongly convicted prisoner, will be met with military force.

"I do not need to remind the Council that the original idea of Gaoln, as it was discussed in the very first days of the Age of Peace, was that this would be a place for war criminals only, people who had committed atrocities— people who had burned piles of still-living people. These would be people who had forced sons to murder their fathers, and then murdered those sons. These would be people who surrounded villages and burned them, killing anyone who attempted to escape. These would be people who raped women in front of their husbands and then made those husbands kill their wives— then they proceeded to kill the husbands. There were one thousand men on the original list. Their punishment was not hereditary.

Many of the men I see before me today were there when this original Gaoln was designed less than one hundred days ago.

"The original Gaoln worked, by my estimate. It was designed for people who had no capacity for human emotion. That Gaoln has absolutely nothing to do with this Gaoln. Those who have gone before me have already discussed the difficulties of identifying pirates as distinguishable from pirate captives or people forced to become pirates who plan escapes. But I would question the legitimacy of any government which signs on to this treaty, and I state that openly. It provides governments a way to throw away men and women who they see as problematic for any reason at all, and they don't need to worry about their families or their offspring, oh no— because they all go to Gaoln together, and they never get out alive!"

Menuld sighed. "I am the least experienced person in this room, but everything I know and everything I feel tells me this is wrong. I read the signatories: Laen, Foremost Sponsor. Skaen, Cosigner and Sponsor. Phenen, Cosigner and Sponsor. Aniania, Cosigner. Keay, Cosigner. Las, Cosigner. Those against the proposition: Gonaka, Dissenter. Kale, Dissenter. The United-Independent Territories of Bautaulan, Dissenter.

"I have nothing more to say, but I will close with the dissenting statements attached by The Kingdom of Gonaka, and I read these directly from the statement I hold here in front of me: 'The reasons for and beliefs behind our dissent are as follows: That a human being must never be born into a life of captivity; that a human being who has committed no crime must never be stripped of his or her opportunity to make a life for him or herself; that a human being must be allowed to pass his or her time with some labor, but must never be forced into slavery when he or she has not committed a crime which justifies him or her becoming a slave under law; that states cannot be trusted with the power to do whatever they like with any person whoever, and that the Council of Nations should not overlook state abuses of that power which would be allowed for under the terms of this proposition; that the ability to escape from a life of poverty and to make a better life for him or herself and his or her family is the right of every human being and cannot be taken away arbitrarily; that the basic necessities described in passages four through nine do not actually qualify as basic necessities and would in fact cause starvation, dehydration, disease, and hypothermia on a wide scale; that it is the inherent right of every person in this world to be free from arbitrary and unwarranted punishment which deprives that person of the happiness and peace which is the right of every person to earn and enjoy.'"

Menuld sat down. For some time there was only the pounding of the rain outside, and the rumbling of the thunder as it approached from somewhere off in the distance. Then one man rose from the other side of the table, and spoke: "I thank you all for attending this meeting, and I hope that this Council of Nations will continue to meet at all times when the problems of our world require our attention. This session will break for a time, and then we will return with our decision." The council, and Menuld, vacated the room, while the group of three indifferent council administrators met alone. The representatives returned later in the evening, and sat around in silence while one of the three administrators rose to address the Council of Nations.

The administrator spoke as soon as he rose from his seat. His voice was devoid of any care—it was brief and abrupt and cruel. "The proposition passes."

SHADOWS OF LAEOLIN
Preview

A dark cloud descended upon the city. It covered all the land from the boundary hills of the east and west to the river's mouths in the north and south. A great thunder rolled in the distance, approaching— threatening.

The first night had descended, and there was a solemn silence cast about the entire Tower of Laeolin.

Kamira could see it in their eyes. It was a confusion filled with terror and surrender. It was everything lost— dreams died that had hardly even had a season yet to live. Cries broke the silence. There were few who did not cry.

Kamira refused to. She did not yet believe in the death of all their dreams. As such, she sat by the narrow window slit and observed as the storm gathered around her. There was no speaking, no arguing, no crying. There was just watching and waiting.

Arguments fumed around her. "They will kill us" young women said, "we need to leave! Break out!" The elders would sigh. "Our only chance," they retorted, "is to wait. We stand no chance against soldiers in a hostile city. Protesting will earn us a sudden death, and no sane man could commit such a crime as it would be to kill us in the open purview of all the world!" The young women, with an energy the elderly had long forgotten, would still protest: "Complicity will kill us! If we wait, we die. If we fight, we have at least a chance for escape!"

The cries drowned out all of these arguments. The cries drowned out everything. They became louder and louder, echoing in her ears. Even the smallest whimper was as a wailing sob in Kamira's mind. The arguments faded.

She did not notice when the tears began to fall down her face. Until the taste of salt fouled her lips, she had been fully unaware that she had been crying as one among them. She was not disappointed. It was empowering to experience this weakness, this terror and sadness. *I know now from what terrible depths we must rise*, she reassured herself, *and I know we must rise*.

ABOUT THE AUTHOR:

Photo by Arianna Fischer, rendered in black and white by Elizabeth Linares

Matthew R. Bishop is a traveling storyteller and adventurer. When not in his home library, he enjoys hiking, climbing, swimming, and exploring the open world. Check out Matt's author website at MatthewRBishop.com to find more books and embark on new adventures.

Matt's first series, *The Kingdom of the Free*, is a humanist low-fantasy adventure set in Fengorian. His most recent series, *Legends of Elyria*, is a mythological high-fantasy epic set in Elyria. These two projects take very different approaches to the fantasy genre, and challenge its traditional boundaries in different ways. Explore both of Matt's original worlds to complete your journey and find your own story.

Matt also has two degrees in history and political science. Outside of his fiction and fantasy work, Matt writes non-fiction news articles and opinion pieces on current political issues and global affairs. To view his recent work in non-fiction journalism, visit his blog at https://matthewrbishop.medium.com.